SLEEPWALKING

SLEEPWALKING

A PROPHECY

ROBERT STEVENS

Content Warning

This story contains graphic descriptions of suicide, cannibalism, cruelty, violence and depravation. Discretion is advised for the fainthearted.

Published 2025
by Robert Stevens

ISBN 978-0-473-76443-2 (International Edition)

Designed and distributed in New Zealand by CopyPress, Nelson, New Zealand.

www.copypress.co.nz

For all the climate change warriors who have tried,
and failed, to make a significant difference to the
path that mankind is on. Not many people are
interested in changing much about the status quo.
I take solace from the words of M. Gandhi:

What you do in life may seem insignificant,
but it is very important that you do it.

CHAPTER 1

The Drifter is Born

He was in his mid- to late thirties, but too many nights sleeping rough had left him looking somewhat older. There was still a sparkle in his eye that the ladies liked, so once in a while he would get taken to the house of some 'woman-alone-tonight' and have a long shower, fresh sheets and eager sex. But not today. And he didn't think it was likely to happen anytime soon in this god-forsaken corner of Arizona. He had been walking for hours. This wasn't the longest walk he had ever taken, but it sure was in some of the most desolate country he had ever seen. Scrubby bush seared by ten thousand suns and precious little rain lay scattered along the edge of the highway, along with the usual signs of civilisation: empty cans and broken cars. No respite from the afternoon sun that he could see, just more clear blue sky. Big sky country out here. His wide-brimmed hat was doing the job required, but it was still bloody hot at five in the afternoon.

He had discovered a while ago that it didn't really matter whether you walked or stood between rides. If somebody was going to pick you up, they would. The last ride had been many hours ago. So today, like so many before, he decided to walk. He found it borderline meditational, the slow-changing scenery and occasionally seeing something of interest. The side of the road was always a curious place to walk, even in these remote parts. All the crap and rubbish of society just lying around after it had been casually tossed from the window of a fast, passing car. But nothing special so far. Just the usual crap: cans, bottles, plastic of all types.

So he walked. In the distance he could see a small mesa – little more than a stark column of rock. He knew it was difficult to gauge distance in the shimmering heat of the desert, but he figured he'd try and get there by nightfall. If somebody didn't pick him up before then. But he didn't think that was very likely. Not today. So he walked on …

— ◈ —

Once he'd been somebody else, had a previous life. Robert Borman, a man who used to wear five-thousand-dollar suits and ties worth hundreds, a financial trader. He'd earn tens of thousands a day in an average week, just five years out of college. Better days *were* better. He had a fine house in the suburbs, wife and daughter, and a fine younger lover in an apartment just down the road from work. Life had been good. He'd been a trader in international securities: governments, the IMF and World Bank all lending money to each other as fast as they could. All at a small margin to his company, of course. The company he worked for made a lot of money lending to everybody during the boom of the 1980s and 90s. He had just started as the markets peaked. And then the surprise of the Global Financial Crisis, the great credit crunch. He had been stunned at the time, along with all the other traders in the office.

Looking back, it still brought a smile to his lips. Like hot air could rise forever? The only thing that amazed him was that so few could mislead so many for so long. How stupid were people? No end to it apparently. He now knew that credit couldn't be issued for ever, that it wasn't underpinned by anything except the quenchless thirst of consumerism, hopeless hope and greed. They hadn't seen that the massively inflated ball of nothing would eventually pop. So they kept on blowing more air into it with all sorts of new instruments: derivatives

     ROBERT STEVENS

and bundled equities and shady deals. It had been fun and he made millions in commissions.

They managed what people wanted – credit. It hadn't even been money, really; it was *credit*. So they went to work from ten till six, with long fat lunches and fatter expense accounts, and yes, he had put on some beef. But nobody complained. His dutiful wife made the meals and made the home, and his lover banged him stupid a couple of times a week, and it was good.

When Lehman Brothers finally fell over, they made even more money. It was obscene, but it was a hell of a ride. After a week of indecision from his American brothers, the governments threw money at the financial institutions so the lines of credit could be kept open. They printed money and bought assets at inflated prices with electronic money, all to stop banks from failing. He became a multi-millionaire within a year on bonuses and incentive payments. They focused on maximising returns to themselves: this was the basis of the capitalist system, and it was good. The bonuses flowed.

He wasn't really surprised to go around to Mandy's apartment one afternoon and find another bloke there. They weren't in bed, but the look in their eyes said it all. *Just a friend, huh? Ungrateful bitch*, he thought as he closed the door behind him. Didn't really expect the relationship to last forever. *What the fuck, there'll be another.* He was getting a little tired of her now anyway – there wasn't the same enthusiasm as there used to be. And once you'd screwed a woman so many times, it was like the same ole, same ole. Time to move on. He wondered about that new secretary at the office – tight little ass and cute tits. What was her name? He caught a cab back to the office.

A few weeks passed and his resentment faded a little. He had cancelled the lease on the apartment and advised Mandy by text that she had a month to find somewhere else to live. *Sorry, you've been dumped.* It had been another excellent day. He'd started at ten thirty that morning, which was pretty normal these days as that was when the machinery of government hit first gear and the announcements and money from Central Bank started to flow. He'd done a couple of hours and then had lunch. The new secretary's name was Savannah. Who would name their child that? Wasn't it some place in Africa? Lunch had included taking Savannah out and making nicey-nice chat. Yes, he was looking for a new PA, so yes, this was kinda like an interview. He was one of the high-flyers in the office, and while not quite getting carte blanche, it was close. *Too soon to put out a fishing line*, he thought. *Get to know her a bit, stroke the ego before you stroke anything else.* Some things don't change. The sun coming up in the east, the stupidity of governments, people's gullibility, and the insecurity many women suffer. Yes siree, things were good.

She came into his office that afternoon and asked some irrelevant question and then chatted a bit more. Yep, she was getting ready. Next move? Too obvious with the 'come-out-to-dinner' routine. She knew he was married, so he'd have to play that card. Imply that things weren't good at home. He'd rely on the mothering instinct: she'd want to mother him even though he was close to ten years her senior. Women just wanted to be wanted, wanted to be nurtured and loved and given a good servicing from time to time. Not that he was going to make out the marriage was on the rocks. That tactic was too obvious. More along the lines of he worked hard, was diligent and made a good living, made good money, but never seemed to have much in his bank account. Savannah would fall for the line that he was unappreciated and worthy of better … Give it a couple of weeks. He knew that she wasn't seeing anyone, so she could keep on the shelf for a while.

He was a sexist pig, but completely unaware of it. In his own eyes, he was a brilliant man. An amazing combination of loving husband and father, a great provider who made a lot of money, and he had a high sex drive. So long as his philandering was discreet and the wife didn't know, where was the problem?

ROBERT STEVENS

That evening he worked a bit later, nothing special in that. He'd caught the train as usual and then drove home from the station. It was close to nine by the time he drove into the garage, which wasn't 'late' with a capital L by any means. At work they had closed the computers and had a quick drink (happened most nights now, but hell, things were good), and then a drink and snack at Jay's Diner. Afterwards, he'd taken the 8.10 from Central, the car parked securely at the local station.

The house was dark. Nobody home? He parked the car in the garage and let the door roll down before he unlocked the access door. Her car wasn't in, which was strange. Maybe she was visiting her mother, although she always told him when she did. The kitchen was dark and quiet, which was the first time he'd seen it like that for many years. No note on the counter. *Damn, what a nuisance*, he thought. They usually didn't eat until past nine anyway, once Katie was all tucked up. He could do with a drink, though. He went to the liquor cabinet and poured a fat finger of twelve-year-old single malt whisky and sat down on the couch. In the darkness. It felt okay.

After the first drink, which was only four minutes later, he called her mobile phone, but his call when straight to voicemail. He went up to the bedroom. All her stuff was there, scattered around the bed and over the dresser. No, she hadn't left, but was becoming a bit of a messy bitch. He looked in Katie's room – messy in there too. But when you were three years old and a proper little madam to boot, your room was allowed to look like a bomb site. He rang her mother, who lived on the other side of the UK from London, where he and his family lived. *No, she had not seen nor heard from them.* He tried his wife's mobile again – same result. He had another drink and a look around the fridge, but the drinks after work, and then the pair of straight whiskies, killed his appetite. And he was tired. He tried her mobile phone for the third time, but once more it went straight through to voicemail. He rang the cops, but after twenty minutes on hold, gave up. He had started to worry. He'd rung her mobile many times, but always it went straight to voicemail. So, after two messages, there wasn't any point. Damned if he knew. He had rung the local hospital: *No, sorry. They couldn't help.*

So after another whisky that put a fair dent in the level of the bottle, he fell asleep on the couch, too smashed to even fantasise about Savannah and her cute little tits.

It was not until one in the morning that the police finally arrived. The registration plates of the car were barely legible after the fire. But they had had to make sure about the identification. Better to be sure. And the dental identification had involved getting the dentist out of bed and down to his office, and then down to the morgue. It all took time, and they had worked as quickly as they could.

It took a fair hammering on the door to wake him; he'd been in a deep sleep. The news, when given to him, didn't really sink in. His wife and daughter, T-boned by a truck running a red light. The police thought the severity of the crash would have concussed both occupants straight away, even Katie in her child seat. The car had fire-balled when the fuel tank had ruptured. It would have been an instant blinding flash and that was it. He was told it would have been quick. And no, sorry, he wouldn't be able to view the remains. The fire had been very fierce. That is why it took so long for the police to positively identify them. And who could they ring to come around and be with him?

He wasn't sure about that one, which spoke volumes.

He'd taken a week off work, but the truth was, he was rattling around and wanted something to do. The funeral service had been all arranged for him. Her parents were distraught; he was numb. His parents had disowned him many years ago because of his womanising and materialistic ways. But he rang them back in the good ol' USA and left a message on the machine.

He didn't quite know what or how he felt about the tragedy. The coffins were appropriately sized and weighted, although he chose not to think too much about that. They were buried in the same grave, daughter over the mother. There was some legal crap about them not being able to be placed in the same coffin. Fucked if he knew. She didn't have a will, although she did talk about being cremated. Given the circumstances, he thought there had been enough fire for the time being. So they had buried his wife and child in the good soil of England, her home, and he rattled around the house until he couldn't stand it any longer. He went back to work because he needed to do something.

— ◆ —

The collapse of their computer system two weeks later was entirely unexpected: all backups wiped, irretrievably lost. How could that be? Their company had been selected as the trial ground for an early EMP test, but they never knew that. The device had been hidden in a small pallet load of paper 'incorrectly' delivered to the offices next door, and the delivery guy had come back and picked it up the next day.

The bosses didn't know what to do. They had no information with which to operate the business as everything was kept electronically. The failure of their business did make front page news in the *Financial Times*, and page five in *The New York Times*. Sixty people lost their jobs, which was reasonably unremarkable. A power surge through the computers was identified as the likely cause, and they were fairly close to the truth. The backup systems had also been fried. Some backups were on USB sticks and remote hard drives, but they had been fried as well, which didn't make sense.

He went home and got smashed for a couple of days, but in truth he wasn't cut out for hard drinking – he couldn't stand the hangover. He made a few calls to competitor companies, but they were all under the pump and business was flat. "Yes, email your CV," was the standard response, and they would keep his name on file and give him a call if something came up. Yeah, right. Same old crap, different day. He didn't really know what to do with himself. He felt nothing – no joy, no sorrow – just empty. No purpose in life. He missed his daughter more than his wife, but he missed them both.

He was cleaning out the drawer of the dresser one day when he came across the .38 Special revolver; he'd forgotten about it. Quite illegal in the UK. *Would have been pretty useful if they had a burglar*, he thought, cynically. It wasn't even loaded. He hadn't even remembered that it was in the drawer. It took him some time to find the box of rounds – they were in a dusty corner of the garage. He had a couple of bourbons under his belt and was feeling quite mellow. *Gee, I hope the zombies will wait while I find my rounds and load up*, he mused silently to himself as he slotted rounds into the chambers. He flipped the cylinder closed and made sure the safety was off. *Just like in the movies*, he thought as he opened his mouth and shoved the barrel up against the roof of his mouth. *Now just squeeze the trigger*, he thought, *this life is over. All done, all gone.*

Five or six plus million pounds net worth last time he went through it, and it was completely worthless to him now. *This life is over. Yep, for sure. Nothing here worth staying for.* He was still for a moment, mustering his courage.

Why not start a new one? The thought came from out of the blue.

He eased the pressure off the trigger and quietly pulled the gun from his mouth. It hung by his side.

But what the fuck would I do?

Doesn't matter, went the silent conversation in his head. *This life is over. You tried, it worked for a while, then the wheels come off. You were an arsehole. You could continue being one, or not. Doesn't matter what you try, anything's gotta be better than a bullet in the head. Ain't that the truth. You'll die in good time, one day.*

He sat down on the bed and, for the first time, cried for his lost loved ones. He howled for the lost lives, his and theirs, and the lost dreams.

He lay on the bed for a few hours, emotionally drained. The revolver placed beside him as he just lay there, not thinking much at all.

Over the next months he sold it all – the house, the car, household furniture and the computers. He gave away his suits and shoes and all Katie's toys and clothes and his wife's clothes. He sold and gave away stuff with reckless abandon, and in the end he had an even finer bank balance. He kept the property in California. Maybe he would go there one day, try farming or some damn thing. There had been a nice little insurance payout for the car and his wife's dead body, plus the cash he had stashed away. The shares were still worth a bundle, not as much as they had been, though, and he cashed in all of those as well. It was truly a new beginning. What had been valuable to him before was no longer so. Transferring the money to the US, converting it from English pounds to US dollars, was even better. More money. What the fuck? He flew back to Los Angeles, his old hometown.

He purchased a very sensible family station wagon, and with two suitcases of clothes, he hit the road. He didn't even know which way to drive. He laughed when he realised that. "Probably not a lot of benefit in buying a GPS," he said out loud to himself. "Why do I need accurate directions to a place when I don't know where I'm going!"

After a week, he realised he was just driving, not seeing anything, just signposts rushing by. Unhelpful. He didn't know what to do, just knew that he didn't want to keep on driving along those infinite roads. So he stopped in some nameless town for a week and read the paper and just 'was'.

CHAPTER 2

The Plan

As the American-led assault on the Iraqi dictator Hussein intensified in 2003, a group of men met in a small nondescript house on the edge of Baghdad. It included two members of Saddam's inner circle who, for at least a decade, had miraculously managed to survive his infamous purges. Many were bearded and older, but one stood out for his youth, pale skin and good looks. Mikael was an Iraqi-born French citizen, who normally worked as a corporate lawyer in various countries. Besides Arabic, he was fluent in French, English, Russian and Swedish. He had been asked to attend this meeting, as had all the others.

After the traditional introductions, the *istikans* of hot, sweet tea, and the obligatory small talk as they settled, the leader and senior imam began. "With the guidance of Allah and, somewhat ironically, the help of the Americans, a fantastic opportunity awaits us. A power vacuum will inevitably occur after this invasion, and this invasion will succeed as we witness and remember the power of the Western military." He paused, framing his next words. "This is an opportunity unfolding before our eyes. Our hopes can be realised. An Islamic Nation built on the word of Allah. We can rid ourselves of the Western ways of thinking and return to the true path." He cast his eyes about, confirming he had their full attention.

"We need to move quickly," he continued. "With the friends in this room and our closest circle, we can seize what we need. We shall not underestimate our enemies, nor pretend we can fight their military machine and win. Nor will we forget the treachery that friends can bring when poorly chosen. We shall strike down our enemies and establish a nation with the words of the Prophet Mohammed."

There was a general nodding of heads. There was no need to say a word. They had heard it before, and usually they would be more cynical, for in the past similar words had been spoken in similar rooms. But this time things were different. The Americans, and hence their allies, were enraged by the attack on the World Trade Centre, and had conceived a vague story to justify this retaliatory attack on Iraq. Having witnessed the early stages of the Coalition attack, the men in the room knew that they could not match this enemy on a conventional battlefield.

"We need the following: weapons, and men and women to use them. These martyrs must not be afraid to be reunited with Allah in paradise. We are not short of such people. This will strike fear into the hearts of our enemies, which is a good start. We will need money to buy influence – American money. Gold and cash, for this is another tool we can use to build an Islamic Nation. The Infidels have already given it to us, they just don't know that yet. And we need true believers of the faith to lead us."

He paused again, knowing that it created a dramatic effect and allowed his words to sink in. "And we need to be cunning, for we know of the drones in the sky above us. We know they monitor every word spoken over a cellular network, and they monitor our computers. So we shall not use these".

"While it may seem an impediment – nay, a curse – that we cannot trust these methods of communication, let the curse be on them. Let us fool our enemy with false words, false hope and false leads, and thus lull them into a false sense of security. We shall offer up fools and the unworthy to the insatiable thirst of the capitalists to find terrorists under every bed. We shall give up some to them to let them think they are winning. But our plans will go much deeper than that."

The old man paused again and sipped his tea, giving the others time to reflect on these words and thoughts. This was new, and they would need some time to digest it. They all wanted more precise guidance, clear action outlined, yet courtesy demanded that the old man be allowed to speak for as long as he liked.

"Sunnis and Shiites have been fighting each other for too long over an interpretation of the Prophet's words, an argument that is over a thousand years old. Are we to continue to be divided and downtrodden? Are we to be too scared to practise our faith in our mosques for fear we may be slaughtered? Or are we to walk freely in our own lands, not looking to the skies for the enemy's drones and bombs? It is this vision we need to heed as we make our plans."

"Muslims and Christians and Jews have been fighting and slaughtering each other for over a thousand years. This is not new. And how the apostate capitalists like to pour fuel on those fires! It is easy to wage war, good business for the French, the Americans, the Chinese and the Russians too." He paused again and sipped his tea.

"But for now, we shall plan for the next year by thinking about where we want to be in the future. Our long-term vision will always be in sight as we make our short-term plans. All our decisions and actions must lead us towards this vision, an Islamic Nation."

The men got down to discussing what key alliances they would need to forge as they started dreaming and creating an Islamic Nation based on the words of the Qur'an. Who could they trust, and who could they use and discard when the time was right?

The next day, the senior imam met with Mikael privately. He didn't want too many people to know of the specifics of the secondary plan. Secrecy was critical, as was the placement of the spies.

     ROBERT STEVENS

"Mikael, you are the smartest amongst us, you need to be thinking far ahead. Many decades. You have studied in the West and speak their language. You look like them, talk like them. You understand how they think, and you have remained true to the faith.

"As previously discussed, the primary objective is the establishment of an Islamic Nation, a united people growing from the ashes of this invasion, and its long-term survival. This group who will lead us towards achieving our vision, let us be called 'the Directors'. The Directors shall not only plan for the establishment of a true and glorious Islamic Nation, we shall also plan for its eternal life in this world, by using attack as the best form of defence, for we can be sure that the Infidels will react against our new Islamic Nation sooner or later. We shall not attack the giant directly, because we shall lose. We need a plan to attack the heart of their society, so their military machines become useless.

"Let us learn from the Vietnamese, who won against the Americans. We do not have enough time to make all the mistakes others did, so let us learn from the mistakes of other. Let us also learn from an ancient text written by the Chinese: *The Art of War*. This is a text, more than two thousand years old, that discusses how to fight and win wars. We have been at war with the West for over a thousand years. We shall learn from our past mistakes and losses. We shall make fewer mistakes than our enemy.

"We shall attack their confidence in their system. Their whole economic system is built on confidence, no matter how foolish we think that is. They have so much debt. They create money to pay for it, and the average citizen thinks that everything is just fine. They have their Sunday roast and Thanksgiving and Christmas celebrations, and for them, things are mostly just fine. All based on credit, spending money they haven't earned yet. The idea is to shake that faith in their system, undermine what they take for granted."

He paused for moment, and Mikael was smart enough to let the moment hang. No need to fill the space with empty words.

Mikael collected his thoughts. "Please excuse me. What will be destroyed by our attack?" he asked.

"Ah yes. I ramble somewhat as I embark on our cause," replied the imam. "And yes, thank you for your question, because we must be honest with each other and be clear about what we are trying to do in bringing down an elephant with a small company of ants." The imam shuffled uncomfortably for a moment, then settled down and continued, "The capitalist system is based on ever increasing consumerism. They have no concept of a steady state."

"This I understand," said Mikael.

"Their god is money and never-ending credit to fuel endless consumerism. The wars in the Middle East and support for the House of Saud are about oil for their cars. If we can create enough doubt about the future, if we attack their confidence through their banking system … If we can create enough doubt, enough confusion, and create a large enough crevasse in their financial and economic machine, they will begin to lose faith in their society. And that doubt is the corrosion that will bring them down – they won't believe any more."

He stopped, then pointed to Mikael. "Your work will be to gather and use people to assemble information on the Western financial system and its weak points. Also the internet and telecommunication systems, the power grids, and the water supply. When you attack, it will not be against tanks and drones, but against the soft underbelly."

Mikael nodded, beginning to understand the enormity of what was being planned. He would need more time to think about how he was going to go about this task – how to bring down the capitalists. He left Baghdad a week later, having sketched out a plan. It would evolve, of course.

— ◆ —

     ROBERT STEVENS

And as the battle on the ground in Iraq reached its conclusion, and the inevitable period of confusion followed afterwards, the leaders began the next stage of their plan.

A number of dissenters and key threats to the establishment of an Islamic Nation were assassinated during and after the American campaign. Just a few more deaths amongst thousands. Weapons that Saddam had accumulated were taken from the massive storage sheds. Gold too. So much of it that they needed heavy transport trucks to shift the crates in the middle of the night from the secret hiding places to new ones. And there was money. Pallet loads of American cash, so neatly packaged in plastic that it looked remarkably unremarkable until you opened it. They didn't count the cash – there was no point as there was so much. The Americans had given the weapons and cash to Saddam to fight the Iranians, just as they had given weapons to the Iranians previously.

The cash, gold, weapons and explosives were hidden in caves that had served as secret hiding places for thousands of years.

A call to jihad was put out over social media platforms for those of the true faith to join the rebirth of the Islamic Nation, and the faithful, disenfranchised and angry from around the globe joined up. Many were cannon fodder, but in some conflicts you needed people who are prepared to die.

There was also money from Libya, and the same saga was repeated there many years later. Muammar Gaddafi, hardly an Islamic sympathiser, also recognised that the enemy of his enemy was his friend. He saw the end coming and made some strategic phone calls. More pallet loads of cash and crates of gold were spirited away on fast patrol boats in the middle of the night, as the overland journey through Egypt and Israel was far too risky. The Libyan loyalists left Benghazi late in the afternoon and landed in Beirut the next day. The local militias were well rewarded since money was the oil for the machine of war. They didn't need weapons. They already had more than they could use.

A lot of the gold was used to finance the establishment of the new Islamic Caliphate. Buying influence and support. Pallet loads of cash, along with significant amounts of gold and small arms, were sent in containers around the globe: a number to America and Canada, some to Europe and India, some to Chechnya, some to Indonesia. At every stage the shipment was managed by friends of the faith who could be trusted.

And thus a seed fund was established. And it was many hundreds of millions of US dollars, provided courtesy of Uncle Sam.

Mikael planned carefully over the years that followed. Once he had digested what the senior imam had laid out, he had a clear idea of the type of person he was looking for. Many of the recruits who answered the call came for jihad, and most of these were not the ones he wanted. Many of these jihadists were just haters, and acted too quickly, without thought. But there were some who were more intelligent and thoughtful. Those who had seen through the thin veneer of consumerism in the capitalist society. Those who had seen the injustices and killings in the name of Western bankers and the industrial–military complex. He identified and recruited the smartest to be his controllers. The ones who could effectively deploy the sleepers being developed in the old compound in the Republic of Bashkortostan in the Russian Federation. While the USA, the great Satan, was an obvious focus of his endeavours, the plan was wider than that. The British and French were hardly blameless, and their fate was tied to that of the Americans.

Mikael used his French passport to travel freely, avoiding the mosques wherever he found himself, as he knew the security forces were monitoring them. Instead, he attended private prayer sessions; his faith

     ROBERT STEVENS

was strong enough to eschew the need to be seen praying at a mosque. He listened to the conversations afterwards, offering provocative ideas when the opportunity arose. One by one he identified men who could be trusted. Women were also recruited, but in far fewer numbers; it was just the way that it was. He wanted one controller for each country, and below that a manager for each of the operations. He would talk to them privately about the vision for an eternal Islamic Nation and what had been the constant war with the West. They talked of the futility of a conventional war against the massed armies of the West and their superior technology. How could this be countered?

Constantly he was looking for dedication to the cause and the possibility of informants. Only one of his recruits was doubtful, and this person simply disappeared one night. There was too much at stake, and had it been a mistake, so be it. There was always collateral damage.

During the first years of the new caliphate, the Islamic State of Iraq and the Levant (ISIL), they witnessed the atrocities that Muslim perpetrated on Muslim, let alone the minorities, and despaired. These were not the wishes of Mohammed. It made their planning efforts go faster; they knew it would only be time before the West reacted to this new development and ultimate threat. Thus they also prepared for the time when they would not have the comfort of this newly-born Islamic Caliphate and would once again be cast to the wind. They also planned on how to communicate covertly since the Western eyes and ears appeared to be everywhere and all seeing.

Mikael was a very intelligent man and worked closely with the leaders, who had also been smart enough to keep on living when so many hadn't. With the demise of ISIL in 2018, they saw the failure of their dream of the Islamic State, and they evolved. The Russians and Chinese, both of whom had no love for Western economic imperialism, were quietly approached and cultivated. They, too, had the same objective in mind, as the enemy of your enemy is your friend.

CHAPTER 3

The Australian Farmer

David Hammond had been born and raised on this land, as had his father and his grandfather before him. Ten thousand hectares of low-rainfall stunted eucalypt scrub and salt bush, located five hundred plus kilometres northwest from Sydney, Australia. They had tamed the bush and fenced it into one hundred to five hundred hectare blocks, installed a stock water system once they had drilled the wells and found good enough water. Without water, nothing could survive the harsh conditions – even the goannas needed to get water from somewhere, albeit infrequently. The flies seemed to do alright, though, he mused. He had grown his crops, raised cattle and a family, just as earlier generations had done. He had infrequent good years, some okay years, and just recently, too many very bad years.

Dave stood on the sun-bleached porch in front of his heat-buckled house, looking out over the parched land. He tried not to think too much about what was happening on the farm; it was too depressing. He chose to think about what he could do that would be meaningful.

It was going to be hot again, unbelievably, mind-numbingly hot. The old thermometer had gone up to 110 °F, a warmish 43 °C. Today was going to be well over 50 °C, a heat that just pushed you into the ground. It shrivelled the few remaining plants left desperately holding on in the red dust called soil hereabouts. Even the leaves of the hardy mallee scrub turned crispy. When this died, there would be nothing left to hold the dusty soil in place, and the great sandstorms would sweep it all away. The winds stirred by the heat differential across this vast land caused these devastating sandstorms, which were happening two or three times a year now. He wasn't sure how much longer he could hang on, and he wondered if that sentiment had ever crossed the minds of his forefathers.

He did not know that, at the time, there were many other farmers around the planet asking themselves that very same question. And this number would balloon as the climate changed and the seasons failed.

Dave had made enough money to keep the bank quiet in the good and average years, but that had been a long time ago now. This drought had gone on for eight years, and he wasn't sure what he was going to do next. Even the kangaroos were dying; the place where each fell marked by a cloud of flies until the body became a desiccated mummy.

The dry had persisted, and the terms 'mega-drought', 'a thousand-year event' and 'civilisation changing' had been bandied about on the airwaves by various people with diverse opinions. But they needed to sell advertising spots, and sensationalism was the traditional way. Though the rainfall records, spanning well over a hundred years, showed a similar story. Less rain overall, much less reliable in the 'wet season', and big weather events where it would rain hard for a week and then stop. This made the calculation of averages meaningless. These downpours were often highly detrimental because of the rapid runoff from the rock-hard ground. Soft soaking rains were a rare thing indeed.

Covid-19 had come and gone, eventually, along with another stock market correction, not that either had affected them at all. They were the definition of isolated. They owned no shares and had no interest in other people's businesses; they were flat out looking after their own. People still needed food, although some days you could wonder about priorities when you listened to the news on the radio.

The week before, he had travelled the hundred and fifty kilometres into the local town with the family. He had taken along a single piece of paper, a printout of a spreadsheet of expected costs and income for the coming year – the income column was empty.

The previous year's barley crop was a complete failure, and he had wound up feeding it to the cattle. He'd only started the harvester to get it out of the shed for a thorough service, doing what he could himself because he couldn't afford a mechanic. Then reversing it back in, he'd put it on blocks and removed the wheels, then he drained the fuel tank. The calves they had bought and raised had shown a small return, but a lack of grass had meant they hadn't been finished. Feeding the barley crop had helped them, but in the end, it was just dry-standing dead matter they were trying to digest. Not suitable feed for finishing animals, and he had sold them for little more than he had paid for them twelve months earlier.

The winter rains, required to refill the soil and the soul, hadn't come. There had been a day when the clouds built and darkened, and it had started to drizzle. Then it got progressively harder and harder, and Dave had dared to hope. And then it stopped, like turning off a tap. Only 5 mm. Better than nothing? Probably not; grass seed long dormant may germinate, but then it would die unless more rain arrived. A huge amount more. Rainfall records going back over a hundred and fifty years, when the old-timers had hunted Aboriginal people on this land, showed a wildly fluctuating line averaging 200 mm annually, with eighty per cent of that falling in May, June and July. In the past five years, it had averaged 40 to 50 mm, coming any time.

The bank manager, Barry, had been good, understanding even. A young guy, fresh-faced, used to air-conditioned offices. But well trained. Barry appreciated that Dave had come all this way, and they had talked. It wasn't good. No, the bank wasn't going to foreclose or doing anything special – Dave was not the only farmer in this position. The bank had

     ROBERT STEVENS

no interest in starting any more rumours about foreclosures or people being forced off the land. There had been enough suicides already, and many more were allowing that sort of thinking to enter their heads. Even though the Hammonds, like many others, now had negative equity in the land and plant, this was not unusual. It had been a long time since the bank had seen anything like a capital repayment on the mortgage. Interest repayments were infrequent enough. Forced sales only brought the land price down, which affected all farmers and all positions the bank held. It was tough all round, but they had endured before.

The bank wasn't happy, but at least Dave was still talking to them, answering the mail, trying his best and living on a pittance. Barry had confided to Dave that he could tell the level of denial in a person from the size of the pile of unanswered mail on the table or mantelpiece when he called on them. Because it was never good news that came in the post.

Having teenage kids didn't help, and the boarding school fees had been recognised as unaffordable four years ago. So the two boys and one girl were now home-schooled, with a monthly trip to the 'local school' the same hundred and fifty kilometres away. Paying for the fuel in the car was becoming an issue. It had been a long time since the price of fuel had gone down, especially so since the Arab/Persian War was now in its second year. His wife, Caitlyn, had looked for work in town – office clerk, counter jumper at the struggling main street shops, check-out chick. The one day a fortnight trip into town made that unworkable, so they had to rethink that one. If nothing else, the Hammonds were flexible in their thinking, which made them a bit unusual in this small rural town. This improved their chances of survival.

Moving the family to town was a tough call, and this drought would end sometime, but only God knew when. You had to adapt. It would pass, one day. Surely. Wouldn't it?

Tomorrow, Caitlyn would finish packing the Camry, plus trailer, and move into town with the kids. The cost of the rental house they had found was easily met by the savings in fuel and income generated by the work she had found with the local accountant. There were many semi-derelict and abandoned houses in town at this stage. The drift of the young people to the big cities, the economic impact of Covid-19, and the ongoing economic uncertainty had created that situation. So the kids were packing. It was scary but also an adventure for them. *No*, Mum and Dad weren't splitting up. They had had many conversations around the dinner table about the need to do something. Doing nothing wasn't really an option; that wasn't the way a Hammond operated. The situation on the farm was self-evident, and pretending otherwise was unhelpful. But Dave knew that this was the default option that many of his neighbours had embarked upon. Yes, most of his neighbours still worked hard, often harder than usual. It was hard to criticise a man who was working long, hard hours. Whether the work was useful or not was another matter. Fixing fences that divided sections of dry dust, cleaning out water troughs that hadn't held water for four years or more, or just riding the horse around dry ground looking for any straggly sheep that weren't worth shearing. It filled in the day and gave a man some purpose – better than sitting inside for sure.

What else could you do when there was nothing you could do?

Dave liked to work on the computer and generate tables and graphs. It saved him from going outside and walking in the dust, looking at the empty fields and getting baked in the unrelenting sun. And the heat was unbelievable. But he did understand, as the generations before him had, that if they didn't get the winter rains, it wasn't good. If they got more than 250 mm over those months, then it was going to be very good. He would put in an extra paddock of spring barley. And there was the weird year, right before it stopped raining, where they had had 600 mm in July and August, and the floods had destroyed fences, scoured out the banks of the waterways, even lost stock in the surging water. The barley crops had drowned, and it took weeks before the

ROBERT STEVENS

ground had dried enough to replant. That crop had then been too late and was no good. That hadn't happened before. And then it stopped raining. He looked at the rainfall records: eight years ago. Land that produced perhaps five hundred to a thousand tonne of barley a year and maybe a hundred and fifty head of stock either fully or partially finished, produced only dust and flies now.

The biggest problem was that he didn't really know what to do with himself. There was a confidence and security in heading off daily to do the normal things that the generations before him had done: sow and tend the crops, shift stock, fix fences, and generally come home tired but satisfied at the end of the day. A cold beer was easily justified as was a big evening meal and laughter around the table with the rouseabouts. They had gone many years ago, and there was little to laugh about now.

"Okay, you lot, let's get this circus on the road!" he called out to the house as he went back inside. Outside, the temperature steadily rose.

CHAPTER 4

The Vision

The young American Indian boy had his first vision one night as he sat outdoors by the fire. He was barely twelve years old, and the experience could have been attributed to changing hormone levels. Yet, even at this tender age, he knew it was a message, one that he should heed. It came from the spirit world, and mirrored the biblical teachings his grandmother had hammered into him, sometimes at the end of stick.

He found himself sitting on the isolated rock plateau of a mesa, high above the desert floor. He didn't know how he got there, but that did not bother him. The words were clear in his head:

Big changes are coming. This society will not last, but many before have failed as well. There will be much suffering, as there has been in the past. This is mankind's lot. Men will fight and kill each other because this is what they do. All have been complicit. Be a friend of the desert, live simply and well. Learn and remember, pass on the knowledge when the time is right. You will know when that is. Do not follow the path that many of your friends are going to take. Go into the desert.

The vision that came into increasing focus was like something out of Dante's *Divine Comedy*, with many emaciated souls calling out for help in the *Inferno* and four mounted Horsemen riding through the screaming crowds. The boy was there, stuck in a thick mud pool, unable to move. He could only watch. And then he was back in the desert, sitting on the high mesa again, with a soft wind blowing and an eagle screeching in the distance. He was at peace once more, and the view of death was swept from him.

As the vision faded, the boy became disorientated, and he took a moment to refocus and recognise where he was. He thought he must have fallen asleep while sitting cross-legged before the fire. When he returned to what he thought was the here and now, he noticed an old man, whom he'd never seen before, sitting opposite him, his face distorted by the rising heat and smoke of the fire. The old man smiled at the boy through toothless gums and said, "You weren't asleep. You were given a vision. What it means only you will know. You will remember it for as long as you breathe, which tells you it wasn't a dream. It is a message – you choose if you want to heed it or not. But it will come to pass either way. Only a rare few see such visions without the help of the herbs."

He paused to let the message sink in, then continued, "Do not be afraid, for you have a gift. You will meet a white drifter in the desert many years from now. Show him where the Yuki people used to live. This, and the other visions you will have, are messages from the unseen spirit world that lives alongside us, and will not harm you. Do with them as you please. You have been given insight, use it wisely."

The boy must have fallen asleep then because he woke some time later and was cold. The fire had died down, and the old man was gone. But the vision still burned. He wasn't even sure whether the old man had been real or part of the vision: a dream within a dream. He watched the dying embers for some time before wandering off to the old caravan he shared with his grandmother. His home.

— ◆ —

As he grew into a man, he shunned the white man's way of life. He watched the rise of the gangs, a subculture that seemed so cool, so rebellious to a teenager. Many of his friends drifted, or ran, to that way of life. He watched his tribe forget the old ways and turn to alcohol. He watched the destruction of the desert as the companies dug it up. They had the unquenchable thirst. The companies had promised money for mineral rights, mining concessions and so on, and that was poured into a casino which apparently made more money. He saw his people living in dirty, run-down shacks on the reservation, with alcohol and other stronger, more addictive drugs decimating families and communities. Men beat their wives and children and did unspeakable things to the pubescent girls. His heart was sad. He knew that he could only change one person in this life, himself, and that his path was different. Anything other than what he observed on the reservation was an improvement. He didn't yet understand why all the money that had come from the mines and the casinos hadn't been shared with those on the reservation to be reflected in their living conditions, not realising that this was an international phenomenon.

Another vision came to him one night as he sat high on a mesa in Monument Valley, a place where he was sure many First Nation people had sat before, experiencing visions. It was, of course, a place that medicine men and shamans had come to for thousands of years to meditate, and their spirits were talking to him because they knew he was a good man. The vision revealed death and destruction, scenes of never-ending war. Brother fighting brother as they starved. He was to come across another drifter in the desert, and he was to share with him the secrets that had been revealed to him.

He wandered the desert, finding peace and solitude in simple things. He avoided contact with others as much as he could because it mostly saddened him. The sun and the wind and the high, screeching eagles were his friends.

 ROBERT STEVENS

CHAPTER 5

The Plan
Twins

The twins were taken from her at birth. Even though she didn't approve, she hardly had a choice in the matter. The fertility treatment had been just right: two babies with one pregnancy. Identical twins have a special bond, some mysterious connection that often leads to them living very similar lives. The leaders had recognised the value of twins, particularly identical twins. They would not betray each other. They thought similarly, and hence the behavioural traits of one could often be seen in the other. And one could easily be mistaken for the other, which was part of the plan. The father had been arranged by the mullahs, and while he was a presentable enough man, once pregnant she didn't see him again for some time. He was a white-skinned sperm donor, she the incubator, and she wasn't even sure what her future would be now that her biological duty was done. She had been told that her duty to Allah was to procreate, and as a devout Muslim, she had no problem with that. In this tough part of the world, love was a luxury most people couldn't afford. To survive and live another day, you did what you had to.

The girls were taken from her straight away, and breast fed by a wet nurse. She did not see them again, and she was sad about that. She was given a recovery period of two months in a little cottage in the grounds of the hospital, which she had assumed was somewhere in Russia. That was all the information she had been exposed to. She had been chosen, and had come willingly. At twenty-four, she had witnessed horror upon horror in her Syrian homeland, and anything else seemed preferable to staying there. It had been a long drive from Syria via Turkiye, and she had seen only gates and armed men as she was finally driven to a part of the large complex reserved for women like her.

It came as no real surprise to her that the bearded men came again one evening and, following all the correct protocols, advised her that her duty to Islam was to provide the same service as before. One of the bearded men was 'Christopher', the man with the light skin, just like hers. He stayed when the others left. And he had the same syringes for the fertility stimulation she had been given last time.

So twelve months after her first set of twins, she gave birth to triplets: two boys and a girl, again taken from her as soon as their umbilical cords were cut. She wondered if she would be required to perform more services of this sort for Islam and the State.

She didn't have to wait long. The answer was no. She had served Allah well, and undoubtedly would go straight to Paradise. There were many other women in the complex who were providing the same service. She had seen them in the dining halls and recreation rooms they were allowed to visit, and she had become friendly with many of them. But they, too, met the same fate when their duty was done.

The children were raised in a very Western environment in another part of the large, sprawling complex in which they had been born. Each knew of their own twin or triplet, as the case may be, but were unaware that they had other brothers and sisters. They were raised as siblings, sharing a bedroom and chores in a mock house that would not have looked out of place in any American town or middle-class suburb in a Western city. They were taught in English by American tutors, and French by French Canadians. The tutors had been especially recruited from their respective countries, and were those who wished to be part of the glorious rebirth of an Islamic Nation and the destruction of the capitalists. All had been personally selected by Mikael as potentially useful cogs in this vast, secret machine. Each tutor was far more useful than a masked man carrying an AK-47, or a woman with a suicide vest.

The correct accents in the selected languages were important, as were the mannerisms, cultural behaviours and traits required for the growing children to one day seamlessly blend into the targeted countries.

The compound appeared to be a hospital-cum-school grounds, with little obvious military presence. It was an old abandoned military facility in an obscure part of Russia: Bashkortostan. And although the Russians had problems of their own with their Muslim peoples, the mullah, the leader of the Directors, assured his Russian 'friends' that the site was needed for secret work that would only impact the West. This was not entirely true, but he did not want to burden them with too much information. He had come with money and an idea: he wanted a secluded training area for spies who would enter the West and be sleeper agents. The Russians desperately wanted the money being offered, large amounts of American cash, and didn't ask too many questions. They granted a fifty-year lease on an old facility, dating from the Cold War, that had been all but abandoned many years earlier.

The enemy of my enemy is my friend.

They knew satellites passed overhead, and in the first few years they kept exterior movements down to a minimum. They built shelters near the large buildings they leased, concealing what was going on underneath. They obtained the schedules for the US and NATO satellites from their Russian allies, and these were drummed into everybody. *Do not forget what you cannot see!* Because the grounds looked like those of a hospital from the air, and there was no apparent military infrastructure, there was little to fear from the eye in the sky. And because they knew the American AI looked for changes in features

– Were vehicles moving? Were more or less people counted? – they kept most things constant. An ambulance with the obvious red cross on the roof would change position every few days. A few people in white lab coats would move about when they knew the spy satellites with their high-resolution cameras were overhead and it was a clear day. They became masters at deception, as they had been taught. *Nothing going on here, just a low-level medical facility.*

The battlefield had moved on, and as usual, their opponents were still fighting the last war.

As well as a traditional 'Western' education, which hardly took a lot of time, these 'bred-for-purpose' students were taught 'extras', such as religious studies, including the obligatory Qur'an and the Bible; international money management and exchange systems; cyber security and computer programming, which were a strong focus. Military training, though, was kept to a minimum. They learned to use a handgun and that was it. The puppet masters had wised up – a person with military training didn't blend in so well. They stood a little too straight; they had a demeanour and presence about them that was apparent to others with military training.

They had been outgunned so many times before, and in response, they became more cunning. Why pick a fight you can't win? The Viet Cong had learned that more than sixty years ago, and they had no intention in relearning lessons the hard way. Time to make new mistakes. So the brothers and sisters were taught adaptability alongside the camouflage of normality, hiding in plain sight.

Each year group, a cohort, had twelve to eighteen students. There were five cohorts, initially seventy-four students in this special school. None of the children questioned why they were almost all twins, both identical and fraternal, and for a while this was considered normal. During biology classes at age four, they were told this was not normal, and they were being trained for a situation that was not normal.

 ROBERT STEVENS

So effective was the training that none of the children questioned this. It was digested and absorbed as everything else had been.

The training had begun early. The first thousand days being the most critical in determining a child's thinking patterns, which they subsequently carried for life.

At age five to six, pairs would start to leave the facility, after a big party with all the Western trimmings of ice cream and cake and Coke, and a long session at the bowling alley and then a movie (the latest ones, such as *Avatar*, *Halo* or similar). Again, none of the children questioned the process. They had been told that they were being separated and that this was part of the greater plan, which they also accepted.

The children who remained continued with their studies – everything they needed to know about Western customs and the specifics of where they were eventually to be sent. The target countries had been selected after much study. While many went to the US, not all of them did. The reason would not be apparent for many years, but the planning had been thorough. Some children went to their target countries at an older age than others; sometimes twins went to different countries, sometimes not. It seemed random, but that was not the case. Technically, the sleepers didn't have a home country, but the Russians, for a price, provided excellent documents that would allow the children to obtain citizenship and passports for the country to which they were each being deployed.

Ultimately, there were twenty-five operative twin sets, along with another sixteen individuals.

The relocated children were sent directly to pre-arranged host families – just in time to start a new school year and appear unsurprising as a new addition to the family. These children were either 'new' enrolments or 'transfers' to the selected school. Sometimes the older children appeared to have come from schools in other countries. Thus the sleepers became either the children or nieces and nephews of the host parents they were allocated. They had money to pay the fees, and the children demonstrated academic ability when put to the test, which was all the schools really cared about. The schools had also been carefully selected. They were almost all in the private, elite category, the incubators for future leaders of business and politics, the breeding ground of the old boys' networks. These children did well at the schools they were sent to; it was difficult for them not to. They became part of the machine, but continued to receive guidance from the radical leaders who had been sent to each country. This was in the form of letters sent via snail mail, and the host families had been given money and instructions on how to raise the children. Under no circumstances at all were the 'parents' to read the letters. They knew better than to try.

The siblings wrote to each other too, via snail mail as well. They did not question why they were living in different towns or countries; it was just the way things were. The clock was ticking, in more ways than one.

          ROBERT STEVENS

CHAPTER 6

Climate Deterioration

Earth's climate has changed before, more than once, without the input of man. The last Ice Age came to an end some twelve thousand years ago when Earth tilted on its axis, initiating the Holocene period, which provided conditions for mankind to flourish. The seas rose about a hundred to a hundred and fifty metres as the ice melted, literally changing the face of the earth.

The current period of climate change is extremely rapid in geological terms, and the ability of organisms to adapt, including man, is limited by the time available. The changes in the atmosphere have been slower than predicted, and it is now understood that the oceans, a massive sink, absorb a lot of the carbon dioxide and the heat.

But as the oceans warm, they expand, and sea levels rise. Large chunks of the Antarctic glaciers calve off and float away, destabilising the remaining ice. This process is massively accelerated by meltwater lubricating the underside of the previously rock-bound ice. Tipping points, where there are irreversible changes, like the loss of a glacier, have come and gone. Sea surges and violent storms, exacerbated by the increasing level of the oceans, have begun to envelop coastal communities. Maps of future inundation areas are developed, showing that many major cities internationally are at risk. Mankind has done little more than look at extra seawalls and argue over who is going to pay for their construction. Emissions rise further still. Superstorms and tornadoes are becoming more frequent. The wildfires in California, Australia, and soon the Arctic Circle, will become more fierce and rage for longer, pumping more carbon dioxide into the air. Countries are, and will, experience flooding and wildfires at the same time. It has an ongoing and accelerating effect. Weird weather is an apt description.

Attempts at establishing international carbon credit exchanges are fraught with bureaucratic rubbish and political correctness. Countries are given credits for not cutting down trees, but the often corrupt politicians support illegal logging in the Amazon and South East Asia. It is good business. Emission goals are continuously being set, and persistently not met for a variety of reasons. The Amazon rain forest burns and the continent-wide droughts intensify. The hundred-year flood becomes the five-year flood.

Funerals are held for European glaciers. Not much changes, man carries on, business as usual. Sales of large SUV-type vehicles surge, a great status symbol in most countries.

Man's thirst for resources knows no end. Forests are still felled for personal profit, well into the 2020s, even though the science has become unequivocal: deforestation accelerates climate change. Shale oil extraction and wars over resources continue. Oil extraction, refining and export aren't the most profitable enterprise on the planet any longer as the world lurches into the 2000s. This sector had been overtaken by the drug trade, the sale of weapons, and people smuggling. An apt reflection of 'civilised' society.

The science predicts that there will be many positive feedback loops. As the hitherto 'permanent' ice caps, sea ice and glaciers melt, there will be less sunlight reflected and additional heating will occur, hence the process will accelerate, not stabilise. The calculations on the contribution of the Greenland and Antarctic glacial melt to the global rise in sea level varies between tens and hundreds of metres. Still emissions rise and the forests fall.

     ROBERT STEVENS

The permafrost and its frozen peat in the vast stretches of tundra in the Arctic Circle have started to thaw, as have the methane hydrates underneath. The peat begins to breath, emitting greenhouse gases (GHG) like carbon dioxide and methane into the atmosphere. As the cold of the Arctic polar regions abates and the permafrost thaws, houses, roads and other infrastructure in northern villages are being destroyed, and trees otherwise anchored in solid frozen ground are falling over. 'Drunken forests' are becoming common.

The global superpowers argue over who owns the ocean and sea floor underneath the disappearing polar ice cap. Shipping companies applaud the opening up of the otherwise frozen Northwest Passage. It will be cheaper to get stuff to people now.

Farmers, carrying massive debt, use ever-increasing amounts of nitrogen fertiliser to boost crop yield and production. But when used in wet conditions, nitrous oxide is produced, a powerful GHG three hundred times more potent that carbon dioxide. It stays in the atmosphere for more than a hundred years.

The world screams out to be fed as the population first topped six billion, then seven billion, then eight billion, and it just keeps on growing.

The global news focuses on the latest war, the latest contagious disease, financial instability, and the transgressions of the rich and famous. Extremism and radicalisation increase. Societal decay is evident, the massive cities that man has built as an edifice to celebrate human progress are starting to collapse from the inside. The sprawl of housing over some of the most productive soils might be slowing, but it hasn't stopped. Few in a position of influence have the courage to say that the many human conflicts are driven by a lack of resources: the fight for what is left. There are just too many people for the planet to sustain.

By 2024, carbon dioxide levels exceeded 420 ppm, whereas previous calculations had predicted that 350 ppm was the 'highest' level at which civilisation could continue without too much disruption. But the irreversible changes began long before. At the end of the day, man appears to lack the will to change.

Save the planet? *The planet will be fine, circling the sun for a few more billion years.* Life on earth will adapt, as it always has. Evolution 101. The earth is a remarkable place for encouraging a diversity of life in what is a very harsh universe.

 ROBERT STEVENS

CHAPTER 7

Marcelle

As long as she could remember, she had been mercilessly beaten; it did not take much: wetting her bed at three, spelling mistakes in her homework, sometimes just because Dad came home in one of his shitty moods. Sometimes he was drunk, reeking of beer and cheap whisky. Sometimes there didn't appear to be a particular reason. He took out his anger, disappointment, perceived slights – you name it – on her, her sisters and their mother. Why her mother stayed was unclear – some mixed-up sense of duty perhaps?

She was eight when the violence became extreme and the neighbours called the police because they couldn't ignore the crashes and thumps any longer. They found her mother lying bloody and broken on the floor, and she didn't survive the internal injuries sustained by her father's kicking and beating. He was charged with first degree murder, but that was downgraded to culpable homicide once the police reviewed the case. Marcelle never saw her father again after he was arrested, and that was fine by her. The kids were all taken into care. Marcelle Rogers was the oldest, and she tried to help her younger sisters as much as she could. But she was angry at her dad, at her mom for not leaving him earlier on, at anyone else who had a family, and at the world in general. This came out as a sullen refusal to do anything that was asked of her. She would help her sisters, and God help anybody who picked on them. Once, in the facility's playground, one of the fourteen-year-old girls pushed her sister from the climbing frame she had been playing on. Two burly security guards had to pull Marcelle off the larger child, who'd had two teeth knocked out and her nose broken. Nobody bothered the Rogers sisters after that. Marcelle got a major telling off, but given what had happened in her life already, she didn't give a shit. *What are you going to do about it?* was her response.

Social Services managed to find a home for the two younger sisters, but people were reluctant to take the elder child, given the reports of destructive behaviour and the sullen resentment that oozed from her. Marcelle agreed it was best for her sisters to go to the foster home and accepted it was her behaviour that isolated her. At eleven she ran away from the facility for the third time and went far enough not to get caught, or more correctly, the authorities made less of an effort to find her. She had stolen food to last a couple of days, and had a simple backpack to hold a spare shirt, knickers and socks. That was it.

Very quickly she developed street smarts: stay with the other homeless people; they know where to go. Keep with the women who had kind eyes, which certainly wasn't all of them. She fell in with a woman called Dor, one of a group of homeless people living in an abandoned building in the centre city. Dor was a part-time backstreet whore and a longtime drug user, but Dor had kind eyes. Dor took the little waif under her wing, shared her safe sleeping spot out of the rain. Started to train the young-un on how to survive. "Mostly you got to do what you got to do," was her adage. Dor made Marcelle promise two things if she wanted help, and Marcelle reluctantly agreed. They were – don't get hooked on drugs, and sell the thing between your legs carefully. This involved the first and only talk Marcelle got on boys and sex.

The teaching section covering male anatomy was straight forward, like many things in this life. "Bobby! Come over here," was the command from Dor. Bobby, a skinny white dude aged somewhere between twenty and fifty, with a straggly beard and long lank hair,

     ROBERT STEVENS

shuffled over. "I'm giving young Marcelle a lesson on the birds and the bees. She ain't ever seen a man's coozer. Flop yours out so she can see what she going to be dealing with for the next little while." Bobby stammered, unsure what to do. "What your problem, boyo? You sure flop it out quick enough for those young tarts over on Broadway. Help this young lass out. It just a show and tell." So Bobby did as requested, and Marcelle learned later on that Bobby was a truly blessed man.

Dor bent down to inspect the instrument more closely. She invited to Marcelle to join. "Look, but don't touch! Bit different to what you got, eh girl! Now, when a man gets all turned on, this becomes full of blood and get all hard and straight, and he gonna fair want to stick it into you. When he does, that is how babies are made. The first few times it hurts a bit, but then it all gets better. All men want to stick it into you, and if you lucky enough, you will find a man that cares about you as well. Help you out, not just fuck you. A special man will also want to take care of you in other ways as well – love you. Those men hard to find in these parts. Be very careful who you let fuck you because you can get with child, or you can get a nasty disease. We're going down to the clinic tomorrow to fix that. I'll show you." End of the lesson.

"Now, Bobby, you and that piece of meat may now leave. If I ever see you showing young Marcelle that thing again, I'm gonna chop it off. You got that?"

"Yes, ma'am. No, ma'am. I'm hearing you loud and clear," was the prompt reply as Bobby zipped up and headed back to his mattress and blanket in his corner of the abandoned building. Marcelle had just turned twelve years old, but they told the nurse at the clinic the next day that she was fifteen, nearly sixteen. She went onto the contraceptive pill straight away. Last thing you needed on the street was to be pregnant.

That night Marcelle's hands did their own exploring, and over time, she learned to pleasure herself. Her first period terrified her; she thought she had gone too far. Dor helped, doing a very good job of suppressing the smile from her face as she recalled her own adolescence and the confused feelings, mixed with a fair dose of guilt and shame. "Ahhhhh, to be young again. How awful." Dor was the best mother, she just didn't know it.

The rest of what she ought to know about boys Marcelle learned the hard way, as many young girls do. At least at the health clinic three blocks away, they didn't ask too many questions. Pads for her periods were supplied along with a shower and essential hygiene information. STDs were discussed. The women there were kind. They did ask awkward questions about her not being in school, and Marcelle had perfected the lie about her being enrolled in a nearby secondary school and attended when she could, when her mother wasn't sick.

Marcelle started stealing. Junk food was easy to squirrel into pockets. A loaf of bread and do a fast run. Share with those who had helped her, Dor and those in the immediate circle. Small compactable items, such as scarves, were easy to stash and resell to the street merchants and Saturday traders. Wear good clothes, which meant stealing them to start with. Brush your hair so you don't look like a tramp. Otherwise the store security was going to lock on to you like a laser. She found a close kinship amongst the homeless; they usually shared what meagre belongings they had. They had no particular attachment to possessions. Things had come and gone in their previous lives. They will come and go again.

She was befriended by other kids on the street. Marcelle was relieved to know her situation wasn't unique. Violent, abusive and drunken parents were more common than she ever imagined. Up until then, she had been living in a terrified bubble, inhabited by an ogre called her father. Kids all around the country had either fallen between the cracks in the social welfare system, or just couldn't be bothered by adult bullshit. Many came from broken homes: violence, drugs, kiddy fiddlers. All sorts of domestic refugees.

Many, if not all, of the problems stemmed from ingrained poverty. Poverty of money, poverty of intelligence, poverty of hope. People so broken they just didn't feel much at all, and had no particular desire to try to improve their lot because they just got knocked down again. If a person got work, it was always at the minimum wage, which just wasn't enough. Work all day to watch your children go hungry and live in second-hand clothes. This bred a smouldering resentment, a disconnect with the rest of society. The drugs and alcohol provided the brief occasions when they could feel no pain, even if it was only for a moment.

Marcelle and her friends scavenged the rubbish bins outside the swanky stores, where they saw the fat cats and their corporate handbags studiously ignoring those 'lesser' people.

Inequality. All sorts of clever people talk about the gap between the haves and the have-nots. For many decades the inequality gap had been widening. The Global Financial Crisis of 2008 and 2009, orchestrated by the greed of the bankers and other financiers, widened the gap significantly. People resented that, as they didn't understand how those who had brought about so much misery at the expense of others, could actually be better off now. And those in the bottom one or two per cent were painfully aware of it, too, as they laughed around the fire at night with their friends. They had survived another day. Tomorrow will bring what tomorrow will bring.

The adolescents had learned it was easier and safer to work as a group: lookouts, shop casers, the scattergun effect of four or six kids taking off in different directions if one was being chased, at the very least it created a moment of confusion. They would rendezvous later and laugh and share stories and loot. Once, two of the gang were cornered by a biker who had just decided to hassle them because he could. As the biker backed the two scrawny kids into a corner under a bridge, another one of the boys snuck up behind with a wooden batten and smashed him over the head. The biker fell, stunned. So a few more hefty whacks around the head and a good kicking finished the job. The two-hundred- pound troll had been felled by a group who, individually, were smaller than him. Evolution 101: Hunting as a pack has benefits. The biker was stripped of valuables – a wallet containing over two hundred dollars, a .45 automatic pistol, a goodly bag of dope, and a plastic bag with an unidentified white powder, maybe coke? "Bobby's nose will do the lab test," one of them said, and the group fell about laughing, partly in elation at felling the troll. But the joke wasn't too bad either. His cell phone was smashed and the keys to his bike thrown into the river just to piss him off.

They left that part of town straight away, disappearing into the nearest subway station. They didn't really want to be present when the biker troll re-awakened.

 ROBERT STEVENS

CHAPTER 8

Money

At the compound in Russia, the cohorts learned about the IMF, international banking, the European Banking Committee (EBC) and the World Bank. The children were young, and all their lessons became deeply entrenched. It didn't take much reinforcing to demonstrate how the entire Western capitalist system was systematically corrupt. The rich growing richer on the backs of the working class with mortgages and the suffering of the peasants in the indebted countries. Debt levels were so high in developing countries that they could never be repaid, but still so many people struggled onwards, as did all the countries with crippling, mind-numbing debt. Austerity had been the call after the first Global Financial Crisis: you balance your budget by spending less. *You must make your debt repayments, or there will be no more*, the wealthy nations admonished. As usual, the poor suffered the most, but that has always been the way of it. Corruption at high levels in rich and poor countries alike was also endemic, but that has also been the way of it too.

The concept of debt is fairly new, but the levels to which it had risen to fuel expansionism and consumerism was breathtaking. Debt is, of course, a belief that tomorrow will be at least as good as today. Why would a person lend money to another, or a country, if they didn't think it was going to be repaid, plus some interest?

Governments also created money. Some of it was literally printed and put into circulation. The central banks provided the lower-tier banks with new money through a reverse bond system to reduce the chance of panic, as many investors felt more content with a pile of notes in their hand. Nonetheless, it led to rampant inflation. Some of the quantitative easing was electronic money: lines of credit that would appear on a bank's ledger sheet overnight, less commission.

The banks and international financiers loved it: making commission on money that only existed as binary code in a computer somewhere. Often they couldn't tell you where that somewhere was, even if they were interested. Many banks did regular backups in the cloud, but security was always an issue. Usually they had their own servers, secure, underground, protected.

The first Global Financial Crisis demonstrated to everyone just how corrupt the whole system was: banks had lent foolishly, and the taxpayer wound up footing the bill – under the government's direction.

This part of the Islamists' plan was to destabilise the capitalist system and make impotent their war machine. They wanted to create doubt about the security of the future, instil a sense that perhaps things will not always get better, then the paradigm of never-ending and increasing debt as a growth strategy would be destroyed. It was this ever-increasing flow of credit, the ability to borrow money to fuel economies, consumerism and the military, that kept the world on the path that it was on. It was debt that armed the capitalists and enabled them to be more technologically advanced at every level. This spending beyond their means had gone on long enough.

In the old days of imperialism, the English, French, Dutch, Portuguese and Spanish would go and conquer new lands and bring home the wealth of the conquered countries to fuel their own expansion and lifestyle. Many of the great cathedrals of Europe are testimony to

	ROBERT STEVENS

this plunder, from a time when there was little distinction between church and state. But now there were no new worlds to conquer. No new plunder. Nations were fighting over the diminishing hydrocarbons, forests and minerals, but these were not limitless either. And soon potable water would be a scare resource.

Mikael's team identified the key financial institutions that the Western capitalist machine relied on, rather that the small, independent local banks, of which there were few left. He was interested in the big machinations of international money. He contacted the sleepers individually when they were fifteen, at their homes.

"You know that you are special," he would start, once the pleasantries were done and they were left alone. "You will still have memories of your early childhood in a different country," he would prompt, then wait for the recognition to appear in the sleeper's eyes, before he carried on. "You will also have found your schoolwork at this prestigious school not to be difficult and that you are consistently top of your class." Again he paused and waited for the non-verbal confirmation, a recognition that he spoke the truth. "This is not by chance, nor is your ability to make friends easily. Nor it is by chance that you know at least two languages and can speak them fluently, once you dust off the cobwebs." He smiled. All the children had such deep conditioning that they did not ask questions until they were given the opportunity. "You have been in touch with your brother or sister, yet have not met them for many years. From now on you can do so. The next stage of your life is about to begin, and the reason for your unusual lifestyle will become apparent. Any questions?"

All the sleepers digested these revelations. They knew they were 'special' and had a higher calling, an expectation that they would play pivotal roles in what was coming. Now the realisation of their purpose was unfolding; it was sitting in front of them in the form of this moderately handsome, middle-aged man. Such was the early conditioning that few asked any question at all, apart from, "What am I supposed to do?"

It was then that Mikael, who had introduced himself as Ian, gave clear instructions as to what subjects they should major in at school and at university, for which they were all destined. He gave them directions as to the institutions they should be learning about, at which they would seek employment when the opportunity arose. And that, if they chose wisely, followed this path and did what was required of them when the time was ripe, they would become true heroes to the world. And then they would be able to live in luxury for the rest of their days. They would be remembered, which would be an understatement.

Then, to reinforce what was expected of them, he got each child to repeat back to him what they were expected to do over the next few years. While these sleepers were highly trained, they were still teenagers.

CHAPTER 9

Sophia the Teacher

Sophia had wanted to be a teacher for as long as she could remember. As a child in South Africa, she had 'taught' her baby brother reading and spelling by reading the words on grocery cartons as he variously devoured or otherwise destroyed them, and would read to him every night before bed. At primary school she idolised nearly everyone who taught her; they were angels. She was a sponge when it came to knowledge, knowing that if she learned and was the best she could be, then everything would be okay.

And then the family had moved from the Cape Province to Canada, and it was cold. She only found out a few years after the shift that her father had been held up at gunpoint, in his car at the traffic lights in South Africa. He had been carjacked, hit with a rifle butt as he protested, and left sprawled in the street while his assailants fled with his car. He considered himself fortunate not to have been shot. A passing motorist called the cops, as his cell phone and wallet were still in the car. The police had not attended the incident, it was unremarkable after all, a routine carjacking, not even a death at the scene.

Her parents, who had been questioning a whole series of developments in their beloved homeland, lost faith in the future of their country at that point and decided to emigrate ASAP. Dad was a qualified civil engineer, and Canada was actively prospecting for engineers at that time. Four months later, they had sold their house, packed everything into a container, shipped it off, and were on their way to Montreal.

Sophia, at the age of thirteen, entered a secondary school that had high expectations of their students. It took a while for her to settle down, but flourish she did. The interaction of hormones, the transatlantic move, the colder climate, the cultural difficulties and 'discovering boys', all made the initial transition awkward. But she adapted. "Do what you have to," was her mother's response to any challenging event. "Harden up," was the somewhat more concrete response from Dad to her tales of teenage woe.

When her school days were over, she went straight into primary school teacher training. Once qualified and employed, it took three years to discover that while it was okay, the role didn't really challenge her. She started correspondence courses to train to become a secondary school teacher. Science and maths were her core subjects; there was a chronic shortage in these fields. She had left home many years earlier, and was flatting with two girls, one a teacher and the other a law student. She kept working at the primary school while she studied. *Pay the bills, do the right thing, fly straight*, was what her father always said.

The conversations around a bottle of wine, or two, with her flatmates were dynamic: the usual stuff about boyfriends and their deficiencies, the politics of the now, and work. Who had played up in school, who had done what. The two teachers agreed that within a day or so, you could tell who the kids were who hadn't been loved, the ones who were going to play up in class. The legal student refused to profile kids in such a way. Surely they can change; they are just children. The brain is still developing in the young, behaviour patterns can change. The debate would rage into the night, becoming more turgid as the level in the bottle declined. Nature versus nurture versus environment. They would still all be good friends in the morning, even if they didn't see eye to eye.

    ROBERT STEVENS

For three years they shared the flat, adventures, broken hearts and the trials and tribulations of starting to make their own way in the world. She graduated first in her class and was quickly snapped up by a prestigious private secondary school in Montreal. Her salary doubled from what she earned at the primary school. It was her dream come true.

She shifted out of the flat and rented a small one-bedroom apartment closer to her new place of work. The students were great. They mostly devoured knowledge, as she had done. After three years she had saved enough for a small house on the outskirts of the city and was on top of the world, mostly.

Another stock market correction came and went. Unremarkable, if you don't own any shares. Sophia and her friends read the stories of traders and bankers jumping out of tall buildings because they had gone from being paper millionaires to bankrupt in the span of a week. This would generate a whole new conversation around the Pinot: Western capitalism and the perceptions of wealth. Credit was not quite so easy to obtain.

Sophia weathered this as well as anyone. She had learned to live frugally, her credit card was always paid off every month, and she met her mortgage payments with a bit to spare. The roll at the school started to fall as wealth evaporated, and all staff worried about job stability. She wanted more, but just couldn't put her finger on it. An annoying itch that wouldn't go away.

It was an incident one morning that was the trigger. She was on road duty before the start of school. A car had driven up to drop off one of the students, one of her students in fact. Jacques was an average student, privileged, but average academically. As the car stopped and the door opened, Sophia heard the end of what must have an argument in the car with the driver.

"Fuck you," shouted Jacques. "Just do as you're bloody told or you'll be sacked," he shouted into the car. "Pick me up from Carlo's place at five thirty." And with that, he slammed the door and stalked off towards the classroom, without a look back.

As Sophia watched this, somewhat stunned, she turned and looked at the crowd of people coming and going. No response. *Nothing happening here.* The argument was unremarkable, simply somebody telling the staff what to do. *And your point is?*

At that moment Sophia realised that these were all privileged arseholes: well-off to rich and used to getting what they wanted. Maybe the parents were feeling a little pain right now, but nothing like the pain the poor felt every day. These teenage children were, of course, insulated from the reality of life for the less-affluent classes. These children were all in the position where they treated others the way that Jacques had treated the driver – make it clear what you want and then just get it done. Money talks. There will always be somebody else to do your job if you don't like it.

During the course of the day, as she reflected on this, she made a decision. She was moving on; this was not the future she wanted for herself. These people didn't need help.

Sophia met Karl, a policeman, while on holiday in a rural Canadian town close to the local ski fields. She had decided on a ten-day skiing holiday during one of the school breaks, and detested it. She tried it for two days, had a weepy, hissy-fit session while laying on her pained hips one more time, then came off the mountain for good. She had booked into the four-star hotel for nine nights, so decided to do some walking, reading and unwinding in this unfamiliar yet comfortable environment.

She had been out walking along a remote snow-covered secondary road when the four-wheel-drive patrol pulled alongside.

"You all fine there, ma'am?" came the friendly, slow drawl from the wound-down window.

"Yes, fine, thank you," was her automatic reply with the faint South African accent still apparent.

"Well," came the considered reply, "mostly the bears are still hibernating at this time of the year." Then, after a pause for effect, "But some of the early ones are now awake and fairly hungry." A long pause followed, allowing her time to consider this. "Would you like a ride, ma'am?" The words and a smile came floating out of the window.

They rode in companionable silence for a bit, and then he asked, "Where does that accent come from?" And they didn't stop talking until he pulled up at the hotel ten minutes later, and it took another five minutes for her to get out of the car. They had dinner two nights later, and it was good.

He was eight years her senior, a decorated policeman, still grieving over the loss of his young son in a car crash two years ago, plus some. The marriage did not survive the grief. He had left the city where it all happened and had settled in this small rural community for a while.

They seemed to gel straight away, the age difference irrelevant.

She had sensed something under his overpowering grief, a suppressed rage perhaps, but didn't know him well enough to explore it. She luxuriated in the feelings of being wanted and loved, and the sex wasn't half bad either.

Saying their goodbyes at the airport that final morning wasn't easy; she had never felt that way about a man before. Could it be love? They traded email addresses, and she set up a personal Facebook account for Karl. He was happy and intrigued to be led through the process.

Sophia thought she had identified the gnawing uncertainty regarding her job – she wasn't being challenged. Of course the money was good, as were the working conditions. And yes, the school had high expectations, but wasn't that the way to get on in the world? Most of these kids would follow in their parents' footsteps. Money makes money. Can't have too much, you don't know what may be around the corner. They were all part of the old boys' network, and there wasn't a problem, was there?

Sophia went to school one weekend to do some of the infinite paperwork and report writing. While in the staff room making a coffee and generally stalling, she started flicking through the education-related magazines, initially not giving her browsing much thought. She found herself looking through the Situations Vacant sections, and idly wondered why she was doing that to herself.

It was another month before Karl accumulated enough leave to come for a visit; it was after all a three-hour flight to Montreal. The sex was even better. Anticipation – what an aphrodisiac!

Sophia shared her reservations about the school and her position. Yes, the kids were well-behaved. Yes, everybody had high expectations. Yes, the students were the privileged elite. Wasn't that just the way of the world?

Karl struggled to understand the problem. Most of his work involved people at the other end of the social spectrum. "What is the problem?" he asked at two in the morning as they lay on the sheets, satiated. She had been gabbing on about her discontent.

"A very good question, Officer," was the cheeky yet thoughtful reply. "I think I am tired of my current job and want a change. I think I want to try something different, perhaps with less-privileged kids. Try and make a difference, maybe reach a few … But, with the current economic uncertainty, it will put my finances in a tricky spot."

"Okay, just do it," was his response. "There will always be economic uncertainty. We should not put our lives on hold because of that. And I'm thinking of a change too, thanks for asking. Had enough of small town, outback frozen Canada."

After six months of the two of them flying backwards and forwards in their long-distance romance, Sophia saw a position as head of the science department of a medium-sized school in a disadvantaged area of Montreal. Women, being more cunning than men, don't so much as plan. They just know how to raise issues in a way that makes it seem a logical idea. It was sprung on Karl the next week after the edge of his passion had been dulled just a little. "Honey, what do you think of us both moving to a new city and starting afresh?" was the opening gambit.

"Taking advantage of a guy when he is down, eh?" was his immediate response, but he was happy. And it had been a long time since he had been happy.

CHAPTER 10

Steve and Carol

Steve had worked hard for as long as could remember. Apple picking or labouring in the school holidays, odd-jobbing after school, always banking most of what he earned. *Old-school stuff*, as he had been told by his father.

He studied hard, a combination of instilled discipline from his parents and high expectations from grandparents and the school. Coupled, of course, with the usual threats of short-term punishment and the longer-term consequences of underachievement. It was also in his comfort zone, or perhaps it was a conformist routine. This way of doing things had been instilled in him for as long as he could remember – work hard, study hard, be good. Get a good education and a good job will be sure to follow. It was hard logic not to follow.

He went to university, passed his engineering degree, did stupid stuff like most of those around him. Did a small stint overseas, initially travelling, and then by sheer fluke, a job in the coal mines of Australia. *Right place at the right time*, as his father had told him. And more: *Put yourself in the position to be open to ideas, surround yourself by things that will give you inspiration, and get off your arse and do something. Follow this advice, and I can guarantee something will happen. The only thing we can be sure of when you do nothing is that nothing will happen.*

The Protestant work ethic kept him there for three years. It was good money, of which he managed to save most. Yes, he drank too much, spent too much on fast cars and faster women, and he also squandered some. But he saved a much higher percentage than most.

He went back home to North Bay, Canada. He stayed with his parents for a couple of weeks, drank beer at the local watering hole, chased up old acquaintances. He soon realised that small-town Canada wasn't for him. He had grown in more ways than one, which his parents accepted even though he was an only child. They encouraged him to go to the city, see what he could find. So he did. With his degree in mechanical engineering, world travel behind him and a mature outlook, it didn't take long to get a job at one of the larger engineering consulting firms in Montreal, where he quickly settled in.

On Friday nights he went with the boys to the pub. On one such occasion, he met Carol, a friend of a friend, as is often the case. Not a raging beauty, nor a corporate go-getter. Nice. Pleasant. Good company. She had travelled a bit, like himself, and now had a good steady job as the service manager at a local garage and car dealership. They dated for a year before Carol moved in. And two years later they married. Old-fashioned stuff, with a traditional wedding. It just seemed the right thing to do. It was a bog-standard, white, upper-middle-class story.

After the honeymoon they settled back into their work. Steve was getting regular promotions and increased responsibility, plus he studied to improve his qualifications. After a year, they were able to buy a modest house not too far from where they both worked in Montreal. It was a bit of a doer-upper, on the outskirts of town, but that was okay. They both subscribed to the same work ethic, and it enabled them to turn their spare time into capital gain. So for three more years they scrapped old woodwork and replaced rotten timber and painted and replaced windows. They were happy in a comfortable way, even though there wasn't any spare money.

Both had joined retirement funds years earlier; in fact, when they both had started work. So that was a consistent drain, as was the mortgage and rates and insurance and the continuous flow of bills that never seemed to end. They had bought a car that turned into a regular inhabitant of the workshop at Carol's work, and even though the accounts were fair, it was sold after a year at great loss. Hard lesson. They borrowed more money to get a better one. The fridge stopped working.

And then, not entirely unexpected as Carol had gone off the pill eighteen months earlier, she was pregnant. Steve was in mild shock. He could understand that this was what they had talked about and considered, and one of the decorated bedrooms was even called the baby room. He was both thrilled and scared all at once. Money, though? How would they manage on one income, and would Carol want to go back to work? The mortgage was still a mountain even though they had increased the payments by a little bit every month. How would it work?

But it did, like it had for all the generations before them. Jane was born four weeks premature. BANG. *The waters have broken. I'm on my way.* All over within ninety minutes, and this little piece of new life in an incubator, Carol resting peacefully, and Steve not quite sure what to do with himself. He went home, finished the lawns, talked with the neighbour over the fence, and painted the wall in the lounge, which had been prepped some weeks before. One of the many jobs that never got quite finished. It looked good too. He sat down and had a beer. A few of them actually. The couple next door plus one, Karl the cop and Sophia the teacher, came over the next day with congratulations and more beer. What an excellent idea. Remy and Philippe, the gay couple from next door on the other side, came and offered congratulations too, but no beer. They were all good neighbours.

Carol did go back to work for a while, but they were both constantly tired, quite drained. The stock market correction came and went, and while they didn't own any shares directly themselves, their retirement fund was a diversified portfolio which included shares in

 ROBERT STEVENS

all risk categories. The 'correction' created a downturn in the economy. The businesses that employed the two of them struggled, and Carol's employer was quietly relieved when she handed in her resignation. It saved an awkward situation developing.

One local bank, where Steven and Carol used to bank earlier, failed. Hard to imagine a bank failing given they seemed so persistently greedy with their fees and charges.

Steve and Carol were concerned about what was happening at their own bank, and he managed to secure a meeting with a mid-level manager a day before the manager was made redundant. Fortunately for Steve, the manager knew this was coming, so could speak openly and truthfully, perhaps the first time in a long while.

The manager didn't beat about the bush. "We all invest depositor funds in what are usually considered safe investments, not a shoebox under the bed or a concrete vault in the ground. The money needs to be out and earning a return. The group retirement fund invested quite heavily in the share market. Returns had been good for a long time. A balance of infrastructure, blue-chip and some a little more speculative. Overall, the ranking was conservative. In any share market there are corrections, and this one was a good one." After pausing a bit to consider his response, the manager continued, "Your personal investment portfolio has lost at least half of its value, and we are not sure at what level the market will stabilise."

Steve was distraught. *How the fuck could this happen?* "You guys were tasked with being prudent!" he said, furious.

The bank manager countered, "The large correction in the share market is unfortunate, but not entirely unexpected. This is what markets do. You were happy to take the gains when they happened. The actions of rogue traders in the market have affected our bank as well, and we suspect a complicity between staff, which is quite illegal. This is being investigated. It appears they may have gambled with between 1.8 and

2.4 billion dollars, which is more than the bank's capital. So this bank is also technically insolvent. Many people's savings were wiped out, along with the retirement savings plan that your employer, the engineering firm, had." The bank manager could barely look at Steve, such was his discomfort at Steve's silent, escalating anger.

"I'm sorry," he continued, his voice wavering slightly, "but if this bank does fail, then your mortgage, which is an asset of the bank, will be on-sold. You are encouraged to keep up the repayments even if this bank does fail because any missed payments will downgrade your credit rating and can affect your subsequent interest rate. Any missed payments will also have to be caught up on. Thank you."

And that was that. Steve went home and broke the news to Carol. He had bought a bottle of wine on the way home, but it didn't help much.

CHAPTER 11

Dave Hammond

A year had gone by, and the winter rains had failed, again. Hammond Farms had, for the first time ever, not purchased any cattle. They had no money to buy them; the overdraft was maxed out. But more significantly, they had no feed. If Dave had some feed, or had been confident that the grass would grow because the rains had come, then he would have gone to the annual sales and purchased stock – whether he could afford it or not. He would've had them delivered and then let out into the farm paddocks, knowing full well it was unlikely anybody would come and retrieve them because the cheque had bounced. Dave would eventually have paid the bills for the cattle and transport because, at the end of the day, there would have been money coming in. But none of these things happened.

Dave spent a lot of time sitting on the porch, not doing much at all. Just watching the dust blow and wondering what to do with himself. Watching the heat shimmer was somewhat mesmerising. The irony was not lost when Dave recognised it, most of the time he just sat and didn't think about much at all. What do you do when there is nothing to do?

Caitlyn and the kids were really enjoying town. Mandy had a boyfriend, which concerned both parents, and the boys were playing cricket most weekends. Caitlyn loved her job, and the money was okay. She was making her own way and providing groceries for Dave and a bit of beer money. *Mental welfare*, she called it. She had lost weight and there was a new vibrancy about her, and while their sex life was the same as usual, Dave did wonder.

He had thought about it many times, as he did now. Why not shift to town himself and get work at the coal mine? Leave the farm. There was nothing meaningful to do here now: no stock, no crops, just flies and wind-blown dust. The odd brumby or kangaroo wandering through, but they were becoming rarer as they slowly starved.

There were two problems. One was his own intergenerational pride when it came to leaving the farm. He could get around that one by saying he wasn't abandoning the farm, just adapting. If, no – *when* it rained again, he would come back and pick up where he had left off.

The second problem was the marauding gangs, travelling in cars. Stealing, raping, burning and killing. The cops were struggling to control them. Yes, they pulled them over, and the rule of law, while weak, was still in effect, theoretically. Sometimes the cops managed to pin a crime on the gangs, sometimes they found weapons in the cars and arrested the occupants. And sometimes, increasingly often, it dissolved into a gun battle, which didn't always go the best way for the cops. The police were undermanned and outgunned, and while double crewing was now obligatory, sometimes even two of them struggled. Last trip to town, four weeks ago, Dave had been pulled over, and the cop had his hand on his gun all the time. His partner had his automatic rifle trained on the car until cop number one gave the all-clear.

The police's overall workload was horrific. Domestic violence had skyrocketed. Stress created by the drought, and the subsequent decrease in cash flowing through local communities, had shut many businesses and laid off staff in others. Both Dave and Caitlyn had wondered how long her job would last, but they had learned not to worry about that type of thing anymore. If you worried about too much these days, you would quickly go insane, because there were no answers. Take each day as it came, adapt. Water, shelter, food, the kids. Maybe not in that order. They just didn't realise it, yet.

He recognised that he was doing nothing useful on the farm. The windmills worked fine in the increasingly gusty weather – there was just no water to pump. One windmill had been blown down by a freak gust, and after surveying the damage and what was required to repair it, he decided it just wasn't worth it. That was a pivotal moment.

He rode his trusty horse back to the house, fed it a little meal and realised there was no point staying. He opened the gate so the animal could go when it wanted. The horse stood there and looked at him.

Dave packed his suitcase and put it in the battered, gas-guzzling Nissan, which he had tried trading in on a more economical vehicle. But he had no money, and nobody wanted such a beast now, so he had no collateral. The tank was never more than a quarter full, and the red fuel light had come on as he drove home four weeks ago. The phone had been cut off a year ago; they had let that expense go. They had not had line power for six months, not since the tremendous tornado and sandstorm had taken out kilometres of power poles and the company had decided not to replace them for just one customer. "We regret to advise …" the letter had stated. The generator the power company had provided worked well, but they left it off for extended periods now because the fuel was so expensive when you could get it.

He had found an old jerry can that had a few litres of diesel in it, and although he couldn't testify to its purity or lack of diesel bug, there wasn't a lot of choice. He siphoned another fifteen litres out of the generator and into the jerry can. That should be enough. The harvester and tractors had been drained of fuel a long time ago. A hundred and fifty kilometres was a long way to walk when the thermometer could touch 50 °C now. The new thermometers that went that high had been distributed by the public health agencies two years previously.

Heat stroke and dehydration now killed thousands every year. Despair killed more.

He looked around, trying to figure out what else to pack, but for the life of him he couldn't think. He had the guns and ammo. A few tools from the workshop. Perhaps he could get some handyman stuff in town. He loaded a plastic twenty-litre drum of very warm town water that tasted like a swimming pool, but at least it was water. He had put in the last of the kids' clothing, and while he knew they had long ago outgrown them, he couldn't bear the thought of leaving that kind of stuff behind. He had cleaned out all the food from the pantry. In truth, there was not much there to start with. He had boarded up the windows as best he could and packed and nailed towels around the wooden window frames to try and stop the dust from coming in. Yeah, right. The bloody stuff was everywhere as the house warped and contracted in the heat, so much now that the wooden windows and doors no longer sat well in their frames.

He went to the yard where his friend, his horse named the Old Nag, still stood. He gave her a cuddle and a good brush down. She nuzzled him; she knew something was up. He then walked away, blurry eyed.

He stood variously by the rear door of the Nissan or wandered into the house, the workshop, or the barn, looking for something he might want to take. After an hour, he realised what he was doing. For one of the few times in his life, he was lost. He sat down in his favourite seat on the porch and wept. He wept because he felt he had failed his legacy. He wept because he felt so powerless. He wept because for the first time in his life he was afraid. He didn't know what to do.

He fell asleep in his chair, drained.

He woke at close to midnight. It had cooled down to a mere 35 °C. He drove into town that night, as the days were too hot now to do anything. The Nissan coughed and spluttered, and he stopped once to clear the fuel pre-filter cartridge, which was clogged with black strands

ROBERT STEVENS

of the fuel bug. But he got there, with the low-fuel light solidly on for the last fifty kilometres and the first light of dawn touching the horizon. He fell asleep in the driver's seat, too drained to even undo his seat belt.

Caitlyn found him there half an hour later when she came home from a night with her lover, who happened to be the chief accountant at work, and just left him where he was. She was grateful that her husband hadn't gone inside to find her not at home. The affair had been going for close to a year, and she liked things just the way they were. Dave was a good man, but he had been beaten down by the drought. He had enough on his plate, an unfaithful wife was the last thing he needed to know about. So she left him sleeping and went to prepare breakfast for her daughter. The boys were away playing cricket, and her daughter slept like a log, which she was grateful for. She would wake her husband with a nice strong coffee and a new sense of commitment. The affair was over, and a new chapter started.

Flicking through the news on her iPad, she saw that that lettuces in New Zealand cost ten dollars each because a cyclone had slammed the main horticultural areas of the North Island. BLTs were definitely off the menu.

CHAPTER 12

Sophia and Karl

Karl managed to get a transfer and shifted back to Montreal. An opening for a senior officer existed in one of the older suburbs closer to the middle of town. Karl secured the position, accompanied by a pay increase. Tougher neighbourhood, many issues. Sophia had applied for and got the head of the science department job she had seen in the *Education Gazette*. It was a public school, a somewhat lower socio-economic situation than she was used to. A lower salary too, but she accepted that.

They were still desperately in lust and love, and decided to buy a house together. They bought a modest three-bedroom stand-alone on a standard section, in an older strip development on the edge of suburbia, and started playing house. It was good, and they had good neighbours. Their immediate neighbours were a gay couple, Remy and Philippe, and a young couple, Steve and Carol, with a young baby. Then further along the road, a professional couple, Michael and Micaela, who were cheery enough but generally kept to themselves. An empty house followed, up for sale, and some unbuilt sections. The previous housing boom had run its course. Across the road was sparingly used farmland, awaiting the next housing bubble.

There were some real behavioural problems in the school, quite different to where she had been teaching. This was one of the questions in the interview, and she had anticipated it: "How are you going to manage disruptive and disengaged students?"

Her response was well rehearsed: "High expectations, rigid but fair rules in the classroom strictly maintained, knowledge of school disciplinary system for referrals, and consistency. Build a relationship with the students so you have a sense for what is going on in their lives. They will try me out, see how far they can push me. That is their job. They will find a rock that is immovable, borderline unreasonable to start with. I will not be their friend."

It actually worked most of the time. But some of the kids were damaged goods. It wasn't rocket science to see why when you met the parents – if you could. Not exactly regulars at the parent–teacher evenings. The poor little buggers didn't stand a chance. The school provided breakfast for any who wanted it. The school canteen had modern music in the background, creating a relaxed atmosphere. Out of a roll of close to nine hundred, fifty to eighty kids would turn up at least twice a week for breakfast. It was an eye-opener. Sophia was volunteered for breakfast duty one morning a fortnight.

Sophia managed most of the troubled and disengaged kids fairly well. Some days better than others, though. Over the course of a few months, she managed to get them mostly settled and mostly on task. Senior management were impressed, and in the science department they actively shared ideas on behaviour control and changes to the curriculum to improve student engagement. She was exhausted but happy-ish. The staff in the department were okay, mostly just exhausted from the constant struggle with students' behaviour. New guidelines for student time-out were established to generate consistency, and some professional development was provided. Improvements started.

Sophia was exhausted, and while not yet disillusioned, she did wonder about the joy component of teaching. Where was it again?

— ◆ —

A new strain of flu swept the globe, colloquially called the NuFlu. Karl went down like he had been hit by a truck, and alternately shivered and sweated all night. Sophia wiped him down with a wet towel and packed ice into pillowcases, which she put under his armpits, her knowledge of science guiding her actions. The bed was saturated, but she didn't care. She felt a little dizzy herself, unsure if it was from the flu, her concern for Karl, exhaustion or a combination of all of the above.

Karl recovered, but it took two weeks. He was weak and had significant muscle loss due to the violence of his shivering and the enzymic breakdown in his tissues. He hadn't eaten in ten days. Sophia played nurse for a while longer.

Financial instability ruled, and a national bank collapsed when it was revealed that a rogue trader had taken unmoderated risks in the stock market and his speculation had wiped out the bank's resources. This was the final straw: a collapse in trading activity and the fine margin the bank made on every transaction. Remy and Philippe had worked hard all their lives in the retail sector, putting in long hours, scrimping. They had bank deposits and quite a portfolio of shares, which provided them with the extra income needed to supplement their meagre pensions. They saw their life saving evaporate over those few weeks.

It was not clear when Remy took his own life, but they had both been dead for at least a week before they were discovered. The postman had noticed the mailbox was not being cleared and had called the police. Philippe was in the bed, showing all the signs of having died of the NuFlu. Remy lay beside him, holding Philippe's hand, the bottles of sleeping pills and the bottle of vodka to wash them down still on the bedside table. Not exactly a crime scene mini-series.

The stock market sagged even further, and more banks started applying for emergency relief from the government.

Karl was back at work part-time. In the district, there were two 'formal', patched gangs heavily involved in drugs, more than adequately

ROBERT STEVENS

assisted by two well-known but poorly respected lawyers who could often find fault with police procedures, unearthing obscure but significant loopholes in the machinations of the legal system. Drug dealers, burglars, rapists and arsonists walked free far too often. The frontline cops were becoming discouraged, and the formal statements from the police to the public were becoming increasingly bland and meaningless as they tried to hide the fact that the statistics were becoming worse. In brief – they were not winning.

One night, after a particularly turgid night of rushing from one event to another, and a responding ambulance officer at one scene had been bottled, Karl sat down with his crewmate Phil over a beer in the staff room.

"Fuck," Karl said quietly. "Back in Banff, there was enough rough country. We could take a couple of these arseholes, shoot them, and the bodies would never be found," he added, half-jokingly. "The world would be a better place."

A short pause while they sat there and reflected on the night.

"Didn't we arrest that skinhead prick with the swastika tattoo a week or so ago? What is he doing back out?" Karl asked.

A long silence from his partner ensued, and then the quiet little comment, "Funny you should mention that. And yes, we did arrest Mr Richards a week or so ago on firearms charges. But he was released the next day on lack of admissible evidence."

"Fuck me, what do we have to do?" Karl remarked. And then, after a bit of pause, "Okay. What now?"

Phil carried on, "We all know we aren't winning. There are more drugs, more assaults and shootings. More burglaries and sexual assaults. More gang intimidation because they control a fair chunk of the drug trade. Disagree?" No comment was necessary from Karl, just a quiet nod of the head.

"Perhaps this experiment in neo-liberalism isn't working, especially as our legal friends keep on bending us over and giving us one," Phil carried on. "The assholes will say all the right things in front of the judge, but once they get back with family and friends, it doesn't take long for the old behaviours to return."

"We would all be better off if they disappeared," Karl said.

"Save a *lot* of money and trouble," ventured Phil.

Karl was troubled and elated at the same time. *Were they to become vigilantes?* "Can't pop anybody we've arrested," fell out of Karl's mouth, "too risky." Perhaps he was more tired than he realised, not to mention the two beers that had slipped down very easily. This was a conversation many frontline police conduct in their own head; few are willing to say it out loud.

"That's not the idea," Phil said. "We wait, we plan, we identify a target and know their movements. We nab them when they don't expect it. They vanish. Into the garbage dump is good. Just another piece of crap."

"Count me in," said Karl. What he had revealed to Sophia just two nights before was that his son had been caught in an altercation between two gangs; it wasn't a car crash that took him. He had been in the wrong place at the wrong time. Despite a pile of evidence from CCTV cameras, eye-witness accounts, and cartridge casings at the scene, no one had ever been charged. He was a very angry man on the inside. He thought he had managed to control the emotion, but no; it still festered.

Phil knew all of this. Earlier on, he had checked Karl's record thoroughly, and had taken a calculated risk in raising the idea of a bit of street justice. The other kind wasn't working. And when something doesn't work, change something. Don't keep on repeating the same old stuff and expect different results.

"Who?" asked Karl.

"Manu," was the simple reply. Leader of the Rancheros, one of the main drug supplying gangs in town. The power of the media, with

   ROBERT STEVENS

programmes like *Sons of Anarchy* and *Mayans M.C.*, had romanticised biker gangs, but the Rancheros were an affiliate of the Triple Sixes gang, a powerful, organised biker group believed to be responsible for fifty to seventy per cent of the drug supply in Canada.

"Okay," was Karl's response. No need for much elaboration.

And so it was, six weeks later, that the door at the motel where Manu was sleeping with his girlfriend-on-the-side was quietly unlocked. The night duty girl at the motel had happily handed over the key to the two armed and masked men who confronted her at 2 a.m.

A quick taser to Manu and his lady friend shut down any conversation or disagreement, and Manu's limp body was quietly bundled into the back of the stolen pickup truck. A tarpaulin covered the deck, the common kind that can be found for $1.99 at any hardware store or supermarket. They made sure they had Manu's cell phone: intelligence gathering. They drove out of the motel parking lot and then a distance down the road to a darkened lay-by. Manu was rolled up into the waterproof tarpaulin, taped in with his arms taped outside, rolled off the back of the truck, and then kicked in the chest to wake him up.

The first question: "Cell phone passcode?"

"Fuck off, pig," was his immediate answer. Manu knew a cop when he saw one. He had disappeared the odd undercover agent from time to time and knew what cops looked and smelt like. He wasn't the leader because he was shy.

"Okay," Phil replied, and then they amputated his right hand by shooting through his wrist with the sawn-off shotgun brought along for such contingencies.

Once the screaming subsided, Manu offered, "Two-four-six-eight double hash."

"Much better," said Phil. "Now, who is your major meth supplier?"

"I don't know the name," was Manu's inaccurate answer.

Phil and Karl had a twenty-litre drum of water and a towel to further encourage the flow of information. It took two rounds of waterboarding, where the brain believes the body is drowning, before Manu changed his answer to something more useful. He gave up the name of a prominent businesswoman in town, which surprised both the cops. It took fifteen minutes to get that information plus whatever else they could get out of him, and then they shot him in the head.

Manu's corpse was then fully encased in a second, larger plastic sheet to contain bodily fluids and his severed hand, all of which was then fully taped over and heaved back onto the truck. The two men drove back to the edge of town. Manu's body was thrown into a dumpster that had no surveillance camera nearby, and which they knew would be cleared in a couple of hours. Some wastepaper was thrown over the wrapped body. The half-used roll of duct tape was also disposed of, having first been wiped down for accidental fingerprints. They set fire to the pickup truck under a bridge where they had left their own car and dumped the surgical gloves in a rubbish bin at the police station. At precisely 5.00 a.m., as per schedule, the dumpster was cleared, and at 6.30 a.m., as soon as the dump was opened, the contents of the rubbish truck entered the compactor and the problem was gone. Just like that.

Phil and Karl clocked off shift at 7.00 a.m. and both slept like babies when they went home.

 ROBERT STEVENS

CHAPTER 13

Marcelle

The strategy of hunting as a pack was effective, and they learned to work as a team, whether burgling a house, selling dope, or rolling some drunk. Just looking after each other. Marcelle was now fifteen and very street-smart. Her sixth sense that alerted her when things weren't right became well-honed. Other kids began to hang out with her and her gang because they were prosperous. She and her gang found their own place in town to crash, another boarded-up building about two blocks from where Dor and the others lived. Dor didn't approve, but how many mothers ever did when the kids left home?

The tighter economic conditions that followed the stock market correction had a significant flow-on effect for these scavengers. As spending was cut across the board, the quality of the garbage deteriorated in the suburbs and the city. There was less discarded food, and fewer still-functioning appliances that they could take and sell for a few dollars at the op shop. Things were getting leaner all around.

Marcelle had been casing the suburbs for two weeks, breaking into empty houses. While there was rarely anything of value inside, she had a list of requirements: tall fences all around, long drive, big house, preferably two-storeys, easy escape route out the back down an alley or similar. At least one empty house beside the target house, which could be an escape route, and it would be nice to have an empty house each side, but that would be a bonus. She was looking for a new place to stay. It took her ten days to find what she wanted.

CHAPTER 14

The Antarctic Ice Shelves

The Antarctic glaciers hold a vast amount of frozen fresh water, and they are best considered slowly creeping frozen rivers. They flow downhill at a slow pace, with the leading edge eventually floating off on the ocean and calving into icebergs. It is usually so cold in the region that the surface of the ocean freezes, so the combination of the frozen sea ice and the inertia of the floating glacial fresh ice slows the rate of the flow of the glacier down off the Antarctic plateau. Thus the glacial ice may be tens of thousands of years old before it reaches the ocean. Icebergs don't affect the level of the ocean as such. It is the volume of glacial ice and meltwater entering the ocean that has this effect.

Icebergs calve all the time, and like most natural processes, these processes ebb and flow through geological time.

Glaciers move downhill under the force of gravity, and there are many processes that affect how fast a specific glacier moves. Two of the most significant are, first, the volume of meltwater on the surface that runs down natural cracks and pools underneath the glacier, providing a lubricating layer between the ice and rock underneath. And the second is the effect of the combination of frozen ocean ice and the mass of partially grounded and partially floating glacier at the leading edge. This mass 'holds back' the slowly creeping frozen river. Climate change, specifically an increase in temperature, influences both.

The Larsen Ice Shelf is made up of different components: Larsen A was a moderately small section that collapsed in 1995. Larsen B collapsed in a period of two to three weeks in 2002, with some icebergs that were produced being as large as 3,250 square kilometres by 200 metres thick. Larsen C is undergoing rapid changes, with Iceberg A68, which calved in July 2017, being 5,800 square kilometres by about 200 metres thick. The melting of the balance of the Larsen Ice shelf may raise sea levels by perhaps a few millimeters, but will destabilise the grounded ice behind it, adding to further sea level rise.

Glaciologists are usually reluctant to make predictions about the speed of glacial change as yearly weather patterns vary. The temperature and amount of snow being deposited at the head of the glacier have an impact, as do the effects of the lubrication underneath and the 'brake' of sea ice and grounded icebergs. What they can say with confidence is that the rate of change is accelerating and that warming temperatures are not good for ice.

If all the ice in the Antarctic melted, which all agree is not going to happen soon, it is estimated that global sea level would rise by perhaps fifty to seventy metres.

The Arctic is different. Besides encompassing areas where the ice has formed on solid land, the Arctic Circle also encompasses areas where there is no land underneath the ice, so all the ice that forms there is frozen seawater, called sea ice. The vast ice sheets of Greenland, Alaska, Canada and Russia are fresh water, which will affect sea level as they melt. In the Northern summer of 2021, temperatures in the Arctic Circle reached 38 °C (100.4 °F), a new record. The Arctic is warming twice as fast as anywhere on earth, and the sea ice there is declining by about one per cent per year. That accumulates to a forty per cent loss since 1980.

     ROBERT STEVENS

CHAPTER 15

The Twins
Imbedded

Fifty-eight sleeper agents were inserted into various countries. In one case, one of a set of twins had died in a car accident back home, and it was decided to leave the imbedded twin in the target country as they could still be of use. In another case, one of the imbedded twins stopped clandestine communication with control entirely. Consequently, this person was being tracked by specialists, and would be found, eventually, and dealt with.

While the numbers of embedded sleepers were less than they wanted, it was still enough, hopefully. Part of the plan was for the leaders in each country to enlist local discontents and anarchists for a separate segment of the operation, which was a different story altogether. That component was always recognised as being more risky, but what high-return endeavours are without risk? They just needed to create enough damage – they knew it could never be total destruction all at once. But, like a brain, do enough damage to essential components, and it will stop working.

Handwritten letters were the preferred method of communication. They had been taught that all electronic communication probably was, or could be, monitored. And it left a trail that was hard to erase.

Letters were sent to an innocuous address in Washington DC, where they were forwarded on to the recipient. And mostly there was no rush, no urgency. The entire strategy was going to succeed through slow and thorough implementation, the exact opposite of the impulsive and immediate world of social media, the rhetoric and knee-jerk reaction of Instagram, Facebook and other platforms. Things were ticking along nicely.

Twenty-four agents were groomed for, and had achieved, national and international positions in banking and were being promoted to senior management roles. Another two were embedded in the Department of Homeland Security (DHS), in the cyber intelligence/warfare department to keep an eye on whether or not the enemy suspected anything. Two were embedded in the tech-heavy telecommunications industry and were short-listed for senior leadership roles. Three were graduates of advanced computing courses and military doctrine and had either been snatched up by the internet industry or various military contractor organisations. All the military personnel were involved in the highest security clearance areas: digital control systems, drone operations, cyber warfare. Two worked for the National Security Agency (NSA). None of the positions they had applied for had been by chance; they had all studied their target companies or agencies and had groomed themselves to be the ideal fit. And this was just the operatives in the US. Many were deployed internationally in similar banking and security roles.

There was no interest in nuclear weapons systems; they were so yesterday. Why poison the environment further? Why destroy useful infrastructure?

All they had to do was report at least bi-annually with updates, contacts, addresses. Opportunities and threats. Progress on their specific task. Targets they had identified who could be eliminated when the time was right, and where they lived. Remembering always to destroy the writing pad once they had finished the letter, and then post the letter alongside other innocuous bills and postcards when the opportunity arose. They were never to post the letters from work; it might be noticed.

     ROBERT STEVENS

All was going to plan, mostly. The loss of one due to 'falling off the radar' showed that they had arrogantly assumed that all would follow their assigned path and remain devoted to the cause. Because they were the types who learned very well from their errors of judgement, the Directors recognised and acknowledged their own arrogance, and vowed not to make that mistake again. Just like they had vowed not to repeat previous mistakes, such as provoking a more heavily armed enemy without having the means to completely destroy them. Sun Tzu's *Art of War* had been compulsory reading for the leaders.

It was also recognised that the number of operatives they had was marginal, but they did not plan to fight a conventional war. The 9/11 attack in 2001 and its aftermath had shown the impact a few could make. They just needed to create enough damage in critical systems to precipitate a cascade of failures. And the way computer systems were now linked, they could hopefully create such a cascade. While the standard computer virus was the ongoing battlefield of the internet, imbedded programmes set to trigger at a certain time were much harder to detect. Especially when it had been written by the very people who had created the programme in the first place; it was not an 'add-on' but already a part of the integral code.

They did pay the Russians, Chinese and North Koreans well to continue cyber operations against the West. They wanted to keep the capitalists distracted, focused on the usual suspects, thinking that everything was 'normal' and that the West was winning.

CHAPTER 16

EMP

The fact that nuclear explosions create an electromagnetic pulse (EMP) had been known for decades. The fact that an EMP could be created by other means took a bit more understanding.

EMP weapons have been on the research and development agendas of many countries since the 1960s, usually employing a chemical reaction to produce the high currents necessary, or capacitors and a Marx generator. Advancing battery technology, mostly driven by electric car development, improved the ability to store and release energy quickly and efficiently, especially when using lithium ions. A few countries had functional EMP weapons – their existence a top secret – to be used judiciously in battlefield situations.

One of the development groups at the Russian facility in Bashkortostan had focused on electromagnetic energy, with physicists recruited from around the globe. The traditional view of a university professor is one of a staid, absent-minded, snowy-haired old man with spectacles, which is only partially correct. Yes, there are still a few like that. But at the facility there were also young people, about two-thirds of them female, many from India and Pakistan, and they were smart, deep thinkers. They were innovative, which snowy-haired, absent-minded professors rarely were. They understood the physics of nuclear reactions and how the EMP was generated.

These kids were bright in many ways. Yes, they understood the science underpinning their respective fields, but they also thought about the world they were inheriting and what they were creating, and realised that if they kept on doing what had been done by many previous generations, they would simply get the same results. And things would not improve. Many of their colleagues had gone off to work in prestigious scientific organisations, or in the R&D divisions of the big conglomerates. The people here, at the compound in Russia, did not choose that path.

Disillusioned with the status quo to the point of anarchy, another path seemed attractive, especially when postulated after a suitable period of assessment and grooming. *You could become just another part of the machine, another brick in the wall, or not.* Six carefully selected physicists were recruited. Two from the field of energy storage, the battery/capacitor interface. Two from the field of electromagnetic energy, and two from the specialised area of very high energy circuitry. They were all in their twenties and early thirties, all mature, single, and highly intelligent. Their remuneration packages were attractive, generous even, but their work would be conducted in isolation, as they were advised once their recruitment was a done deal. No conferences. No journal articles. No Facebook, Snapchat, X or other social media of any kind. Limited contact with those back home; what they were doing was classified.

It is not often realised that most of the real breakthrough ideas and technology, the disruptive ones, were conceived by people who were young, often under twenty-five years of age at the time. The young brain is not yet too tainted and restricted by conventional thinking. A technical person working in the same field for a long time often knows a lot about that field, and tends to see it from a certain perspective: their own. At a core level, they believe they know the field well. While they may be capable of making incremental advances, a paradigm shifting idea, the disruptive technology, is rarely generated by an oldie.

For those who chose this different road, it was exhilarating. They worked in a pure environment – no distractions like budgetary reports or petty jealousies between departments. Their site in southern Russia was an underutilised Cold War-era military base. The facility was clean, well-managed, and the food was good. Philosophical conversations around religion, world politics and history, and what they were striving to achieve were encouraged. Friday night was open forum night, where they gathered at a small bar that would accommodate perhaps twenty people. Everyone was allowed an opinion, and they were all smart enough to digest contrary points of view or conflicting ideas, and ruminate on them.

One enduring theme was that mankind had somehow lost its way and become overly focused on material possessions, status and money. Incremental change was unlikely to work. Climate change was a building threat, and unusual weather events around the globe were noted – any storm, rainfall event, sea surge, tornado, wind speed. Any weather event that was at least five per cent greater than the largest one recorded to date. Or an unusual weather event for which there was no precedent. An increasing number of points began to appear on the coloured graph in the bar. No one in the current 'establishment' was taking these accumulating threats seriously, nothing was changing in the rest of the world. As Alanis Obomsawin, an American Indian, said many years ago: *You cannot eat money.*

Time to start again. Collapsing the global financial system would be fun. The fat cats would lose everything. It wasn't going to affect the massive number of poor in the world –you can't lose what you don't have.

It was clear what they had to do: develop the technology to produce a device, small enough to fit into a briefcase, that could deliver an EMP of the desired strength and frequency. Yes, a larger model may be useful, but miniaturisation was the goal. The workers were well paid, although they didn't realise that their accumulating bank balances wouldn't be much use to them later on. The leaders did not like to leave loose ends lying around, and this was merely one project amongst many. While they were confident of success, it wasn't guaranteed. And the leaders wanted to avoid any retribution coming their way if they were less than completely successful. They wanted to keep on fighting. The hate was strong and getting stronger as international affairs continued, business as usual.

The world had become almost entirely dependent on the humble personal computer and the internet. Most banking was now done electronically, cash now constituted barely five per cent of total monetary transactions, and many people went to work and shopped without a dollar in their pockets.

This dependency was a weakness. The internet itself had been hacked many times with varying degrees of success. General malicious viruses created by angry people had done some damage, but these weren't too difficult to protect against. The wins, the damage to the system, was transient at best. Ransomware had come and gone. The states sponsoring such activity had eventually been coerced into stopping their support of these hackers, mostly.

So the cyber battle raged at a level below the awareness and comprehension of most. But it would not be the decisive blow that the leaders were looking for.

The technology behind the generation of an EMP was not difficult, miniaturising it was the problem. This had taken many years, but progress was made. A car-based system was first off the block, with a built-in power source that could charge and recharge the capacitors required to create the massive initial flow of energy. Making a car that would work after the initial pulse was not too difficult if the car was equipped with a diesel motor; they just needed to lobotomise the electronic control systems. They wanted to be able to drive away afterwards, hide the evidence.

The concept was tested in a street in Mumbai. It was ideal – lots of electronic equipment in the vicinity and not too much follow-up. When the pulse went off, silently, all electronic devices in a seventy-metre radius immediately went dead. Some passers-by felt a sharp pain in their head and, for some, temporary disorientation. Others suffered a residual headache for a day or two. No one was killed or significantly harmed. This was the goal of the leaders, as they had planted watchers and test computers as controls within the pulse impact area. While generally not too concerned by collateral human casualties, they wanted to kill computers, not people.

The Directors were very thorough and intelligent men. Not the goatherders that the West likes to portray. They had kept the trial well away from the financial districts. A significant event like this would have caused too much disruption, would have attracted unwanted attention, and a follow-up investigation would be launched. They didn't want that, not yet.

Smaller, less powerful versions of the EMP device were fitted into boxes and made to look like a delivery of printing paper or some other office supply. The problem was that while they could be remotely activated and create massive, localised computer damage, they would ultimately be discovered. This was *not* the objective.

Fear comes from the unknown, and the attackers wanted to remain unknown, in the shadows, striking at random and building battlefield experience for the bigger attacks to come later. They wanted the first trials to look like a general computer failure and leave the company IT guys scratching their heads.

Two months later, the next trials involved incapacitating two more soft targets: an accountancy and a financial trading company. English firms were chosen.

A simple delivery was made at 4.45 p.m. on a Friday to each company. At the accountancy firm a load of printing paper and toner cartridges was delivered and signed for by the office junior, someone who wouldn't have the confidence to query the delivery. Once signed for, the delivery guy was kind enough to wheel the trolley load of heavy boxes to the printer room. The young lad appreciated that because he just wanted to get out of there and down to the pub.

The pulse was programmed for 11.00 p.m. that night, and the burglary to recover the device early the next day. It was thought that the pulse would disable the alarms. The four to five hours between the pulse and the burglary was sufficient time to see what the security response would be. And who burgles an accounting firm anyway?

The results were as good as they dared to hope. All the computers were now just inert pieces of plastic, and backup hard drives were completely scrambled, both at the accountancy and the financial trading company.

At the financial trading company all data was lost, but there were backups in the cloud which would be accessed as soon as the computers were replaced. IT was confused. Initially the cause appeared to be a malicious virus that had locked up the machines, but even the most experienced IT techs could not get the computers to boot. Even company mobile phones left in the office overnight had been fried. Very strange. In the end, they put it down to a power surge, although the power company denied this. And how would a power surge kill a disconnected mobile phone stashed in a drawer?

It took a week to get the computers replaced and data downloaded from the cloud before they were back online and running. It took another nine months before the insurance company paid out the claim, but the financial and reputational losses were grievous. The business ultimately collapsed with the loss of sixteen jobs, at a time when it was increasingly difficult to find employment.

No one thought to ring the government's internet security agency. Why would you?

The last trial involved a bank. Robbery is when you take something from somebody without their approval. So in one sense, this was a planned robbery, but they did not expect to make much money from it. This was the new, cutting edge of warfare, and like all weapons, it needed to be tested. They used two of their human drones. Over the years they had recruited hundreds: the useful idiots who could be paid in money or drugs, or otherwise coerced into doing simple tasks with no questions asked.

The first drone's name was Alicia, she was twenty-eight years old, looked good, and was a high-functioning heroin addict – for the moment. She was becoming increasingly unreliable, but that wasn't going to be an issue for long because she would become a liability after the trial; she knew too much. The bank that was chosen was a nondescript suburban branch in the USA, where the second drone held three accounts and a mortgage, all accessible via the internet.

Alicia carried a large shoulder bag, perfect for shopping, and as she walked into the bank the metal detector went off. But all she had in her bag was a large, old-school laptop. She still had a good figure, and the fat guard always appreciated a bare mid-riff and a pert set of tits. Yes, siree. He managed to get a nice long peak down her top while he did his inspection.

Alicia waited in line patiently and then, at the counter, presented the cheque she wanted cashed with the correct ID: her own. Her account had been topped up to ensure the cheque would not bounce; the leaders wanted no drama. While the details were being entered into the computer, Alicia pressed the send button on her pre-programmed cell phone. There was an almost imperceptible buzz from the shopping bag at her feet, and all the computers in the bank crashed.

The teller was confused; the transaction had stopped halfway through. Alicia had been told to wait at the bank for no more than five minutes. She was to act like a normal customer. Initially, she should

     ROBERT STEVENS

feint surprise and wait, and then after five minutes, state she had another appointment, retrieve the cheque and quietly leave. Even the front door wouldn't open automatically and had to be forced open by security staff.

Follow-up work included the second drone trying to access her accounts that evening and every day for the next week. It took the bank a week to replace all the computers within an eight- to ten-metre radius of the front counter where Alicia had been standing, and to reload data from the external backup storage that many banks now employed. Few trusted the cloud and had decided to manage backup themselves. They didn't even think that there may have been a pattern to the damage. It was just another random computer hissy fit, perhaps. It just didn't make sense.

The controller paid Alicia at the corner café ten minutes after the attack, as agreed. A small bundle of twenty-dollar notes and a bag of white powder changed hands. She returned the laptop, then immediately went to purchase the new handbag she had seen the previous day in the upmarket, my-shit-don't-stink-look-down-your-nose-at-me shop. She got a real thrill paying the three hundred dollars in cash for it and seeing the surprise on the counter jumper's face. That night she snorted back a nice line of the heavily fentanyl-laced cocaine the controller had supplied as a bonus, and died.

Drug overdose, no suspicious circumstances, was the coroner's conclusion. There was no investigation, no analysis made of the residual white powder on the table, and no attention paid to a brand-new, three-hundred-dollar handbag owned by a junkie. Just another statistic.

The field testing had gone well, and now it was a matter of upscaling the production of the three variations of the weapon. The support technicians knew the designs and workings of the devices.

The loose ends at the facility were tidied up the following night, once testing was complete. The rice didn't taste any different to usual, and none of the six noticed that they had been served from a different container to the other staff and security in the workshop. War is brutal, and there are always non-combatant casualties. Although, the six were definitely active participants in this new type of war, they just didn't know it. They never would.

	ROBERT STEVENS

CHAPTER 17

Roman

Roman was a regular guy. Very regular. A nice apartment in downtown Manhattan. Every morning during the week it was up at six, twenty-five minutes of callisthenics, and then a quick shower with the temperature a bit below just warm. He liked the paired ideas of saving a bit on power, thereby reducing his carbon footprint just that little bit, and keeping himself a little more hardened by having a cooler shower. He was mildly contemptuous of those around him – the fat, unfit, gossiping and backstabbing hordes. He kept to himself. He was a year shy of forty, and he thought it didn't bother him. He paid his rent on time, and bought groceries on Thursday after work, regular as clockwork. Just the way he liked it.

His routine was established: walk four and a half minutes down the road to the subway station. Catch the No. 25 train on Platform 9 at 7.15 to York Street Station. Take a seat in car No. 4. Then up seventy-eight stairs to York Street. *Gee, what a surprising name!* he thought every day. Then three minutes down to Mack's on the corner for his breakfast, a lightly toasted panini with Italian salami, French parmesan cheese, and a dash of their homemade tomato relish, plus his double-shot, trim-milk latte. Yes sir, indeed. That set his day up well, mighty fine.

He would arrive at work, Musgrove's Accounting, scan his ID card, and be at his console five minutes before he was required to be.

He would not speak to anybody during this routine. Perhaps a brief thank-you as they passed over his breakfast in the crowded deli.

He liked his life just the way it was. No partner or pesky kids, his working week nicely organised, and enough to pay the bills, plus a bit. Friday night down to the gay club was enough for him. Maybe the occasional Saturday too, if he had that unsettled, pacing thing going on. While there had been lots of guys who had sought his cell phone number afterwards, he didn't want that. He didn't want a relationship with all the drama and needy behaviour and the requirement to compromise. He was happy just where he was.

His weekends were his own to do as he pleased. He could lose a whole day on the computer, nothing special – a bit of news, a bit of porn, trolling through Facebook, getting some form of social interaction.

Sunday was sleep-in day and then to the pistol range where he took one of his children: perhaps the .38 Special, or the Glock, or the Beretta. Each Sunday he would fire perhaps eighty or a hundred rounds. Each Sunday he practised with just one handgun, but he ensured that he was proficient in them all. He had a permit to carry one, but he rarely did; they were uncomfortable.

The stock market correction had hit months ago, and his modest investment in a large banking conglomerate took a mighty hit. He could intellectualise that the market did go up and down, and historically it was persistence that paid off. Do not maximise your losses by getting out once it has crashed. But he did not enjoy the feeling, and for the first time in fifteen years, his net worth decreased. It unsettled him. Many things were unsettling him, and he didn't like it.

Trips to the supermarket were a series of frustrations. His favourite, Black Doris plums, had been out of stock for months now, and he missed them. And then over time, more products disappeared. 'Sorry, temporarily out of stock' signage appeared with increasing regularity on the shelves, and he did begin to question just how long 'temporarily'

     ROBERT STEVENS

actually was. Crushed garlic, bran flakes, jasmine rice – random stuff that just wasn't there when it should be. One Sunday, having taken the 'kids' to the range, he counted how many products were out of stock: more than sixty-five in one supermarket! WTF? It was their job to keep products in stock. Couldn't they do that right? It troubled him, and for the first time he could remember, he was sleeping badly.

Roman watched the news religiously at 7.00 p.m. every night and was finding the recurring thread somewhat disconcerting. A drought that caused the crops to fail in some far-flung country, and somewhere else, a flash flood that wiped out a remote village in a place he didn't really care about – nothing new there. Unprecedented wildfires in Australia, which he was pretty sure was an island just off the coast of China. But more recently this was happening in places which he *did* know the names of. Sacramento Valley, for instance, experienced a massive drought, wildfires and heavy irrigation restrictions that wiped out most of the produce – the high temperatures just baked the crops in the field. There was a modest price rise in vegetables at the market, especially the kale and broccoli which he loved, as they now came from the West Coast. Whatever. Then there were the rallies and riots. Again, nothing special about that when they were somewhere else, but the riots and destruction in Miami and then in El Paso. The US President blamed illegal immigrants, but it just didn't ring true. The TV footage showed a lot of white guys beating up on the cops.

The cost of the insurance on his modest little apartment went up thirty per cent the past year, and he wasn't sure why. He paid on time and had had no claims. WTF? Fuel going up, which didn't affect him too much since he didn't own a car, but it increased the price of taxis and Ubers. It was just never-ending, constantly chipping away at his budget and sense of ease. The subway, usually a great example of timeliness, was becoming more irregular to the point that he was late to work twice last week. *Fuck, they only have one job!*

One Tuesday, an extraordinary rainfall had temporarily flooded the subway, making it impossible for him to go to work at all that day. He had initially been confused by this, and had wandered in and out of the subway station three times, perhaps in some hope the flood would have abated in the interim. Eventually he realised that he wasn't going to get to work that day, which was just a mind-fuck as he didn't want to spend any more time in his apartment. He had looked around for a taxi, but there were hundreds of other commuters doing the same thing. No way was that going to happen. He tried his cell phone, but the system was either overloaded or water damaged. Either way, there was no connection made. After thirty minutes of considering options and repeated attempts to call for a cab, he gave up and walked home. His shoes had managed to stay mostly dry on the walk to the subway station but had got soaked on the way home because the runoff overwhelmed the capacity of the street drains. His fake-leather shoes were ruined, and he was not happy about that either.

Then the next Monday, for no particular reason, things started to fall apart. He was at Mack's at 7.35 a.m., as usual, and they knew what he wanted. After eighteen years, how could they not? Staff were known to adjust their watches based on what time Roman walked in the door. But this Monday was different to the previous 4,325 – they didn't have any French parmesan cheese. There had been a problem with the supply. *So VERY sorry Mr Roman, no French parmesan today.* But they had some parmesan from New Zealand, very good, apparently. Would that be okay? And also, so sorry, there had been some problem with the lettuce supply, but they had a nice coleslaw which they were sure would make a tasty change.

Roman was taken aback. For some reason this threw him. He knew it was a trivial thing, but it bugged him. He was caught. The polite, don't-make-a-fuss Roman wanted to do the obvious and say, "That'll be just fine." But he didn't. He stood there a bit stunned. More

    ROBERT STEVENS

stunned by his indecision than by the change in country of origin of his parmesan, or coleslaw not lettuce. He stammered, swallowed, and eventually said, "Yeah, that'll be fine," but in his mind it was far from fine. And he didn't know why.

What the fuck? Why can't these useless twats just make his filled roll, lightly baked like he always gets it, so he can be on his way to work as usual. Nothing unexpected about what he was going to order. Why didn't they have *his* fucking cheese, and not some other crap?

The news this morning. Nah, the news over the past years was unsettling. Shit, was news ever settling? Floods in Pakistan and Bangladesh he couldn't give a flying toss about. Another few million displaced and few thousands killed in the succession of super-typhoons and torrential monsoon rains, or some ignorant tribal conflict in Africa. Who gives a toss? Not like it was anything to do with him. And not like they were short of people. Nope, that just did not bother him. What was grinding away at him was the way the wheels just seemed to be slowly falling off everything at home. Some boat with the wrong containers. Really? That was all they did, couldn't they get it right?

Then his computer at work. First day back at work and already an especially nasty virus crashed the system. And half a day to get it back up and working. Nothing for him to do but listen to the idle twaddle of the staff. What their kids did on the weekend, or what little Johnny was doing at school, or at university. Really? Who gives a shit? And then the company computers did not sync properly with the bank computers. Apparently a glitch somewhere in the system was at fault, which just compounded his frustration.

Little did he know that these issues were linked to a covert trial EMP attack on the other side of the good ole USA, the pulse echoing around the world.

The ATM at his bank had initially spat out his card: not recognised. Had to reinsert it twice before it would read, and then he had thirty-five million dollars in his account. Yeah right! The error was fixed the next day, and the bank was apologetic. There had never actually been a millisecond when he had considered withdrawing it, but what a classic fuck up. And now this – the wrong cheese again.

And it happened again on Tuesday, and he was just a bit more annoyed, and he did ask the nice little Asian girl who was serving him, perhaps with a slight bite in the tone, as to when they thought they would get the proper cheese? Because, while the New Zealand stuff was okay, it just wasn't the same. And it had thrown him all day, quite unreasonably so. He had made several mistakes at work. Given that he rarely made mistakes, three in one day was not right.

Wednesday was even worse, and even though the logical part of his brain was screaming at him to stop being a tool and get over the lack of French parmesan, he couldn't. He was making mistakes regularly, and for the first time in almost nineteen years, his supervisor came down to Roman's cubicle, mainly because she was concerned. Roman was continually muttering under his breath: "Fucking New Zealand cheese, fucking French, fucking coleslaw, fucking Asian bitch not able to get what I quite reasonably asked for …"

The supervisor sat with Roman for a bit, and while the muttering had stopped, it was obvious from the flushed colour and keyboard hammering that Roman was having a bad day. So after the obligatory pleasantries and solicitations about how Roman was feeling today, the supervisor suggested, in all sincerity, that Roman take the rest of the day off. The supervisor had noted the previous week that Roman, Roman the invisible, had not had a day's leave or sick day once since he had joined the company, apart from when the office was shut for the statutory holidays. She needed to talk to Roman about that. Now was her opportunity, but not until Roman had calmed down a bit. There was a large amount of accumulated leave to take, why not take some?

     ROBERT STEVENS

So Roman went home at an unusual time of the day for him. And because he didn't have the familiarity of the train he normally caught, he sat in the subway station for close to an hour. He was lost, and he wasn't sure why. He just knew that he didn't like it. There were some unsavoury people hanging around the station, hoody types. Probably unemployed wankers who took, never gave.

Once home, he got the kids out, oiled them, checked the loads and his spare ammo, of which there was quite a lot, and sat watching the TV. Two trains had crashed head-on in France. Where his fucking cheese was! How could it be that two trains would crash in this day and age? Maybe his container of parmesan cheese was on it, he idly wondered. Super-tornados had swept through Russia (ha, ha on them), and the Australian wheat harvest was a total disaster due to the drought which now covered the whole country and had been going for eight years already. Like Roman could give a flying toss about some ignorant Aussie farmer. Didn't affect him in his little apartment.

He tried going to work the following Monday. Still no proper cheese at Mack's, and he noticed that the cute little Asian thing he had spoken to was resolutely in the background like she didn't want to serve him. Tough shit, he was the customer, and the customer was always right, wasn't he?

He chewed halfway through the lightly toasted panini roll and then, for the first time in eighteen years and a few months, threw it away half-eaten. He almost got it into the rubbish bin, but his focus wasn't quite right, and he missed. Couldn't give a shit. He stomped up to his cubicle and began to work, but it wasn't going well. The supervisor came down after an hour and politely suggested Roman go home again; his swearing and cursing were upsetting others in the office. Why not take the week off? The new kid, Rashif, would be able to cover.

Roman wandered down to the park, fed some pigeons and advised the God-squadder harassing folks in the park that *no*, he didn't think about God, and *no*, he wasn't too worried about what was going to happen to him when he died. The Jehovah's Witness knew when to retreat, which was a good move, because today Roman was carrying the little .38, and while it was mostly unobtrusive, it was there, a comforting presence. But Roman couldn't actually remember clipping on the holster that morning. Must have been because of those arseholes at the subway station last week. That had unsettled him too.

The following Monday didn't go well. He slept in. Missed his morning ritual and for reasons he never could explain, clipped two pistols to his belt and carried a box of fifty rounds for each. The Glock and Beretta were his choices.

He was beyond out of sorts; he had mayhem on his mind. These people had fucked up his ordered life. They were responsible for his angst and anger. They had collectively fucked up international trade, so his Black Doris plums and his French parmesan cheese weren't there when *he* wanted them. He was going to show them in no uncertain terms that he knew what was going on, and they were going to pay for it. As he walked into Mack's, he was ready. He was ready for the, "Sorry, Mr Roman, no French parmesan again today." He was going to lay into them.

But, as he walked in the door, his hand already on the butt of the Baretta securely clipped not quite in the small of his back, he noticed three uniformed cops also ordering breakfast. His world crumbled. *FUCKKKKKKKKKK!* To draw now would be suicide. The staff saw him walk in, and asked, as always, "The usual, Mr Roman?"

He stammered, he stalled, he was a gasping fish. After an inordinately long pause, he said, "Yes, please," and walked out the door. He stood on the sidewalk, hyperventilating. It wasn't supposed to be like this. Because he didn't know what to do, he reverted to habit and walked to work, minus his lightly toasted roll this time. He only lasted thirty minutes before he got up from his console and simply walked out.

     ROBERT STEVENS

Sophia and Karl

A low-level drug dealer went missing, his bodyguard found with a single stab wound to his chest. The money the bodyguard carried was gone, and the investigating officers surmised it was a hit from a rival dealer. There was essentially no forensic evidence at the scene, which was unusual as drug-related killings were typically sloppy jobs.

The drug dealer had given up a lot of information before he was dispatched. This was cross-checked with what information they had managed to glean from the recently deceased Manu. The phone had been ditched, of course, once the list of contacts and recent calls were copied onto paper. Old-school, but undetectable electronically, and big brother was definitely watching. Phil passed on the essential summary of it to a tame snitch who duly gave it to a fellow senior officer. As hoped, the receiving officer used the information wisely, and eventually the CIA from across the border was called in since they had far superior intelligence-gathering systems, and this was an international drug and money laundering ring after all. The well-connected business woman initially named by Manu was also monitored, and while she was more cunning than most, she eventually revealed her true colours and contacts. Cell phones were monitored, and tracking devices and face recognition software employed. Over a period of six weeks, a vast interconnected network of heroin, cocaine and methamphetamine importers, meth labs and cannabis growers were revealed. It was massive, and the information revealed that the group was heavily armed. Canada's Special Forces were called upon; this was beyond a few cops holding handguns or AR-15s.

Karl and Phil were unaware of what the ripple effect of their little escapades was until the night of the 'Big Raids'. Machine-gun fire could be heard across not only their city, but also in Quebec City, Chicago, New York and Miami. It was the mother of all busts, and at the end of it, the street value of the seized drugs and cash was hundreds of millions of dollars. Twenty-two bad guys and two Special Forces operatives had been killed, which they accepted stoically. There were more than a hundred arrests with more pending, based on interviews with those arrested. Drug-related crime in Canada and the States in the Northeastern United States dropped fifty per cent as the supply of product evaporated. Some previously well-respected business people were caught in the net as well, which rattled a few middle-class cages. Money is a very powerful drug indeed.

If Karl and Phil ever needed justification for their actions, this was it in bucketsful. Neo-liberalism was dead as far as they were concerned. It didn't work. Move on.

Karl and Sophia's immediate neighbours had been a professional couple, Michael and Micaela, but Michael had died suddenly of a viral infection of the heart, and Micaela had sold up. The property was now a rental. They did not know who lived in that house now, but like most suburban situations, if you knew your immediate neighbours then things were going well. The next house down was Steve and Carol, a good, regular, hard-working couple who had a young baby and were doing their house up in stages. Karl occasionally heard the baby crying at night, but one of the parents would soon be up and tending to it. The lights went on, and the crying stopped.

Next down the street had been Remy and Philippe, the old gay couple, who seemed to have spent a fair bit of time travelling the world, and then moaning about it. The flu had taken them both, either directly or indirectly. That house was now deserted.

They made a point of inviting Steve and Carol plus baby Jane for dinner from time to time. They liked to know their neighbours, and given the empty sections on one side and the transient occupants on the other, they just liked to stay in touch.

Two weeks after the Big Raids, Karl and Sophia were sitting at the table after dinner, talking. The topic of the raids and their stunning success was discussed. Sophia commented that at the school there had been a drop off in drug detections, which was a good thing. And then, in a throwaway line, she added, "Two of the worst students in the school, the ones who take a massive proportion of our time to the detriment of other students who want to learn, had parents who were either killed or arrested in the raids."

Karl pondered this. It wasn't really surprising. The parents mostly determine the child's outlook. He ventured a thought, taking a risk. "From an investigative point of view, the parental information in the school data base is a valuable resource, you know. Teachers know who the bad kids are. We can dress it up in all sorts of fancy New Age speak, but generally, bad kids often come from bad parenting. And bad parenting is often associated with criminal or antisocial behaviour. The police need all the help they can get. Information is the key to effective policing."

"You want me to supply confidential information about students and their caregivers to you?" asked Sophia once she had digested this. She had never been stupid.

Karl paused, thinking how to best respond. "In short, yes. But I understand your professional reservations. So how about a test? You provide me with the names and phone numbers of the caregivers of a student who you know comes from a troubled house, but keep the name of the student out of it. I'll bet you we can draw a link between those names and numbers and criminal activity within a week. Just as a trial, just an 'I wonder' exercise. I promise to report all the findings to you and to action none of it unless you agree."

Sophia considered this. Last week her car had been coined while parked at the school. Stupid, senseless vandalism. The school had agreed to increase the number of security cameras, but at the end of the day, you are treating the symptoms of bad behaviour, not the causes. "Okay. One set of names and numbers. One week."

It took three days to get results. One day to get the warrants to place surveillance on the phone numbers and get approval for a watch on the house. The cell phones quickly revealed a network of burglars and the movement of stolen goods both within the city and through to America. Another great find. Karl bought a nice bottle of champers that night to go with the Chinese takeout. It was his week to cook after all. Sophia was simultaneously stunned, surprised, and not surprised by the information Karl had managed to glean in such a short time from what appeared to be insignificant contact details.

Of course the police would raid this group. "People would only be hurt if they resisted arrest," was Karl's response to Sophia's voiced concern. She had others, but wanted to cogitate on them for a while. The school had been burgled the night before. Karl wasn't aware of that yet. Who breaks into a school?

The raids went ahead the next week. The police had learned a lot from the Big Raid, and speed was one of the critical factors. Don't fluff about because, somehow, the lowlifes get wind of the police moving against them and they shift. There was more than one leak in the police force and the legal system in general.

Another half-dozen arrests and large quantities of drugs and stolen goods recovered. The student whose details had led to this result didn't

 ROBERT STEVENS

turn up at school the morning of the raid and wasn't heard from again.

The school settled down. Student behaviour improved, and consequently, academic achievement rose. Sophia still had major professional reservations about revealing the confidential information, and told Karl about her concerns. She could intellectualise the value of the information and see the benefits of the absence of the troublemaking kids, but wasn't so sure the end justified the means. That age-old uncertainty.

Sophia had been at a departmental meeting, and it was dark when she emerged from the office to make her way to her car. She was the last out, and set the alarms as she went. The school was well lit, and she had walked this way hundreds of times before. As she rounded the end of the fence, there was a blinding flash of light, and she lost consciousness. She had been hit over the head with a plank of wood. She came to perhaps thirty minutes later; she couldn't tell. Everything was hazy, and her head throbbed. She was confused. She felt cold, and realised after a moment that her clothing was ripped and half off her. She couldn't sit up, and couldn't find her handbag or phone. She tried to call out, but could only manage a feeble croak. She drifted in and out of consciousness, and was found by a jogger twenty minutes later. The emergency services were called. She woke up properly in the hospital some time later.

Karl was there, and another policewoman whom she vaguely recognised from one of the Christmas parties. Sophia was confused, and her head hurt. Karl sat by the side of the bed and held her hand. Finally, she asked, "What happened?"

Karl spoke slowly. "It looks like you were walking towards your car from the school, and somebody smashed your head with a blunt object. Probably the fence paling we found close by. Your handbag has been stolen. I've stopped the cards." He paused.

"What else?" asked Sophia in a croaky and trembling voice.

"You were raped," was Karl's simple answer through a mist of tears. He was struggling to hold on to his emotions. He knew he had to be strong. Sophia lay back on the pillow and tears flowed.

"Why? Why me? What did I do?" All the unanswerable questions flowed through her mind, and she went into a blank state.

Sophia spent a week in hospital. Mostly to recover emotionally. The blow to her head did create some concussion, but the doctors were not too concerned. Her reflexes and cognition were fine.

The school cameras revealed a hooded shape walking along the school perimeter. The person was carrying the fence paling, patently ripped from a nearby fence. No prints as the suspect had been wearing gloves; there were microfibres in the wood of the paling. The hoodie had been pulled around the face so even with computer enhancement there were no recognisable facial features. The handbag was found the next morning, thrown into a hedge, only the cash missing. It had been a random, chance attack. The hooded shape had seen Sophia walking towards him and had waited by the fence.

There were no leads, and after a week the investigating officer admitted they had little apart from the DNA in the sperm; no match was found in the database. They were not allowed to do a familial DNA trace as a protracted legal argument a year previously had disallowed this practice under civil liberty laws.

Sophia decided to go back to school after a fortnight. She couldn't stand being in the house, and Karl was like a caged lion, pacing about. She would just tell the kids she had been unwell, and get on with life.

Two days later, as they kissed goodbye for the day, she spoke to Karl in a quiet voice: "One contact, every month, on the condition that you are honest with me and fully reveal what you find as a consequence." She looked directly into his face, her expression sombre.

"Okay," Karl responded. There was no need for further comment.

 ROBERT STEVENS

Seventy-five per cent of the contacts produced results, a criminal activity of one sort or another: low-level drug dealing, burglary, car conversion, theft, prostitution. Although not illegal in Canada, prostitution was often associated with illegal activities, including pimping.

Over the period of half a year, another four of the most troubled students left the high school due to the arrest of their parents or caregivers, and they moved on to some other place. Frankly, Sophia didn't care what other place they moved on to, just so long as it wasn't near her school. Academic achievement at the school continued to improve.

Unbeknown to Sophia, the technicians at the genetics lab did have a quiet word to Karl a few days after the rape. There was some spare capacity in the DNA profiling regimen, so a few extra samples, not a large number, could be processed without the need to log them into the system. The DNA results could be run through the computer and its linked systems as 'check runs' and similarly not logged. Finding familial links took some serious computing power. They had that power. The technicians knew what had happened to Karl's wife, and they were essentially policemen at heart. They wanted the cowardly bastard caught and if they could help provide the tools, so be it. Not everyone fully engaged with the edicts that came down from the courts.

The technicians put the word out and like-minded helpers started to collect DNA samples from suspects. Sometimes a few strands of hair from an altercation in the cells were enough. Where there is a will, there is a way.

It took four months before they found a satisfactory familial link. A person living in a city shelter who was caught shoplifting and who became stroppy with the attending officers. The charges were upgraded to assaulting a police officer. The DNA sample showed that he was directly linked to the rapist: probably a brother. The police knew the family; they just didn't have any DNA up until that point. There were two brothers, one with a previous conviction for sexual offending.

The technician rang Karl the moment she discovered this, and he shared the information with Phil. Three nights later a group of four masked men burst into the bed-sit where the rapist was staying. Later that morning, while Karl was at work, a severed penis and scrotum in a simple brown box was thrown over the front gate of their house. Job done. The Lord may have said that vengeance was His, but for some on this mortal plane, that is just not good enough.

Karl found the box when he got home at lunchtime, and decided not to share the information with his wife. He pondered how to tell her that things had been settled, then realised that would not be what she would want. He kept the information to himself and bought a case of whisky for his police mates and the lab technicians to share.

— ❖ —

Access to the entire education department's mainframe came easier than she thought. Sophia had been trawling the paper copies of student enrolment documents at her own school for close to a year – untraceable, no link to any computer. The admin staff were always so busy that she didn't really register to them. When she was asked once what she was doing, the lie was easy: "Just checking a home phone number as I need to ring a student's parents." Nothing was thought of it. Teachers routinely did this. But she had discovered that with the 'removal' of perhaps ten or twelve of the most troublesome students, she was now scraping the bottom of the barrel and was perhaps considering kids who were just being stupid teenagers.

She was doing her paper data search, identifying the relatives and contact details of a kid she thought may be dealing drugs, when Clarisse came into the office. Clarisse had an unusual character trait: she voiced out aloud everything she was doing. "Department mainframe," she began, followed by, "Update school student attendance. The system didn't do it automatically, again!" And then seamlessly, "Login password, Administration 2018, because that was the year they installed the new system, followed by the school number." As she went gaily about her task, she provided a running commentary of what was going through her head. Rather annoying for anyone working beside her. Sophia was gobsmacked: this gave her anonymous access to the entire Canadian education system. To retrieve student and caregiver information from any school in Canada, all she had to do was enter the school number after using the login code. Identifying troublesome students was easy even if you didn't know them – just look at the pastoral information. Pass on the name of the student and their parents or caregivers, along with the school location, and Karl could quickly check that against anything in the police database.

The correlation, while not perfect, was remarkable. But the pattern was unmistakeable: troublesome students usually came from troublesome homes. Usually the damage had been done early, in the first three years of the child's life. While the bleeding hearts thought that everyone could be saved, the science and data indicated that this was not likely.

Her own school was blossoming under this new regime. She didn't care about the kids who had left – good riddance. Inside, she did wonder if it was one of these kids who had attacked her.

That night she went down to the public library, which had a pretty good download speed on their wi-fi. She knew there was no camera outside, and the download speed was unaffected by short distances, so she sat on the bench conveniently located immediately outside the library. She had had a second laptop for many years, and it was quite powerful. She logged in and went straight through to the state's website. She logged out again, making it look like a mistake.

Sophia knew what she was doing was illegal. It could put her in jail for conspiracy, but this was now the point she was at. She was smart. *How to do this without looking suspicious?* she wondered. Having a cop for a husband was an advantage. Time of day would be important, so best done during normal school working hours. The plan was to milk this magnificent source of information for as long as possible. While nothing lasted forever, a lot of work could be done while this resource was available. Do what you have to do, was her motto.

She logged on from school the next day using her backup laptop, sitting on her own in a communal office at lunchtime. Information from one of the other large public high schools was quickly perused; a download would possibly be too blatant and noticed. Three sets of data quickly screen-saved. Next time she would do it using the library wi-fi. *Keep changing the method*, Karl had advised her when she revealed what she had found out.

Karl passed on the information to an informant, but this time it was a typed note. Names, addresses and phone numbers of three potential targets. Other police stations were aware of Karl's station's brilliant arrest record, and word of mouth to trusted confidants promised they would be given useful information in due course. They were to monitor the contacts – cell phone surveillance had proved the most productive – and should then act accordingly. Ask no questions, just do your job.

Of the three students who were tagged from this new target school, two were drug dealers and the third a suspected pimp. The suspected (and actual) pimp simply vanished. There were two house fires, with fatalities. The blazes had erupted violently in the early hours of the morning. But meth labs do burn pretty good. No loss. The police appeared to investigate, but they didn't try too hard.

CHAPTER 19

Steve and Carol

Petrol was becoming expensive, but it suited Steve to bike to work most days. When it rained, he caught the bus and walked a block. If was really tipping down, which it seemed to do more frequently now – heavy, heavy rain, and then nothing for weeks or months – he would take the car. One day it flooded so badly while he was at work that his newish car was drowned where it was parked in the lower levels of the parking building. The insurance paid out, but it wasn't enough. They had to go back to the new bank, and the mortgage was up for its first review since they had resettled following the demise of their first mortgager. Yes, they would lend them the extra to get a modest, reliable car, which they needed with the baby, but unfortunately the interest on the mortgage would go up because the car loan was now secured against the house. Sorry, the policy terms and conditions had changed six months ago. In fact, they were lucky to have had such a low interest rate previously. Yes, they had a great repayment record, but they only had one income now, which made them a riskier proposition.

The repayments were an extra fifty dollars per week above what they had been paying with no tiny extra bit being taken off the principal.

The house renovations came to halt as they struggled to balance their budget. Some of the products they looked for in the hardware store seemed to be constantly on order, and they noticed that the fresh vegetable section of the supermarket just seemed to have less selection and often sold out by lunchtime. Weird.

Then six months later, more great news from the insurance company: they could no longer get flood cover for the house. Because they lived on a flat section, quite some distance from the coast and quite a way above the stream that ran at the bottom of the hill, it had never occurred to them that there was a risk of their home flooding. The house had never been flooded, but the ones further down the road had, only once, during one of those heavy thunderstorms. But that was at least twenty sections away. The insurance companies had revisited risks associated with extreme climatic events. Previously, this area had been a flood basin, a natural ponding area that had been drained by the developers. It was naturally low-lying. It took a few months for them to realise that this did not improve the value of their house. What bank would lend against it when there was a perceived risk of flooding? They rang around, consulting various insurance companies, but they were all the same in their response. They both fretted about it; they were used to having everything covered.

The value of a house became a multi-tiered thing: Those with houses that were insurable, albeit at ever-increasing cost, had a property that the banks would lend against. These were worth the most. The same house in 'riskier' areas was worth less and required different asset-to-debt ratios from the bank to secure a loan and also insurance, and it was repaid at a higher interest rate to reflect the risk. Houses at the coast, houses in flood- and wind-prone areas, and houses not attached to the town water supply or without fire-hydrants close by, were essentially worth the least as there was no insurance and hence no bank funding available. Speculators with cash started to invest in these properties, until the floods and wildfires made them realise that there was no insurance cover for a reason. Investors not only lost the house, but because they were usually highly leveraged, often the bank would have taken a lien over other properties they owned. When the loan was called in, and the money found to be wanting, the other properties were subsequently put on the market as well. But the timing was bad. There was now a boost in the houses for sale in all the Western economies. The suddenly less wealthy had decided to get rid of the rental and holiday home, which had seemed like a good idea at the time. House construction essentially stopped. House prices plummeted, creating a vicious downward spiral that was much faster than the gradual but seemingly unstoppable increase in house prices people had experienced in the past few decades.

Things were tight financially for Steve and Carol. Who would have thought it cost so much to raise a child? They started using old-style cloth nappies and endured one of the trials of parenthood – cleaning and washing nappies. They struggled to pay off the credit card bill every month, and the interest on that was starting to bite. Steve rang home and asked for money. The parents could help a bit, not much. The investments his parents had had in real estate had taken a bath with the changes in insurance and the greater economic downturn, and with the stock market correction, their share portfolio had gone backwards as well. Steve finally realised that a lot of these 'investments' his parents had talked about – the shares, the properties – also carried a fair amount of debt.

His parents were struggling too, but they could lend them a couple of thousand, which would clear up the credit card debt. They had already cut the card in half.

Steve's parents' visits became less and less as transport became more problematic, as did the phone calls to touch base, although often the cellular network struggled to provide cover twenty-four seven. And then one day they appeared unannounced at the back door, and his father did not look well.

"Cancer," was all Murray said, after they had all sat around the kitchen table and traded the obligatory small talk and made tea.

"Riddled, in fact. I just thought I was feeling weak and shitty as I was eating poorly and getting old," explained Murray. "Perhaps a few months," he added in his usual abrupt style, recognising the unasked questions. "I am content. Just sad that I will not see my grandchild grow up into a young lady, but I know you will do a good job". To say the conversation struggled a bit after that announcement would be an understatement, and after a while Jacky and Murray went home. The news had been delivered, and they needed time to digest it.

And when it all came to pass six weeks later, Jane was not old enough to understand. But the couple began to feel a sense of isolation as there was only Grandma Jacky left now, and her grandchild wasn't yet three years old. This wasn't the way it was supposed to be. Grandparents are supposed to be there to spoil the grandchildren.

Carol went back to her old place of work to see if anything might be available, but no, things there were quiet, and they weren't looking to take on more staff. Just the opposite in fact, unless things picked up a bit. She got some afternoon work as an aged care worker and cleaner while daughter Jane was at preschool. Minimum wage, which meant by the time fuel and day care costs were taken into account, they didn't actually make any money. But it did get Carol out of the house and feeling like she was more than just a stay-at-home mother.

A group of young people moved in next door. They never seemed to lack money for a party. Initially, the requests to keep it quiet at night were accepted and the stereo turned down, but over time it became more difficult and eventually turned into a straight "Fuck-off". The local council's noise control officers, and then ultimately the police, were called. They were met with a barrage of bottles, a number of which were thrown through Steve and Carol's windows in retaliation for calling the cops. The insurance wouldn't pay the repair bill (Sorry, clause 82 paragraph C, malicious damage), so cheap plywood was screwed in place to leave intact the money being saved for noise-reducing double glazing, to be installed later.

They tried to find out who the owner was through the real estate company managing the property, but they wouldn't say. Because the tenants were paying the rent on time and there was no damage to their client's property, technically they couldn't evict the noisy tenants. The property management company did write the tenants a letter.

They struggled on, noting that the pattern of noisy parties was one every fortnight, coinciding with welfare payments. They rang the cell phone number of the agent assigned to the property as the noise level grew the following fortnight, but the agent had left their phone turned off at night. Noise control at the council were called more than once, but to no avail. There was no reduction in the noise level. In fact, it got noisier. The most recent party grew quickly, with many large engine cars and Harley Davidson motorbikes coming and going. Baby Jane was screaming. The party turned into a near riot when a large bonfire in the backyard set fire to the fence between the properties. Steve did his best with the garden hose until the bottle throwing got out of hand, and he took a glancing blow to the shoulder. The police and fire brigade had been called, and the first responder units quickly called the riot squad, who dealt swiftly with the problem.

Steve and Carol thought this was marvellous. They had no particularly kind thoughts about the people next door, and the sooner they all went away, the better. They went to bed once the fire brigade had extinguished the bonfire and what remained of the fence.

No one lived next door for the next year. The grass grew long and rank and became a fire risk. The company in charge of the property eventually paid for half of the fence, claiming the old one, now destroyed, was at the end of its useful life and would have needed replacing anyway. Steve and Carol could take the matter to court if they felt that the offer of half the replacement cost was unreasonable.

They took the cheque, signed the indemnity, cleaned up the damaged remains, and got rid of the worst bits in a controlled burn. They used the money to get a new window to replace the plywood.

Carol became pregnant again. They discussed an abortion. While they really wanted another child, the financial burden was just too great. They decided not to go down that route, mostly for ethical reasons, and surely this downturn wouldn't last forever. Even at Steve's work, staff were being made redundant, and it was the fact that he had studied and improved his worth to the company that he was kept on. There was no annual bonus or pay rise, and the desire to pursue one was tempered by the increasing number of empty desks throughout the building. He didn't want to put himself in the position of asking and being turned down. That could have been awkward. Now was not the time to be looking for another position.

He sold his beloved mountain bike for a song, but he hadn't ridden it in ages. The old road bike was fine for commuting. They established a small vegetable garden in the modest area of the backyard. There was a small section of fence which had not been damaged. He dismantled it and re-used the posts and rails to make a trellis for beans and tomatoes. The hardware company had to order the couple of posts he needed: they were trying to carry minimal stock. Where they lived was a fair way north, but the growing season just seemed to be getting longer and longer. Like all novice gardeners, they made classic mistakes. Wild fluctuations in rain and temperature limited what they could grow.

Their second child was born, another girl, Stephanie. On time, not premature. Jane was almost five now and more than a bit jealous, so she was given extra 'grown-up' duties in the garden and extra time at the playground down the road.

They had squatters move in next door, who seemed reasonably blasé about their inhabitation of somebody else's house. They chatted

     ROBERT STEVENS

amicably through the non-existent boundary fence, and shared ideas about vegetables and other topics that came to hand. They were a couple in their late middle age from a farm that had gone broke due to the ongoing drought inland. The couple had been forced off the land their family had owned for three generations. The final blow had been a tornado that had ripped the roof off the house, only to discover after the event that their insurance company wouldn't pay. Bitter would not even begin to describe their feelings towards the insurance companies, banks, lawyers and accountants.

Often they would sit in the backyard sharing home-brew liquor, which Stan, the ex-farmer, seemed to have become reasonably adept at fermenting. "Call it gin, vodka, methanol fuel. I don't mind. I call it sanity in a time of increasing insanity," was his remark on being asked about what label he wanted to put on it. And yes, after the throat had finished constricting on the first shot, it did kind of mellow you out, as they found sitting around the fire in the backyard while the heat of the day abated. There was a general fire ban in the district, but Stan had become staunchly anti-establishment. This was discussed with more vigour as the level in the bottle lowered.

Shortages at the supermarket were common now, and it paid to know when the delivery trucks were scheduled. They regularly exchanged information on what they knew about different stores.

Stan was usually the agent provocateur around the evening drinks.

"You guys work hard, keep you place tidy, and raise your kids well from what we see," Stan offered one night. His wife Samantha, Sam, who didn't say much generally, nodded in agreement.

"Thank you," was Carol's simple reply.

"Best guess is that our neighbourly chats through what is a missing fence are due to an insurance 'fuck-you' and that the house had lowlife tenants before we found it just sitting here, empty," Stan followed up.

"Yes, very perceptive, Stan," Steve said.

"Paid your bills and thought everything was covered until push came to shove. And then they left you just standing there, didn't they? And some shiny-arse lawyer would have said, 'That's correct. The specific circumstances mean the insurance company is under no obligation to pay,' or something close to it," said Stan.

Steve recalled the conversations they'd had with the insurance company representative about the windows, the fence and the plantings they'd lovingly done to enhance the property, and the lack of care on the rep's part. "That is frightening close to what they actually said. You a mind reader? Perhaps you have a contact at Big Brother Google, or something spooky?" Steve replied.

Sam spoke up. "You're not the only ones who are being dicked over by those bastards. Sorry, you're not that special." They all smiled at that and had another sip.

Stan put out his fishing line. "Notice how the bastards at the top – the lawyers and insurance company CEOs, the bankers and other parasites – don't seem to be doing it too hard. They are still able to drive around in their flash cars and look down their noses at us dispossessed and underemployed. They are not feeling the pain like we do."

"Yes, we had noticed that. But isn't that the way of the world? Doesn't the boss lion have a harem and the lower males just have to wait a bit, wait for their opportunity. Life is not fair. To struggle is to be human," said Carol. The depth of the comments took Steve back a bit. He had not realised that his wife and the mother of his two daughters could come up with that type of stuff.

"Yes, if we still lived in the jungle then we would be happy to get through each day without being eaten by something bigger. Pinnacle of life would have been producing the next generation so your line doesn't die out. But. Always a but …" Stan said, then paused for effect before continuing, "We are supposed to be a society, not individuals focused on our personal needs. Collective good and sharing the wealth. Isn't that supposed to be the way of it? *Homo sapiens* lifted himself out of the jungle and introduced the idea of taxes so we could have a government to lead us and to redistribute wealth for the collective good."

They all sat around watching the fire for a bit. Carol got up and went to check on the kids who were both sleeping well. She checked the front door and the windows, which now all had extra security stays on them. When she returned, the other three were still quietly sharing the bottle, the level of which had dropped alarmingly. Alcohol – always a great conversational lubricant.

Once she sat back down and had taken a small sip of the firewater, she collected her thoughts, ruminating on the last comment Stan had offered. "Okay, then," Carol started. "The government and the taxation system have not worked as planned. I don't think any of us are really surprised by that. There will always be haves and have-nots. You guys are clearly more attuned to the shifting economics, given your change in situation over the last couple of years. Well, if you were king, what would you do, then?"

Stan took the bait. "I don't think I'll be king any time soon, so I prefer to think about what I could do to address some of the social issues that assail us. You can join any one of a number of do-good agencies that are trying to help the poor. We even get to go and have a nice cup of tea and a biscuit ourselves every Tuesday and Friday if we need somebody to chat to. Wonderful. The tea is fine, but nothing changes. Helping those at the bottom is an endless task; they are legion."

His words hung in an awkward silence, all of them watching the fire as mankind had done for tens of thousands of years. If there was a clear answer to the conversation that had been left suspended, they knew it would come up at some other time.

Five days later the internet crashed, and two days later, so did much of the international financial system, all due to a series of co-ordinated attacks on server farms and electrical substations. Steve's position was made redundant two weeks later as engineering consultancy work on new infrastructure projects dried up. He was lost. What would he do now?

A late frost wiped out their pumpkins and potatoes the next morning.

ROBERT STEVENS

CHAPTER 20

Marcelle
The Raid

Marcelle stayed at the chosen house for three days, along with two of the most trustworthy boys. It was a large double-storey house in a modest suburb, subway station just down the block, big front yard behind a high fence, and tall hedges on the other three sides. The electricity company hadn't got around to turning off the power yet, and there was gas. The large bottles were still by the back door.

Once she was content that this was a pretty good option, they returned to the city building. It paid to move around, and this move would be unexpected. Homeless people lived in the doorways of city blocks, didn't they?

Only nine of the team wanted to move, the other two just felt comfortable where they were. Freedom of choice. Easy. Stay. Whatever. No removal van was necessary. They stuffed their meagre belongings into bags and rucksacks and walked to the nearest subway station; the trains were now running irregularly. The group moved in under the cover of darkness. They had learned to trust Marcelle's instincts and instructions. Thanks to her, they had stayed out of trouble for some time now and had a reasonable standard of existence. And being told what to do on occasion was a comforting thing; it saved thinking.

The new place was great. Access through a poorly latched back door was just too easy. The previous residents had stopped caring about the house, and it was now owned by the bank, who cared even less. All the windows were in place, and quite a bit of the furniture was still there. It was not surprising that many of the goods sold on a dollar down were never repossessed. Nobody wanted nearly new second-hand goods anyway. They had no value and thus were not worth recovering.

There were beds, and it had been many years since any of them had slept in a proper bed. There was even some linen, which was a novelty for many.

There were rules as always, but rules to ensure they survived. Winter was always coming, and it got bloody cold. Foraging for blankets was important. While the house was well insulated, there was only one gas fireplace, but lots of electric heaters. Marcelle realised that using these would draw the attention of the electricity company. This she did not want. It had a gas oven, gas hob top and a gas fire that all worked well. Stealing the large 110-lb bottles of gas was tasked to the oldest boys, as it took a lot of effort to wheel them down the street once they had been unhooked. They had to steal from properties well away from the house, quietly, at night.

The kids mostly slept during the day. One crew was rostered to do daytime break-ins, usually three of the team at a time. One with a phone to act as a lookout, the other two to quickly break in and steal what they could. Once in the house, provided there was no alarm, they took their time going through drawers and clearing out the pockets of jackets in the wardrobes as these were favourite hiding spots. Even if an alarm went off (these were usually conveniently noisy, so they knew went it happened), they wouldn't panic. Yes, it did speed up the process. They knew that in many situations a rent-a-cop would turn up in five or ten minutes. The kids would either hop over a back or side fence, or just quietly walk out to the designated escape route. Nowadays, not many neighbours bothered when an alarm went off in a neighbourhood, so the chance of an immediate response from a neighbour was remote. And if they did poke their noses in, a quick pull of a knife normally made them backdown. After a few burglaries, they had a nice assortment of guns and knives, as well as the jewellery and money they found. Selling the jewellery became more difficult as that market steadily dried up; fewer people had disposable cash for these trinkets now. Alcohol was also a favourite item for obvious reasons. All loot was shared on returning to base, but often the returnees would be well pickled because they tried to guzzle as much as possible on the way home. Marcelle let it slide. Pick the fights you could win.

Marcelle also had other plans. Drug use amongst the group members was common. Freedom of choice. If it became excessive and the user was risking others, they would be given one clear warning, and then be packed up and put on a train. They knew the rules: The collective good was more important that any one person's needs.

They had got to know many of the small-time dealers, and had, over time, got in contact with some of the larger dealers. In the drug business, relationships and trust are paramount. The money was excellent, but the risks were high. Backstabbing, double dealing, informants and undercover police were all real hazards, as was the chance of just getting caught. The suburban malls were brilliant cover. Teenage girls doing random stuff in a mall was not exactly unusual, so they could hide in plain sight. During the winter, malls were warm, and in the summer they were cool. Great places to do business. They started with marijuana, dope. The toilets were the place of choice to do the deals. The second lounge in the house was dedicated to cutting and packing the dope as it came in. The money was rigorously policed. More than ten dollars out per deal on a daily load of twenty deals was cause for a severe reprimand from Marcelle, and back to doing break-ins after a week of house duty, which sucked.

The kids were paid on commission, which for a twenty deal daily target would equate to two hundred and fifty dollars a day: Good times. The money rolled in. The kids were given advice on what to do with their money. Marcelle purchased a safe and looked after the surplus that each kid wanted to save. They had no idea what to do with such newfound wealth, and thus Marcelle gave very good budgeting advice: spend some, save most, have a goal. Most of them had no idea what a goal would look like. They had lived all their lives simply getting by from day to day, just surviving. Want something? You gotta be joking! It was just going to get further and further away, or somebody would steal it from you as soon as you got it. Car? Yeah right. Buy a house? Why? There were plenty of abandoned houses now, empty. Nice clothes. Yeah, okay. That works. Need to blend into the crowd at the mall.

Feeding the gang took effort, and each contributed weekly. Prices on basic items like milk and bread had been steadily increasing as farms struggled with the changeable weather. Many crops had been ruined by the wet weather, followed by the unseasonal heat wave. It was now late autumn, and the ground was cold. But they had enough money at this stage to buy decent food.

Marcelle travelled back to the industrial part of the city to see how the others were getting along. The old building they had been in was completely abandoned, nobody home. She went down to see Dor and the crew. She noticed there were more people living around the area now, many more. Some had lost everything in the stock market correction and were homeless, and they were adapting to their new circumstances.

They were a new kind of urban refugee. They had come from high lives: big house, bigger mortgages, maxed credit cards. They were still in state of shock, having lost everything so quickly. How the house of cards had tumbled!

After the brief visit, Marcelle went 'home' to the suburbs, not realising she had been followed.

— ◆ —

     ROBERT STEVENS

A massive tornado came through the city. This had never been seen before, since the city was hundreds of kilometres from the 'normal' tornado belt. The destruction was massive, a wide swathe ranging from a hundred to a hundred and fifty metres wide and more than a kilometre long, simply ripped apart. No building it the tornado's path survived. Walk twenty metres to each side of this swathe, and apart from thrown debris, nothing. Weird. It had been preceded by a hailstorm where the hailstones ranged from two and a half to eight centimetres in diameter. The death toll from both events was remarkably light, only twelve souls. Many of the buildings destroyed by the tornado were warehouses, and these were often operating with skeleton staff because everybody had downsized. Many of the building owners found out in the next few days that tornadoes and many other weather-related events were now excluded from their insurance policies. The wording of the new policy had been available online for some time, they were informed. *Hadn't they read it? Sorry, but that's the way it is. You are not covered.* The death toll went up by two: suicide. Both these building owners had invested heavily in commercial property because it seemed a rock-steady investment. The combination of everything that had been going on was too much for them. This was the final straw, albeit a goodly sized one.

The prospector who had followed Marcelle had been watching for a number of weeks. It was his job, and his objective was to recruit two or three kids in this cohort and train them as drivers. Find the dispossessed and angry, the garbage of society that no one cares about. Tell them there is another way, that they can strike back at the bastards who have never cared.

He chose three of the older kids from the two groups of homeless he had been monitoring, and another kid whom he had befriended on the subway. The third kid seemed to spend most of his time just travelling on trains and doing graffiti surreptitiously. They all used drugs, of course, but his intuition told him that these three weren't yet too far hooked to be of any use. They could be straightened up. Well, enough anyway. He found opportunities to talk to each of them privately. No, he wasn't a cop. No, he wasn't some kind of spy (well, yes, he was, actually), nor a paedo. Yes, he needed some help with a project, and he had money. He needed workers – well, more like warriors, actually. But they had to keep it quiet. He gave each of them a hundred dollars and said they could do what they wanted and to meet him in three days if they were interested. He made sure that none of them knew that there were others being recruited as well. All three met with him at the designated time; he was a good judge of character. He gave each of them another hundred dollars.

The police raided the house in the suburbs the following week. It was brutal. They had seen the uptick in the number of burglaries and the amount of drugs being sold in the area, and surveillance had identified at least two teenagers who were involved. While they were slippery little buggers, face recognition software identified them on the subway and their entry and exit stations identified. Simple surface surveillance after that identified the house in which they were squatting. The cops raided in the early morning, 5.00 a.m., when the highest number of people were present. They had been told that guns would likely be present since a number of burglaries had netted firearms. The police were taking no chances and went in heavy-handed. Everyone had been asleep when the front door was smashed in, even though the cops could have walked through an unlocked back door.

Tony, one of older lads, lurched sideways across the bed. "Fucking pig-cops-scum," he yelled as he grabbed his knife from the bedside table and swung off the bed, trying to slash the nearest cop. The cop was wearing his bulletproof vest, which undoubtedly saved his life. The extensive, never-ending training cut in. He grabbed the arm that held the knife and twisted it viciously. Anybody else would have dropped the knife, but not Tony, who was still moderately high on a combo of cocaine and methamphetamine. He was invincible. He hung on to the knife and twisted it around to try and castrate the cop. The cop was momentarily off guard, then went for a quick knee lift to knock the knife away. The cop's knee hit Tony's hand obliquely, shoving the knife into Tony's inner thigh. It cut the femoral artery, and the blood instantly spurted out in a pulsating stream. Both men looked at it in surprise, and then the cop commented, "Doesn't look too good for you, bro." The pressure in Tony's circulatory system dropped quickly, and he lost the strength in his legs. He collapsed onto the bedroom floor and tried to stem the blood flow with his hands. The cop picked up the knife and smiled into Tony's face. "Die slow, fucker."

The cop upstairs called downstairs, "We have one man cut up here, but the situation is not stable. We have not secured the area. We will advise when the area is secure." Then the cops proceeded to watch young Tony bleed out. It didn't take that long, and the cops watching were a little disappointed. They knew this type: mouthy, uncaring, self-centred. Fucking zombies.

A while later, a paramedic called out, "All clear upstairs?"

The cops still in the bedroom with the recently departed Tony all nodded to each other, acknowledging that they knew the story, and one of them called out, "All clear, but there is no hurry."

The rest of the kids, including Marcelle, were all dragged from their beds and given a smack around before being bound, hands behind the back, with cable ties. They were thrown unceremoniously into a van. Two lost teeth, and one girl, who was five months pregnant at the age of fourteen, miscarried. Given that she had been kicked in the stomach, it probably wouldn't be classed as a miscarriage, but an involuntary abortion. She bled heavily in the cells, and despite her cellmates calling out for help, she slowly bled out and died that night.

Marcelle, who had been approached by Mr Mysterious over the past month, was in the cell with the dying girl. She screamed for help until she was hoarse, cradling her friend until her body was cold. Her rage at the police and 'the system' was cemented in place. It became a cold, dark thing inside her, and she pledged herself to Mr Mysterious since he had made it clear that he would be able to help the dispossessed strike back.

The group appeared in front of a judge later in the day on charges of being in an organised criminal group, vagrancy, theft and drug dealing. When the judge heard of the death of one of the girls in the cells, the death at the house, and the circumstances under which these happened, he paused. He observed the level of bruising and cuts amongst the defendants, and dismissed all charges. "People are innocent until proven guilty," was his starting line. "In this country we still believe in the due process of the law. We do not mete out summary justice. No resistance was offered, yet patently these people have been denied their rights and have received unlawful treatment from the police and other agencies. One died in her cell from blood loss, an indefensible position for the arresting agencies. All charges are dismissed. You are free to go."

This was unexpected. *What were they to do now?* the young people wondered. They were close to the centre of town and felt lost. They decided to go and stay with Dor and her crew for a few days. They knew they would be welcome.

What now? There was no answer to that yet, but it would come. They had always done what it took to survive, and they would do it again. They had started with nothing but the clothes on their backs when they first became homeless, and that was where they were now. Marcelle was thinking about Mr Mysterious and what he had said. She had previously agreed to meet him again, and now that was definitely what she planned to do. The rage inside her had become an immovable dark part of her now. She left two days later.

 ROBERT STEVENS

CHAPTER 21

Roman

Roman arrived home that lunchtime, shaking on the inside and the outside. Even though it was only Wednesday, his agitation was such that he went to the infrequently used sideboard and rummaged around for a drink. In a long-neglected corner, he found a nearly full bottle of Napoleon brandy. He had no clear recollection of where it had come from or how long it had been there, but decided it was what he needed, now.

He poured himself a good-sized glass. The first mouthful burned the back of his throat while he still stood there, but he was surprisingly okay with that. He then went to his favourite armchair and sat down.

"So, what the fuck's up with you?" he asked himself aloud. Why had he been so upset by the type of cheese in his panini? *You were ready to shoot someone over fucking cheese!* Really? *Because it's more than just the cheese! It seems like every bloody thing!* went the conversation in his head. His Black Doris plums, the flooding on the street that wrecked his shoes, the recent heat waves and the unbearable humidity. The cost of living so high that he was barely making ends meet. It seemed like the wheels were just coming off everything. Another goodly gulp of brandy set the fire going in his empty stomach, and he liked it. It had been a long time since he had felt that glow. He was smart enough to know that it was just a transitory moment, but it did feel good.

After some time, he picked up the phone, and for the first time in many years, dialled his brother, Justin.

After the surprised pleasantries, Roman got to the point. "Truth is, bro, I am way out of sorts, borderline manic. I know that I'm a very regimented guy, must have all my ducks in a row, borderline OCD if you like. Because of this, I have chosen to live alone and live a very organised life." He paused, feeling quite uncomfortable since this was the first time he had really opened up to anybody.

Justin was equally surprised; he didn't know his much younger brother well at all, and had hardly seen him since Mom and Dad had passed away years ago. "Okay," was his initial reply. "I knew this. Carry on. Oh, by the way, nothing borderline about your OCD." To which he received a cynical grunt in response.

For Roman this was cathartic; there was more than a crack in the dam now.

"There's this deli I have gone to for the past nineteen-odd years to get the same goddamn panini every day, how sad is that? Anyway, they didn't have their usual cheese, and I was thinking about shooting them because of it! What the fuck? I was going to kill somebody because they didn't have the right sort of cheese! How fucked up have I become?" He barely held back a sob. The brandy glass was now empty, but it had done the job it was required to do. He lurched out of his armchair and walked to the sideboard.

At the other end of the line, Justin gathered his thoughts. In the not-so-uncommon quirk of nature, he was of a completely different temperament to his full brother.

"Okay, dude, sounds like you're at the end of your rope. Why don't you come and stay with Amy and me for a few days, get your head straightened a bit. Take some leave, you must have a few decades saved up by now ..."

Roman was again surprised by his own reaction. His brother had

     ROBERT STEVENS

offered before, but he had always made some limp excuse. But now he was relieved. It was something that he could do that he actually wanted to do. He actually wanted to go and see his brother whom he hardly knew. After a further exchange of pleasantries, and just about as they were to finish the conversation, Justin added, "Hey, bro, look after yourself. Slow down and take a deep breath more often. And remember what the old man used to say, 'You always have a choice. Which choice you make reflects the type of person you are.'"

The next morning Roman was up early, slightly hungover. No calisthenics, and a hot shower. He left fifteen minutes early and caught the earlier train. He walked into Mack's fifteen minutes early, much to the surprise of the counter staff. "The usual, sir?" asked the small Asian girl, who hadn't had time to retreat to the kitchen.

"No, not this morning, thanks," he said pleasantly. "I have been a dick the past few weeks and would just like to apologise to you for that. And just an espresso, please. And a question. I was thrown a few days ago by the fact that you couldn't get the normal French parmesan cheese, which is pathetic, I know." He paused. "Do you know why you didn't have it?" he asked in a pleasant tone he hadn't used for ages

The girl took a moment to digest this development, and replied, "Thank you for your apology. And no, I don't know, sorry. I don't do the ordering. Mr Singh, the owner, does that, and he gets here about eight thirty. I could ask him if you like?"

"Thank you," replied Roman. "I will come down and catch up with Mr Singh myself. I think I am on a mission." His espresso arrived two minutes later, and he walked down the street to Musgrove Accounting, as he had done for almost twenty years now.

"You know, old son, I think I have now had enough of this routine," he said to himself as he walked through security and caught the elevator. Once there, he went straight to the supervisor's office, the steaming cup of takeout coffee still in his hand. He knocked gently to announce his arrival and walked in.

Marie, the supervisor, looked up in surprise. Roman *always* went straight to his desk. "Oh, hello, Roman. How are you?" she asked politely.

"In truth, not so good," replied Roman. "Yesterday was not a good day for me, and I'm sorry I got up and left soon after I arrived." Marie nodded, she had planned to speak to Roman about that, and a few other issues as well.

Roman carried on, "I'm not doing too well in my head, for reasons I don't understand. I am not coping with life too well at the moment. I am not on top of my game, and I would like to take some extended leave, please. Effective immediately, thanks."

Marie digested this. This was not what she expected from Roman, the OCD, anal-retentive, socially inept plonker. She gathered her thoughts. "Hmmm, you have a lot of leave accrued, as you know. I would have to check precisely how much. How long were you thinking of taking? And we would need some notice so we can arrange cover, probably at least two weeks' notice."

"Hmmm," Roman countered. "I think I have about sixty or eighty weeks accrued. I have been here almost twenty years and have taken essentially no leave. And, um, sorry, I don't have two weeks' notice to give just to take some long-overdue leave. I really do think I shouldn't be here at all. So, sorry, I give notice of my resignation effective immediately. If you could arrange my final pay as soon as possible that would be great, thanks." And with that he unclipped his security tag and placed it on her desk. With an enormous grin on his face, he turned around and walked out the door. He hadn't yet taken a sip of his coffee, which was still a little on the hot side.

Three minutes later he was back on the street, stunned at himself and feeling reborn. "Well, fuck me," he said to himself. "Didn't think

     ROBERT STEVENS

you had that in you, did you, you OCD wanker." And still with the stupidest, widest grin on his face he went back to try and catch up with Mr Singh, in a good way. It is true that grins are infectious. He felt reborn seeing people smiling back at him. First time he had seen that, too.

CHAPTER 22

The Drifter

He'd pick up hitchhikers from time to time for company, mostly not having any type of real conversations with them, just watching the countryside roll past. He wasn't sure what caused him to slow down and pick up the huddled shape at the truck stop. It was getting late and he was tired, and he should have been looking for a place to sleep.

The back door swung open, and a backpack was considerately placed on the seat. Then the door was shut properly, the front passenger door opened, and a soft voice said, "Thanks for that." He looked across. This was no guy, rather a woman, in her early to mid-thirties, with short hair. She was not pretty but attractive in another way, the way that means more. She climbed in and shut the passenger door, then clipped in the seat belt. She'd already sussed him out – you don't go close to a car if you don't like the look of the driver. Common sense, really.

He pulled out and began the next chapter of his life.

"Where are you heading?" The words came out simultaneously from both of them. They laughed, and he knew this was different, just not sure in what way. He didn't even bother with the usual chat.

"Where am I heading? Good question. A mythical place called New Beginning, I think. I was at the end of my rope," he said, "and I was curious to know what happened if you let go instead of tying a knot in it and hanging on, as all the books say."

"Okay," was all she said.

"About six months ago I lost my wife and daughter in a car crash, and some weeks later I quit my job," he stated simply. "I'm not looking for sympathy, or anyone to mother me, or a pity shag. I just sold it all up and hit the road. Not really sure where I've been or where I'm going. I don't burst out crying, I just feel kinda empty inside. I had a gun in my mouth a while back, and then realised that I could start all over again. So I did. No plan, no thoughts, just driving and looking to see what happens. I'm leaving my mind open."

"Okay."

They travelled for a while in a companionable silence, not much of a gulf between them at all, and she hadn't actually said anything. He drove on.

They travelled together for nearly three weeks, but only became lovers on the last night. Robert was stunned at himself. Normally, he would have made a move in the first few hours, certainly within a day. But it just didn't feel right, and he was smart enough to look at this new behaviour objectively. He smiled on the inside. They talked about jobs and maybe-careers and the world in general. They both agreed that it was a pretty stuffed-up place. He confessed that he had been a money trader; it was the 'had been' that saved him. She spoke about trying to be a New Age hippy but not really getting into the drugs or enhanced mind states scene; she just liked observing things around her. She noted that not many people seemed happy, that the consumer age and having lots of stuff didn't seem to actually make anybody happy. She'd been a young wife in suburbia and had done part-time work in a secretarial pool, which was a slow death, along with the new house and all the appliances and a young lawyer hubby. And he'd been banging the secretary as well. So she moved out, although she'd been unhappy at a core level for some time, the cause of which she just couldn't put her finger on. Long before hubby jumped the fence. Guess he wasn't that happy either, she realised. Robert felt a deep sense of shame at that moment, realising he had been that husband once. He didn't say anything, there was no need.

They discussed a broad range of topics as the countryside rolled by. For instance, they agreed that TV programmes, the internet and the billboard adverts were all deceptions. One of the roving and animated conversations focused on the culpability of government, any government. Did they consciously lie? Or did they have such short-term vision and such a long-term vested interest in the status quo that they couldn't see where there was a problem?

Ministers, senators and politicians of all flavours were surrounded by advisors and consultants who just wanted to maintain the status quo. "Climate change? Yeah, we are onto that one. Financial instability? Just a glitch. Inequality? Nah, looks okay from our perspective. Here's the latest data showing that ..." Were people stupid or just too lazy to really think about things?

They talked about what was important. Was it more toys, or a bigger car, or the fattest bank account? What made people happy and healthy? More lovers? They drove past schools and looked at the kids smoking and loitering, and the armed guards at the gates in both the seediest neighbourhoods and the upmarket ones, and they talked about that. They saw the homeless living in make-do shelters. Not just the scruffy guys who had obviously been doing it for some time, but also families, burned by the collapse of the stock markets. Robert tried not to think too much about that, as he had been an integral part of the machine that created this situation. There were the angry ones, mostly youths with no jobs and no prospects of a job. What do you do when there are no jobs to be had? They were pissed at 'the man' who seemed to have everything, more than everything. No trickle-down effect here.

They drove quickly through slum neighbourhoods where you didn't look too hard at those on the sidewalk while parked at the

     ROBERT STEVENS

lights, and then ten minutes later, they would be driving through an affluent neighbourhood with gated villages, security cameras and slow-driving patrol cars. And they wondered why it could be so close and yet so different. And he realised that if it hadn't been for fate and a runaway truck, he would have been in one of these mini-fortress houses somewhere, and he wouldn't have even seen the slum and the never-to-do-well types from the other side of town.

When he woke the last morning, after a night of intense passion, the best he could remember, she was already finishing her shower. He walked in on her and marvelled, what a night! His thoughts must have been fairly transparent.

"No," was her simple answer. "I'm moving on today. I haven't finished my journey, and the next stage isn't with you. This is something I need to do on my own. Last night was wonderful, thank you. You have your baggage just as I have mine. Our paths crossed, but now they diverge again. We met for a reason and taught each other something that is essential for our own journey. Now we move on, with sweet memories." She smiled and looked at him steadily.

"Okay," he replied and went and made coffee. He sat down at the cheap table in the motel and thought. They weren't good at small talk. He wondered what the next step was for him. He had been driving for quite some time.

She re-appeared from the bathroom ten minutes later, washed and clean. The atmosphere was awkward. They had spent many weeks together cruising and talking, and he had found a whole new world – ideas around conservation and destruction, wilderness and the American Way, inequality, stuff that had never entered his realm before. That there isn't equal opportunity for everybody. The vast swathes of farmland dried and brown, crops withered. They had seen the great strip mines and the dying forests and the dead streams and the nuclear power plants rising like puffballs. The abandoned and shuttered houses.

"Here's the deal," he said. She watched in silence, her backpack half-packed. "It's been a very interesting time for me, with you." He smiled, then carried on, "When I left my previous life in London, I didn't know what I was going to find. Being with you, and talking with you, has opened up my mind, stimulating all sorts of ideas in my head. You are right, our paths now diverge, and we go our separate ways. Great time last night, thank you, and perhaps fitting that we part this morning. I think I am now ready for the next part of my life."

He paused, and then thought, *What the fuck*. "I want you to take my car and my two suitcases. I'll write down on this piece of paper that I have sold the car to you and will sign it, adding my driver's licence number and social security number. So I guess it's legal. Part of this is a gift to you as thanks for the learning and knowledge you have shared with me over the past weeks. The other part is that I want to trade it for your backpack, less the knickers and other girly things. I think my next stage is getting rid of even more stuff in my life. I would like you to help me do that."

She stood for a moment, looking at this man and considering what he had just said, and gauging the look in his eyes. "Okay," she said. They had both come to enjoy simplicity and honesty in communication. Not so much of the usual crap passed between them.

And a while later he stood at the side of the road, thinking that Texas sounded interesting and stuck out his thumb. It was on the route to California, and he knew he had something to do there. Not quite sure what he had to do, but he had purchased sixty or seventy hectares there many years ago. A lifetime ago, in fact. On with the next stage.

     ROBERT STEVENS

CHAPTER 23

Abu Khan

Abu Khan was a fisherman in Southern Bangladesh. He struggled away in his small boat each day, going further and further out into the Bay of Bengal to catch fish when the weather suited, which was becoming less often. Especially when he had to travel that much further to catch anything apart from jellyfish and plastic bags. Gradually, over the years, he was consistently catching fewer smaller fish and more plastic. But he survived and managed to feed his wife and three children, who would soon be old enough to help out on the boat with simple tasks.

There was additional pressure in the small village with outsiders coming in, looking for food and a place to live. Usually they managed to accommodate a few, but feeding them and their children had become steadily more problematic as the human tsunami just kept rolling in. While there had always been people wanting to move in, the influx of Rohingya from Myanmar had made the problem ten times worse. While most of the refugees were held within camps dozens of kilometres away, not all wanted to live semi-permanently in those rat-infested shitholes. So they sought work, food and shelter elsewhere, and not necessarily in that order. The small village rarely had spare food, and feeding extra mouths, no matter how genuine they were, was difficult at best. Even the international aid agencies were struggling to provide food, water and shelter to the hundreds of thousands who arrived.

The report over the radio of a gathering storm was initially nothing to be too concerned about. This was a region well-versed in storms, storm surges, monsoon rains and floods. They picked up the pieces when the rain and water receded and carried on, as his family had done for many generations.

The weather built up ominously over the next day, as predicted on the radio. Massive storm clouds gathered, and the atmosphere became dark and heavy. There was no wind initially, but that soon changed. He had tied his boat to the old pier that ran for many tens of metres out into the Bay; it had been safe there before when other storms blew in.

When the pressure quickly dropped, he felt an unfamiliar tingle down his spine and body – something was coming. He knew of no 'Dark Man' but did understand evil spirits, and he had an uneasy feeling. The wind started to pick up, as it had many hundreds of times before, as the cyclone approached land. Initially, it had been classified as a Category 3 when he had last listened to the radio, but he did not realise that it was rapidly gathering strength as it travelled over the unusually warm waters of the Northern Indian Ocean. He had tied ropes to concrete blocks and thrown these over the roof of his family's shanty as he had done in the past. The storm shelters inland were just too far to travel to.

The cyclone was a Category 4 by this stage. Its centre was about thirty kilometres from land, although the land–sea boundary was now quite confused as large waves swept inland. It was very slow moving, but growing rapidly as it sucked up moisture and energy from the warm ocean. The storm surge was ultimately gauged as being between ten and fourteen metres. The cyclone was probably a Category 5 at its peak when it hit the landmass, but that was somewhat academic for Abu and his family. He had retreated indoors when sheets of corrugated iron and tree branches started flying around, and he had put the battens in place to hold the door closed. He realised they were in trouble when the first waves lapped up against the door and washed in underneath it.

They hopped onto the beds to try and stay dry, but this did not delay the inevitable. The kids were screaming and his wife crying, while he watched in terror as the door bulged and then flattened rhythmically as waves hit it and then receded. The wind was a screaming roar, and the shack gave a huge shudder just before the roof was ripped off. The noise was stunning, and he could only watch on helplessly as his meagre household contents were sucked up vertically, along with his second youngest child, and simply disappeared. The walls of the shack caved in, and a large wave overwhelmed the door. Water washed in, soaking them all as they huddled together on the bed. The last minutes were indescribable as water swirled around them, the wind tore at the remains of the building, and the combined noise of his family in panic and the storm overwhelmed him. He went to a quiet place inside himself and started to pray. He could not comprehend what was happening to them.

The prayers did not help.

A wave larger than the others gushed through the disintegrated shack and swept them all off the bed and into deep water, well over their heads. He could swim in a dog-paddle style, but his wife and children could not. A piece of fast-moving debris in the water speared through his right shoulder, and he could no longer hold on to his wife. Both of them slipped under the swirling mass.

When two of the bodies were found five days after the storm had receded, no autopsies were performed. Whether they died from drowning or debris impact was irrelevant. The bodies were decomposing in the heat, and the rats and flies were having a field day. Most corpses had been chewed somewhere; the nose appeared to be a favourite starting point.

The body recovery had to be done by hand because the ground was still of a toothpaste consistency and walking on it was difficult. The heavy machinery had not yet arrived because the access roads had been destroyed. The recovery agencies were quietly happy that so many had been washed out to sea. It took a lot of effort to lug a stinking, bloated body in a plastic bag kilometres inland to where the trucks were waiting. They had only so many walking boards to keep themselves out of the sticky mud, and had improvised as best they could with the debris of destroyed buildings and tree branches. For weeks thereafter, many bodies would continue to be washed up by the now tame waters, though many simply vanished. The final death toll was only a guestimate, probably around three hundred thousand. The Khan family's village was not the only one that disappeared.

The seabed had been completely reshaped, so the few shellfish and crustaceans that had previously survived the onslaught of washed-out nutrients, plastic and other pollutants were irredeemably destroyed. Now the entire ocean in that region became a dead zone for hundreds of kilometres offshore, and the few fishing boats that had survived the carnage were useless – there were no fish to catch. What would they eat?

Since the fishing village had been completely erased by the cyclone, aid and government officials could only guess how many houses had originally been there. The salt contamination of the land meant that it was probably impossible to even try growing crops there in the future. The long distance that this storm surge had carried inland meant that rebuilding in this location was unwise, to say the least. The survivors came back to devastation and bleak prospects. After eventually realising they had nowhere to live, they joined the echelons of displaced refugees. Stay behind and either starve or drown? Not much of a choice, so they moved inland. Where else could they go?

The cyclone did not make front page news anywhere else apart from Bangladesh, India, Pakistan and Myanmar. It got a single column on page four of *The New York Times*. There was plenty of news like this nowadays, and local wildfires, heatwaves, floods and landslides sold more papers and click-time than another disaster in some other country, with most having no idea where Bangladesh was anyway.

     ROBERT STEVENS

CHAPTER 24

Roman

It turned out Mr Singh was unable to help Roman much in pinning down the reason why French parmesan cheese was off the menu. "According to the supplier company, Yummy, they just can't get it. Sorry, Mr Roman. Did you not like the New Zealand replacement?"

Roman was unsurprised by this; it was as he expected. "No, the New Zealand product was fine, thanks. Almost identical in flavour. For reasons I don't understand, or maybe because I am losing my mind, I have grown curious about all the product shortages we are experiencing in this time of enhanced consumerism and instant gratification. Thank you, though." And he walked out, never to return.

That afternoon he caught the subway and then changed to a surface train to visit his brother. It was only a five-minute walk from the nearest station to his brother's place, and he had packed just a medium-sized backpack. He was looking forward to seeing Justin and Amy, but didn't think he would be staying that long.

He knocked on their door, and Amy, a tiny Vietnamese woman with a delightful laugh, opened the door and gave him a long, heartfelt hug. "Justin told me you nearly did something silly the other day. Thank goodness it was *nearly*."

As he disengaged himself from this charming bundle of happiness, he smiled. "Yep, nearly did. And over the past day I think I've now come to understand why I nearly did. Let's go inside. You can make me one of those insipid green teas you like, and I shall download to you." She laughed, and then laughed again, as this was not the 'Justin's brother' whom she had known and disliked. This was somebody new, and he seemed far more likeable.

Justin arrived home just as the second cup of tea was poured. Roman explained his growing unease at just about everything: the shortages in the supermarket, the lack of French parmesan cheese and lettuce and Black Doris plums, his insurance, politics and a dozen other niggles that had contributed to him losing his shit, big time. Justin and Amy listened. Parts they could resonate with, like the cost of living explosion, and the general frustration at life in general for the working class.

"Okay, bro," said Justin as the download slowed and eventually stopped. Their tea had gone cold. "All of us have similar frustrations about the way things are at the moment. Generally, we have to suck it up as there is no other option, unfortunately. But not everybody loads up a gun to shoot some blameless counter jumpers at the local deli. Any idea what pushed you to that point?"

Roman had and had not thought about why he had lost it so big time. There had been no clear single thing he could pin it on. "I think it was just a culmination of a whole lot of shit not going right in my life. I have deliberately isolated myself, living alone and lonely, because too often I found people to be a pain in the arse, just too needy." He paused while he gathered his thoughts. "I guess that having nobody with whom to discuss what is going on, all the small shit just accumulates in your head, compounding the problem. Social media was just reinforcing my point of view, as it does. So your world view becomes distorted by this accumulated clutter, just like a bit of crap in your eye makes it water so you don't see straight until you clean it out."

For a minute they all sat there while they digested this.

"I quit work today, rightly or wrongly. While quietly getting pissed last night, I realised I hated my life. I thought I was in control by keeping people out, and look where it got me. In truth, we have been more like cousins than brothers, which is one example. I don't expect the brotherly love to instantly materialise, but I would like us to get to know each other a bit better over the years ahead."

Justin smiled; he hadn't met this Roman before. All he knew was the OCD model. "Cheers, I would like that," he replied.

"I think we should go to a bar tonight, my treat. Dinner and way too many drinks. I'm on a mission, not quite sure what the mission is yet, but I'm on one."

And that is what they did, eating pub grub, drinking beers and shots, playing poor pool and generally having a good time. Laughing, which Roman realised he hadn't done much of in his life. In the morning he awoke on the couch, fully clothed; he had been too drunk to make his way upstairs to the guest bedroom. He was hungover again, and black coffee and paracetamol were high on the list of priorities.

"Nice night, last night," Justin opened once he had emerged from the bedroom and sat down bleary-eyed at the table. "And really nice hearing you open up, too. Seems like you've been reborn in some strange way. A nicer you, by the way." Roman smiled. After a moment, Justin carried on, "What now, you unemployed bum? Us working-class types got to go to work shortly. You staying longer? You're welcome, doubly so if you keep buying. Must have cost you hundreds last night."

"Cheers, my pleasure last night," Roman said, thinking at the same rate as he was talking. "You can pay another time, when we go to somewhere really expensive and drink Champagne. Thanks, but I won't stay tonight. I think my mission is to pack up my apartment, put my shit into storage, and go to France and find out why they can't provide me my cheese." He concluded with a dead straight face, and Justin realised he was being straight up.

"If my life to date has led me to walking into my favourite deli with a loaded gun and every intention of using it, then I think I can safely say that my life was pretty fucked up," Roman said. "And what could be more important than finding out 'who stole my cheese', or at very least, who moved it." The grin on his face at his own joke gave it away, and they both burst out laughing. Solid laughter, from the stomach. Headache forgetting, choke-on-your-coffee laughter.

Amy appeared, and with the two of them giggling and chortling away, she shook her head as she headed to the kettle. With a wry grin, she muttered, "Men!"

And that is what he did, without a shred of reason. He packed up his flat and put most of his stuff into storage. Some of the contents he 'lent' to Justin and Amy, and he purchased a one-way ticket to Paris, France, without a word of French in his vocabulary. He was on a mission.

     ROBERT STEVENS

CHAPTER 25

The Market Gardener

Richard Chung's family had been growing vegetables in the Horowhenua, just out of Levin, New Zealand, for well over a hundred years. His great-grandparents had come out with the last of the Chinese gold miners indentured to the New Zealand Government to dig for gold in the dry and hostile Otago gold fields in the late nineteenth century. Much of the best-paying land had already been well worked over, but his forefathers had worked on stoically, saving what they found. After many hard years, his great-grandfather and great-grandfather's brother left the gold fields, searching for somewhere and something less brutal.

Travelling north, the climate steadily became warmer, and they found good river soils on the coastal strip above Wellington, a growing city with a continuous demand for fresh vegetables. The west coast of the North Island had good, regular rainfall, and they thought they had found paradise. They purchased forty hectares, or a hundred acres in those days, with some of the gold from their finds in Otago, to which they steadily added parcels of land over the years, being shrewd businessmen. Other Chinese immigrants came out and joined them. They liked having Chinese workers: they worked hard for little pay. The Chungs intermarried with the local Māori and also the Pākehā, the white fellas. They became a true mix of colour. They worked hard and, over the next hundred years, developed one of the largest vegetable-growing enterprises in the country.

Richard Chung, a great-grandson, was worried. He had seen problems before – new pests and diseases, restrictions from the local council on where they could farm. They had to establish set-backs from waterways to reduce runoff, costing them precious growing land as the best sedimentary soils were right along the edges of the waterways. There were restrictions on the amount of fertiliser they could apply, but there were easy ways of getting around that. Ever-increasing 'requirements' were imposed on them by the people who chose to live in the city. Those who had never seen dirt under their fingernails.

Restrictions were placed on the amount they could irrigate. They had been known to take all the flow from the local stream in the past, until the locals complained. A bore was sunk quite some distance from the stream, as the local council hydrologist had specified. It had been a good well, with what initially seemed to be endless volumes of crystal-clear water, fed from the nearby ranges.

After the past four years of highly irregular rainfall, the once abundant supply of feed water going into the head of the underground stream they had tapped, was dwindling. The static water level in the bore started to fall, and last autumn they had drawn out more than the underground stream could supply, and the pumps sucked air and sand, not water. They cut back the take and started installing smarter metering systems, and employed a local consultant on ways to better utilise the water they did get. They struggled on, but the static water level in the groundwater continued to fall despite his reduced take. Richard recognised the farm had come a long way in the past twenty years in terms of efficiency of farming, production yields and overall environmental impact. Yet he felt he was running flat out just to keep place. Profitability was down; the overdraft soared. Consultants and legal costs with the local council and electricity costs; it never stopped.

Richard called in the local drilling company after the interminable paperwork associated with getting consents to drill three new wells.

     ROBERT STEVENS

There had been considerable objection from the community, even though he was a major employer in the area. He had eventually been granted consent to drill for two new wells with restrictions on how much additional water he could take. Growing vegetables was thirsty work.

One hole was a dud, the second was better. This was developed, pumps installed and the underground pipework and necessary control gear fitted. It worked adequately for a year.

Even with the new well supplementing the falling supply from the original, he struggled to fully irrigate all his crops. Increasingly he was irrigating at night as the middle of the day was too hot from late spring through to mid-autumn. Watering plants in such heat caused leaf burn. This was not a major problem, as he had employed good field managers to ensure all went as well as it could.

The weather was weird. They'd had an extremely heavy downpour three weeks ago. It rained so hard the ground could not absorb the water. More than ten centimetres in three hours, an insane amount of rain. It beat the bare surface of the soil flat. It ran off in sheets, taking many of the small lettuce and other salad greens seedlings with them. Precious centimetres of topsoil had washed away, some was now sludge, piled against the flood protection banks of the river, the rest washed out to sea. It was a week before they could get tractors back onto the ground to begin recultivation.

It had rained in the ranges as well, as the multiple slips testified. But it would take years for the water to percolate down through the ground and into the underground streams he now relied on. And the ranges had suffered massive runoff as well, with flooding in all the local rivers and streams. The bottom eight-hectare paddock was a write off, the fertile topsoil scoured away and now replaced with stones washed down by the river. Some of the sweetcorn plants had survived, but not many. Most were either washed out of the soil or were bent over and half-buried by silt and stones. The crop was a loss. He was not even sure if he would ever be able to use the paddock again.

Then it got hot, like an oven. It was early summer, and he would expect temperatures in the low twenties. But it was persistently well into the thirties, conditions he, his workers, and the crops were not used to. The rain-battered crust on the bare soil baked hard, like concrete. It was sludgy wet underneath with hard jigsaw-like pieces of baked silt on the surface, which impeded the emergence of seedlings. Big crops like garlic endured, but late-sown onions struggled, with perhaps ten per cent of the seedlings emerging in the gaps between the jigsaw pieces.

He was not sure what crops would actually survive to harvest. The recently established broccoli should be okay, and the cabbages were surviving, but the infestations of white butterfly and aphids just seemed to persist. He had sprayed insecticide three times already but was getting limited control. He had sown new brassica crops as per schedule to maintain supply to the supermarket chains as contracted. The planting machines, once he could get back onto the land, had broken nicely through the crusty upper layer, and the seedlings had established.

A plague of black field crickets, steadily spreading southwards as winter temperatures rose, allowing such a move, had eaten the brassica seedlings within two nights. One afternoon the seedlings were there, just doing fine in the hot midday sun. Then when the field manager conducted his scheduled inspection, the crop had just vanished as if it had been stolen. The manager sat on his quad bike, stunned. He double-checked that he was in the right paddock. He got out and walked along what should have been neat rows of little green plants throwing out their third and fourth leaves. They simply weren't there. There was the odd plant, looking chewed and bedraggled. He pulled out his phone and speed dialled Richard. "You want to come down to paddock eighteen. It is hard to describe. This is not good."

     ROBERT STEVENS

Richard drove down in the ute. Normally he would take the pushbike, get some fresh air, take the time to inspect the estate. But he was worried. If the crop of new brassicas failed, then he was in big trouble. He had precious few crops left in the ground; he would be in breach of contract with the supermarkets. He was their biggest supplier by far, and they couldn't ditch him. But they would look for other suppliers, which was the foot in the door he did not want the other suppliers to have. But with no crops, there was no money coming in. While his operation was big, he worked on fine margins; the supermarkets worked that way too. Big volume, small margin.

There was a stack of bills in the red folder: fertiliser, sprays, maintenance, new gear, wages.

He arrived at paddock eighteen five minutes later, and got out of the ute without saying a word. He looked around at the bare soil. He was stunned. A total loss. If there had been anybody else there, he would have gone off, yelling and shouting, demanding what had gone on. Luckily for Richard, it was his best manager, Tomai, a well-respected and intelligent man. By this stage, Tomai had found numerous black crickets hiding under the remaining flat flakes of baked crust. He had found the culprits. He held out his hand for Richard to inspect. There was nothing to say.

Fortunately, Richard had kept his cool, even though he seethed inside. The aneurism in the blood supply to his frontal cortex pulsed with each heartbeat, the bulging thin walls of the artery just ready to burst. It would burst next week while he was working on the accounts, working up a case for extended credit from the bank. They found him sitting slumped in the chair a couple of hours later, having had a massive brain bleed. He never fully recovered, having difficulty speaking and walking. The management of the farm shifted to Tomai while they figured out a longer-term strategy.

The accountant and the bank manager went through the records, and realised the perilous state the finances had been in before Richard had his bleed. They hadn't realised how bad it was, and going around the farm in all its separate blocks, realised how harsh the season had been.

The sun beat down, and the levels in both wells continued to fall.

The farm continued to struggle on after the foreclosure. It was still some of the best-producing soil in the world. Tomai was retained as interim farm manager while the estate was settled. Richard needed to be living in town, close to where the care workers were. His wife stayed by his bedside while everybody adjusted to the new reality of Chung Farms' bankruptcy.

The farm's properties were broken up, with large areas of beautiful productive soil being used for housing subdivision because this was the most profitable way to use land. Smaller blocks were established for market gardening, but they did not have the scale of operation that existed before. Lifestyle blocks were also established, a great boon for builders and real estate agents. The supermarkets had to negotiate with many new potential suppliers, and found that their dictatorial terms were not acceptable to many. Smaller operators combined and set up 'old-school' fruit and vegetable shops, and the supermarkets struggled to get product.

The cost of broccoli and just about every other vegetable went up, when they were available, as supply dwindled due to a combination of loss of land, unpredictable weather, restraints on irrigation and spraying, and a move to farming operations that were less risky than vegetable growing. Like all good cock-ups, a series of things were going wrong. Chung Farms wasn't the only farming enterprise affected by the weird weather.

     ROBERT STEVENS

CHAPTER 26

The Training

Mr Mysterious had been at the court hearing and acquittal, sitting in the back row. He had previously introduced himself as Tom. He didn't look like a Tom, but if that was what he wanted to be called, then whatever. He was one of Mikael's recruits, and had been working for him for five years now, gathering information, making contacts and recruiting. Two days later, he texted Marcelle, as agreed, suggesting a nice diner to meet for a chat. Marcelle was hungry, and the bruises on her face were still purple, just starting to fade to yellow. Tom knew of the raid, but played dumb.

"And the bruises?" he enquired, after the obligatory introductions and small talk. The food arrived.

Marcelle gave a rough account of the raid, the death of her friend, and her reinforced cold hatred of the law, society at large, and her father.

"You know that the police agencies were formed to maintain peace and order?" Tom said as his opening gambit. "They maintain the status quo, which is how things are at the moment. Many people, especially those who are doing well, like things to stay exactly as they are." He paused, making sure he had her full attention. "The police, the army, the secret services, all are tasked with maintaining the status quo. They protect a system that produces and rewards the bankers, the lawyers, the accountants, the fat cats. Try and fight the police and the army straight on and you will lose, every time. You following me?"

"Yeah …" was Marcelle's caged response.

"Have you heard of the Vietnam War? Or, if you are Vietnamese, the American War?" asked Tom.

"No idea," was Marcelle's short response between mouthfuls of sauce-covered fries.

"Long story short, the American military is the best equipped fighting force in the world and has been for some time. Basically, in the nineteen sixties, the Americans were trying to prop up a dictatorship in Vietnam. The locals wanted change, but had no weapons to talk of, initially. So the Vietnamese people fought a guerrilla war again the dictatorship, which is a hit-and-run sort of fighting strategy. They knew that they were outgunned, and to fight the enemy front on was a quick way to get killed.

"The Vietnamese used captured enemy weapons against the Americans and won in the end. It was a complete humiliation for the Yanks as they didn't adapt to the new conditions and kept trying to fight a conventional war.

"You, along with many others in this country, are sick and tired of the fat cats at the top taking more than their fair share and fuck all the rest. The technical term is inequality, the difference between the richest and the poorest. You, young lady, are in the latter category, if you ever needed reminding."

She looked at the man with suspicion. She wasn't being talked down to, which was unusual. She was being told stuff she didn't know, which was curious, different. She decided to keep listening. "Okay," was all she muttered.

"Given what you have been through recently, things are not getting better for you," Tom continued. "There is no chance for you, or the rest of your housemates, the way things are." He paused, looking at her attentively. "You want to get even and to kill cops. But these are two different things. If you want to kill cops, then away you go. Lunch is on me. *But*, if you want to change the system so there are no downtrodden like yourself and your friends, then I can help you. You will change the very thing that the police and the other agencies are trying to protect. The status quo. Things as they are now." Another pause while Marcelle digested this and her fries.

"So, some friends and I are looking for warriors who are prepared to train and take action to get even. To fight like the Vietnamese against what appears to be an invincible enemy. It will take time. And at the end of it you will destroy the system that perpetuates the status quo. You will disempower the cops and those who led the raid on your house and caused the death of your friends. Interested?"

Marcelle was impressed. Somebody wanted her, and she was not being treated as stupid, which was often the case when people looked at her clothes and unkempt appearance. Even though she didn't understand some of the words, she understood the message. The answer was too fast, too ready: "When do we start?"

"Now if you want. You can go home and get your stuff if you like, but we can get new stuff. The whole point is that this will be a new direction in your life. You can leave if and when you like, but consider this as one of the greatest adventures you will ever be on. All you have to do is simply come and hop on a train with me."

Marcelle made her decision impulsively. She wanted to get even. And just like that she was gone, another teenage girl disappeared.

The majority of the sixty-two other American recruits from six different locations across the US just walked away from whatever life they had. The selection process had been based on observation and then determining that these teenagers and young adults didn't have much to walk away from. That was the point. They wanted the younger dispossessed, the unwanted, the angry and frustrated. Risky behaviour associated with sex, drugs and booze were all seen as useful traits that could be developed and exploited.

There were plenty of prospects out there, but not everyone went with the offer. The recruiter just walked away and started looking again. It took five weeks to finish the recruitment process once they started; they wanted the cohort moving forward as a group.

Tom had also been in contact with a white supremist gang of Neo-Nazis, who hated just about everything. They hated the government, the system, Blacks and Asians, the elite and just about anybody else. They did not need a lot of encouragement to sign on because they responded well to a speech about the status quo. But this category of recruit would be managed and treated differently. They responded well to money, guns and drugs, and provided a lot of logistical support. The controllers knew such white supremist groups were being monitored by Homeland Security, so electronic communication was kept to an absolute minimum. Contact was face to face and money transacted in cold hard cash. They were also going to be an integral part of the initial attack.

Marcelle and Tom caught a series of trains to the semi-rural cottage he had leased for this purpose on the outskirts of a small town. It had been chosen because it had a lot of rooms and a large kitchen. It was one of six cottages they had leased for a year. Each could sleep ten to twelve when they doubled-up in the bedrooms. There was a cook-cum-cleaner who spoke a little broken English to the trainees, and a manager-cum-trainer. A driving school was situated in the vicinity and each cottage equipped with a people mover van. Some of the trainees could drive, but none of them had a licence. That was the second task, the first being to get them settled in. Then they would undergo psychometric testing to gauge their ability to be controlled through psychological means. Blood testing identified the level and type of substance abuse each recruit practised, for which they readily gave samples. They had been promised an ongoing supply of what they desired, but in controlled amounts. It was not expected that all would make it. They wanted twenty-five to

     ROBERT STEVENS

thirty warriors in this cohort by the end of the training in six months' time. A pass rate of fifty per cent was considered optimistic.

Progress reports were sent back every two weeks, as written letters sent via snail mail to a clearing house in suburban LA. There was a schedule to work to. First, the kids were taught how to drive a car, both stick shift and automatic. They were given lessons on the road rules, but not in a traditional classroom sense since most people don't work their best in that artificial environment. These kids hadn't enjoyed school, so there was little point repeating that exercise.

"Do not keep on repeating the same mistakes of the past," the American controller had advised the managers at one of their rare meetings. "Make new ones. What we are doing is innovative, and we don't know what will go wrong so we will try new things."

The recruits did most of the driving and road-rules training on the road in the people movers, each taking a turn to drive with the L plates firmly affixed while getting lots of advice from the others. Some advice was more useful than others. It was hilarious, and they were keen to keep on doing it. All the time the students were being assessed. One of them 'decided' to leave and just took off in the middle of the night and was never heard from again. This trainee just did not have the eye, hand and foot co-ordination to master the driving skills required and was not doing well with the controlled detoxification either.

As the trainees became more proficient at driving a car and a van, they were introduced to trucks of different sizes, and taught how to hot-wire them. Yes, they were planning to steal some heavy vehicles. Never mind what kind of trucks, they were just big, and they needed to be driven. They were also given a small revolver each, just in case. The feel of the gun in the hand was good. It gave them power. For the first times in their lives they were in charge. It felt very good.

The conversations at night were directed by selected opening comments such as, Why was there such a difference between the street people and those at the 'top'? Those at the top being the bankers, the lawyers, the corporate CEOs, the financial leaders, the judges. All the professionals, career politicians and government administrators whose positions were supported by the status quo. Other conversations were around the structures and institutions that supported or maintained this inequality. Not surprisingly, those at the top didn't see what the problem was and thus, where was the imperative to change?

Only the people who benefit from change will support it.

"The tree of liberty must be refreshed from time to time with the blood of patriots and tyrants," wrote Thomas Jefferson. What did it mean?

All the recruits enjoyed this discussion. It reinforced their world view with a logical argument, which they were increasingly able to follow as their substance dependencies were better managed.

Another ongoing conversation was about the value of life. Was a banker worth more than a street person? Was a trophy wife on the arm of an investment financier more valuable than a suburban housewife struggling with a house full of teenagers, or a young solo mother who had fallen on hard times and had to turn a few tricks to make ends meet and feed her baby? Who was making the most effort, making the most significant sacrifice, and was the most valuable? They all vaguely recalled their own departed friends.

What was the legacy they would leave behind? What was the legacy anybody gets to leave behind? Was it the size of your house or the number of toys you gathered? Was it the size of your bank account or the number of people who called you boss? Or was it doing the best in the circumstances you were cast into?

None of them had really thought along these lines before. Up until then, their thoughts and efforts had all been focused on staying alive, getting through one day at a time. The value of one life? They had all considered their lives to be cheap – nobody gave a shit about them. They had all lost friends, left them at the side of the road for the coroner to pick up.

How could they, in their lowly positions, hope to make any kind of difference?

One night, a new song was introduced because the trainees were being given a day off the next day. A party was developing, and the drugs of choice were handed out. The song had been recorded separately and now played over the sound system:

Here I am, still alive.
Surviving, much to my surprise.
Got some drugs so I can get high,
'cause sooner or later, I'm gonna die.
'Tis much, much better to die while high
Than to drift along and simply die.

The simple ditty was played to a catchy tune, the type that sticks in your head even when you don't want it to. "Better to die while high" was the catch phrase, and it took the world of drug abusers by storm.

"What is going to be asked of you is a big thing. There is a risk to your life. Some may not make it. But your name and legacy will live on; you will have made a difference. Back on the street, your life was meaningless. You talked yourselves of how a friend would pass during the night, and it was sad but unremarkable. Nobody gave a shit, just buried them with all of the others who had died, unnoticed.

"You are going to change the world so radically that the old ways of doing things just won't work. The whole system that led to you living rough on the streets and the fat cats at the top not even noticing that you exist – this is what you will change. You are going to make one profound statement to them: you do exist, and you are pissed off with the way things are. The police and all the systems that created and maintained the fat cats will have no purpose because the system is going to come crashing down.

"It is what we achieve during our time here that is important. Are you going to go quietly into that long dark night, or are you going to rage and rage against the system?"

Tom was a well-educated man, and he knew he was misquoting Dylan Thomas, but he wanted these kids to do something extraordinary. *You got to do what you got to*, he thought, and a misquote or two would not be the greatest of his sins.

The trainees liked the way that their brains sparked, and they had to stop and think about what he was saying. They enjoyed the higher level of conversation and the fact that their opinions were listened to. Most had already figured out that they were perhaps on a suicide mission, and the fact that Tom had admitted that some wouldn't make it was not surprising. This dude was honest. But most would live? That they could make a difference? That their lives would be more than just a brief wet flicker of hopelessness and despair.

"Insurrection is when you fight against the boss, the man, the system, and you lose. Revolution is when you fight against the boss, the man, the system, and you win. The difference between insurrection and revolution?" asked Tom. The kids paused, thought about it. They now knew the answer was more than the initial thought that popped into their heads. They waited. They had learned that if you waited …

"Timing. The difference between insurrection and revolution is timing. You are trying to achieve the same thing, but you have to wait until the right moment. And that moment, my young warriors, is going to be in two weeks' time."

Theirs was not the only training camp that was getting the call to arms that night.

CHAPTER 27

Climate and the Beginnings of the Shortages

On the vast steppes of Russia and Ukraine, far from the attention of the general public and well below the radar of the news channels and social media platforms, many of the grain and summer crops were ruined due to a week of late frosts followed by persistently overcast and moist conditions, which encouraged moulds and opportunistic bacteria to flourish. The crops rotted in front of the farmers' eyes. What few sprays they tried were ineffective. There may have been a temporary knock-down, but the weather conditions were so favourable for mould and so poor for the crops, that there was really no contest. The crops died.

It was only when the minister of agriculture of the Russian Federation mentioned it at a cabinet meeting that the other leaders became aware of the situation. Grain yields in Russia and Ukraine were expected to be down eighty to ninety-five per cent. Carry-over grain levels were down due to the widespread drought that had affected many of the world's crops last summer. The grain was needed to feed the chickens, the pigs, the dairy cows and the beef that produced most of the calories consumed locally and internationally. Potato crops were being affected by a blight that was resistant to the normal fungicides used to control the disease. The impact on yields was not yet known. The Russian Government was confused. "Grain shortages? Couldn't they just buy off the Americans or the Australians as they had in the past?" But yields had been slashed by weird weather in the US, Australia and India, the great grain-producing countries. Australia in particular was still in the grip of the decade-long drought. Widespread famine was expected.

News of this was kept top secret, and a news embargo imposed. Because of the embargo, social media became alive with gossip and rumours. Withhold information and people will make up their own story.

The Russian Government pondered what to do. The futures market had a sense of what was happening, and the futures trade for all grain rocketed. An embargo was placed on information relating to the grain futures market, and trading was summarily halted across the globe.

To those who trade in this sort of commodity, it was an unmistakable alarm bell. A number of Russian and Ukrainian-speaking emissaries were sent to the grain-producing regions to see for themselves. Those countries with circulating spy satellites re-tasked them from monitoring the uneasy 'truce' between Russia and Ukraine to looking at agricultural areas. UV and IR cameras told the same story, confirming the dire situation.

The agents, when they returned a week or so later, had sombre news. It was worse than expected. Instead of displaying seas of golden grain heads gently swaying in the breeze, entire regions showed blackened plant stumps with hardly a grain to be seen. It was all they saw – disaster. And to blame was the weather: the crops hadn't seen a sunny day for months.

The price of grain soared. The world normally tries to carry a 'forward' grain supply of around a hundred and fifty days' consumption to cover potential issues with the Southern and Northern hemispheres' harvests. In spite of wars, political posturing and rhetoric, most nations understood the need to co-ordinate on matters such as this.

　　ROBERT STEVENS

But, as is the norm, as resources become more limited, so does civilised behaviour. The Russians, on finally accepting that there would essentially be very little grain harvested that summer, stopped all trading and export of their own reserves. In fact, they started to buy in as much as they could from the Americans until they, too, stopped all international sales, recognising they needed all the grain they had, irrespective of the type. The Australians had little to trade with now.

The great bulk grain-carriers were laid up: sorghum, wheat, barley, maize, soya beans, rice. The trade slowed and then stopped within a period of weeks. Seafarers and traders alike were made redundant. Payments on the ships stopped and many were repossessed by owners who didn't want them.

The price of a loaf of bread doubled, and then doubled again, internationally. And then purchases were rationed: one loaf per family per day, and then two loaves per family per week. But it wasn't just bread, rationing of cereals, red meat, chicken, eggs and milk all followed. All foodstuffs increased in price as supply gradually dwindled. Farmers had cattle killed because they couldn't afford to feed them, and these animals were not replaced.

At first anger and then aggression at the local store or the supermarket was bubbling over. How would people feed their families?

CHAPTER 28

Sophia and Karl

Karl and Sophia both kept on working, and on the weekends they would review what had happened at work. How were the kids in the classroom? What was she teaching? What was the crime rate doing now that there appeared to be an improvement in crime detection and clearance?

The clandestine war against the organised crime, the drugs and the burglaries was going well. The authorities knew they would never stamp out the drug trade while there was such an expanding and lucrative demand, but for the first time the police thought that real progress was being made on cutting supply. The source of the information leading to this success was a mystery, but no one was looking too hard.

The Zombie Dogs were another matter. They weren't organised like the drug gangs, so were harder to pin down and get information on. They were a lot more random.

It was a barbecue with the neighbours that really took the conversation in a new direction. They enjoyed sitting around with Stan and Sam, who squatted two doors down, and Steve and Carol, a good, regular couple, struggling away like so many. The potent home-made brew from the neighbours got things going once again as they sat around the bonfire in their extended backyard that doubled as a developing urban farm. They had got to know each other better as the months had drifted by. To ease their visits back and forth, holes had been made in the remaining fences across the backyards, including the empty house previously occupied by Philippe and Remy.

They regularly got together over the fire and shared a drink and laughs. Stan was the protagonist as usual, after a few drinks. He was seeking something: clarification, justice, redemption, approval. Perhaps a combination of these? He was the one to lead the discussion on this particular evening.

"They had all worked hard?"

"Yes," everyone responded, a few nodding.

"They had played by the rules and not much improved for them, did it?" Stan continued.

Karl and Sophia just nodded in agreement, and at that moment, chose not to share their part in *not* playing by the rules. While not necessarily agreeing with what Stan was banging on about that evening, they felt it was always more entertaining to keep him going.

"The Zombie Dogs were created by our generation, through inequality and lack of hope for the future," Stan explained. Yes, this was true, the rest of them felt, looking at one another for confirmation of this shared understanding.

"They may not want to become 'part of society' because it was this society that created them." This was a hard logic to escape, even though somewhat inconvenient.

"And what were the main causes of this inequality, this system that keeps all of us oppressed with an illusion of democracy?" Stan asked.

"The establishment, the status quo, those who have benefitted most from the system and who do not particularly want to see it change," said the ex-farmer. "Initially, I just thought I was angry at the bankers who had foreclosed on me. And for sure, I was. Still not over it, may never be, I admit. But as I spoke with those who used to be my neighbours, or those down at the shelter where some days I am reduced to go to get clothes and food, the story is repeated, just with different players. Is there any justice? Not that I can see!"

Karl became very reserved at this point. This conversation was not much different to the one he'd had some time ago one early morning in the squad room. Just the subject of that conversation was different: druggies and other lowlifes. But essentially it was the same – the system doesn't work, and it is not getting better. Now bankers and lawyers were being discussed in the same terms.

"Can we rely on the normal channels of justice to help?" Stan continued. "And I am aware, Karl, that you are a cop, and a well-respected one, I understand. And one that I have heard is achieving great results locally against the drug trade." Stan smiled at Karl, dipping his head in respect. "I am happy to shut up now. This is a conversation I have had in my head many times, and just occasionally, out loud. I have thought long and hard about it, and have an idea, but it is illegal … and possibly immoral. But we seem to be living in the age of immorality."

They all sat in silence for a bit. Steve threw another log on the fire and then hauled another bottle of his firewater out of the bucket full of cold water. He had been experimenting with his own home brew, and that was evident. All good fun. The power had gone out a few days before, and the fridge-freezer wasn't working. They were getting used to that, and they adapted.

"Okay," said Karl. "I'll bite. What is your idea, then? And let's pretend I'm not a cop at the moment. I'm just another working-class dude who feels somewhat disjointed by what he sees around him. And feels for the next generation."

The baby inside the porch started to whimper and cough. Carol got up with a smile to tend to her.

Stan paused because he was about to make a leap. "Make them feel a lot less comfortable. The lawyers and bankers and accountants and insurance agents who never seemed to become disadvantaged

     ROBERT STEVENS

themselves." A small pause. "A *lot* less comfortable. In the eighteenth and nineteen centuries, the Scottish did it to the English who owned the lands and fancy castles in Scotland and Ireland while the locals starved. Burn them out, I say."

"Fuck. Okay. Ummmmmm. What did they do to you exactly?" asked Steve. "To create such rage?"

"They took my land. I accept I am biased about that. And they, the bankers, had arranged for some foreigner to buy this place here, where we squat in modest discomfort. And they did not give a shit that you originally had awful neighbours for six months, people who made your life hell. The bankers also increased the interest rate on your loan, so you struggle to make ends meet, yet their profits do not alter one drop. Where does that extra repayment money go? That extra money you pay goes straight back to those who lent it to the banks in the first place: international financiers, the fat cats. And there are always the bank fees and charges and penalties and small print in the contract, which are always in their favour.

"And they sit smugly in their flash cars and their fine houses, fancy corporate wives, and, my man, they don't even know you and I exist while they chat away at their cocktail parties."

They all studied the embers for a while.

"Yes, I guess that is an option, although not quite legal," offered Sophia, after a pregnant pause. "But burning them out, isn't that a bit over the top? And vengeance is mine said the Lord," was her final rejoinder. Samantha looked at Sophia with a faint smile on her lips, and they held their gaze for a moment. Sophia looked away first.

"Legal or not is often related to how expensive your lawyer is these days," Stan followed up, "and while the Good Lord may, or may not, have anything to do with sending an unambiguous message to these bastards is unclear. I am of the mind to do something more tangible in this life. People only respond when pain levels are high enough.

And I'm not the only one who thinks that way. But I have rattled on too much, and the booze has gone to my head. Please excuse me."

Stan downed his last swallow, mumbled goodnight, and wandered off to his back door. The rest drifted off to their respective homes. Steve had not broken the news to Carol, let alone the others, that he had been made redundant that morning. Some kind of gnawing inadequacy chewed away inside, some unreasonable embarrassment at his failure as a man.

Karl sat there quietly reflecting. Was what he was doing much different? Working way outside the boundaries of the law and what 'modern' civilisation had deemed appropriate behaviour? But the old system was broken, as Stan had implied. And the direct approach seemed to be getting results at the one end of the spectrum he was familiar with. Would it be hypocritical to condemn this other form of action at the other end?

ROBERT STEVENS

CHAPTER 29

The First Attack

Of the sixty-two who initially went with one of the two recruiters, forty-two were left in the six rented cottages. These were considered the ones who were susceptible to subconscious manipulation, and who could be trained to drive a truck and use a pistol semi-effectively. A substance dependency was an advantage because when the time came, drugs could be used to induce a state of enhanced consciousness. Generals had been giving their troops drugs for thousands of years – a tot of rum, amphetamines, cocaine. All to boost the performance of their troops at a critical time.

Three days before the planned attack, the houses were vacated. They were cleaned from top to bottom, thoroughly vacuumed twice, and all surfaces wiped down with alcohol to remove any trace of fingerprints.

One by one the 'warriors' were picked up by private car. These were all driven by members of various extremist groups who wanted the generous money offered and understood the concepts of 'no questions asked' and 'just do the job'. Money had been paid, sixty per cent up front, with enough being withheld to make it worthwhile to deliver on the job.

The warriors from around the globe flew to destinations in various European countries: Finland, the UK, France, and many others. The USA had many, too. When the warriors arrived, they were met by a local contact, who also happened to be a member of an extremist organisation. The vast numbers of immigrants around the world had reignited latent racism and Islamophobia in many, not to mention the age-old fear of the new and the unknown.

This cohort of forty-eight was one of eight around the globe, and they all decamped simultaneously.

A great deal of planning and preparation had occurred before the cohorts were deployed. The locations the warriors were taken to had all been selected for very specific reasons: there was either an internet server farm or a significant power switching or load control station close by. These local contacts knew the roads and had been well paid to watch them for the past two to three months. They had been watching truck movements, specifically fuel tankers. They had been taught the Dangerous Goods (DG) codes for petrol, diesel, LPG, methanol and ammonium nitrate fertiliser. These were always displayed in a diamond-shaped sign on the rear and the front of a truck. They had been shown that if you parked your car close to an interstate flyover and had a good set of binoculars, you could easily identify the trucks as they sped by. Both ways.

The information on the tanker movements was relayed back to the controllers and leaders. In all cases, the notebooks were posted to a suburban address in Los Angeles every week. They trusted nothing to the internet or cellular network. They had been given very specific instructions on what to write about the tanker and truck movements. Date, time, direction, location (overpass number), highway number, trucking firm and DG number. That was all. There were on average sixty entries per day, per book. A computer programme was used to assess the regularity and time variation of the various movements, and then to calculate the optimum timing to move on the trucks and tankers on the road. The next step was to assess how many of these vehicles could be stolen from yards or nearby. These tankers and trucks had to have a full load, but few of them would be stored in yards while full.

        ROBERT STEVENS

But there were a few, and that was just fine.

Some of the truck and tanker movements were then independently verified. The USA controller, for instance, only had two weeks to do this. She managed to get around most of them in the US, and the information proved correct. She had to assume the rest of the information locally was also correct, which it subsequently proved to be. A similar process was conducted in the other targeted countries. The model of vehicle was confirmed and the information sent back to the trainers, which enabled the best match of warrior with location. The attack procedure was calculated using a computer algorithm due to the many combinations and permutations. The ideal was to have less than thirty minutes between the discovery of the theft of the tankers and trucks, and the impact. The leaders could not know precisely what the response would be; the only thing that was certain was uncertainty.

There were also entries and maps of local electricity substations: the number of transformers, the fencing and security. The United States controller already had a map of the main electricity grid for Continental North America, including the importance of particular nodes.

The day of the strike in the USA and internationally was planned. The cohorts would be shifted into their locations two days beforehand. They did not want these 'warriors' sitting around too long. They just wanted to make sure they were in place when required, and they didn't want any skills degradation or loss of focus in the interim period. The various gangs and extremist organisations were sent a timetable for their attacks on specific electricity substations and relay points. They couldn't hit every substation, but the twin of the electricity systems engineer gave them sound advice on how to destabilise the entire system.

A dozen smaller trucks that delivered bottled LPG gas were also stolen, and these could be hidden once the GPS locators were ripped out. The Neo-Nazis were a good prospecting area for this type of weapon. Hateful, fatalistic, and they already had driver's licences.

They knew they were considered trash and more than willing to strike back at the 'system'. There were nine in another group, all terminally ill, who agreed to the offer of substantial money for a suicide mission. They were equipped with people movers, packed with homemade explosives as well as enough C4 to make sure there was an effective detonation. This group was notorious for sloppy preparation and had a history of bombs that didn't go off. Extra technical skill had been provided free-of-charge. The front ends of these cars were reinforced with steel to improve the impact penetration characteristics.

Money was being spent at a prodigious rate, but they had plenty of that. Each group, internationally, had been given twenty million dollars as a seed fund, and they were chewing through it. The fact that it had originally come from Uncle Sam via Iraq, Iran and Libya, was by-the-way.

The warriors had each been given a cell phone. It had one pre-programmed number, and they were told clearly that they were not to use this unless there was an emergency.

The instructions were individually phoned in the night before the attack. In the USA, Marcelle was one of the warriors who made it through the training, and was in a small motel at the edge of Lenoir, North Carolina. It was cold, and she had the wall heaters on max, but they were struggling with the late snowfall in the nearby mountains. The contact person who met Marcelle gave her a map and pictures of the site she would target. Her route was planned and programmed into the GPS unit she was given.

Marcelle was walked through the stages of the operation. How it was going to go down, when and how the truck would be taken, how far she had to drive it, and how she was going to get away.

Each warrior had been given a backpack to take along. It contained a water bottle, a head lamp, the necessary tools for boosting the truck or tanker, and the GPS unit, which contained a small but significant

     ROBERT STEVENS

amount of C4 explosive. Each GPS unit was programmed to send a signal revealing its location, which it was already transmitting. Unbeknown to the warriors, each of their backpacks also contained a small receiver, detonator and an incendiary substance in the padding. Nothing was being left to chance.

In all cases, the warriors were picked up from their hotel rooms by the same people who had done the surveillance locally. Again, this cost a lot of money, but no questions were asked.

To steal the trucks and tankers from the overnight holding yards was easy. Each warrior was given a location, vehicle registration and type, and a time to break in. While alarms went off as expected, the vehicle was long gone by the time the security people arrived. The local helpers assisted with the truck heist and knew the route the security response would take to get to the yard, so they simply avoided it as they drove away. The thefts would be reported to the police, of course, but generally, theft was not considered a high-priority offence these days.

Some warriors were taken to storage sheds or yards where previously stolen trucks and tankers were stored. Many of these vehicles had old tyres added to their storage spaces or were loaded with LPG bottles festooned with old tyres. The controllers wanted a lot of black smoke to create further damage, confusion, and a chance to escape.

Some vehicles were hijacked while they were parked at traffic lights in built-up areas. Easily done, just a simple case of follow the vehicle and take the opportunity when presented. Hijacking a truck or tanker on the highway was somewhat more complex. Some were taken while they were parked at a gas station, some stopped due to 'accidents' ahead, or were flagged down by a pretty young thing with long legs standing along the road, beside a car with the hood up or just hoping for ride.

If all else failed, the vehicle was stopped by a carload of men with machine guns, hired from the same organisations that had done the initial surveillance.

These types of crimes, and their particular modus operandi, were happening in many different locations simultaneously – in the US, Europe and Asia – but no one would be aware of a pattern until well after the event.

Of the seventy-five tankers and trucks targeted in the USA, sixty-eight hijackings were successful. There were another twenty previously stolen trucks around the US that carried LPG gas bottles, and these had been fitted with collector pipes, so only two gas taps had to be opened for the gas to start flowing. Nine 'suicide' people movers had also been acquired through various means.

The extremist organisations mobilised their warriors, driving cars with armed men to the designated electricity substations and switching stations. They were under instructions to kill as few as possible and to burn the computer control gear. Attacking the transformers was not very efficient.

Marcelle drove her petrol tanker well, following the directions on the GPS. She was five minutes behind schedule, but they had been told that that didn't matter too much. The hijacking on the highway had essentially gone as planned, and the follow car that was to pick her up afterwards was tailing the tanker as expected. The controller estimated a thirty to forty-five minute window before the authorities realised what was happening and launched a response to stop any further destruction. She turned off Highway 64 as directed, and it was about that time that the trucking company control system noticed that the e-road and GPS systems weren't sending any messages to them. The dispatcher got on the radio. "Truck 57, please advise your location. Your GPS does not seem to be functioning."

Marcelle had been told to expect this, and she turned off the in-vehicle radio communication system. That was a distraction she did not need at this time, and it wasn't going to change a thing. She quickly peeped into the small backpack she had been supplied. Along with the 'energy' drink she had already been sipping on, there were five thousand dollars in cash, with another twenty thousand promised once the job was done. There was also a small revolver, and she put both the cash and the pistol in the pocket of the heavy jacket she was wearing. After ten minutes of driving down secondary roads, she approached her destination. About two hundred metres from the target, she stopped in the middle of the side road she had been navigating along. She kept the truck idling and went to the side of the first tank, turned on the pumps, and cracked the tap that fed the main outlet. A thin stream of petrol spurted out. She turned the tap open even more to produce a steady stream, careful not to get any on herself. She did the same for the trailer tank, and noticed the follow car had pulled up just a little behind her. All was going to plan. Dribbling a wick of petrol, as she had been trained, she hopped back in and started moving again. Marcelle had been told the plan was for her to crash the truck into the target, walk back while there was still confusion and people checking to see who was hurt, and ignite the strip of petrol with a flare from the backpack, which would detonate the trail of fuel and set the whole forty thousand litres of petrol in the truck and trailer on fire. *Ka-bam*, straight out of the movies. Then into the follow car and gone.

Doing sixty-five kilometres an hour, she drove straight through the perimeter fence, and the simple wire mesh on the five-centimetre steel poles topped with razor wire just gave way. Some of the razor wire wrapped around the rear wheels as she powered towards the large, plain grey building. That didn't matter now.

The fifty-five tonnes of steel and fuel, still doing sixty-five kilometres an hour, hit the roller door on the side of the building and just smashed through like it wasn't there. The tanker ploughed through the wooden-framed insulated walls inside the loading bay and then hit some kind of concrete bund. The planners knew where the roller door was, but were unsure about what was on the other side of it. Clearly it was a loading bay of sorts, but they been unable to get plans for the building. The tanker lost some speed and Marcelle lost control of the steering as the front wheels and tie rods buckled. But she kept her foot on the accelerator; the plan was to get the whole truck and its two large fuel tanks inside the building. Rows and rows of black cabinets, about two metres tall, as far as she could see, were being gathered in front of the truck as it continued to plough forward, but now it was losing a lot of speed and pressing harder on the accelerator wasn't changing anything. Both the truck's tractor unit's tank and its trailer unit's tank were now well within the building, and there was a great mass of these cabinets piled up crazily in front of the truck. She was planning on getting out as instructed and waited until the truck came to a complete halt. Amazingly, there was no one around, yet. She could hear shouting. Petrol was pooling rapidly beneath the long vehicle.

The door of the cabin wouldn't open. The cabinets were piled everywhere, and she could only get the driver's door open a fraction. She started to panic, wondering what to do. She pushed and shoved against the door, but it would only open perhaps fifteen centimetres. Not enough to squeeze out. What to do? The smell of petrol was quite strong, and the first people to arrive at the tanker smelt it too. They very wisely decided to retreat.

Marcelle gathered a breath, the air now reeking of gas. She tried the offside door, and because of the angle at which the tanker had been ploughing the cabinets, she was able to get this open enough to squeeze out. She reached back into the cabin to retrieve her backpack.

All the while the controllers had been monitoring the progress of their guided missiles via GPS. They saw Marcelle's tanker stop in the middle of the complex they were targeting. All good. The commands to detonate the C4 in her GPS unit and the incendiary explosive in the backpack were sent. But they didn't ignite straight away – there was a fusing, sparking sound from the backpack, and it started to emit

     ROBERT STEVENS

smoke. Marcelle quickly realised that something was very wrong. The backpack was a bomb of some kind, and it was going to explode soon.

"Oh, fuck me," was all Marcelle said before she threw herself backwards out of the partially open offside door and fell heavily to the ground. Instantly she was on her feet and turned to run. There were flames in the tanker's cab now, and she knew it would be only moments before the fuel outside ignited. The smell of the petrol fumes was almost overpowering. She ran out through the hole in the wall the vehicle had created in the side of the building, easily hurdling the small bund that had impeded the assault. Once outside, she sprinted for the hole in the perimeter fence.

The tanker's cabin exploded and ruptured the front of the tractor unit's petrol tank, as well as the vehicle's two diesel tanks. In combination with the incendiaries igniting, there was a terrific flash, and the pooled petrol ignited. It flared back down the trail that had been left behind, which unsurprisingly caused a minor panic in those coming to investigate what had just happened. They had seen a figure appear from the building and run away, which seemed like a very good idea at that moment. Those who had ventured towards the disappeared roller door turned and ran. They couldn't see the destruction going on inside, but knew this was a serious accident.

The fire was fed by the fuel escaping from both the truck's fuel tanks and its two massive petrol tanks, and it became fiercer by the second. The residual fuel in the tanks began to heat and expand, giving off more flammable fumes. The smoke and heat were terrific, and after about two minutes, the petrol tank of the tractor unit exploded. The fireball lifted the roof of the big building, which then came back down pretty much exactly as it had been, minus its supports. The smoke generated by the fuel, burning plastics and the fibreglass truck cab, plus the vehicle's many tyres, was thick, black and toxic. The vehicle was partially trapped under the fallen roof, and fire swept through the entire building. The trailer tank didn't explode quite as spectacularly since it was partially starved of air, but it still made an impressive thud as the last of the petrol finally ignited. By the time the fire brigade arrived, the fuel was mostly burnt off. The smoke was thick and oily and had spread through the entire building.

Google's data centre was a smouldering wreck. It took two days to find out how many had died, which turned out to be three technicians caught in a corner of the building with no way to escape, but there was no sign of the attacker.

Sixty-five other data centres around the US were hit with similar results. Three of the trucking units failed to get to their destinations for various reasons. All the suicide vehicles exploded, one very prematurely on the highway as it made its way to its target.

Similar attacks, using similar methods, were simultaneously launched in Canada, Europe and Asia, including India. The Swift financial operational centres in Zoeterwoude, Western Netherlands; Culpeper in the US; Diessenhofen in Switzerland; and the control centre in Hong Kong were specifically targeted. In all, more than one hundred and fifty data centres were either destroyed in the blasts, the fires and the toxic smoke, or by an EMP pulse. Precise electronic circuits do not respond well to smoke contaminants. Eighty-five electricity facilities in the US were also hit, with fire being used to destroy the computerised control gear at each facility. While normal switching is used to share and spread load in the case of an accidental outage, the simultaneous 'failure' of multiple nodes in the system caused a nationwide blackout. Emergency generators kicked in instantly in hospitals and other critical care facilities where installed and maintained.

The effect was immediate. While traffic lights were supported by backup generators or batteries, as was most of the cellular network, in most places of work the lights went out, and the computers shut down. The rail network stopped working, and many people had a long wait for buses or taxis to take them home when it finally dawned that this was not a temporary outage. TV sets didn't work, so battery-operated radios, where available, were used as the magnitude of the attack unfolded.

Homeland Security, the FBI and other agencies were dumbstruck. There had been a small leak to the FBI from an informant in one of the extremist organisations, but it had been unsubstantiated and involved a garbled description of watching a highway for trucks. It was not followed up at the time.

The Pentagon was not attacked. Firstly, it was too well defended, and secondly, it was considered irrelevant – it was still fighting the last war.

Following the attack on the civilian data centres, the load on the remaining data centres throughout the world was extreme, and the servers there were unable to cope. The internet, originally designed to be a communication network that would survive an attack on the lines of communication, failed. Alphabet and Azure were high on the list of targets as they dominated the world of data centres and cloud computing. Searches went nowhere. Some telecommunications, cloud backup, internet banking, and EFTPOS systems just didn't work. And they didn't come back online after ctrl/alt/delete either.

It would take years to repair. To start with, most of the computer servers in the world had just been destroyed, and it would take time to build new ones, let alone ship them and hook them up.

A few of the drivers survived the chaos of the crash and the subsequent detonations and fire, and some figured out they were not supposed to have survived the attack. Mostly, those who did survive immediately tried to run, but were soon found by the authorities. Even though they admitted what they knew after a significant amount of persuasion, in truth they didn't know much. Marcelle had made it to the follow car, which had been given instructions to only wait a minute after the tanker crashed into the target before leaving; it was expected that the tanker driver would not survive. Marcelle was fortunate. The driver of her follow car was a fire bug, and he waited until everything was well ablaze before he realised that 'his' driver-cum-passenger was panting wildly beside him, urging him to "wake up, and get the fuck out of here".

The authorities eventually recovered some CCTV footage of the comings and goings from the training houses and the monitored extremist groups, but without the internet, they could not access their own databases or those of other law enforcement agencies. They had decided to store data in the cloud some time ago because it saved money and, apparently, was more secure than their own networks. Most of the original drivers of the hijacked and stolen vehicles survived, but they could offer little information, only a sketchy description of the hijackers, but most of these were dead now anyway.

Well, it turned out the cloud was not a wispy collection of high-altitude condensed water vapour. The cloud was now a series of burnt-out, smoke- and water-damaged, smashed-up computer servers currently being dumped at the local tip.

    ROBERT STEVENS

CHAPTER 30

Failure of the Wet Season

For ten thousand years, large areas of the planet have relied on the wet, rainy or monsoon season, depending on your home address. Many heavily populated places, such as Northern India, Southern China, and South East Asia, rely on the wet season to replenish soil moisture levels so the annual planting cycle of their staple crop, rice, can continue. Often the floods associated with the rainy season bring silt and nutrient-rich water to the lowlands.

As weather patterns changed, the reliability of the rainy season changed as well.

After a few years of particularly wet seasons, which created abnormal flooding and destruction, one year it just didn't rain. Across Northern India, Southern China, Taiwan, Thailand, Cambodia, Laos, Burma and Vietnam, the skies would darken with cloud as usual, but they would not turn to rain. For weeks, and then months on end, starting in May, farmers in all these countries looked to the skies and prayed to their gods. While late rains had happened many times before, it had never been this late. June and July came and went, and still, it did not rain. August the same. In early September, it did rain, but a fraction of what was required, maybe ten or twenty millimetres, variable over the entire region.

The farmers were distraught; they didn't know what to do. For generations the rainy season had been variable, but never this dry. It had become increasingly variable, either too wet or not wet enough. But nothing like this. Would they wait a bit longer and see if it rained some more, or plant now? Many chose to plant when they could, in the expectation of further rain to come, which it surely would. Wouldn't it? Always better to be out doing something than sitting around home being nagged. The paddies were just wet enough to get the plants into the sticky mud. They prayed for more rain, but it did not come. Within a month most of the rice, barley and sorghum plants had withered and died. The farmers turned out the pigs and the chickens to get what little green feed was still standing before it was a complete loss.

The irrigated crops were no better off, as the reservoirs in the high country that had traditionally filled during the wet were dry as well. And what water was available was being used to supply water to the people in the cities. For many years now, an ever-increasing number of cities around the planet had become reliant on water trucked or railed in as the normal reservoirs ran dry through a combination of lack of supply, increasing demand, mismanagement and decaying infrastructure. The glaciers that initially spawned these rivers had been in retreat for decades. There was just less ice and thus less fresh water.

The crops were failures, and while individual farmers usually had some livestock from which they could get basic sustenance in the short term, there would be no rice harvest.

The agricultural agencies in the various South and South East Asian countries reported to their local government officials that there would be no, or very little, rice or other grain harvested this year. Initially, they talked of famine in the farming regions. As the information filtered upwards with various degrees of misinterpretation, the minister of agriculture, or the equivalent in each of the countries, finally got the report which detailed the unfolding disaster. It would be a slow-moving train wreck unless something was done: they needed to buy in grain.

The all-seeing eyes of the satellites above documented the same: parched brown earth where there should have been a great green patchwork across vast areas above the equator, some of the most densely populated areas of the planet. The CIA and other international agencies were interested, and not only in the North Korean situation. Millions had starved there before – nothing new about that. The nukes that Kim Jong Un had developed were what was new, now firmly in his sister Kim Yo Jong's control since his untimely death.

The international agencies and grain trading companies started to look at the bigger picture. Ongoing drought in the vast grain-growing regions of Australia and the USA. The Russian and Ukrainian crops had failed. Now this unfolding situation across large sections of the rice-producing regions. Grain reserves had been steadily declining while demand had been continually rising over the decades as the world population just kept on increasing, and the overall grain production decreasing. Usually, if one region of the planet had been hit with a weather event and production was down, other regions had a good season and compensated. To see such problems in just about all the grain-producing regions of the world was unprecedented.

The word 'famine' was used discreetly and in hushed tones at the UN, but a worldwide shortage certainly existed. Local famines were nothing new, but something of this order, on a global scale? What could be done? There was already evidence of countries withholding what stocks they could. The US stopped selling its depleted stockpiles of wheat, corn and soya bean. They would be needed for domestic consumption. China and India followed suit, what rice and barley they had on hand would be required for their own people.

The attack on the internet had no significant impact on agricultural production. It just made trading more difficult: they had to revert to phoning. People were going hungry. Some countries cared more than others. For hundreds of years the Chinese have been beset by agricultural uncertainty, and millions have starved to death before, as they did this time.

Some subsidies were paid to Western meat producers to kill off livestock that were dependant on grain: chickens, pigs, dairy and cattle. It is more efficient for people to eat the grain themselves than to feed an animal, the argument went. There was a brief drop in meat prices as extra stock were slaughtered in the short term, but grain prices rose steadily as more traders and importers-exporters began to acknowledge the basics of Economics 101: Supply and demand determine price.

A loaf of bread in the supermarket became more expensive, as did pasta, and all forms of rice products. Shelf space in the supermarkets was quietly shrunk to disguise the fact that as well as the prices going up, there just wasn't the same volume of product available. Stock was kept past its use-by date to extend supplies. Grain was being rationed to the mills to try and extend the life of the stockpiles, which, while delaying the inevitable, did help by a few months. An emergency reserve was held back in government-controlled stores, earmarked for the police, armed forces and emergency services.

Those who depended on food charities and a dive through the supermarket dumpster went hungry. But it was always the poor who suffer first.

The impact of food shortages in all countries was expected to manifest as social unrest, at best. They were not wrong. Initially, the protests were about increasing prices. Nothing changed. As stores and supermarkets began to run out of bread in the early afternoon because of reduced supply, anger was directed at the store staff: "What will we eat?" Variations of the same question were directed at the hapless counter staff with various levels of aggression. Eggs were in short supply since chickens eat grain. Milk, in most countries, and associated dairy products shot up in price as supply shrunk: most cows are grain-fed.

     ROBERT STEVENS

As the price rises continued and the shortages intensified, anger was directed at the government – local or national, it didn't matter. People wanted to blame somebody. They were hungry now. This anger quickly turned to rioting, which was quelled with increasing brutality by the police and army.

As the shortages intensified over the next months, becoming severe by January and February, people just stayed at home, quietly fading away. Mothers and fathers would give up eating so their children could eat. With such weakened bodies and immune systems, simple coughs and colds became fatal. Most simply died in bed, and many of the survivors were only just strong enough to drag the bodies of their loved ones outside. Invariably, it was the job of the army and civil defence organisations to collect the bodies, which were taken to mass graves. There was neither the time nor energy for individual burials.

It was no consolation that some places that were traditionally wet did get unusually high rainfalls. Places like the West Coast of the South Island of New Zealand, for instance, where rainfall is measured in metres. This doubled and sometimes trebled, and although the rivers and pastures were used to high flows and rapid drainage, it was just sodden. Grass drowned in the waterlogged soil, and many rivers changed course numerous times, depending on circumstances. Farmers struggled, and for some new to the industry and thus burdened with high debt loads, it became too much, and they took the only way out they could think of at the time – a permanent solution to an overwhelming problem. It was possibly trying to decide what to do about the moss, lichen and mould that grew on the backs of the sheep and cows that may have been the final straw.

North Korea, well accustomed to food shortages and famine, was hit again. This time the oppressed populace had had enough, and Chairwoman Kim discovered that her troops were rebellious as well. Many of the soldiers had families who were affected by the growing famine. This time it did not affect only the countryside, which could usually be quietly ignored. People in the cities became restless as food shortages intensified. The soldiers needed a distraction, and what better way than to provoke the South, their archenemy. On the made-up pretext of a border infraction, Kim Yo Jong ordered the heavy shelling of South Korea over the border, which included Seoul, as the city was well within the range of their heavy artillery and rocketry. The South and its ally, the USA, responded in kind, sending rockets, shells and drones over the border, progressively wiping out the artillery batteries. Chairwoman Kim had mistakenly thought they were well dug in and camouflaged. Tanks were mobilised to crash through the border into the South, and they were partially successful through sheer weight of numbers. Superior Western technology dealt with them one at a time with uncanny precision. Much had been learned from the Ukrainian conflict. Kim Yo Jong felt it all slipping away, her illusion of superiority was eroded with each report from the battlefront, which was now thirty kilometres deep.

Initially, she had the generals who presented these unflattering reports shot on the spot, which didn't help the situation on the ground. Finally, she ordered a nuclear attack on Seoul by land-based missiles and New York by submarine-based missiles aboard a vessel which she again, mistakenly, thought had slipped undetected into US territorial waters off the eastern seaboard. As the nuclear missile site in North Korea ramped up preparations for the launch under a heavy cloud cover, the orbiting drones and ground-based SEAL observation teams detected this activity. A flurry of Tomahawk missiles put paid to that launch, and the sites will remain radioactive for thousands of years, although no one cared apart from those who still remained alive in the region.

Similarly, the diesel submarine that carried the sea-launched nukes had been tailed by a Virginia-class, hunter-killer submarine ever since leaving the naval dockyard in North Korea. The Americans had

     ROBERT STEVENS

intercepted the top-secret communication authorising the launch. As the unmistakable sounds of missile fuelling aboard the North Korean vessel were detected by the Americans, two Mk 48 ADCAP 'fire-by-wire' torpedoes were sent on their way. The first inkling that the North Koreans were not as clever as they thought was when their sub's sonar operator yelled that two torpedoes had just been fired at their port side and impact was in two minutes. The captain had no idea what to do, and that is how he died, a hundred and thirty-five seconds later. He did not tell the crew to expect the impact, there was no point.

Chairwoman Kim was assassinated by her personal bodyguard two days later as the war on the ground sputtered to its inevitable end. But there was still no food.

CHAPTER 31

The Drifter and the Old American Indian

The sun was just on the horizon as the rock finger drew close. Robert could smell smoke, which was encouraging, though couldn't see any sign of life. He was hungry, but there was nothing unusual in that; he'd been hungry before. There was little in his recently acquired backpack: a fresh shirt (that was clean-ish), socks, underpants and another pair of shoes that may or may not be as worn as the ones he had on his feet. Plus a toothbrush and a few mementos of his past: a picture of his wife and daughter in happier times, his wallet with the stash of dollars he harboured carefully, his EFTPOS 'get-out-of-jail' card. His favourite bandana, which he swapped with the hat on his head depending on the conditions of the day, was wrapped around his arm. His water canteen was half-full: he took conservative sips. You didn't want to waste water when you were walking in this type of country. Not everybody stopped, even if you were in trouble. And some who stopped were more trouble than you may have already been in. You could never be too careful these days. He walked on towards the end of the rocky outcrop that supported the finger-like projection. He was lean and hard, clear-eyed and well-tanned. It had been many months since he had given away his car, and he was content. He didn't care for the news any longer; little happened that affected him personally now.

It was almost fully dark when he rounded the side of the rocky outcrop. He saw the dancing light of a fire and idly wondered who else would be out in the middle of nowhere at this time. Probably another drifter, although he preferred the term 'itinerant traveller'. Into the gathering darkness, he called out, "Hello" – a universal courtesy – but there was no reply.

He picked his way through the jumble of rocks surrounding the mesa, almost completely shrouded in darkness now. The glow from the fire outlined most of the rocks, but he still managed to hit his shin on a low-lying one that he didn't see clearly. The injury was heralded with the usual exclamation that announced the arrival of unexpected pain. There was a low grunt, not quite a laugh, from the other side of the fire, and the young man knew he had company for the night.

As he walked into the fire's glow, he could see the man sitting opposite. He was of indeterminate age and long-haired and looked at Robert with a steely eye. 'Seasoned' was the word that best described the man. Whoever the man was, he accepted Robert's presence. He sat by the fire, smoking an old long-stemmed pipe, and silently watched the young man find a nearby rock and sit down. The young man rubbed his shin and looked at the older man, who then grunted a greeting. The young man looked around and saw a battered old pack lying beside the older man and wondered what it held. Guns? Drugs? Spare undies?

The two men contemplated each other. The pipe smoker broke the silence. "Just my personal stuff, a spare shirt, enough food for a couple of days. Don't play poker, young man, I can read you like a book."

Robert was startled. He thought he had barely glanced at the battered old pack. The American Indian smiled. *Yep, this one was easy to read. Good heart, good aura. Hiding nothing. Unusual these days.*

"Walked far?"

The young man nodded. "About ten hours." Distance here was measured in hours.

The old man nodded.

"Not many people out this way, and even fewer stop to give a man a lift," he added.

The old man nodded again.

"How long you been sitting here?" he asked the old fella. There was no reply.

The young man knew enough to let the question hang. Sometimes it is good to talk and sometimes it isn't. He'd just bide his time with the old-timer. In his previous life, he would have gabbled on, always something to discuss: the latest stock figures, bond rates, competitor activity, the latest war. The usual crap.

After a while, the older man asked, "You had any dinner?"

"No." A simple answer and the truth.

The old man rummaged around behind the rock he sat on and in his hand appeared a frying pan with some beany-looking goo in it. He nestled it on the edge of the fire at arm's length and sat back to suck on his pipe. "What you running from?" he asked.

Robert considered that for a while, and then spoke slowly. This wasn't going to be one of those conversations where you had to say your bit quickly before somebody came in and talked over you. Words could be considered.

"I hit the end of my rope. I was doing everything that was expected of an intelligent, white, up-and-coming guy. Rich upper-middle class, not quite gentry. My wife and daughter were killed in a car crash, and I was ready to eat my gun. I now realise that what happens in our lives is always for a reason, even if is not obvious at the time. We have a choice. Self-destruct, or do something different. I chose the latter. I have come to enjoy being an observer, to watch the machinations of our civilisation as it smashes and destroys nature and ourselves. No, sorry. The white man's civilisation. I am not a good consumer any more, therefore I didn't fit in."

The older man considered this answer for a bit. "If you've come for some sort of peyote-induced spiritual enlightenment in the desert," he said, "you've come to the wrong desert."

"Nope. Done my fair share of shit, got high, got laid, got rich, had lotsa stuff. Didn't really satisfy much," Robert countered.

"Mmmm," the old man said, then paused to consider the matter. *Many threads here.* "Sorry to hear of your family. We always have a choice in life, like the biblical apple thing. To learn and grow through our experiences. It's the bad events that give us the opportunity to learn the most, unfortunately."

The man watched the younger one, looking for some kind of response. The young man nodded, realising the other was no fool. He was clearly well educated and literate. This was no drugged-up waster taking time-out in the desert. This was something else.

The bean goo was bubbling away and starting to crisp underneath, so the old man spun the handle around for the younger man to grab. "Dinner is burning." He smiled. It was a test.

Robert smiled to himself as he unwound the bandana he had wrapped around his forearm and used it to insulate his hand from the hot handle. *Got you, you cunning old bastard,* he thought as he deftly picked up the frying pan from the fire and settled it onto a nearby rock. A sudden movement behind the old man turned into a dog moving closer to the fire and the hope of dinner.

"Sit down," growled the old man. The dog quietly ignored him, came up to his master's feet and lay down beside him.

Robert scooped beans from the pan to his mouth slowly, using the spoon he dug from his backpack. Even though he was famished, he had learned to savour food when it was available. He was in no hurry. It had taken some time for him to learn that skill. He slowly chewed his way through the refried beans and thought it was possibly one the best meals he'd had in years. It gave testament to the adage that an excellent meal was mostly about the company and timing, and the food often came a distant third at best.

"The dog will clean the pan once you have had enough. That's his dinner you're eating. And he knows it." Robert looked up and studied the dog, who was studying him. He smiled at the dog, who glowered back. *Hmmm, smart dog too.* He deliberately took another few spoonsful just to make his point and, even though still hungry, put the pan on the sand in front of the rock. The dog waited until the command from the boss and then took to it with gusto. He was not going to let this new human have any more of his dinner.

The old man spoke: "I heard about the fall in the stock markets and how people lost their homes. I read about what the white fella has done to the oceans and the sky and the earth, and I feel sad. I am sad because it could have been different. I am sad because our ancestors warned of this, and we did nothing. The teeming masses, they want to be fed, and they envy the white fella with all his stuff. So, the unquenchable thirst, it is still there. Although, you are one rare individual, having let go of stuff."

He paused, looking first at Robert, then scanning the night sky. "This planet's been around for a long time. You can see it in the rocks and the dust. The planet will be fine. It has changed before, and it will change again. The world isn't going to end any day soon, but this current civilisation, that is another matter," the man concluded. He paused to suck on his pipe and was rewarded with a little smoke, which he rolled around in his mouth before slowly exhaling.

"The hungry white fella, he hasn't even come close to finding any kind of balance. The unquenchable thirst, what a bastard. Biggest surprise is that the wheels hadn't fallen off earlier, which is probably quite a testament to man's ingenuity. But the longer you deny a problem, the bigger it grows. The end of this civilisation is very close."

"Do you think there is anything that can be done?" asked Robert.

The American Indian was never in a rush to say anything, so a long pause was expected. "For reasons I don't understand, modern man thinks that the destruction of the physical environment has nothing to do with

 ROBERT STEVENS

society's health. They think that societal decay and the fighting that is going on is not related to the exploitation of the Earth Mother. Dumb fucks. There is an energy that binds it all so that everything is related. We are all bound to the earth, but I guess living in a concrete tower in some concrete jungle, a person becomes a bit disconnected from it all. You been there," summarised the old man.

"Short answer. Most people just don't want to change. They are mostly content with the way things are. The pandemic viruses of 2020 and afterwards created a window of opportunity. Just a few weeks of the economy at a dead stop and the skies cleared, and the planet was given a momentary chance to heal. And she did, as best she could. Everybody saw it. But as soon as he could, mankind ran straight back to rushing here and there, endless work and producing things we don't need, and doing everything the same old way.

"I have watched, just as you are learning to do. Man has lost touch with the spirit of nature, and while mankind may avoid extinction, it will survive as a much diminished species. Man has no interest in changing. Not even with the precipice immediately before him. He will fall.

"The time of man is not yet over, but the reckoning will be soon. I have read in the Bible that there will be seven plagues. I do not think they will be of the biblical kind this time. Not hordes of locusts or flies, although I am sure something similar will happen before the natural balance is restored. I think the reckoning will be from within, and many will not even recognise it for what it is. They will die in misery and confusion. But this is also known. Entropy, impermanence – this is the nature of things."

The fire put out more warmth than heat, which they both enjoyed in the flickering light. The old man puffed his pipe for a few moments, then continued, "Each life is a path, often strewn with many false trails. The goal is to find one's purpose in life. Many never find it, and I am sure they stay in a loop of reincarnation until they find out what they are supposed to learn in this life, so they can move onwards with purpose in the next life. The initial goal is to be the best version of yourself that you can be. To understand your mistakes and learn from them. To live with the gifts or disabilities with which you were born and to do your best, for everybody. Even the highest individuals make mistakes, for this is when we learn the most. Well, I bloody well hope so 'cause I've certainly made my fair share!" he said, guffawing. "We must learn to make new mistakes, not repeat the ones of old. In each life, we have a lesson to learn, an impediment to overcome. If we do not recognise this and fail to improve ourselves, then we simply repeat it in as many lives as is necessary, until we do."

He tapped out his pipe and repacked it, then lit it with a hot twig taken from the dying fire. Robert watched and waited, knowing he was being tested again. *Just let the silence be. There is no need to continuously fill it,* he thought.

The old man soon resumed. "I did not know your wife and daughter, and I see that you still grieve for them, which is as it should be. In time, you will understand that you needed to move on, and that their time to move on had come. You may think that these were senseless deaths, especially your daughter, taken so early in her life before she had really lived. The way the universe works often seems unintelligible to us mere humans and our logical way of reasoning. Trust me when I say that everything in the universe is exactly as it should be. The days of reckoning for man are close, but he cannot or will not see the evidence in front of his nose. So be it.

"I wish you well on your journey and that you may recognise your path when it appears. I think you are on it, even out here in this parched land where nothing seems to lead anywhere. There is so much that could be done, needs to be done, that it is easy to be overwhelmed and to feel that anything we do may seem insignificant. In spite of all of this, it is essential for the spirit that you do what you feel is right. It may seem

      ROBERT STEVENS

unimportant, but it is not so for you, and we never know what impact our actions will have in this life or the next.

"You know the ways of the white man. Use the skills that you have, do not lament what you do not have. Go to California, to your piece of land. Create a refuge for others, create hope when there is none. Keep on learning and changing as you have done so far. You are a leader, and the people will need that. This is your path."

Robert was startled. "How the fuck …" he began, then decided mid-sentence not to question how this old codger knew he had land in California. He knew that this American Indian had true insight. He was a shaman, a medicine man, a visionary – whatever you wanted to call it. Don't ask why, just accept.

The man smiled and carried on. "You must plan for what you are going to need."

And so the two men talked into the night, thinking about what was to come and what would be useful, or not. Much later, just on the point of sleep, so he was not sure if the words had been said or imagined, he heard: "This is not the end. It is a beginning."

In the morning the old man was gone. Robert knew that he had been real, that it wasn't an apparition or a realistic dream, for the remains of the fire were still there. The frying pan, left by the fire the night before, was gone, and Robert wondered if the old man had cleaned it or not after the dog ate from it. He smiled. Probably not, water was too precious out here. The words circulated in his head, and he knew he was not meant to wander eternally.

With an open heart and an empty stomach, he walked back to the road and put out his thumb. The first car came along five minutes later and picked him up.

"Where are you going?" asked the middle-aged, overweight travelling salesman who was behind the wheel.

"California," was Robert's simple reply.

CHAPTER 32

The Desert is a Place of Extremes

To most people, deserts appear to be hot, dry places, inhospitable to life. They are mostly correct in the first two instances, but not the third. Usually, the desert is in a quiescent state, waiting. And there are many different types of desert. Sandy ones with large shifting dunes. Flat and arid ones, or stony ones. Or there is the great frozen desert of Antarctica. What they all wait for is the opportunity, in whatever form it comes, for life to flourish, albeit for a short time. Usually, in the arid places, it is rain that is desperately awaited. Sometimes seasonal, sometimes not. In the great plains of Ethiopia, South Sudan, Central African Republic and Nigeria, there are areas that have experienced increasing desertification through a combination of overgrazing, climate change and war. All with the added element of people pressure. The swathe of land in western and north-central Africa known as the Sahel, which stretched from the Atlantic Ocean to the Red Sea, a vast semi-arid region separating the Sahara Desert to the north and the belt of humid savannas to the south, had now become a desert. The few remaining hardy souls from the region had either died through malnutrition after too many crop failures, or migrated south in search of hope. Islamist extremists had established themselves in the western regions, invoking their brutal form of administration until they, too, discovered that you can't live without water or food, irrespective of what you call your god.

While war has the overall impact of reducing human population, it also reduces the recordings and observations made by people whose task it is to monitor conditions and events. Specifically, the recordings that were not being made were related to locust swarms. Plagues of locusts were well known in this part of the world, ever since people had been living there, and the biology well understood by those employed by the World Health Organisation (WHO). The devastating impact of massive swarms had been known for many generations, and the WHO had hoped, in a land of lost hope, that the monitoring teams would be able to advise when a population explosion was about to happen – not if, but when. And preventative action, such as spraying, could be undertaken in a timely manner. But alas, no. These monitors had long gone, either due to local fighting or just not being paid.

It hadn't rained for many seasons, and the areas classed as semi-arid were increasingly dry and arid. People moved away as the grazing for the small goat herds became even scarcer, and crops withered and died. Previously, the pastures and soil produced just enough to support a family and the clusters of small communities. The resident locusts, in their solitary behavioural pattern, did what they normally do – hanging around, not breeding excessively, just keeping the population ticking along based on the limited food supply available in this increasingly arid environment. But after years of drought, came an unusually early heavy downpour as a prelude to what was to become an unusually wet and prolonged rainy season. The desert locust, *Schistocerca gregaria*, moved from its normally solitary existence to the small islands of ground not flooded by this sudden downpour. An individual locust's proximity to others shifted its behaviour from normally solitary to gregarious: they mated, and mated, and mated. The good rainy season that followed produced the green carpet they required to maintain this behaviour, as it had for thousands of years previously. Numbers started to build, and as the rainy season carried on longer than usual, so did the increase in locust nymphs. They were always there for people to see, if anybody had been looking.

The first swarms were just localised and in areas with few human survivors; it was simply not noticed. But with the plentiful grass and sprouting shrubs to graze, and continued proximity to other desert locusts, the breeding cycle extended. Unusual, ongoing rain continued the process for much longer than normal. South Sudan was the first to record the larger locust swarms, but they were probably not the first ones. Neighbouring Ethiopia had probably had the swarms for longer, but the ongoing dire situation in that particular corner of Africa meant there were few who would have noticed.

The breeding continued, and mega-swarms developed, comprising billions of individuals. Such plagues required massive volumes of green material to survive, so the swarms moved up to a hundred kilometres every day in search of anything to eat. Over a period of two weeks, they travelled both west and south, devouring everything in their path.

Kenya was engulfed, as was Uganda, Central African Republic, Cameroon and Nigeria. The rains had washed right over central Africa, and the plague of locusts started to move further south. The desert areas in the north were a natural barrier, and since these areas had not received the rains, there was nothing to feed the swarms.

Pleas for help went out from various governments; they needed pesticides, and the aerial means to apply them.

But Western governments were struggling themselves. Internal social unrest and the collapse of the internet had stymied them. Who would pay for the chemicals and the planes? And they were tired of Africa; the needy hand had been held out for help for too long now. Though Australia sent a plane, as did Canada.

It was like farting against thunder. The swarms continued to move west and south, leaving a totally denuded landscape behind them. Cattle had nothing to graze on; goats would eat dead locusts. While the grass

     ROBERT STEVENS

and shrubs would eventually regrow once the plague had moved on, the livestock did not have the condition on them to survive the temporary feed shortage. Crops vanished, even corn stalks were reduced to mere stumps in the field. Waterways were polluted by millions of decaying locusts, their lifecycle complete as the youngsters moved on, devouring everything. There are ways to prepare and eat locusts, but it was too late for many humans who had forgotten that knowledge.

There was the unusual sight of billions of dead locusts being washed up on the western shores of Africa, from Mauritania to South Africa. The remaining fish fed well, and that food chain flourished for a while.

Hundreds of millions simply starved to death in a vast swathe sweeping through Tanzania, Kenya, Uganda, Central African Republic, Congo, Cameroon and Nigeria. Mostly, the West chose to remain blissfully ignorant of this disaster. They had their own problems. It was becoming very difficult to keep supermarket shelves stocked.

CHAPTER 33

EMP Attack on the Banks

The technicians at the base in Russia had made a larger version of the EMP generator, which weighed about thirty kilograms. This version was disguised to look like a backup battery supply for a large computer bank. It took some time to design the device to be modular so the components could be broken down and later reassembled to look like part of a 'normal' computer array. The goal was to be able to reassemble it within an hour. Some of the cabling was much larger than that required to carry an electronic message between normal computer server modules, but it was necessary to cope with the extremely high current created by the capacitors. One of the sets of twins had been trained in the field of computer design and installation. She worked with her sister, one of the few times they actually worked beside each other. A wig, glasses and judicious use of make-up helped cover the similarities. And who would expect a senior executive at one of the world's largest international investment banks to have a close relative working for a high-end computer supply company? And Sarah, the senior vice-president of IT at World Investment Bank, based in New York, wasn't married and had advised she was an only child. Hence her dedication to the job. She had been given, and had taken, every opportunity, and was one of the youngest senior VPs the company had ever had. But the technological boom had generated the demand for younger brains across the board, therefore her rapid movement up the ranks in the world of global finance was not surprising.

The device was part of the systems upgrade that had been planned for the past two years. This was a major upgrade of data processing, backup and communications systems. The company had decided, particularly with the guidance of the senior VP of IT, not to rely on cloud storage – too open to infiltration and corruption. And the costs of 'secure' cloud storage were not insignificant. But for this company, money was not a problem. Reliability and security were critical. They would have mirrored computers: one to do the work and one as backup. They could turn one off for maintenance and the other would keep on doing the work.

The room these computers were housed in was armoured in many ways. Apart from the power supply, only one cable went in and out, and everything could be monitored. As well as the regulation reinforced concrete, there were layers of lead and aluminium shielding to prevent electronic penetration. Plus, there were motion and vibration detectors and a state-of-the-art firewall on that single cable. Cell phones would not work in the vault. It was on the third floor of the building since the basement had become too risky with the heavy rainfall events causing recent flooding of the underground garages.

The regular computer components were installed, as were the additional parts. There were two technicians cleared to work in the vault. The backup system was installed first, along with the EMP device. The second technician was advised this was an emergency battery-based backup power supply to support the diesel generators. They provided a seamless power supply if and when the mains power supply was down, and it took a few seconds for the generators to start and cut in. He didn't question it; he was the second fiddle to the lead technician who was extremely bright and did not tolerate inane questions or incompetent work. He kept his head down and did as he was bid; his boss was a bitch in every sense of the word.

Once this initial bank of computer equipment was installed at great cost, all the company information, which included trillions of dollars of investor fund information (who owned what, and who owed what), was transferred to the new computers and the system switched over. It went almost seamlessly, which was a testament to the ability of the twins. The mirror system was installed next, which also included an EMP device. It had to look identical, and it had to work when required. The two systems were brought online, backing each other up but also operating independently in case of a failure of one. The board congratulated itself: forty-five million dollars had been spent, but the investors were happy. More money and debt flowed in. The old, redundant computers were scrubbed of data and dismantled. The company also controlled a fair share of the international credit card debt as well as interbank lending. Where do you think the money came from for you to overextend yourself financially? This paled when compared to the international debt the US Government carried, of which they also managed a fair slice, a lucrative portion of this very large and ever-expanding international pie.

The plan was to activate the EMP within a day or two after the attack on the internet and the electricity grid. Complacency followed by fear was the goal. All Western societies are based on confidence – confidence that tomorrow will be better than today. Somebody will lend you money to invest in either new equipment, or the ability to buy the stuff that the new equipment will produce cheaply, in the belief that you will pay it back in the future. Fear is uncertainty at a very base level.

The precise day of the attack wouldn't be known until the other components of the plan had been put in play. Sarah, VP of IT at World Investment Bank, would be advised through a simple phone call to her second cell phone, and she would activate the timer on the twin EMPs.

They were not the only operatives working in the targeted financial sector attack. The development of the EMP technology,

     ROBERT STEVENS

and its miniaturisation, was far too valuable to be used only once and ultimately discovered. While World Investment Bank was a 'direct hit' at the centre of the system, there were plenty of other targets around the planet that were not as well protected. London, Mumbai, Shanghai and Hong Kong were targeted, amongst other major financial centres. The Swift command and control centre in Hong Kong was targeted by one of the larger devices delivered to an office one floor below. EMP pulses go through normal office walls and reinforced concrete. While enough protective steel will ultimately halt an EMP pulse, standard reinforcing won't. A number of the sets of twins worked in financial institutions and were able to lay their hands on building blueprints that identified the level of protection an individual computer system had. Often the protection was inadequate against a large, directed pulse. Another twenty-one devices were planted as close as possible to the main computer systems of the major banks in selected countries. The insiders were able to provide information on backup systems, and these were targeted as well.

Some banks were targeted using car- or small van-based devices. The larger the device, the larger the impulse that could be delivered and the greater the impact radius. The operatives had worked hard on finding out where the banking computers were housed and what protection they had. Some, but not many, had EMP protection. Many blasts went straight through exterior walls. Sometimes it was as simple as parking a car in a precise location outside a building.

A lot of effort had gone into identifying the most critical targets. There was little point in targeting a small suburban bank when far more significant targets existed elsewhere. Getting drones to drive the vehicles to the targets was easy. But they had a very specific schedule: the weapon had to be in place at a certain time. Surprise is a huge element in the success or otherwise of an operation.

Like the internet, while it was not possible to attack every target, the plan was to do enough damage to the interwoven system so it would stop working. The financial system was now a complex neural network with many parts interconnected and relaying information between the different components. There was no 'heart' or core as such, but like a brain, do enough damage and it will stop functioning properly. Some parts were more important than others.

Stock markets were targeted in a more traditional way. Operatives in the industry provided enough insider information for a range of specific viruses to be quietly installed in discrete blocks of code, so they did not fit the traditional 'look' of a virus and hence, could avoid detection. The blocks would find their own unobtrusive way to unification. The whole idea was to create enough permanent damage to key trading platforms to erode confidence in the system. They were under no illusions they could permanently collapse entire international stock markets.

Immediately prior to the global co-ordinated attack, sets of twins and operatives around the world made massive cash withdrawals, helping fund the attack, confident in the knowledge that the information on the withdrawals, overdrafts and loans would be lost in the data corruption. They also planned to decamp either prior to the attack, or immediately after when confusion reigned supreme. There would be an intense witch hunt after the event so it would be best not to be anywhere near the wounded beast. And cash would be handy, given that they didn't expect EFTPOS or credit card systems to work afterwards.

The impact on global financial and stock markets was immediate. Not only did any client or employee linked by computer to World Investment Bank (WIB) find they could no longer access their information (as it no longer existed), but most of the other major banks and financial institutions around the globe also suffered a similar crippling loss of data at precisely the same time. The repercussions were immediate. Credit cards, EFTPOS, mortgage loans, sovereign debt and

     ROBERT STEVENS

interbank loans – cumulatively the largest sums of money on the planet – evaporated. Stock trading houses could not identify who owned what stocks. Global financial trading, which involves billions of dollars daily to finance global trade and the operation of governments, froze, as a large cog in the machine of money magically vanished at 10.00 a.m. Eastern Standard Time. At that precise moment, Sarah, the senior VP of IT at WIB, who happened to be in London, having activated the countdown on the EMP when instructed, hopped onto a plane to Paris and was never seen again. Financial markets froze, and no banks would open the next day. Or for many days after that. The crowds outside the banks became louder and louder until eventually there were smashed windows and overturned cars. It was those with money on deposit who were most concerned. Those who owed the bank money quietly prayed it was a total meltdown. This included the US Government, which had defaulted on its international debt repayments three days earlier.

Afterwards, the FBI, Homeland Security, and MI6 investigations showed a well-planned and heavily financed terrorist attack, and like the 9/11 Twin Towers attack in the US many decades before, the security agencies were beyond embarrassed by the lack of prior knowledge of this new type of warfare.

It took a day to identify the devices in the vault, but weeks to try and get some movement in the flow of money around the globe. Trillions in electronic money had vanished. Not all the money in the world, but enough to take a quite a few links out of the money chain. Much international trade either stopped or slowed to the rate of molasses flowing out of a small hole on a cold morning. The desired result was achieved – a serious blow to Western confidence, and it undermined their ability to conduct economic war. It was considered an almost complete success by the Directors.

Economies that had started to recover from the stock market correction three years earlier and had accumulated debt burdens, spiralled into depression. Even the spin doctors could not call it a recession. This time it was much worse for the bankers because no government bailout was forthcoming.

Treasury or central reserve bank computers had also been hit in the affected countries, as was the ability to print money. That old, perennial fix-it had been targeted as well. There was no help from up high this time.

ROBERT STEVENS

CHAPTER 34

Paper Money

The attacks on the Treasury Bureau of Printing and Engraving locations in Washington, DC, and Fort Worth, Texas, could not have succeeded without insider knowledge. Both buildings were heavily armoured against external attack for obvious reasons – they printed all the paper currency for the USA. And given that one policy of the United States Government was to print money as a strategy to literally create wealth and repay loans, removing this ability was a significant part of the Directors' long-term plan. Two of the sets of twins had been groomed for positions in each location, and now held senior management roles at the Treasury Bureau at relatively young ages, due to their stellar progress in the industry.

Using two sets of twins in this situation had been strategic; it allowed each senior vice-president to be in two locations at once, which accelerated progress. The plans had evolved over time as they learned the strengths and weaknesses of each facility, and as usual, the opportunity appeared after they had looked long enough.

The buildings themselves were technological marvels of industrial strength; even a guided missile, of which they had a few older models, was unlikely to penetrate the exterior. The Russians had offered newer models, but it was considered they would have limited chance of total success. The underground spaces were similarly protected, so tunnelling wasn't going to work. The arsenal of weapons available to the highly trained security personnel made a ground assault unworkable. But they found the weakness. Like all modern production systems, the high-capacity printing presses were computer controlled. While it was difficult to gain access to the printers for obvious reasons, the computers were somewhat more vulnerable.

Some thought went into the most appropriate attack for each of the facilities: an EMP attack on the computer control systems, or an internal bomb? A bomb would be quite effective because the strength of the exterior walls would contain the blast, maximising damage inside. It was decided to use explosives, which would be smuggled inside each facility.

The substrate or 'paper' for the money printing machine at each facility came in specialist rolls delivered by truck every week. Familiarity breeds not only contempt but also complacency. At both facilities it was a routine delivery with the same drivers rostered on a regular basis. Any change, and the supply company would advise. Every load was X-rayed, so it was initially problematic to get around that, until the senior vice-president of supply at the Treasury Bureau of Printing and Engraving noticed that he could get access to the X-ray computers through an ingenious hack, provided by the team now based in Los Angeles. They could get around the X-ray by playing back a previous scan of an earlier delivery for each site.

The plan was to get a bomb into one of the barrels of paper for each site. It had to be a large bomb with a very high yield to overcome the internal walls between the storage rooms and the printing presses and ink banks. The planners had the blueprints of both buildings, of course. The rolls of paper, which weighed well over a hundred kilograms, were in barrels considered large enough to accommodate a bomb. Local private investigators were used to build a profile of the CEO of the company, Standard Paper, that supplied the substrate to both sites. Mikael was looking for a flaw that could be exploited or a way to get the device into a shipment on a very specific schedule. It all had to work simultaneously, in sync with the other operations being planned.

He found out after a while that the man was bisexual. Nothing special about that, a lot of married men are, and struggle with it. So the CEO would head down to the gay club when he could, which the watchers discovered. Finally, a compromising fact that could be exploited. The CEO had a wife and two teenage daughters, so he would have preferred to keep his little secret quiet. In the end, they did not have to use any form of coercion or blackmail; it may not have worked anyway. While the CEO was away on one of his little encounters at the club, the watcher managed to take 3D scans of his master keys, which were kept in an insecure locker. The operatives now had access to both the paper store at Standard Paper and their offices. They already had the latest security code for the offices due to the position of one of the twin infiltrators, and once inside, they could access the delivery schedules for both Treasury printing presses – the one in Washington, DC, and the one in Fort Worth, Texas.

With the master key to the paper supplier's facility and the access codes, they were able to drive into the paper store and identify the drums scheduled to go to each location the next day; they already had the delivery staff roster and schedule.

The drums of paper were all on pallets, preloaded for delivery. It took some time to unwrap the pallet, pull out two drums from each proposed delivery, unload the paper and reload with explosives, then repack. The redundant paper was loaded into the stolen pickup truck brought along precisely for this reason. It took two hours and a courtesy call to the security company to ensure they were happy.

The operation's planners could not rely on cell phone activation. Security levels at the printing presses were so high that cell phone signals were disrupted. Even management at the Treasury Bureau's plants weren't allowed cell phones inside the 'red line' zone, and every landline call was logged, of course. So timers were used, and the risk taken that the devices would get through security, be delivered into the respective paper stores, and not be discovered. The planners had, of course, measured the time interval taken for delivery from the paper store to each Bureau plant, and the time taken to get through security. They knew from information provided by the infiltrator, who knew the layout of the printing presses and stores, that a powerful enough device activated in the paper store at each of the Bureau's printing plants would penetrate through to the computer suites as well as the printers. All computer programme backup was internal, they did not trust external suppliers. It would be difficult for them to recover from this in a meaningful way. The printers were very specific due to their purpose: they printed money.

Early that morning, a delivery truck left Standard Paper and made its way to the plant in Texas. Another delivery to the Bureau of Printing and Engraving in Washington, DC, went out as scheduled a bit later. The trip across to Texas took twenty-four hours longer than the delivery to DC. As planned, all four devices went off as scheduled the following day, completely destroying the buildings, printing presses and computer control systems of the Treasury Bureau's printing presses. The blasts were huge, internal damage absolute since the external walls had acted as expected, containing the blasts inside. More than a hundred people were killed. Civilian casualties are inevitable in a war.

The ability of the US Government to print money to finance itself was destroyed. It would take months to rebuild the plants. There were old printing dies, but they had been held at the same facilities. These were not the kind of things you could get off Temu. The President was advised within thirty minutes of the simultaneous blasts. She sat down in the Oval Office and was seriously concerned for the future. She had a lot on her plate, and had no idea it was actually US Government money that had financed the attacks.

    ROBERT STEVENS

The Chinese extended a helping hand by offering the large amounts of US cash it happened to hold, but this was politely declined. It had been suspected for some time that the Chinese had been printing US dollars as a form of economic warfare they had not yet deployed.

The plan had been to shake confidence in the entire financial system, and it worked.

CHAPTER 35

The Lecture

The man was in his mid-sixties, grey, but well-built. He had looked after himself. As he strode into the lecture theatre in Washington, DC, he commanded a presence, and the waiting students and assorted alumni stood as a mark of respect. This particular lecture had been extensively advertised over the past few weeks and was genuinely anticipated. Since the stock market crash and subsequent instability in the financial markets, concern about what they were witnessing in the local and global economies was exacerbated by global tensions that were spluttering into open conflict. The internet had crashed, and power supply had been unstable the past twenty-four hours. It seemed like the wheels were falling off everywhere, and they were all looking for some kind of insight and enlightenment. If anybody could provide it, it was this deep-thinking, intelligent man.

Professor Shaun Jones had been one of the youngest graduates at Eton and had gone straight to Harvard on a full scholarship. Unusual for an English lad, and he still had a quiet English accent that the Americans loved. He had excelled in geopolitics and international relations. He had been awarded a PhD for his work on the role of big business, particularly the armaments industry, in the escalation of relatively minor local conflicts into cross-border wars. His work had involved fieldwork in some of these conflict zones, which had provided him with an insight rarely seen in academia. The conflicts were about the same old stuff: minerals, oil, tribalism, religion, land. He had been tenured at the White House for a short period until his strong sense of ethics had forced him to resign and follow academia. He decided that you couldn't help fools – there is no vaccine for stupid.

So he had tried to mould the next generation, realising that the paradigms of capitalism and old money ran deep, and that trying to influence the captains of industry was slow and painful, often with little reward. It is hard to teach an old dog new tricks. Better to work with the puppy.

He had married another academic, a bright and vivacious woman with a PhD in medical research. They had produced one son, who had blossomed in the rich atmosphere of culture and education that pervaded their home, contributed to by the intelligentsia who came to dinner. The conversations around the table were deep and varied, opinions considered and debated.

In the early 1980s, the professor had been one of the first to recognise the potential impact of catastrophic climate change brought on by cascading effects, the tipping points that were to subsequently come and go, ignored by nearly all. His own area of study and teaching evolved, graduating more towards the response of governments to climate change, the slow-moving disaster from an economic perspective. He also examined the subsequent influence of big business and the banking industry in funding the deniers and sceptics, creating a climate of confusion and doubt, just as the tobacco industry had done. Doubt and uncertainty prevailed, thus delaying critical response strategies that may have been implemented in a timely manner. His work, not surprisingly, attracted the attention of various intelligence agencies, including that of the US, the bastion of 'free' speech. He became aware that his personal communications were being monitored.

The title of this seminar, which he claimed would be his last, was simply 'What's next?' He fussed about, setting up the laptop that held his presentation and connecting the cables for power and the projector. His briefcase sat beside the laptop. He began simply. "What we do defines us. Talk is cheap, as we see in the UN, the World Bank, plus many other bodies, and any other government caucus you may choose to listen to. What we do, or not do, in times of need defines us as people of worth, or not. Those who stand by and criticise the actions of others who are trying to effect change, usually while doing sweet-all themselves, are just as culpable as those who created the situation that precipitated the required corrective action. Those often criticising the efforts of others while filming on their smart devices and then posting to social media, are just as culpable as those who created the situation they are filming. Well, shucks, it seems you cannot post online at the moment. What a loss to your self-worth!"

At that point, many of the smart phones that had been filming this address were put down and turned off. Some in the audience carried on though, hoping for a future post.

Professor Jones continued, "It is not good enough to observe, even if you feel the greatest sympathy for the cause others are fighting for. For decades, Americans have sent prayers and thoughts to the victims of the endless mass shootings in this land. Prayers and thoughts never changed a thing. Maybe it assuaged a conscience or two, but achieved little." A table and accompanying graph presenting US mass killings statistics by year were flashed up onto the screen. Gasps from the audience. "Was there any meaningful action on restricting the sale of assault-type weapons? These are specifically designed to kill people. No, nothing changed. It is convenient for us, the older generation, to blame the younger generation for their thoughtless consumerism, their short attention spans, and the ease with which their thought processes, votes and purchasing patterns can be manipulated by 'social media'. It is, of course, social engineering on a massive scale." A pause. The audience shuffled uncomfortably, his words settling uneasy on their minds.

    ROBERT STEVENS

"It is difficult to look at the man in the mirror, as Michael Jackson sang many years ago, and acknowledge that there is where the problem lies. When I see the echelons of modern students, young people who resemble a zombie apocalypse in the way they sit or walk, glued to their devices and oblivious to their surroundings, I am saddened. They don't even recognise the person beside them, let alone communicate in a way that matters, which is called conversation, and it is done in person. Young people are so easily led, so easily fooled. Yet it is my generation who created this situation."

An image of the Cambridge Analytica emblem appeared. "Not only did we devise the technology that made the cell phone possible, or the TV for that matter, with its mass-produced, mindless pap, but also thought up ways of using it for advertising and promotional purposes. The modern manipulation that we have seen in these so-called democratic elections was the natural extension of this. And with developments in AI, there isn't much online you can trust nowadays.

"Did your parents or caregivers create the algorithms that fuelled internet and social media addiction and consumption? Or were they part of the advertising machine that drove people to buy things they didn't need or want? Or a clever psychologist who knew how to manipulate basic human desire by stroking the pleasure centres of the mind? Do you come from a family who has benefitted from this greed, overconsumption, and subsequent destruction of our ecosystems? That supplied the money that has seated you here to perpetuate the myth? The million-dollar holiday home you use for six weeks a year while others are homeless? Do you wonder why they are pissed? Have you slept in your car for a week with your partner and a young baby to see how your perspective may change? Some-how, I doubt it."

A graph of homelessness over time in the United States and the UK appeared behind him. This was followed by the number of people receiving food parcels in the same countries. At this stage, just about all the handheld devices had been put down and the laptops folded. Many of the audience felt a sense of embarrassment. They had been called out in a not-too-delicate manner.

"We are now entering a stage of cataclysmic climate change, when it will be impossible for modern civilisation to survive." The now famous graph of atmospheric carbon dioxide levels appeared. Immediately overlaid was the temperature graph and an extrapolation fifty years into the future. "The projected temperature rises are pretty much locked in due to what we call the lag period. The planet will be fine. This rock will continue to circle the sun for many more billions of years and life will evolve, as it has done for many millions of years."

A graph of the world's ever-increasing population replaced the inexorably climbing carbon dioxide line. "We have known since the 1960s that there are too many people and that such rapid, borderline exponential growth is unsustainable, but nothing changed. Shame on the UN. You also did fuck-all except talk. Talk is cheap. Extinction is not new. What is truly ironic is that we arrogantly named ourselves *Homo sapiens sapiens* – the wise, thinking modern man. Yeah right. We are authors of our own downfall, and we knew that this was a likely outcome of our own actions and greed.

"It would be very PC to think that the graph of the human population on the screen will flatten out in a nice, controlled curve, that we will implement the technology we have to control birth rates. Never before in the history of studied biology has this happened. Such a steep rise is *always* followed by a cataclysmic crash, and then there will be the 'ECG heart fluctuations' as the population tries to find a sustainable level. The crash in the human population is inevitable, and it is upon us.

"Covid-19 wasn't even the beginning of the great cull, but it certainly gave global indebtedness a great upwards nudge. Covid-19 was a mass media event, perhaps ten or fifteen million died if we take into account

     ROBERT STEVENS

the false reporting by many governments, yet over the three years that comprised the height of the pandemic, the human population rose by perhaps two hundred million. Still we carried on."

A graph of international indebtedness appeared. "The apparent economic meltdown and social instability we are experiencing at present are not the big story. They are a predictable symptoms of the much larger problem. Spend more than you earn, both financially and biologically, and eventually the system stops working for you. Ecosystems are collapsing around the world, and yet we choose not to draw the link between ourselves, sitting in a usually air-conditioned lecture theatre or the latest model electric car, and the biological systems that sustain us. The reason we do not consider our predicament to be intrinsically bound to the ecosystems of the planet is due to our mindset. We have been degrading and exploiting the natural environment for so long that we believe it is our right to gather all the fruits of the land. Because of our collective arrogance, we choose not to think too deeply about the consequences of our consumerist lifestyles.

"Many of the captains of industry seek sustainable growth, not recognising the term is an oxymoron. Unfortunately, they have run the world for the past seven to ten decades. Who are we to criticise a Third World economy, say China in the 1970s, or Uganda in the 1980s, seeking a higher standard of living for its citizens? They watched the First World Westerners, you and me, and envied our consumerist lifestyle. Who wouldn't? The developed world's consumers achieved their lifestyle through consumption, fuelled by the exploitation of resources from other countries, including the people of their countries." A graph of consumer goods consumption by country appeared, with an overlay of expenditure per capita.

"The slavery of the seventeenth and eighteenth centuries is but one example. Modern human trafficking is yet another. The demand is for cheap labour and sex. So who are we to criticise China for their coal-fired power stations? All we did was shift the production of the consumer goods we buy to China. Thus we shifted our pollution in the manufacturing of these things, which we want rather than need.”

A graph of the number of operational coal-powered electricity stations over the past hundred years appeared. Most were shocked to see the ongoing upward trend: 'Made in China.'

“We collectively chose to ignore the impact of accelerating climate change for too long. We ignored it because the bottom line was that business as usual was no longer an option. But too many people liked business as usual. Perhaps your family made its money in big oil, or you have an uncle or family friend in big oil. The oil industrialists knew back in 1977 that climate change was real, that it was at least fuelled in part by oil and gas, and that there was little time to act. But as recently as 2021, the oil industry still funded climate denial groups, and have been actively emphasising the uncertainty in climate science. Americans have twice elected a climate denying clown to the Presidency. You are about to find out, as an old American Indian saying goes, that 'wealth is not held in bank accounts, and you cannot eat money'. In truth, your privileged positions mean you will hang on longer, but the final fall will be harder.

“Not many of you will know, but two weeks ago my son was shot in a drive-by shooting in Washington, DC. Just down the road from here. He died two days ago, just as I finished preparing this address. I guess I knew what the outcome was going to be. This has taken from me the greatest joy in my life, my wife having passed many years ago. I had thought that, perhaps, I could carry on with the work I had been doing. Trying to get a new generation thinking in a different way, moving away from our consumer-based society. After thirty-odd years of trying, I do not believe I've had any effect, which is a bitter pill to swallow. To keep on doing what I have been doing would be insane. My son was most likely killed by those who are now known as the Zoms – the Zombie Dogs. The dispossessed. A direct consequence of inequality."

A graph of the international measure of inequality, the Gini coefficient, for the main nations over the past fifty years appeared. The oft-used logarithmic scale had been removed, making the differences even more obvious, not masked by deceptive practices.

"But even more telling than the Gini scale is a look at what proportion of total wealth is held by the top one per cent of the globe's population." A table and graph appeared beside those for the Gini scale, showing the proportion of the world's wealth held by the most wealthy over the past hundred years. There was a collective gasp from the audience.

"Today, the wealthiest one per cent of the global population own forty-five per cent of the world's wealth. The greedy at the top kept on sucking up the money and the resources, and those who were without knew this. There is no trickle-down effect. Why does a CEO earn four to ten million dollars a year? You cannot spend that kind of money meaningfully. A lot of what we teach at this prestigious institution is about maintaining that inequality. How the laws can be used and manipulated. How money buys justice, power and influence. Why would the top echelon of society, those with the greatest wealth and power, want to change anything? As far as they are concerned, everything is just fine. 'I'm doing all right, Jack! What's your problem?'

"Well, my fellow alumni, the problem is that our society has been far from sustainable for many decades. And we knew it, but did nothing concrete to correct the situation. Give a few dollars to Green Peace maybe. Conscience money at best. Put out the recycling next to the larger rubbish bin. Did anybody actually look inside their rubbish bin? I mean tip it out and go through it, noting that everything in it has been purchased. Now about to go to a landfill somewhere else, a place out of sight and out of mind. 'Did I really need to buy this?'

you should be asking. Did we change the way we lived? Nope. Did we stop buying the things that were in the packaging that's in the recycling? No. We just hired storage units for the tsunami of stuff we purchased."

A table and graph of the number of self-storage units appeared behind him. A student in the second row muttered, "Where the fuck does he get all this information?" There was no reply.

"How many of you have carbon farming businesses in your investment portfolio? Sorry, rhetorical question. Did we create the inequality that ultimately led to my son's murder? Yes. Did we buy stuff that we didn't need? Yes. You or your family have an electric car? Ever give any thought as to how the electricity is generated to power said car? We cannot consume ourselves towards an enhanced sustainability. Are we the authors of our own fate through our actions, or lack of action? Yes. So, fellow alumni. To my students, all future scenarios are bad. Carbon dioxide levels continue to track upwards and climate change will easily exceed 2.5 °C, which will be catastrophic. The polar caps will continue to melt at an accelerating rate, as will the last of the glaciers, and the sea levels will rise tens of metres – multiply this by three for feet. That means that most of Manhattan Island will not be above sea level. Where will those people go? And if you think about that for a moment, it means that vast areas, globally speaking, of currently densely populated flat land along the coastal margin will also be under water. Do you think those residents will just stay put and drown? Or stay put in a place that is just too hot to live in?

"In the past few weeks I have thought about what is to come. It is not good news. Biologists have long talked about the multiple interactions between the organisms of this planet and the inevitable cascade of ecosystem collapses that will occur if we do not change our ways. This will no longer be in some remote part of Africa or Pakistan, viewed as a video bite on the new high-definition TV, to whom we can send our

     ROBERT STEVENS

thoughts and prayers. You are all biological creatures, and it will affect you, and I can't comprehend what it is going to be like.

"The recent disruption to the internet, power grid and stock markets has created a loss for you; your investment funds have all but vanished. The latest credit crunch, created by the banks once again, means your ability to buy stuff is much reduced. Curiously, this should have happened decades ago to give the ecosystems half a chance. I can guarantee, however, that your recent lack of internet access is the least of your problems."

The good professor paused for effect, then resumed, "Food scarcity and eventual starvation is inevitable. Superstorms, storm surges, flooding and drought are inevitable. They are upon us already. Heat waves followed by freezing. The mega firestorms in Australia are a symptom, not the cause. It is difficult to comprehend when all you have experienced are conditions that are pleasant, mostly sitting on your arses in air-conditioned rooms not unlike this one. There will be legions of displaced and homeless people in your own backyard, and you won't know what to do. The Zombie Dogs. There are a lot of them, they are pissed off, and they have nothing to lose because they have nothing. They are street smart and have a much higher level of aggression than you. Handbag puppy meets wolf. You will be scared and confused, partly because much of your life you have waited for the world to come to you though your device. Ooops.

"The ecosystems that maintain life on this planet, including your own, are now in an advanced state of decay and it is far too late to do anything about it. The collapse of these interconnected webs of life will not be as photogenic as the collapse of the Twin Towers, but the impact will be many orders of magnitude greater. I have decided not to watch, it will bring me even more sadness, which is hard to comprehend. I would take questions, but I do believe we are out of time. I wouldn't know what to say to your questions anyway."

The audience sat in stunned silence. They didn't know what to say, what questions to put to this man. This man whom they all respected, whose words were always considered and thoughtful. While they sat there, dumbfounded, trying to process this dark message put in very blunt terms, the professor unhurriedly shut down his computer and disconnected the projector's USB cable. He then quietly opened the briefcase that had been sitting on the lectern. He pulled out a .38 revolver, put the muzzle in his mouth and pulled the trigger.

Quite the full stop.

     ROBERT STEVENS

CHAPTER 36

A Brief History of Climate

In its earlier geohistory, during one of Earth's icehouse climate states, the planet was a 'snowball', completely covered in snow and ice. Scientists and academics postulate the period of such a global ice age is likely to have been some time before 650 million years ago, during the Cryogenian Period.

And then it changed, over an immense geological timescale.

Volcanoes originally created the planet's atmosphere, pumping vast amounts of gas during a time of massive volcanic activity. This enabled the first organisms to evolve, possibly in a chemical soup, possibly with divine intervention. Who knows? Interestingly, a modern volcano, while being spectacular by mortal standards, pumps out roughly the same amount of carbon dioxide as six hours of man-made emissions.

The climate on earth has changed significantly before, without the help of man. About twelve thousand years ago, Earth tilted on its axis, bringing an abrupt end to the last Ice Age and basically heralded in the modern era.

Pre-industrial atmospheric carbon dioxide levels were around 280 ppm, and by 1970, had climbed to around 325 ppm. In 2020, they were 418 ppm and rising at about 2 ppm per year. There is seasonal variation based on the carbon dioxide absorption in the ring of forest surrounding the Arctic in the northern spring.

The UN Climate Change *Conference* in Glasgow (COP26) in 2021, produced a climate pact after intense negotiations amongst almost two hundred countries, one of its aims being to keep global warming below 2.0 °C, whereas the scientific community has long maintained that a maximum of 1.5 °C warming, while still creating large fluctuations in weather, is the most that modern civilisation could probably cope with.

Researchers are now interested in the Pliocene Epoch, specifically around three to six million years ago, as the earth was about 2 to 3 °C warmer then than it was in pre-industrial times. It is believed that at that time sea levels were about fifteen to twenty metres higher than they are now.

During the Pleistocene Epoch, informally called 'The Great Ice Age', about twenty thousand to a million years prior to the present time, the global temperatures were generally colder, fluctuating around -1 to -4 °C colder than the pre-industrial average.

The dinosaurs ruled during the Cretaceous Period, about 145 to 65 million years ago, when the temperature was about 6 to 12 °C warmer than pre-industrial levels. High levels of volcanic activity kept atmospheric carbon dioxide levels at around 450 to 600 ppm and the Gondwana landmass was still breaking up. Antarctica and the Arctic were ice-free. Sea levels were perhaps a hundred to two hundred metres higher than the present day.

Remember: *The planet will be fine, and the climate has changed before!*

Mankind has been wandering around the planet for perhaps a quarter of a million years in organised groups, and building recognisable buildings and social structures for perhaps fifty thousand years. The earliest Neanderthal cave paintings date back about sixty thousand years, that is twenty thousand years before *Homo Sapiens* arrived in Europe. Jesus walked the planet at the time of the Roman Empire, two thousand years ago. Man has 'flourished' during a period of relative climatic stability that had prevailed for around the past twelve thousand years, the Holocene Epoch. This period of climate stability would have

        ROBERT STEVENS

enhanced settled communities and reliable agriculture, surpluses of which would have been traded between groups.

Food security meant that less time was required for hunting and gathering, and this enabled more time for thinking, the arts, socialisation and trade. Fully-fed creatures are much more likely to successfully breed and raise their young to adulthood. Like bacteria, numbers will grow until the nutrient source is consumed. Usually, once this happens, the population will decline to a level that can be sustained by the supply of nutrients.

During the 1980s and 90s, extreme climate events were relatively uncommon and could be mostly attributed to normal climatic variation. The science community were the ones who generally talked about global warming. An understanding of climate change was developing, and the collection of data accelerated. Satellites improved the measurement of things like ice cover at the poles and the changes in glaciers, and the evidence began to accumulate. In 2004, Al Gore first presented his keynote address 'An Inconvenient Truth'. At that time, global carbon dioxide levels were 379 ppm, and in 2008 the 350.org movement was born. The movement campaigns and organises "locally and globally to create a world powered by just and accessible renewable energy that will move us away from fossil fuels, for good".

In the new millennium, the severity and frequency of extreme weather events accelerated, with record-level droughts and floods beginning to impact large areas of the planet. Urbanisation, deforestation, swamp drainage and land use changes all accelerated rainfall runoff, having a direct effect on the severity and speed of floods, landslides and mudslides. Wildfires are now common in both the Southern and Northern hemispheres. Many countries have reported variously record temperatures, rainfall intensity, wildfires and drought. Often in rapid succession. Potable drinking supplies are increasingly threatened.

For the past fifty years, global carbon dioxide levels have increased at around 1.5 to 2 ppm, annually. Politicians applaud when the rate of increase begins to decrease. The signs have been there for some time now – they are just getting larger and will continue to do so.

ROBERT STEVENS

CHAPTER 37

Dave in Town

Life in town hadn't worked out too well, or too badly. There was no work, like *no* work at all. There was plenty to be done, but no paying work. The collapse of the internet and global financial markets affected them not one jot, apart for the whining coming from disconnected teenagers. The coal mine had been shut down for care and maintenance and most of the men laid off. The new carbon taxes and the meltdown in the global economy had put paid to the production of the low-value thermal coal.

The day Caitlyn saw her husband asleep in his clapped-out Nissan, she told her lover that it was over. Her husband had come in from the farm, and it was just not right. The accountant was miffed; no one enjoys getting dumped. And he liked having a bit on the side. Caitlyn's hours were cut, but in reality there hadn't been as much work going through any of the accountants in town for some years now. As businesses closed, there was less going on. Simple devolution. Things winding down. Entropy. In previous situations like this, the government would embark on a campaign of quantitative easing or public works programmes, creating money or jobs, or a combination of both. But indebtedness was one huge factor that had reduced the ability to do this. Every government owed so much money to everybody else that there was no appetite for more risk. Like a business that had traded at a loss for too many years, eventually you must face the music.

But more relevant was the deep loss of confidence and trust that had stewed and grown over the years. The attack on the banking system had evaporated trillions of dollars of deposits and loans. Financial paralysis resulted. The droughts and floods, the superstorms that were ever more common, had all but collapsed the insurance industry. Farm production had been slashed across all forms of agriculture and horticulture. The aquaculture industries fared no better – they were seriously impacted by increasing sea temperatures and increases in ocean acidity. And the terrorist attack on the internet had left a generation of young adults unable to function effectively because the lack of connectivity in their devices was too disorientating, with many becoming completely erratic, irrational and depressed. The symptoms closely mirrored a junkie unable to get a fix.

There were water restrictions in town. There were water restrictions everywhere. He had spent an afternoon digging a vegetable patch in the scorched earth of the backyard, thinking that he could water it in the middle of the night while no one was watching. But the water meters would show what was happening, and a quick inspection would reveal a patch of green amongst the pervading brown. The local council now prosecuted for this type of behaviour. Some people didn't care, and stealing water in novel and creative ways became the new pastime. Some places had their water permanently turned off at the street, which was a new way of telling somebody to fuck off.

They collected the water from the kitchen and shower – the grey water. This was bucketed out to the vegetable patch and applied in the evening: watering during the day was insane. Technically, it was late autumn, but temperatures were still in the mid-forties in the middle of the day.

They grew some potatoes and beans. It helped. The prices of fruit and vegetables, when they were in the shops, were very high. Many couldn't afford them. Bread too, as wheat crops around the world were affected by the weird weather.

   ROBERT STEVENS

They all lost weight, and they had to go to the welfare office every fortnight to collect the cash payments because internet banking had evaporated. Armed guards were on duty at the welfare office. Not only were tempers more fragile, which often exploded into shouting and pushing, but there had also been an attack on the office the previous month while the armoured car carrying the cash was unloading. Zombie Dogs had got themselves armed and organised, which was a worrying trend. The shoot-out was more noise than impact, with one Zombie Dog and a bystander wounded.

The rent payments they made they simply cut in half, and then stopped. Going down to the real estate agent building was a pain, and they realised that the agents didn't really care that much. A large bank of empty houses now stood in town anyway. Dave and Caitlyn were looking after the property, which was a lot more than others were doing. And the kids were going hungry because of the cost. If they were asked to produce the rent or be evicted, then they would cross that bridge when they got to it. It didn't pay to try and think too far ahead these days.

People started to trickle back from the city. The crowding was just too much in urban areas, combined with the heat being more extreme in the city, as the concrete jungle held daytime temperatures for longer. Without air conditioning, you couldn't sleep at night, and the power cuts were becoming more frequent, some of which were planned by the transmission companies. Electric arcs across the power lines above tinder-dry gum trees were a recipe for disaster. The power companies were steadily retrofitting safer gear, but it all took time and money. Trains now ran at night as the extreme heat of the day buckled the tracks, making train travel during the day hazardous. In fact, a lot of human activity now happened in the early morning or later in the evening as the heat of the day dissipated.

The gangs did not go away. They became even bolder. Dave, Caitlyn and the kids were aware of this increased threat to their personal safety, and they took a lot more care where they went, and went in pairs when possible. The girls never went anywhere alone any more. Dave walked with Caitlyn to the office on the two days a week she now worked. They both suspected they may not have to do that for much longer. *Worry about that when the time comes*, was their attitude.

Late one morning there was a knock at the door. A shifty-looking lad aged in his twenties asked if he could use the phone as his car had broken down. Dave advised that they didn't have a phone, not even a mobile phone. Sorry. He looked around and could see no car. A second lad appeared in the driveway, and Dave sensed trouble. And it was here, now. The first lad quickly turned into an arsehole by pulling a small pistol from the pocket of his baggy trousers and tried to push his way past Dave, while the second ran towards the front door to support his mate. Dave did not hesitate, and in a reflex move, he head-butted ZD number one as he moved forward. It was a glorious strike, breaking the kid's nose and laying him onto the floor, half in and half out of the house. When Dave looked up from his handiwork, ZD number two was coming up the front steps, and another had appeared at the front gate, looking for guidance. Dave stepped forward to meet the second prick and swung an uppercut into the face, hard. The combined forces of Dave moving forward with an upwards punch, along with the second prick moving towards Dave's accelerating fist, with years of pent-up anger behind it, broke the prick's nose off neatly where the cartilage of the nose joined the skull, and pushed the whole ragged-edged bone and cartridge into the frontal lobe. Arsehole number two dropped even faster than the first, who still lay semiconscious on the floor. It was difficult to know who was more surprised: Dave or the recently deceased arsehole who now twitched on the front porch of this nondescript house, in a nondescript rural town, with his nose now imbedded in his brain. Arsehole number three looked at his two fallen mates, and his limited mental capacity struggled with whether to go and help his mates or

     ROBERT STEVENS

consider his own safety and run. It was a situation he hadn't dealt with before. Normally, they got into the house just fine and had their fun once inside. No one had fought back so effectively before.

While he dithered at the front gate, Dave did not. Adrenaline now flowing, he stepped back inside over the two prone bodies and got the rifle from behind the door. This was not quite as quick as he would have liked since a semiconscious body was lodged up against the door. But after a few seconds, he had the .308 rifle in his hand, cranked a round into the breach and swung back onto the porch. He raised the rifle and simple laid down his ultimatum: "Fuck off or die, cunt!"

It was all the encouragement that arsehole number three needed, and he fled.

Dave stood for a minute, gathering his thoughts. Dead number two was still twitching, which was a bit unnerving. He had seen dead people before, but had not killed anybody until this. Semiconscious arsehole number one was stirring, and would be troublesome soon. He needed the cops, but it was true – he had no phone. He fired a shot into the front lawn (or what used to be lawn), and a fountain of dust puffed up. That should do it; cops will be here in a minute. He checked for a pulse in Twitchy but couldn't find one. Good. Taking the rifle with him, he went inside and eventually found some cable ties in his toolbox in the garage. The kids would be back from school soon. School now ran early in the morning while it was cooler. During the heat of the day everybody just laid up where they could; find a coolish spot was all one could do. The Indigenous people had it right.

By the time he had returned to the front door, arsehole number one was struggling to stand. He was on all fours, still in the doorway, and there was a lot of blood over his face. Dave gave him a good kick in the balls, which put him down again. Dave had heard stories from his mates at the club and the police about what these bastards had been up to, so there was no interest in talking. He pulled number one's arms behind him and, not too gently, cable-tied them together, making sure they were tight enough to cut off the blood flow to his hands. He gave him another kick to the guts for good measure.

Armed police appeared five minutes later. Dave was ready for them, his rifles laid out on the bed inside while he sat on the porch waiting for them, along with the two bodies. Arsehole number one was moaning — the pain in his head and testicles steadily being overtaken by the pain in his wrists. Not a happy chappie.

Once the police were satisfied that no further risk existed, they uncuffed Dave and listened to his story. The Dogs, as the Zombie Dogs were being called in this part of the world, were known to the police, of course. A Dog, not the four-legged faithful kind, was the lowest form of human life.

The moaning became noisier, so the sergeant who had been talking with Dave on the porch got up, and with his steel-capped boots, kicked the dog in the head. "Shut the fuck up," and then sat back down to continue his yarn with Dave. Number one went quiet.

The small pistol was all the evidence the police needed: an armed home invasion. It was bagged for future fingerprinting. The sergeant said they had been looking for this group for some time. They were believed to be responsible for several home invasions, rapes and murders. Too bad the shot hadn't gone through arseholes three's head was the lament. There would be no charges against Dave, and he could keep his guns. He had acted responsibly and reasonably. This type of prick was now a worldwide phenomenon. Taking advantage of the difficult situation that many people were in made them lower than parasites.

After perhaps ten minutes of talking, the police dragged number one off and bundled him into a police van. One they could wash out afterwards, because some extra treatment would be administered before they got to the police station. These were the types of Dogs who were more than happy to shoot it out with the cops, and an officer from the

     ROBERT STEVENS

sergeant's crew had been killed two weeks earlier. The dead body of the second Dog was thrown in next to the recovered but groggy number one. He had lost all sensation in his hands, and would ultimately lose the use of most of his fingers due to nerve damage.

Dave was rattled. Not so much by the death he had caused, which was a bit of a fluke really and no real loss. It was the randomness of the attack, early in the day. The potential for harm to his family was the real concern. He didn't really enjoy town life, and longed to be back on the farm. There had been no rain in the twelve-plus months they had been living in town, eking out an existence. He knew there was nothing but more dust and flies out there, and he was deeply saddened by this.

The family discussed the events that evening. The kids were both horrified and impressed by what Dad had done. He had gone from being some annoying older person, put on this earth to make their lives a misery, who couldn't even get a job, to a hero in a few short minutes. Cool.

Dave and Caitlyn were not sure what options were available to them. While their thin illusion of safety had been shattered, they were not convinced that it would be better anywhere else. The stories from the cities were even worse: food shortages, riots, robbery and random violence were common. They accepted that Caitlyn's work wouldn't last much longer; everything was slowing down. The farm was technically still theirs, but there was nothing there, not even the restricted water supply they had access to in town. They decided to stay on. No one went anywhere on their own from now on.

Dave became something of a local celebrity.

— ◆ —

There were other farmers who were now in town, so Dave's situation was not unique. Some had been foreclosed on and were required to leave their farms. Their farms, if they could still be called that now, were owned by the bank, who did not want them. A few had done as Dave had, grudgingly accepting the situation. It had been too dry for too long, little could survive. A much larger number couldn't cope, and had taken their own lives. There had been a state-run programme on mental health, trying to reach those who were struggling. But farmers are a specific breed: independent, tough, unlikely to show to others what they perceived to be a weakness. When the strain of seeing years of hard work literally turn to dust before their very eyes, they took that way out. Almost all the suicides were males in their forties and older. They didn't know of any other life than the one that was disappearing in front of them. They didn't know what to do.

The wives and children who were left behind moved into town, if they had not done so already. They did not want any part of what had killed their husbands and fathers.

There had been two clubs in town. There was the RSA club, and a private club secretly owned by the local mafioso. It had the somewhat ironic name of the town's Social League, but the illegal activities that went on behind its doors were far from socially responsible. Many men, now on welfare, went there to spend money which should have been spent elsewhere. Whores and gambling were on offer, as well as illegal booze that was a lot cheaper than the government-taxed booze. Just for a moment they could forget their worries.

The RSA club became the default place for people who just wanted to meet and talk, to share their troubles. People gathered and shared what they had: help with the kids, and an exchange of clothing, recipes and any excess produce, which was a rare thing. Even marrows were eagerly taken. Some human kindness remained. Booze was expensive at the best of times, and while some could afford a beer, over time the liquor sales were so slow that the club decided to let its licence lapse and renamed itself The Community Club. Opening hours were from five till ten in the morning, and then seven till twelve at night. They had air conditioning but couldn't afford the electricity to run it when electricity was available. Because of the layout and orientation of the building, a cool breeze could be generated naturally. The cooler south side of the building slowly absorbed the midday heat but rapidly gave off the heat overnight. That part of the building became a great place for a midday nap. People would come early in the morning, have a cup of tea and a chat, and then sleep on the carpeted floor for the hottest part of the day. Many houses were just too hot to sleep in. Mattresses were found for the kids.

Power supply had been intermittent for some time now, and then it became very irregular. The hospital started to run the backup generators nearly all the time to keep the air conditioning going and whatever equipment they had that was still operational. The supply of parts and the technicians to install these had become increasingly unreliable over the years. Electricity transmission was affected by the very high temperatures that caused the aluminium cables to sag beyond their design point, and with the persistent winds, it made electric arcing more common. In the tinder-dry conditions, many wildfires were started this way. The coal that fired the power stations had become expensive with the carbon taxes, and the power companies struggled as all businesses now did. The hydro-powered stations had been running well under capacity due to the insignificant rainfall in their feeder catchments. Solar and wind power were operating well, but the failing distribution network struggled to get the power to where it was wanted. Demand, especially for air conditioning, nearly always exceeded supply and rationing was introduced.

— ◈ —

An avid conversation about how the residents of Coober Pedy had dug underground to live in the heat was revisited by the townspeople, and a group, including some from the town council, went to the local river to look at the geology. A local school science teacher had advised the town was built on old sedimentary rock, and this would probably be suitable for tunnelling to create caverns and underground chambers. The river had dried up many years previously, and the sheer face of the river bank was a great place to start the geology lesson. It looked promising, and it was agreed that work would begin immediately on tunnelling to explore what would actually happen if they went deeper. A cooler place to sleep would be a good start. They had to keep in mind that this was an old riverbed, and it would rain one day. And the news from around the world was that when it did rain, it could do so with a vengeance. They did not want to be caught like rats in a drainpipe.

Dave went along as well, using his celebrity status. He became active in the group, pleased to be able to sink his teeth into something solid. He was part of the group that went out to the coal mine to see what equipment might be available. The town council was tight for funds, but did have a limited diesel supply, experienced operators and planners. The mine was more than willing to help, and diggers, loaders and a retired geologist were packed off to town. Work began at once, clearing the brush and undergrowth that obscured the smooth rock face of the old river embankment. The council worked on retrospective permit approvals, and as it was tunnelled out, the loose rock was flattened to make an all-weather access way.

One digger, while clearing the old willow trees, found out what the Aboriginal elders could have told them years ago: there was still some water seeping down through the old sandy riverbed, above the impervious sandstone underneath. While not a gushing spring, it did lead to the development of a water seep for limited amounts of fresh water and a community garden in the moister sands. An unemployed agronomist was tasked with taking soil samples and then making recommendations for fertilisers. The local fertiliser depot still had a plentiful supply of old product since farmers had stopped purchasing

     ROBERT STEVENS

many years prior, and it wasn't worth sending the product back. The town was scoured for vegetable seeds.

The work on the tunnels progressed steadily. While the townspeople wanted the cool area, they needed to make sure they were safe from cave-ins. Air ventilation was a series of holes drilled down from the surface. People would come and stay in the partially dug tunnels during the heat of the day and go home at night. Preference was given to the machinery operators and the children. While perhaps in an earlier time, the elderly may also have been given some priority, this was not the case now. The protection of the children was self-evident, and eventually, as work progressed, the primary school was relocated underground. Machinery operators needed good sleep to function well. What they were doing was tricky at the best of times, but now also very important. They were well experienced in machinery operation, but not underground. They rushed quietly at the job.

The elderly were, by necessity, not so important, although it was never quite put in those terms. Where did the priorities lie? Care was being rationed, as was everything else.

The gardens grew well, but there was not nearly enough for the whole town. The area had to be guarded twenty-four seven. It was not only the Dogs who looked to raid the produce before it was ready. Many people were struggling now because food was so expensive, when it was available. The supermarket only opened four days a week, and only in the morning, and they had employed armed guards to keep order. Produce purchases and canned goods were rationed to get the limited supplies spread as widely as possible. A lot more people carried weapons now – shotguns, rifles. Technically, pistols were illegal, and the police often frisked those they did not know.

Over the year that Dave and his family had been in town, it still hadn't rained significantly. They had squirreled away some money and a few litres of petrol, which was also being rationed. After a period of relatively wet weather, when they got thirty millimetres of rain over two weeks, they all went back to the farm, shoehorning themselves into Caitlyn's little Camry along with supplies to stay a few nights, depending. The old Nissan had been driven around the back of the house and was an impromptu sleep-out for anybody who wanted time-out. Tempers were easily frayed these days.

What greeted them was not a pretty sight. Dave had packed a few tools, and he stripped boards from the old sheds to batten over the heat-twisted windows and doors. The kids cleaned the house and Caitlyn made tea in an old billy and scavenged firewood. While it was a desolate sight, they enjoyed doing something positive to the place for a couple of days. It gave them a transient sense of being home, although they hadn't been there for just over a year.

His old horse appeared at the remains of the fence surrounding the property, investigating the noise. She was mostly skin and bone. Dave recognised The Old Nag, but she wouldn't come up to him. Dave retrieved the rifle from the boot of the Toyota, but couldn't do it. He handed his rifle to his eldest son, and told him where to aim, using the stockyard rail as a support. The shot was true, and The Old Nag fell instantly. The over-land cut is a quick way of getting the back steaks and rear legs off a carcass, which was handy as the poor beast had fallen on a mound of large ants, and they were not impressed by the intrusion. Much laughter and hilarity ensued as the two boys and Dad struggled to retrieve the meat and swat ants at the same time. The girls had tears running down their faces by the end of it.

They ate their fill that night. Even the back steaks were chewy strings of sinew, but it was a feast, and they laughed and joked around the fire. It was good, just for a moment. Once the kids had gone to bed and they were just sitting around the fire outside, for the first time in a long time, Dave and Caitlyn made love. In the yard on an old blanket

     ROBERT STEVENS

by the firelight. Even the mozzies gave them a respite for a minute, for they had reappeared like magic after the rain.

There was a tinge of green across the paddocks at the farm, as the seeds in the ground in Australia germinate and grow quickly when there is moisture. They need to get through their reproductive cycle as quickly as possible. There was no stock on the place, not even a sign of the kangaroos that were normally a pain, breaking down fences. The next day was cooler as the clouds persisted even though it appeared the rain had stopped. They all fossicked around the sheds and played the goat, and it was good. Dave was as content as a man could be in the circumstances and was pleased that he hadn't gone down the road of taking his own life, as many of his neighbours had, and yes, the thought had crossed his mind. He wasn't sure what the future would bring, but he was just taking it one day at a time.

They drove back to town that afternoon, and the fuel light was on for the last half of the trip. They were getting used to that.

CHAPTER 38

The Drifter

It took a week for Robert to get to California. He hitched continuously now, not walking much at all, feeling a growing impatience within himself. Head west and get on with what was now a mission for him, on the land he and his wife had purchased years ago and he hadn't visited since then. He couldn't explain it to himself, let alone anybody else. He just knew he needed to get there, and for the first time in many years, he was focused. There weren't many cars on the road, and definitely fewer that were prepared to pick him up. He caught a bus, having withdrawn a modest amount of cash from his EFTPOS account. It felt like the old American Indian was with him, guiding his actions.

In LA he still had bundles of cash in a safe deposit box. He went on a buying spree, getting great deals from grateful store owners. He purchased a good, second-hand Winnebago campervan and filled it with weapons, solar panels, batteries, cabling and controllers. Water tanks and pipe were put into a U-Haul trailer, which he also purchased with cash, along with a myriad of sundry tools and timber. A large range of vegetable plants and seeds were also bought when he found them. The list that he had developed with the old man was etched in his mind.

The price of food continued to climb as crops failed, and now there were genuine shortages of basic foodstuffs: bread, sugar, coffee, dairy products; it was across the board. People were angry. They were angry at everything as their paradigm started to unravel. Bankers still had fast cars and fat lives. The corporate dogs still seemed to live fairly comfortably in their gilded cages. The protective details that kept these elite from the unwashed masses increased in number as the level of anger grew.

Fire-bombing of elite houses became the new Saturday night entertainment. The emergency services were overwhelmed and often attacked themselves. Anybody in a uniform was also the enemy. They were 'establishment'. Even ambulance officers were routinely attacked now, and only went out with armed police. Many quit; it just wasn't worth it.

He had retrieved all his bundles of cash, and for reasons he could not explain, withdrew more money held on deposit. He smiled when the internet and power grid were attacked the next day, followed by the banking system. He knew the old American Indian was smiling too. The timing was too prefect to be a fluke.

While Robert was now entirely disconnected from the web in his day-to-day life, or so he thought, it affected all his electronic transactions. He was aware that the remaining stack of electrons that specified his wealth and 'place' in society had instantly evaporated when the attacks on the banking system happened. He laughed when he realised that he didn't really care about it any more. If a similar thing had happened in his previous life, he would probably have ended himself because money and status was how he had measured his worth. He had learned to live modestly while on the road and appreciate what was actually important: the difference between wants and needs.

The rioting and looting, which had been simmering away at a low level as a symptom of general discontent amongst the populace, was rampant now. Supermarkets were ransacked, as were appliance stores. Perhaps there was a mistaken belief that an appliance without power is a useful thing, such was the level of ignorance or denial amongst many.

Police were overwhelmed, and the army, national guard or its equivalent, depending on the country, were called in. Most countries imposed martial law, and night-long curfews were introduced. Because nighttime rioting and destruction of property continued unabated, initial warning shots turned into deadly force before too long. Pitched battles started in some areas where the populace was well armed.

Robert listened to this on his radio in the Winnebago, a sense of déjà vu washing over him as he recalled the conversation with the old American Indian. He wondered where the old guy might be now and then realised that he would find out in good time. He had his own work to carry on with.

He drove from Los Angeles to his parcel of land. It took more than two days. Although the streets were remarkably clear, burnt-out cars and general rubbish were everywhere. He saw more people walking the road as he drove, walking away from the decaying cities. Robert was well insulated from this, having shifted himself, his mobile home and essentials at just the right moment, but he realised that his little slice of remote paradise wouldn't be isolated from the social decay forever. It was more than two hundred and forty kilometres from the boundaries of the nearest city, which was a seven- to ten-day walk for a fit person.

The next chapter of what was becoming a very full life had begun for him. He liked himself and what he was doing. It was good. He had changed, adapted. He didn't think that process had stopped either.

CHAPTER 39

The Drones

The drones were built in China, just another product from a factory with workers grateful for a job at a miserable wage. There were few records kept. The drones had been paid for with crisp new one-hundred-dollar American bills. A Russian driver who could speak Mandarin collected the order. He was well paid to drive across China for the pick-up, then back into Russia, and then to a secret location that had been pre-programmed into the GPS unit provided. The documents he had been given got him through all the check points with remarkable ease. In fact, the guards often seemed relieved to see the back of the foul-smelling, diesel-smoke-belching machine. A hundred and twenty drones packed into sturdy wooden crates, each weighing nearly forty kilograms, was a small load that did not need any inspection. The documents implied this in no uncertain terms, with 'Priority Shipment' stamped in Russian and Chinese across all the pages, and signed by the Russian interior minister himself, in co-operation with his counterpart in the Chinese Government. They could work together when it suited.

At the compound the GPS directed the driver and his load to, he was escorted to a large shed where he drove inside, away from the prying eyes above. The truck was promptly unloaded by young men who got on with the task with vigour. He was given a generous bonus and sent on his way. He had been given clear instructions to just leave and not talk of this to anybody. He had been given enough money to make that part of the deal easy to keep. And the look of the fit young men who had unloaded the truck – the efficient and systematic way they had gone about it without saying a word – had made him reflect that perhaps discretion was the wisest choice.

The engineers and programmers who went to work on the drones had been well trained in America, the UK and India. The capitalists certainly did produce some remarkable innovations, and everybody had learned from the extensive use of drone warfare in Ukraine. American cash had also provided the computers, the software, the 3D printers and other engineering capacity, plus the explosives – everything they needed to achieve what they wanted to do.

The first job was to empty the crates, strip the drones and reassemble them, to see what the Chinese had got wrong. Sometimes the mistakes were just plain silly, imbalanced nacelles being but one example. Porous soldering, faulty motors. Other specialists were focused on the re-tasking of the drones, adapting them so they would do the job required. This work involved heavier duty wiring to improve electrical current flow, improving computing capacity and optics to enable completely autonomous operation – they did not want to be exposed to external drone disruption technology. Once checked and initially re-engineered, the drones were sorted into groups for further reworking.

The price they had paid excluded the additional battery capacity they wanted, so the necessary components were ordered and installed. This order came from Korea, and again paid for in cash to limit the potential for trace back. Again the customer picked up the order by car, having driven through what remained of North Korea.

The 3D printers produced the new propeller blades, which, coupled with the extra battery capacity and better motors, gave the fleet additional range and speed. But most importantly, it allowed for extra carrying capacity.

     ROBERT STEVENS

A number of drones were sacrificed in the development phase. A mock building had been constructed, photographed and the image fed into the AI system they had developed. Dummy runs were conducted, which cost them twelve drones. It was a small price to pay.

It took just more than two months to get the fleet as they wanted, and then these were driven to France in two medium-sized trucks. Well-forged papers, again supplied by the Russians, got this shipment through with no questions asked.

The launch platform was two delivery trucks, quite unremarkable on the outside apart from the roof, which most people don't see anyway. Each truck had been retrofitted with a retractable roof and a conveyor system inside that would bring six drones at a time into a launch position. It was engineered to be fast: six drones from each truck launched every twelve to fifteen seconds. This procedure was practised repeatedly. Speed was essential as it magnified the element of surprise. The drones could be spun up to launch speed remotely, and the conveyor system was operated by the driver to ensure all drones had taken off and there was no malfunction that would jam the system.

Paris was the site of the planned attack; a location where the global financial leaders were expected to meet in response to the forthcoming financial attack. In attendance would be the heads of the IMF, the European Central Bank (ECB) and the World Bank as well as key banking leaders from the US, the EU and China, amongst others. This is where they had met before in response to the two prior Global Financial Crises. The only question was the location. At present, there was a likely list of four locations. There would be heavy security, of course; these were important people. There would be too much firepower and defensive protection to launch a conventional suicide attack. An exclusion zone of perhaps two to three hundred metres would certainly be in place. Any larger and the Gallic anger at anything that affected what a Frenchman wanted to do would become unbearable. But these were easily surmountable problems.

Local agents provided detailed street maps, distance measurements and pictures of the target building and their surroundings for all four possible meeting locations, which usually included the accommodation for such a prestigious group. The attack plan for each site was developed and converted to computer code. It only took the relocation of the launch trucks and the selection of the correct programme that matched the final location, when known, for the operation to be put in motion.

Two days prior to the meeting, and three days after banks, globally, suffered malicious malware, EMP and direct explosive attacks on their computer systems, an announcement was made that the world financial leaders would be meeting in the Ritz Hotel, Place Vendôme, Paris. It was perfect. This location enabled not only a clear view of the hotel frontage, with few obstacles across the square, but also the opportunity to attack both sides at the same time through the long, grassed courtyard at the rear. The trees weren't too much of an issue; drones could easily be programmed to fly around them.

Twenty minutes before the attack, the delivery trucks were driven into position, one block away from the square that fronted the Ritz. The signwriting on the trucks indicated that these were shopfitting vehicles and thus not unusual in a location such as this. A cursory inspection by a passing gendarme was met with typical Gallic humour and intransience. *No, they wouldn't be long, and oui, they knew they were close to an exclusion zone, and oui, there must be very important people involved as there were so many police around, and oui, the Parisian women were as pretty as ever.* The gendarme departed fifteen minutes before the timed start of the attack, which undoubtedly saved his life.

The first two drones were launched and given thirty seconds hover while the next wave was prepared. These first drones then flew to the rear of the hotel, where the services were located.

 ROBERT STEVENS

These two drones had been specifically programmed to target the exposed water main, which conveniently had an elbow where it came out of the ground and into the building. The hotel fire extinguisher system was thus disabled. A very large hole was blasted into the rear of the building, in the same spot as the water main, when more than ten kilograms of plastic explosive detonated.

The second flight of drones took off thirty seconds prior to the third. These were the window-busters. The plan correctly assumed that all windows in the hotel were bulletproof and that the ground floor windows were barred. All these windows needed to be opened to allow access for the subsequent waves of drones. The second flight of twenty-four drones flew very fast, each with a small JATO pack which would give up to a five-second burn once the pre-programmed GPS co-ordinates were reached. The drones were each programmed to attack a predetermined window or door, with a combination of image recognition software and thermal signature used to enhance precision. At the nose of each of these drones was the impact explosive. As the drone dived to the windows at near supersonic speed, it exploded on contact. Twenty-four windows and the front doors were targeted, and twenty-two were successfully destroyed.

Armed guards and police were dumbstruck, with no idea of what to do. The first inkling that something was about to happen, after the unexplained explosion at the rear of the building, was the collective whine of close to a hundred propellers flying around a building on the square they were covering. And then the drones were upon them, with the whine of the rotors quickly being replaced by the explosive whoosh of the JATO packs all igniting within a few seconds of each other. The explosions from the rear of the building, as the water supply was destroyed, happened only a few seconds before the explosions across the front, and more at the rear, as doors and windows were attacked on all sides.

The detonations were stunning, with over a dozen guards and staff killed in the initial explosions. Within thirty seconds, the third wave of thirty-six drones followed the same path, but these did not have JATO packs. They carried explosive loads and were programmed to detonate inside the building, once they had flown through the holes created by the first and second waves. These explosions killed most of the hotel staff who had been on the ground floor. Fortunately for these victims, it was a very quick death, many unable to comprehend what was happening because it was happening so damn fast. Again, both the front and rear were targeted, and again computer programmes and optics ensured a very high level of success. The objective of this wave of drones was to create highly flammable wreckage inside the building and seriously reduce the opportunity for anybody to escape.

The world financial leaders were meeting in a heavily guarded room on the second floor. While the guards at this level were given a garbled warning over their radios, those inside had no idea of what was happening as multiple explosions hit and shook the building. Many ran to the doors to try and escape, but in the end, it made no difference.

The fourth and last wave of drones carried phosphorus and jellied petroleum: napalm. These, too, were programmed to fly through the gaping holes where the windows used to be and explode a second later, spraying their deadly load throughout the ground floor and igniting the debris created by the previous waves. The plan was to set the entire building on fire and kill all those inside.

The heat created by the fire was intense, melting plastic and Perspex on the other side of the square, some two hundred metres away. By the time the fire brigades arrived, the building was a towering inferno, and the first responders realised the chances of anybody surviving was remote at best. They had never seen such a large building completely involved so quickly. But neither had they ever before seen such a deliberate and well-planned attempt to set fire to an entire building. Well, not since

     ROBERT STEVENS

the war anyway. All those inside died. Only those who had been on the ground floor would have had any chance of survival, but they had been wiped out by the second and third waves. Even kitchen staff, who had escaped the initial blasts and incendiary devices, were trapped by the debris and flames. Normal escape routes had been blocked off as a security measure, but they would have been next to useless anyway. All those inside were stunned by the ferocity of the multiple explosions. Neighbouring buildings caught fire, and the fire fighters struggled to contain the inferno which had created a firestorm, such was the intensity of the blaze. All they could do was spray vast amounts of water from a distance to try and cool the fire to try and prevent it from spreading.

Of the hundred and twenty drones purchased, ninety-eight were used in the attack. Of the seventy-odd that successfully penetrated the building, there were no meaningful remains or clues; they had been completely consumed by the fire. All the investigators had to work with were the scattered parts of those that had detonated at the barred windows, where some residual debris had been thrown back into the Place Vendôme. One drone had crashed into the substantial rock pillars between the windows due to a fault in the optics system, but few clues remained.

The two launch vehicles were quietly driven away as the flames spread through what was once the five-star Ritz Hotel, established in 1898, and taken to a wrecking yard further out in the city.

Those incinerated included the leaders of the IMF, the World Bank, the ECB, the Bank for International Settlements, the European and International Banks for Reconstruction and Development, plus a number of other major international banking groups, including the board chairs of JP Morgan Chase, Bank of America Corporation and Morgan Stanley. Plus all the minions of these prestigious people, and the staff of the hotel who had been on shift that fine Parisian afternoon. All for less than an investment of three million American dollars, which ironically, had previously been donated by the Americans.

CHAPTER 40

Marcelle Matures

After just over two hours of driving in near total silence, the sallow-faced driver of the follow car dropped Marcelle off at a small but well-presented homeless shelter in the centre of the nearby town. She had plenty of time to reflect on what had just happened. She knew she wasn't supposed to have survived the attack. The smoke and sparks from the backpack were likely a malfunction of some kind. It was clear that the treachery had come from those who had trained her. She didn't know the purpose of all the black cabinets in the large warehouse, but guessed it must have been something important. Although the radio in the car was off, Marcelle knew that law enforcement would be searching for her, and the best plan, as always, was to get as far away as quickly as possible.

She didn't know whether the driver of the follow car was aware that she wasn't supposed to be alive; he hadn't given any indication. She kept her hand on the butt of the pistol in her jacket pocket the entire time. The driver seemed relieved when she was dropped off at the shelter.

Marcelle signed in under a false name, making up a story that after an argument in their car, she had been unceremoniously dumped by her boyfriend who was still in possession of her handbag and other luggage. She was told what bunkroom she would be in and was given a towel and two sheets, along with simple rules: no alcohol or other drugs, meal times were set, as was lights-out time, and so on.

Going upstairs as directed, she soon found the small room furnished with two sets of bunk beds. When Marcelle walked in, a young woman, twenty something, lay on one of the bunks, just staring at the ceiling. The two girls looked at each other for a moment. "Margaret," Marcelle named herself in the brief introduction, to which the other replied, "Katie."

After a pause, Katie followed with, "What's your story?"

Marcelle looked at the thin, rusty blonde for a moment before replying, "I'll tell you in a bit after I've had a shower."

Once in the hot shower, all the emotions came flooding out. She had nearly been killed by those whom she thought she could trust. All her life she had been abandoned, unwanted. All her life had been a constant struggle, and she was always so angry. She was tired of it all, and now every cop in the world wanted to find her. Deep sobs racked her skinny frame, and she bawled her eyes out for ten minutes as the hot water cascaded over her head. Eventually she composed herself, and turned off both sources of water, sniffed deeply, dried herself off, dressed and wandered back to the room where Katie waited. Dor's words from a lifetime ago resonated in her head: *Do what you gotta do.*

Marcelle sat down on the lower bunk, with Katie above and unseen. She absently towelled her wet hair and vaguely realised that the meth in the laced drink had worn off. She was desperately tired.

"Okay, you go first. Spill," was the instruction from above. Katie swung down from the top bunk and plonked herself down on the opposite bunk, facing Marcelle, AKA Margaret. After listening to the fanciful tale of woe from Marcelle slash Margaret, Katie offered, "Hmmm, I'm somewhat of a bullshitter myself, but I can see I am in the presence of a master. Please carry on …" Katie smiled, and Marcelle had no other option but to smile back.

"And why do you say that?" asked Marcelle.

"From the look of your eyes, you have just had a good bawl in the shower, which I am sure has nothing to do with this so-called ex-boyfriend of yours, who wouldn't deserve such emotion. Your swollen, red hands suggest you have been very close to a fire recently, which may or may not be related to why the authorities are going apeshit at the moment, and the internet's not working." Katie paused, searching Marcelle's eyes for some feedback.

"And also arriving here, within a couple of hours of said shitstorm, with no luggage, not even a wallet or handbag or phone, is also like just too much of a coincidence," Katie concluded.

The two girls eyed each other, sussing one another out.

Marcelle decided to take the focus off herself. "So why don't you tell me a story then, about yourself," Marcelle suggested, conceding that they were in storytelling mode.

"Hmmm," started Katie. "I am beginning to like you, whatever your real name is. And mine isn't Katie, but I think we both know that. So instead of trying to make up something as feeble as your story, I won't. Let's go and have a late lunch. The food here in the evening is good, but there is a deli down the road that does divine bagels and coffee. My treat."

Marcelle smiled. It seemed that what she needed most had appeared at exactly the right time: a potential friend. Didn't know her name yet, or anything about her, but something just told her it was going to be okay. She had learned to rely on her gut, and it was usually right. The two girls walked out for a late lunch; Marcelle had not even combed her hair.

The coffee was excellent, the bagels borderline dry, but neither cared. It took two hours but eventually they came to trust each other, desperation amongst desperadoes perhaps. They were both on their own, both sought by the law, and both looking for something better.

First up they agreed to exchange real names: Marcelle and Karen, to which they both giggled like schoolgirls. They had a lot in common:

     ROBERT STEVENS

both were orphans and had drifted into petty crime as a survival mechanism. Marcelle conceded she had upgraded from petty crime, to which Karen admitted that her first attempt at bank robbery, while netting some cash which now fed them, wasn't as successful as she had hoped or dreamed. Karen also conceded she had a long-standing problem with the bottle.

The radio had been broadcasting news about attacks on internet server farms in multiple locations across the US and Canada (the news from overseas had not yet filtered through), when the lights and radio in the deli cut out. The power had gone off. Staff went to flick switches and check fuse breakers.

Marcelle took the plunge. "I know I need to get far away from here, and should probably go now, but tomorrow morning will do. I must sleep or I will fall over. I will head south and west, into the big interior. You could turn me in to the cops, but you would be turning yourself in as well. Maybe they'll catch me, maybe not. I am not going to make it easy for them. I don't know if you want to come with me, that is your choice. At the moment, the cops are looking for one female. If I cut my hair short and get clothes from the op shop, I could look a bit more manly. We could be a couple hitching our way. What do you think?"

Karen smiled. She, too, had learned to trust her gut. "Sounds like a plan."

So at the op shop next door to the shelter, they bought jeans, baggy sweaters and hoodies, an out-of-date pack of hair dye, a pair of scissors, and a backpack for Marcelle, all for only a few dollars. Just as well they had cash. The power was out across the whole town and the EFTPOS wasn't working. "Must have been a car crash taking out a power pole or something," suggested the lady behind the counter. "It will come back on soon, I'm sure." The girls gave minimalist replies. They had both learned to not make an impression.

On returning to the shelter, the manager advised that because the power was out, they could only offer cold meat, cheese and bread for dinner, and the showers were also not working. "I am sure it will come back on shortly."

"Maybe a car crash or something," suggested Karen. The girls headed straight to the cold buffet, and were surprised by the volume of meat, cheese, breads and pickles that had been rustled up at short notice. "Road food," was the comment from Karen, and Marcelle instantly recognised what was being said. As no one else was present in the dining room at that moment, they took the opportunity and filled paper bags that were on a counter nearby, stuffing them with a variety of goods. They weren't overly hungry as they had done well on the bagels, but they ate what they could.

"Hmmm, it's a sign," suggested Karen.

Marcelle smiled and replied, "Didn't see you as the religious type." Karen got the giggles. She wasn't.

With the extra food stuffed into the backpack and the large carry bag they had from the op shop, the girls retired to the bunkroom. Thankfully, there was still only the two of them. Karen pulled a half-empty bottle of vodka from under her pillow and took a long pull. "Ahhh, yes," she sighed, and then offered it to Marcelle.

"No, thanks," was her simple reply, to which Karen shrugged and took another long swallow.

"Okay, let's butch you up before it gets any darker," said Karen. During the haircut and dyeing process in the darkening bathroom, Karen told her that she preferred to be called Kat. Marcelle realised she needed a new name, and she decided on Bobby because she had such nice memories of the scruffy, lucky man many years ago. She relayed the story to Kat, which got them both giggling again.

In the early morning they both left the shelter, leaving nothing behind, not even the empty vodka bottle. They wiped the whole room

     ROBERT STEVENS

down to remove fingerprints. The clothes they had been wearing, which may lead to them being recognised, they threw into a dumpster many blocks from the shelter. They hitched a ride with a long-haul trucker who continuously used his earbuds linked to Spotify on his phone. Thankfully, it spared them the inconvenience of conversation and prevented the driver from being up to date with world events. It was only at the next truck stop, ten hours away, when he couldn't refuel because there was no power for the fuel pumps, that he realised a shitstorm was going down just about everywhere. The couple who had been with him for the past ten hours had simply walked away, but there wasn't anything remarkable that he could remember about them anyway.

The police arrived at the shelter some four hours after the girls had left, as they now knew that the person who had driven a fuel tanker into the nearby server farm had got away, and may still be in the area. The manager could only give rough descriptions. Her glasses had needed upgrading many years ago, but volunteering on the pension didn't provide the necessary funds.

And so the happy couple tacked their way south and west, with no particular destination in mind. Kat couldn't pass a bottle store, and she had figured out that Marcelle had money and was an easy mark for a dollar. In reality, Marcelle had very little experience with having money in her pocket, and it was only after the first five hundred dollars had evaporated that she decided they needed to be more frugal. Raising the topic of Kat's drinking was never going to be easy.

They had stopped at a fleabag motel when Marcelle broached the subject. "We are burning through cash at a fair old rate," was her opening line. "And to be honest, how much you drink is your problem. But today, when you started to abuse the guy at the liquor store for no good reason, you were drawing attention to us."

"Fuck me," was Kat's reply. She was well on the way to finishing off the litre-plus bottle from the liquor store. "Are you my mother or

my boyfriend? Or some do-gooder cunt who wants to run my life?"
she slurred.

"None of the above. We are both on the run, and to me it makes
sense that we don't draw attention to ourselves. I just want to stay
under the radar."

"Awww, for fuck's sake. That guy in the liquor store was looking at
my tits. I saw him," Kat said.

"Yep, very likely," replied Marcelle. "If you're going to display them
like you have been, then you better get used to guys looking at them.
That is what they do!"

"Hah, easy for an itty-bitty girl like you, who can pass off as a guy
anyway, to keep out of sight. I like my boobs." And with that, she gave
a shimmer in her braless tee shirt. This left Marcelle with the clear
impression that her travelling partner did in fact have a nice set, and
liked to flaunt them. This was not going to help in the short term. At
that point she decided she needed to ditch this woman who was fast
becoming a liability. She just needed to work out if and when Kat was
going to realise she had to shape up or ship out. Sooner rather than
later would be the best option. She wasn't convinced that her partner
was going to change her behaviour.

Getting anywhere took a long time now. They were reduced
to walking for long distances as the amount of traffic on the road
magically decreased following the attacks. Some of the roadside stops
they called into had emergency generators and hence hot and cold
food, and often a truck or two refuelling. Marcelle was nursing her
cash supplies, as it had become clear that the EFTPOS system didn't
work, even where the power was still on. Kat had headed off to the
bathroom at one more truck stop for one of her "long stops" as she
called them, and Marcelle saw a trucker head out towards his rig after
paying for his fuel. Seeing an opportunity, she put twenty dollars down
on the table, grabbed her backpack and walked quickly out the door.

     ROBERT STEVENS

She caught the trucker just as he reached for the door handle.

"Hey, mister, I really need a ride out of here. I can pay a little, but I need to get away."

The trucker had seen the couple walk in and had noticed the unsteady gait and bleary eyes of the drunk. He understood straight away. "I'm heading west. Hop in, sport."

And with that Marcelle was back on the road with one less thing to worry about. But the remaining list was still quite long. She had learned, however, to deal with the problem in front of her first, and then figure out later what to do next.

They travelled in companionable silence for a while, and then the conversation began easily enough. "You aren't a guy! Gay?" asked the trucker.

Marcelle laughed. "Nope. We just thought we would be a bit safer if we weren't travelling as two chicks," was her honest reply, and the conversation rolled on from there. The travelled through endless paddocks of scruffy-looking, dried-out crops they did not recognise. The countryside looking bleak and run-down. The infrequent houses they passed were neglected, many needing paint and a tidy. And then, quite quickly, the farms became scattered scrub with no fences and no obvious cultivation. The landscape became drier and drier, and the infrequent houses now became no houses at all.

After eight hours, the trucker pulled into another roadside stop and advised, "I am out of hours, which means I must layover for at least eight hours. I am going to grab some food and then bunk down in the sleeper behind us. You are welcome to join me," he offered with a hopeful smile.

"Thanks, dude, I am tempted, and it has been a good ride. But I shall decline. It's a nice thought, though." She smiled back. "Remember, you are a married man, or so the ring on your finger tells me."

And with that they both laughed. She got out of the cab, and they went their separate ways.

— ❖ —

Marcelle had become adept at camping out. She had accumulated discarded gear and bought bits and pieces when the opportunity arose.

Two nights after leaving the horny trucker, she was sleeping under a bridge, somewhere in the vast interior of America. She had smelt the water that seeped from beneath a nearby bank into the dried-up riverbed and managed to excavate the stones and create a small puddle from the seep under the road bridge. This was all she needed, and with a small meal inside her stomach, she was soon curled up in her sleeping bag with the embers of the fire beside her.

The old man, wrinkled and seasoned, appeared before her.

You have come a long way on your journey. Do not spend much time thinking about the past. It is exactly that and cannot be undone. Do not dwell on why you made the choices you did that led you down the dark path. Up until now, you have been driven by the lessons you learned before you knew anything. That was the training you received from your parents, rightly or wrongly. But from now on you can choose another path. You are on it already.

Go to California, north of San Francisco. Seek out a good man who is giving hope where there is none. You will know him when you meet him. You have a lot to offer the world, and in the coming time of need it would be wrong to squander what you have. But always, it is a choice.

Marcelle woke with a start and realised she had probably been dreaming. She threw a few sticks onto the glowing embers of the fire and looked around to see if anybody else was around. Specifically, an old American Indian. There wasn't.

She sat for a while, contemplating the fire, the messenger and his words. After a time it dawned on her what the dream had revealed: her anger was in response to her upbringing. Her dad, the drinking and the neglect, had created her rage. "California it is then. And Dad, fuck you, from the deepest part of me. You are not travelling with me any more," she said aloud. Marcelle lay back, rolled over in her sleeping bag and fell asleep instantly. She was reborn.

CHAPTER 41

The Start of the Food Shortages

For most people in the Western world, famine is something that happens on the TV, in some other part of the world, far removed from the comfort of their living room. While watching the images of rake-thin people, viewers often find it easy to wonder to what degree this problem is something that they should be concerned about. Often in the faraway region, there was a conflict of some kind in the area that disrupted normal agricultural practices. On occasion, the protagonists in the conflict would disrupt food aid supplies, diverting the food to people who supported a specific cause or ethnic group. This had been going on for years after all. But, really, what impact did it have on the average Westerner?

As the decades ground on, donor fatigue and compassionate indifference set in at exactly the time the need in multiple regions increased. It was always called a shortage of food, a combination of factors usually compounding the problem – drought, conflict, corruption, whatever. Never was it called a surplus of people, the population exceeding the carrying capacity of a specific region. There was never one event that led to the famine, it was always a combination of factors coming together. Like all good cock-ups.

Then the great migrations of the early 2000s took place. Millions of people journeyed from the traditional conflict zones of the Middle East, Africa and South America towards the US and Europe. They sought what most humans seek: food, water, shelter, jobs, hope. Many of the conflicts they fled were actively funded and fuelled by the great weapon-producing countries of the world: the USA, Russia, the UK, France and China. The permanent members of the UN Security Council. War was good business.

The resultant impact on the infrastructure and race relations in the receiving countries was predictable: Where would these people live? What would they do? How would they integrate? Many of them would work for much less than the locals. They had seen horror and despair, and any opportunity to get ahead was to be seized. The migrants knew they were being exploited, but it was better than being shot at or seeing your children slowly starve. The tsunami of migrants fuelled the underlying xenophobia, and hate groups blossomed. The far right became more politically and socially active. Because many of the low-skilled jobs were taken by hard-working migrants, gang membership blossomed as the bottom end of the host society reacted to the changing world they had no control over.

For the developed world, many only knew of plenty. All you need is down at the local supermarket or corner shop. Often up to twenty per cent of the food that was purchased was thrown away, such was the level of waste and assumption that 'there will always be more'.

The maths isn't difficult: more people to feed, good agricultural land being swallowed by urban expansion, and climate change leading to increasing instability in food production through rainfall and temperature extremes. The oceans had been all but fished-out, a concept that fifty years earlier seemed incomprehensible. Technology to find and harvest all the oceans could offer was good business too.

Grain is the essential component in most of the meat and milk production in the world. Chickens, milking cows, pigs, feedlot cattle. Few are raised on grass. Meat production fell and prices soared as grain harvests failed.

Around the world, the average customer at the local market initially saw the price of all meat double, and then it doubled again over a period of six months as the impact of a series of crop failures accumulated. At the same time, bread nearly tripled in price when it was available. The same with rice.

Where they could, people established small vegetable patches. But for many urban dwellers living in apartments, this was not always possible. Numbers turning up at the urban gardens began to increase, as did the theft of produce from these gardens long before it was ready to be harvested. Hungry and desperate people do not always think rationally. And while it made people feel better and engendered a sense of helping themselves, you cannot grow enough vegetables on a suburban backyard to feed a couple, let alone a family.

The shelves at the supermarket were not fully restocked. Items like cleaning products and toilet paper and hardware were still in plentiful supply, but the bread, fresh produce and meat sections were steadily being shrunk in size. Canned products sold out as quickly as they were put on the shelf because people recognised a decreasing number of food choices now existed.

The observant in-store shopper would have noticed that the number of shelves in the supermarket aisles began to decrease. Instead of five or six rows of shelves stocked with items, there would be only four or five shelves, and there were distinct gaps between the products that were lined up.

Most shops closed for at least a week after the internet attack, followed two days later by the attack on the international financial system. The loss of the internet had the effect of shutting down nearly all electronic point of sale transactions and online banking, which had dominated business and household financial affairs. EFTPOS had struggled with the interruption to the internet, as many cellular networks ultimately rely on the internet to relay the messages. With

 ROBERT STEVENS

the attack on the financial system, EFTPOS systems evaporated. How could you buy stuff now? Cash money, which had become a bit of relic, was now a valuable commodity in short supply. There were rumours that the money printing facilities in the US had also been attacked, but the US Government refused to answer any questions about that.

The street people noticed that the offerings in the rubbish bins were seriously diminished, and the supermarket dumpster dive was less rewarding. The soup kitchens and other support organisations continually pleaded with the government agencies to supply more food because the demand was doubling every few months. The agencies could offer no more. Extra money helped a bit, as it addressed the higher prices that were being asked, but overall, there was less in the supermarkets and less was being received from other suppliers. Food donations dried up.

Burglaries and eventually home invasions targeted food: canned, frozen, anything. Booze was also a popular target because getting pissed was a tried and trusted method to forget your daily woes, for a while.

Many of the supermarkets, previously open twenty-four seven, now shut at night. The raids by gangs on the supermarkets were initially nighttime affairs: smash and grab. But there is only so much you can stuff into a bag and carry away in the few minutes it took for the police to arrive. The supermarkets and market owners responded by either employing armed guards while the shop was closed, or sleeping on the premises. Or both. Shotguns were the weapon of preference. It was the street people who first thought of an organised raid, and it wasn't too long before other gangs and groups of people cottoned on as well. Perhaps ten or twenty people would go into the store and start loading trolleys. Then in a co-ordinated push, they would all stream out the door and off into the parking lot. Security staff could only physically capture maybe two or three and then their hands were full. Turn your back on one and they would soon flee, albeit without the groceries in many cases. But most got away. And the courts were initially quite lenient on people stealing food, but that would change as the situation deteriorated. For the street people, a few nights in jail was no big deal. It guaranteed a meal, a hot shower and a blanket, a luxury for some.

In one instance, one of the fleeing trolleys had overturned, and the person behind it had grabbed a few items and then fled on foot, leaving much of the food on the ground. Customers in the parking lot initially just looked at the overturned trolley. Then, after a moment's hesitation, they descended on it to fill their own bags as quickly as possible. Nice cuts of meat, small bag of potatoes, some carrots. What a find!

Suddenly there was a maul all around as others flocked to the trolley like a group of seagulls fighting over a bag of chips. Pushing and shoving ensued: "I want that" and "I need that for my kids". The maul rapidly descended into a brawl as people fought for the remaining scraps on offer. The fight was as much about frustration as it was about the food on the ground.

Two weeks later the supermarket was burnt to the ground.

Martial law was declared a week after that because attacks on supermarkets and petrol stations had become common place. Groups of people would gather in protest at the lack of food and petrol. Local policing, the thin blue line, was stretched at the best of times. It was regularly breaking now, being overstretched and demoralised by the far-too-frequent release of criminals because the prisons were overcrowded. The cops were being openly shot at and had started returning fire more and more. The hot summer inflamed temperatures and feelings. Most were looking for an opportunity to vent their frustration at all that seemed to be going to hell and back.

The US Army and National Guard were mobilised, and a curfew between 7.00 p.m. and 7.00 a.m. imposed across the entire USA. A week later, the same was imposed in Russia and the EU. The Chinese had their own methods for managing their citizens.

     ROBERT STEVENS

Bus services were intermittent, sometimes non-existent. Ringing the bus company was a waste of time. The bigger problem was the risk of being robbed while either on the bus or leaving the supermarket. People were hungry and the thin veneer of civilisation was becoming even thinner.

CHAPTER 42

Steve and Carol

They had cancelled the newspapers a long time ago as a cost-saving measure. The news tended to be all bad anyway. Wasn't it said somewhere that bad news sells newspapers? If that was the case, then they should be doing well. The collapse of the internet had dried up that source of information. Many years ago they had had a radio, and then it was found in an old storage box in the attic. The batteries were dead, of course. Surprisingly, Steve found the power lead for it as well, so this became their source of information. Electricity supply was intermittent because the attacks in the USA had a ripple effect across Canada. But they found that during the middle of the night it was more reliable, a time when they were invariably up attending to one of the children anyway. News in their part of the world all seemed to be bad as well. The attack on the banks and financial institutions were the lead articles, along with the disruption to the electricity supply across the border through targeted attacks on strategic load-sharing substations. The government believed it was definitely state-sponsored terrorism, given the scale of the co-ordinated attacks. Investigators were trying to find out who was responsible, and it was clear that the damage was massive. The response was expected to exceed that which occurred after the attack on the Twin Towers all those decades ago.

There were isolated reports of arson in some of the well-to-do suburbs, and armed patrols had been formed by the residents. Police were overwhelmed between searching for and attending to suspects associated with the internet, bank and electricity attacks, and seeing to their 'normal' policing duties in this fraying society. Regular burglaries were not investigated, and when the various gangs of Zombie Dogs figured that out, they became even more emboldened. Their numbers swelled as the police presence shrank, and it was only a matter of time before martial law would be imposed across Canada.

When a very nice house a few blocks down went up in flames one night, Steve couldn't help but wonder if his neighbour had been out doing what he had threatened so many weeks ago. They still met around the fire in the backyard for a drink and a yarn, but the subject of summary justice was never brought up again. The conversation often revolved around general law and order and the Zombie Dog gangs, and how the neighbours could go about helping each other. Steve went and purchased a pistol.

Steve was given welfare payments for the mandatory six months. He had struggled with going to the welfare office to apply in the first place, and then with the continuous follow-ups and form-filling. But it was a condition of the welfare, so he packed up his dignity, left it at the front door as he went out for these demeaning exercises, and picked it up again when he got back home. He had children to care for: seven-year-old Jane, who was a hoot to be around, and two-year-old Stephanie, who was a good kid but just seemed to persistently have a runny nose and cough.

The vegetable garden expanded, but money was beyond tight. They learned to buy the products on special at the supermarket, but there was less and less choice on the shelves, and the people hanging around the parking lot looked pretty shifty. The supermarkets started rationing fruit and vegetables. They heard on the radio of people being mugged in the supermarket, both going in with their money and coming out with their groceries. The supermarket employed guards, who were unarmed initially, but after a couple of fatalities, they became armed. It was disorientating to see this.

They had two children who were expensive to care for at the best of times, and they were buying second-hand clothing from the welfare stores. They had let the insurance on the car lapse and, against the advice of the bank, had also let the insurance on the house and contents expire. It was just too expensive, and they had been let down by the insurance industry before. If the bank wanted to foreclose because they had not maintained the full insurance as required, then they could. But Steve was taking a gamble: the bank did not want to foreclose. The bank already owned many more properties than it ever wanted to, and this was obvious as you travelled around town. These houses were often in an advanced state of disrepair and increasing numbers of the dispossessed were squatting in them.

Steve and Carol adjusted to unemployed life. He pottered around home, tidying the backyard and expanding the vegetable garden even further. It was now late spring and warm. It had rained a lot during the previous months and the ground was saturated, although he heard that inland the drought continued, and farmers were reluctant to sow crops into bone-dry ground. They may not plant at all, saving the expense of seed, fertiliser and running the tractor, but were also looking down the barrel of no income. Which was the lesser of the evils?

And then it got hot. It was cold one day, the ground was soggy, and within two days it was over 30 °C and muggy. The slugs and snails, aphids and mosquitoes appeared out of nowhere, and his garden was decimated. Fuck, would he ever get a break? He went out at night with his torch and pulled off the snails and dealt with them, not realising they would make a tasty meal. With the slugs, he found that small pieces of board scattered around was where they went to hide during the day. They did that only once. He sprayed the re-sown crops with soapy water to try and slow the aphids. It was a continuous battle, and he became absorbed in it. Carol was relieved that he had something to fill his day. He scavenged the neighbourhood and found others doing the same. The isolated fruit trees weren't ready yet, and he could imagine a queue of people lining up for what produce there may be. He found a lemon tree full of fruit, undiscovered by others. He quickly picked them all, shuttling them in his backpack until the garage was littered with boxfuls. He wasn't exactly sure what he would do with them all, he just knew he did not want others to have them. They drank a lot of lemon juice over the next weeks, and it did help with the throat-searing home brew from next door.

Steve struggled with his loss of place, his title, his purpose in life. While he understood the lack of work and hence the redundancy, that it was a worldwide downturn made worse by the attacks, somehow intellectualising it didn't make him feel any better. They economised at every turn, reducing meal sizes for himself and Carol so the kids could be better fed. Despite their best efforts, the remaining welfare money each fortnight wasn't enough, and the reserve of cash slowly dwindled away as the cash paid by welfare never exceeded the outgoings. He wasn't quite sure what they would do when the reserve was used up.

He and Carol both lost weight, with skin sagging in all sorts of places. Even the kids looked scrawny.

The remains of the back fence had long since been cleaned up and burnt in the backyard bonfire. They had started on the fence between themselves and the empty house in which Remy and Philippe had lived, in what seemed a lifetime ago now. They had scavenged the house but found they had been beaten to it by others. Some decent gardening tools and seeds were found in the garage, which was useful, as was the small amount of petrol in the fuel tank of the car in the garage. Over time the fences were demolished, ironically at the same time as the more well-to-do neighbourhoods were erecting even bigger security fences.

They got to know Karl and Sophia better and found them to be regular people, also just struggling on. No kids, but problems of their own.

In another time, it would have been a simple issue. It was an old nail from the fence that went straight through the sole of Steve's sneakers and into his foot. He knew straight away that he had trod on something, and had done a good job. It did not bleed a lot, but he and Carol washed it out with antiseptic and bound the wound. It would have been better had it bled a lot, but that was academic. After three days he knew the wound was infected: it was red and swollen and painful to walk on. He suffered in silence for a day and then decided they needed to go to the A&E department at the hospital. They couldn't afford the doctor. After waiting for six hours in the bedlam of an overworked A&E department with the kids, the diagnosis was not startling. It was an infection requiring antibiotics and, yes, it did seem a fairly aggressive one.

The prescribed antibiotics were picked up straight away from the hospital pharmacy, but made no impact. Two days later he had a high temperature, and the wound was raw and seeping pus. They returned to the hospital, and unusually, they got the same doctor who had seen Steve previously and remembered him. The look on the doctor's face said it all – this was serious. He prescribed a much stronger cocktail of antibiotics; clearly the first course hadn't worked. It was not yet time to admit him, but it did look nasty. The doctor did not advise that the threshold for admitting patients had been raised. In a previous age, Steve would have been hospitalised with this type of infected injury and elevated temperature.

The doctor opened the septic wound with a sterile scalpel. Steve couldn't stifle the moan of pain and fell back on the pillow with a sheen of sweat on his brow. A stream of yellow-green pus slowly bubbled out, and the doctor got Carol to massage around the wound to help expel it

    ROBERT STEVENS

all. They had left the kids with Karl and Sophia, and the kids seemed quite happy with the idea.

The new antibiotic cocktail appeared to help initially but played havoc with Steve's intestines. He learned the hard way that there are no farts when you are on these drugs. He dragged himself to the shower to clean up, and thought he felt a bit better. His temperature was 39 °C, and he felt weak. After two days of seemingly not getting worse, the infection escalated, and his temperature soared. He was zoning in and out of consciousness, and Carol got Karl to call an ambulance. She tried to cool him with moist towels around the head and neck. Sophia came over and agreed to take the two kids home with her for the day while Steve was attended to. The ambulance arrived, and he was immediately admitted to the same hospital where they had been before.

No, they did not have any medical insurance, but Steve was not looking good. The infection had spread, and he was steadily entering the early stages of organ failure. He was put on an intravenous drip of the strongest cocktail of antibiotics they had, and was given oxygen because his breathing had become quite shallow. The wound was brutally opened to try and drain it, again. Clearly it must have been a bacteria with multiple resistance to the antibiotics. The best the medical staff could do now was to try and support Steve as his immunity system fought the bug. It did not help that he was undernourished, and he lost the battle. He died a day later of multiple organ failure due to a bacterial infection of the blood. His temperature had peaked at 42 °C.

Carol was lost. What would she do now? The following weeks were a blur. The body was held at the hospital for a day and then transferred to the county morgue, awaiting burial at the county cemetery. Carol didn't have any money to pay a funeral home, so he received a pauper's funeral. It was well attended by the neighbours and his old work mates. The hospital waived what costs they could, but the bill was still more than five thousand dollars when it arrived. She had no idea how she was going to pay it. There was the indignity and process of applying for a widow's benefit, which was very similar to the amount they had received previously as an unemployed couple. At least this benefit wouldn't expire until the children turned sixteen or left home, many years away.

Over the next months she settled into a new routine. She shifted into the deserted house next door to Karl and Sophia for security and company. "Just for a little while," she explained to the kids. Karl pulled down the last of the fences between the properties. Home invasions had become increasingly common and violent. Keeping friends close was good, and she didn't want to stay in the "old family house" any longer: too many memories. She walked the kids to school on the weekday mornings. Since they had been hassled by street thugs on a couple of occasions, and she and the kids were terrified, Carol now carried the small pistol Steve had purchased. Some days she would stay at the school and help out on a voluntary basis. Keeping herself busy helped her cope with the loss. The school appreciated the extra help, and the kids didn't mind after a bit.

It was now summer, scorching hot, and water restrictions were implemented. They saved all the grey water and would bucket it out to the vegetable garden in the evenings. The bonfire would still be lit if the wind wasn't too strong. Stan and Samantha helped where they could, entertaining the kids and helping around the garden and the house. Fortunately, they lived on the outskirts of town, so the frequency of Zombie Dogs prowling the neighbourhood was much reduced compared to people trying to get by in inner-city apartments.

Daughter Jane got a nasty cut on her arm while out playing. Carol went into a deep funk. She was yelling at Jane about how she could possibly be so careless, and simultaneously washing the cut out with volumes of water. Fortunately, it was a day when the water pressure was good. Jane was crying; the water hurt, her arm was bleeding, and Mommy was yelling at her. Stephanie began to wail in confusion. Sophia

     ROBERT STEVENS

heard the racket and came over, and gradually calmed everything down. First job. The wound was bound to stop the bleeding. The residual packet of Steve's antibiotics was still in the bathroom cabinet, and after a conversation with Sophia, it was agreed that they wouldn't do any harm. Jane was given these at a double dosage.

After a while the wound was unbound and Jane made to lie in the sun and expose the wound to the sun to try and dry it out, cleanse it with sunlight. She fidgeted and complained for the rest of the day. But it worked, and while she carried a scar on the arm for the rest of her days, there was no infection.

Summer was upon them; the vegetable patch was producing well. They had new potatoes, tomatoes and lettuces. They had a shared meal with all the neighbours, and Steve's mother, Jacky, had bused in and stayed for ten days. There was a festive mood, but Carol desperately missed Steve and would often be found weeping in the bedroom. She continued to lose weight as she just wasn't hungry, and everybody worried about her. Steve's mother caught her in the bathroom one day with her shirt off. Her bony ribcage, visible under her much-diminished bosom, was painfully obvious. Jacqueline was shocked, and began to weep. Once she had composed herself in the lounge, and Carol had had a chance to cover her emaciated body, they met in the kitchen. After an awkward moment, Jacqueline blurted out, "You've become so thin. You are not well. We all miss Steve. But you must look after yourself, even if it is only for the kids' sake."

Carol burst out crying, and they both wound up having a good howl on each other's shoulder. "It's just too much. Everything. Of course I miss Steve, terribly. So do the kids." Carol paused. "I have to carry a gun when I take my kids to school. I am scared that the vegetable garden won't produce enough, and I can't afford to go to the supermarket. There's nothing in the supermarket anyway, apart from cleaning products. And they have armed guards inside and out. I have no money left and I have all these bills to pay … I just don't know what to do any more. Why is this happening to us?" she said, weeping.

Jacqueline didn't have any answers. She put the kettle on the gas hob and went about finding the teabags. It kept her occupied while Carol composed herself.

It was the bitterest of times, and while Jacqueline worried about Carol, she worried a lot more about the kids. What kind of world would they inherit?

CHAPTER 43

Weird Weather

The Gulf Stream, or more correctly, the Atlantic Meridional Overturning Circulation (AMOC), is the ocean current that brings warm ocean water from the equator, brushes the eastern seaboard of the United States, and then heads east to warm Northern Europe. England, Ireland and Northern France in particular. The AMOC is a river of warm water in the cooler ocean. This current is strongly affected by the temperature and salinity of the water surrounding the Arctic. The temperature of the Arctic waters had been steadily increasing over many decades due to climate change. Loss of sea ice and hence reduced albedo (the fraction of light that a surface reflects), leads to increasing ocean temperature, which leads to increased ice loss and so on – the classic feedback loop. Scientists had been faithfully recording and reporting this ice loss and rising sea temperature for decades.

As well as a steady rise in ocean temperature, climate change has seen an ongoing increase in large volumes of episodic freshwater runoff from European rivers due to the unprecedented downpours that create flooding and havoc inland, and then eventually drain to the oceans. Fresh water is less dense than salt water. The salinity of the surface layers in some areas began to decrease, also affecting the AMOC.

As the AMOC became increasingly weaker and erratic, average temperatures in Northern Europe began to fall, which would normally seem counter-intuitive because the planet heated overall at the same time. But one of the reasons why the term 'climate change' replaced 'global warming' as the common label for humankind's legacy, was the recognition that there would inevitably be a permanent change to the remarkably stable climate man has flourished under for the past twelve thousand years. And for some, a consistent degree and a half warmer had seemed like a fine idea. But it isn't going to be like that at all. Weird weather is a more apt outlook.

Crops that had been able to grow in the previously warmed Northern Europe, failed to thrive. The wine industry was decimated for one. The growing season shortened, and crop yields had been slowly falling for some time due to the reducing accumulated growing degree days.

It was the winter that was particularly severe. The polar vortex had destabilised and centred itself over Northern Germany. Winter temperatures, normally often below freezing anyway, fell another 10 to 15 °C, a catastrophic amount. People froze to death in their homes. But the biggest problem was more subtle, unrecognised by most – the winter crops. Normally protected from the worst of the cold by a covering of snow, the clear skies and lack of precipitation meant there was not much snow, but rather mind-numbingly cold temperatures for the first weeks of the meteorological winter. Autumn-sown crops were destroyed. Cellular contents froze. Plants died. Across vast areas of Northern Europe, Ukraine and Southern Russia, vegetables, winter wheat, and unharvested potatoes still covered by earth froze and turned to mush once dug. Even garlic froze so hard that it snapped off at ground level.

Tens of millions of Europeans would starve.

      ROBERT STEVENS

CHAPTER 44

The Old Man Comes in From the Desert

The parcel of land that Robert had purchased years ago with his financial millions in a previous life had been a slice of paradise. A river ran along one boundary, and there had been a large grassy area where, a long time ago, he and his wife dreamed they would have a fancy log house built. There had also been a large, wooded area of mature trees stretching back into the hills. All past tense now. The partially forested land was no longer as he remembered. Now it was like no one remembered. The firestorms, two that he had read about in the past seven years, had all but wiped out the mature trees, and chest-high regrowth now dominated. The most recent firestorm, during another round of record-breaking temperatures, had been followed immediately by flooding, which he had seen glimpses of on the TV in the bar of some distant town he had wandered through, somewhere. The meteorologist had used the term 'atmospheric river', which was one he hadn't heard before. It was supposed to be some infrequent event that brought unprecedented rain to an area, metres of it over a week to a region that may get a third of that in a year. The resultant floods had been catastrophic.

The river had completely changed course numerous times over that period. First chewing out about twenty hectares of the better flats on his land's side of the river, and then swinging away and leaving him with a jumbled pile of uprooted trees, rocks and mud. The neighbour who had grazed Robert's land had lost his house and some stock in the fires, and then more prime beef in the flood. After that, the neighbour had just walked away. There was no attempt to clean up. Everything was broken, including the spirit of the land and the man who had tried to wrest a living from it.

Robert set up his camp on the remaining thirty hectares, two hundred and forty kilometres northeast of San Francisco. There was a thin strip of land between the jumbled detritus of the flood and the regenerating bush. He only had the resources he had brought with him. While he had more than most, it was still never enough. He learned, eventually, to not worry about the things he didn't have, but be thankful for the ones he did have, and to make do. His Winnebago was the base, and this he situated up on one of the higher terraces above the river. Even though the river was often no more than a trickle, he was understandably wary of future floods, especially as the rainfall events, when they did occur, seemed to be very heavy. All he had to do was look out the side windows to be reminded of that. And while the river was going to be the source of water, he planned to keep a respectful distance away.

There were packs of wild dogs. He heard them howling as they smelt the new arrival, and it was only two days later when they made an appearance at the bush edge. There was not much timidity about them; evolution favoured the aggressive. The next day he was lucky. He had been pottering around in the awning of the Winnebago when he heard a low growl behind him. His instincts had been honed by his years in the wilderness, and without even pausing to look behind him, he took two quick steps into the wagon and slammed the door behind him. This unexpectedly quick move had just beaten the rush of the dogs, which cannoned into the shut door. A snarling, snapping frenzy of frustration ensued outside as Robert opened up the cupboard and

      ROBERT STEVENS

began assembling his weaponry. The pump-action shotgun would be the first weapon of choice, taking seven rounds of heavy varmint pellet. The two .45 pistols were loaded, and he swung the double holsters onto his lean hips. His large sheath knife was clipped onto the rear of the wide belt that supported the holsters. He didn't know how many dogs he had to contend with, so a look out of the curtained window showed perhaps a dozen. He couldn't see what was outside the awning. "Shit" was the simple summary. He looked in the mirror. *Fucking Rambo.*

He didn't know how long the dogs would linger once he started blasting, but he knew he had to make a dramatic first impression and kill as many possible. It would be easy to pick a few off from the window, but he was quickly developing a strategy. Aggression usually only understands aggression. He took a moment to calm himself by taking some deep breaths, then he threw the door of the Winnebago open and levelled the shotgun at the largest animal that had looked up in surprise. The blast inside the wagon was deafening, but it was quickly followed by a second and third, and he pumped and squeezed, shifting the angle of the barrel slightly to clear a path. The first dog was obliterated, and two others went down with the next shots. Yips of dismay sounded as the remaining dogs bolted, two running to the end of the awning where they were trapped. Robert quickly went down the steps and swung to the right, pumping a new round into the chamber and then dispatching a large Doberman that had gone the wrong way. A smaller collie had also trapped itself, but upon sensing it was trapped, instantly turned and rushed at Robert. He barely had time to crank another round into the chamber, firing with blind luck, hit the charging bitch just as she took off in a leap of attack. The blast hit the collie dead centre, and it flipped into a vertical backflip and landed at his feet, very dead.

Fuck, he thought as he cranked in another round and swung around to check what was still in the awning. It was clear, and having lost count of the rounds he had put through the shotty, he put it down on the picnic table and pulled out his two .45s. *Regular cowboy!* he thought as he strode out of the awning to see what waited outside. Nothing immediate, and he could see at least half a dozen dogs hightailing it to the bush. One Rottweiler had stopped and was looking behind. A simple squeeze on the trigger, and it went down with a howl.

Realising he hadn't checked behind him, he swung around to see two dogs running amongst the tree and rock detritus of the riverbed. He loosed off a few rounds which had no effect, and satisfying himself that he had made his point, went up to a grievously wounded Rotty. The dog knew what was coming, and summoned up its best puppy dog look. It didn't help, and another round was sent through the top of its skull. Again, he had lost count of his shots and made a mental note to himself that he needed to work on that. He walked back to the awning, which now sported holes in two sections from shotgun pellets, three very dead dogs and two whimpering wounded. These too were dispatched with a .45 round to the head.

"Fuck," was all he said, and he sat down at the picnic table that still held the warm shotgun. "I need more guns," he said aloud, and he took a moment to gather his thoughts. He picked up the shotgun and went back inside, cranking out the last shell from the weapon onto the bed where there was already a collection of various calibre cartridges. He reloaded the pistol he had fired and just felt more secure carrying it. He wore at least one of the firearms nearly continuously after that.

He wondered briefly about the holes in the awning, and then decided not to worry about that at present. With shaking hands, he put the kettle on the gas ring, and made a strong coffee, reinforcing it with a great slurp of whisky. He allowed himself a moment to sit, and as the level in the cup went down, he gathered his thoughts. He got a small notebook and started making a shopping list of things to get when he next went into town.

     ROBERT STEVENS

Automatic rifle
Tent repair stuff
More ammunition
Animal traps
Whisky

There was an increasing number of deer in the regenerating forest neighbouring his land; not all had been killed in the fires. There were more goats as well, but the dogs found them easier to hunt. Robert regularly saw evidence of this as he explored. Initially, these excursions were little more than armed tramps, but as his skills improved, they became regular successful hunts. Actually, there was a lot more wildlife, period, since the economic collapse. The two seemed incompatible. The economic expectations of a government and its people on one hand, and the environment on the other. And governments had bulldozers and diggers as the weapons of choice, plus a desire to continuously grow GDP. His recollection was that the neighbouring forest was managed by the forest service, but he didn't think that people would mind too much about the hunting that went on openly now. Feeding people was the priority. The forest was a regenerating shell of what it had once been, and making your way through the regrowth and fallen or burnt dead trees was hard work.

He was gutting a hind he had just shot when a thought came to him that made him pause and smile. How many years had it been since, in a previous life, he had thought about shagging the little secretary back in London? What had been her name? Was she still alive? Had she managed to escape London? What an arsehole he had been back then, and how much everything had changed since. He paused to reflect while the flies buzzed around. He remembered his lost family, and smiled to himself again. The pain had faded, not evaporated. But his memories of them were good. *We have a choice, don't we? We can learn from our experiences and mistakes, and evolve, or not. And we learn more from our mistakes, because the lesson, whatever it may be, can be somewhat bluntly delivered.* He chuckled to himself and carried on with the job.

One night as he pondered the next day's activities, there was a "Hello, the camp fire!" call, which is a common courtesy and reduces the chance of getting shot.

It was a man, thirty-something, on his own, who had tramped from the city for the past week. He was footsore and tired, and relieved to finally find something that looked like a camp. After initial greetings, exchange of names, and small talk about the weather, the man opened up. "There are many others out there, making their way north. They will also find this place." A pause. "I appreciate your hospitality. You didn't shoot at me, and for that I thank you. You seem a reasonable guy, and I would like to stay and be of use." He stopped. It was on the table now. *Would you let me in?*

The terrace he had chosen to set up his own camp had more than enough room for others in tents. He had known that over time others would come, just as the old American Indian had said. He had been expecting this first contact with a refugee, but he wasn't sure how to respond right away. He paused, considering the matter, then said, "I can't offer much. No freeloaders. Everything is in short supply now, and I suspect compassion is on that list as well. You can pitch a tent and feel 'at home' so long as you help and contribute in one form or another. And one condition I can think of now is that if you are asked to leave, you do so without a fuss."

The man pondered this. He understood and nodded. "Thank you. I might sit for a moment and then go and pitch my tent. Thank you again."

— ◆ —

Refugees from the city were escaping in dribs and drabs with what they could carry on their backs once the petrol ran out. Those who had made it this far had shown a large amount of resilience. But they were tired and confused. Many were armed, and they talked about the gangs of thugs that preyed on the weak. Robert realised this was Biology 101: Survival of the fittest, played out one individual at a time. It was always a brutal lesson. Evolution was bathed in blood. Adapt or die. But this was a sermon these people did not need at the moment.

The cities were in full collapse; the army and other instruments of 'civilisation' had been overwhelmed both from without and within. The soldiers all had families too, and they could see what was happening. Many deserted, and some, fully armed, appeared at his campsite.

The people at the small camp realised they needed to work together if they were to survive. Around the campfire, the group discussed what to do now. They had to ration resources, allocate tasks, protect themselves. This is where Robert's knowledge and newfound wisdom, coupled with his innate ability to see things coming, the same skill that made him his millions in the previous world, was invaluable. He was a natural leader and wise enough to listen to others, recognise and acknowledge their fears, and suggest actions in such a way that the group saw it as a sensible option.

A young woman came to the camp one afternoon and immediately asked to see the leader. She was shown where Robert's camper was situated. She called out "Hello" once outside it. It is difficult to knock on a canvas awning. Robert replied from inside where he had been cleaning his armoury. "Come in."

"Hello," she said again as she pushed aside the canvas flap and stood just inside. Facing Robert, she said, "I am Marcelle, and an old Native American guy appeared to me in a dream one night, some time ago. He told me to come here. I just know it is you that I am supposed to meet, but I don't know why."

Robert studied Marcelle for a moment while he digested this surprising information.

"Yes, he does that kind of stuff. Unsettling, isn't it? Anyway, welcome. Sit down and I'll make coffee. I suspect we have a bit to talk about. You can oil a gun while I make refreshments," Robert suggested, and Marcelle knew she had found the right place. "I'm Robert," he called from inside, by way of introduction.

From outside the young woman replied, "Marcelle." And then they both laughed as she had already told him that.

It was an unusual first date. Robert explained, "I met the old American Indian in the desert while I was wandering, and he told me to come here. He has the kind of insight that I don't understand. I have no idea where he is at the moment, but I suspect he will reappear. Do you have any idea why he sent you here?"

Marcelle sipped her excellent hot instant coffee. The relief at finally being where she was supposed to be after so long on the road was still diffusing through her. "I have absolutely no idea why he sent me here. I can't think of any skills I have that would be of any use. In fact, I don't think I have any skills. All my life I have been just surviving."

Robert digested this. "I think that is exactly the skill we need now." The two of them sipped their coffee and contemplated each other and Robert's last comment.

The community became far more organised. Latrines were dug. Foraging parties went to nearby towns to gather food, weapons and ammo, and building materials. Bicycles and handcarts became valuable items as there was precious little petrol. The weather was a nightmare. It started to rain, a rarity in the Californian summer. But it rained and rained, and the river flooded, again. The developing makeshift camp on the lower flats was quickly evacuated, just in time before it flooded. The

     ROBERT STEVENS

people were moved to the highest flat close by the bush edge, which proved fortuitous.

It snowed in May, unheard of. They just managed to survive by burning dried fallen trees and branches and timber scrounged from the now derelict neighbouring fences. The rate of people arriving began to slow as it was just too cold to travel by foot. There were close to a hundred people now, families and young, fit people. Not many elderly. Most people at the camp carried weapons.

Over the next months they settled into a routine. New arrivals would be screened and given a tent if they didn't have one. Anyone who was unwell with an ailment that even vaguely resembled an infectious disease was quarantined in a separate area for a month. It was better to err on the side of caution. The solar panels worked most of the time in supplying power for water pumps and light for security. Extended overcast periods were traditionally rare in this environment. The deep-cycle batteries were okay for now. They had been flat for a long time before being found on one of the foraging missions. The batteries had weighed more than a tonne and had been brought back with difficulty. The foraging parties were currently out looking for more solar panels, control gear, batteries and water tanks to increase irrigation capacity while there was still water in the river and a reserve of drinking water, which was rationed. Weaponry was always on the shopping list.

The packs of four-legged wild dogs were very aggressive, but had learned to stay a respectful distance away from the camp. Many months ago, they had managed to take a five-year-old child who had mistakenly tried to befriend one of the dogs. The screams brought the adults quickly, but the deep bite marks around her neck meant she had bled out very quickly. All dogs, both types, were shot on sight.

As the camp grew, there was a roster for sentry duty, hunting, tending the gardens, firewood collection, cooking, checking the batteries – all the mundane tasks associated with staying alive. Failure to get on with your tasks invoked a first warning, and was often accompanied with latrine duty to make a point. There was no room for passengers.

The plan was for the sentry duty to morph into actively seeking out the Zombie Dogs when the camp was sufficiently established, as well as seeking out other groups who were trying to survive. Recent encounters had spurred the need to increase the number of sentries. The camp's distance from San Francisco was not enough to prevent bands of Zombie Dogs, intent on theft and rape, biking out on periodic raids. One of the key discussions was what to do about this problem. The road was the obvious and easiest access way, even though several bridges had been washed away by cloudbursts in the back mountains or the massive flood of a few years back. The road was also the route that other survivors used to make their way out of the city. The number of sentries was doubled after a probing raid by ten or twelve Dogs had seriously tested their defences and had left three residents killed, five wounded, tents destroyed and food taken before they were driven off. The Dogs knew where they were, and as most had got away, they expected more attacks in the near future. This became a topic for discussion for the whole camp. What were they going to do about it? Just sitting back and waiting for the attack was not a viable option.

It was late one night when Robert went back to his Winnebago, and much to his surprise, there was a familiar face sitting inside the canvas awning when he unzipped the fly and went in. Nobody locked anything any more; it is difficult to lock a tent anyway. He instantly recognised the craggy face and smiling eyes. It was his old American Indian friend from the desert. They had never actually traded names.

"Welcome, let yourself in," said Robert with a smile in his voice.

The old man replied, after a pause, "Okay, don't mind if I do."

They both laughed and hugged, just pleased to see each other after what must have been at least two years and many roads travelled.

"For some inexplicable reason, I am not surprised to see you here," Robert said after they had traded pleasantries and a quick update on the camp.

Robert continued, "I shall make coffee and bring out a bottle of whisky, because I want a drink. While I do this, I shall think about how the fuck you knew I was here. How you have stayed alive, and why you have appeared now. And then I will decide that you don't actually know the answer to any of these questions, that it 'just is', and then I shall consider what you have come to share with us."

The old man smiled. There was no need to talk. This man was just ordering his thoughts out loud, which he was known to do himself from time to time. They were bound somehow.

"I also have a young lady friend in the tent next door, who you decided to visit one night some time ago, in her dream. I am sure she would love to meet the flesh-and-blood version. Soon," Robert added.

So they drank coffee and had a whisky, followed by another, which set a nice glow alight in the stomach. Then Robert cooked up a simple feed of venison back steaks, beans and some of his precious rice, which made a satisfying goo. It reminded them both of a previous time in the desert.

"The dog?"

"Ah," the old man said, smiling. "He passed. Old age, I think. Just didn't wake up one morning. He had been good company, a great listener but not a great conversationalist. I miss him. But everything has a season."

"Sorry to hear that. I am sure the dog never forgave me for eating some of his dinner, which I still remember fondly for reasons I can't explain." He paused and took a sip of the whisky, which was ageing well but not for too much longer. "Give me a minute. I'll go and fetch Marcelle. Her tent is just next door." Robert disappeared, and three minutes later Marcelle appeared. They all hugged.

"Okay, my man!" Robert began once they sat down and recharged their glasses. Even Marcelle was open to a small tot. "Any more you've had 'chats' with who are going to appear and be part of our exclusive little cabal?"

"Yes, a few. But they are in the future, not now," replied the old man. Anticipating the next question, he followed with, "We are here to survive. Those who were asked – and not all will answer – have skills that will help with that task. Over the past two hundred years, great chunks of mankind had become all-consuming, fat, lazy, self-centred, disappointing pieces of work. That was the sugar-coated version. Now the wheels have come off. People have always worked better in small groups, and that is what we need to revert to for a while."

Robert and Marcelle realised that 'a while' could be a long time. This man perceived time differently to most. They sat and pondered the old man's message; small talk did not interest any of them.

Robert continued, "I am concerned about the safety of our people here. We are too close to the city. While it is convenient for foraging and we are building a good place, we are also too close to the Zombie Dogs. They are sure to come back in numbers and try and take what we have."

The older man reflected on this. "This is the nature of all men, to take what another has if he can. You will not change those who want to attack and steal from you, but you will, over time, develop a new understanding amongst those who stay here. You must give people the chance to live so they have the opportunity to learn and adapt to this new world. In the short term, you must protect them. The winter is coming, and it will be very cold. Very cold." He paused and then repeated the words for emphasis: "Very cold. Much colder than usual. There will be deep snow on the ground in San Francisco and LA. This will thin out your enemy, for they do not have your skill in food production, and foraging often returns nothing to them now. They are

     ROBERT STEVENS

eating their weak and the dwindling number of survivors in the cities, but this is not new either." He paused and ordered his thoughts. Robert could see him searching his memory. "Then there will be a very hot, very dry summer, and this will nearly finish them off. But you must make your people safe."

Robert thought about this. And he had been given a clue: the Zombie Dog raiders were going to be naturally thinned out anyway. So the smart choice for him and his people was to shift away, at least for a year or two, and then possibly come back. They had accumulated quite a bit of infrastructure here at the camp, but that was not a major problem. It could be shifted, or hidden and retrieved later. They had built the camp from a zero base, and they could do that again.

The old American Indian continued, "North of here the Yuki people had a winter campground, long forgotten by most people. It was told to me many years ago by an old man similar to myself, and until now, I did not know why he shared this with me. It is probably an eight- to ten-day march, accounting for women and children, walking slow and shifting what you can. A scout could be there in two days, and the same time to return. But if you go, you have to go soon because your enemy is mobilising."

"Hmmm," Robert replied. It was as he suspected. But now he had a secret weapon: insight. He had realised some time ago that there was no point asking this wizened medicine man where this insight came from. He couldn't, or wouldn't, be able to explain the interdimensional aspects.

They talked on into the night, remembering the past, telling stories of their own journeys before they met in the desert, and since. It was comfortable. Marcelle headed back to her tent, but didn't really want to. Eventually Robert unfolded the camp stretcher, although the old man was used to sleeping on the ground, which is where Robert found him the next morning. They both slept well.

In the morning, Robert woke with the predawn light as was his custom. He felt just a smidge of headache from the whisky, but it had been more than worth it. The bottle sat empty on the table in the Winnebago, and he smiled. Well worth every last, precious drop. He rose and dressed quickly, then quietly opened the door and stepped into the awning space.

The old man grunted, rolled over and pretended to be asleep. Robert opened the fly of the awning and said he would be back in five minutes, and that they would have a guest for coffee in ten, so perhaps a pot of coffee on the stove would be a good idea. Then he walked away. The old man smiled inside his battered sleeping bag. He did like this guy, even if he was white.

Ten minutes later Robert appeared with a lean-looking man in his thirties, who was introduced as Carlos. He had been an army ranger, before. The old man, who had made coffee as instructed, nodded. He sized up the new guy, and realised that he was ideal for the job. Marcelle reappeared; Robert had kicked her tent as he walked past and called out, "Want to join us in a minute?"

Once the four of them had settled with coffee and traded brief introductions, the old man began to speak, addressing no one in particular: "North of here, probably two days' fast walk for you" – he nodded at Carlos – "who I think probably walks pretty bloody fast, is an old campsite the previous land occupiers, the Yuki people, used during the winter. It has good water, is close to the mountains for hunting, and is sheltered from the northern winds. It is north of a town called Paradise. You will need to follow the main line of the mountains for nearly a day. And the site is perhaps two days inland from the coast, say eighty to a hundred of your kilometres. You need to find this place and then lead your people there. Or you will fall to those you call the Zombie Dogs, who are gathering their numbers for a big raid on your camp."

Carlos nodded. Nothing to say or ask, yet.

     ROBERT STEVENS

Robert retrieved a map of northwestern California and spread it out on the table inside the Winnebago, where they all sat nursing cups of strong black coffee. Once the likely area had been circled, Carlos was asked if he wanted to take the map with him.

"Not necessary, thanks. I have memorised it in my own internal GPS. If it fell into the wrong hands, it would not be helpful. I will leave in a few hours as I sense there is some urgency to this. I will let my woman know that I will be gone for perhaps a week, and she will wail and cry because she is pregnant, but she will be fine. I will tell her to come and get an explanation from this old man if she needs one. Although, she won't. She is a good woman, but I am a little biased. Be back in an hour or so." And with that he placed his half-drunk coffee mug on the kitchen bench and left.

The American Indian looked at Robert, gave a little nod of approval and asked when breakfast would be ready, because if this was how you white guys treated guests, it was no wonder that they didn't get many. Once again Robert's stomach vibrated with laugher, and he went to see what he could offer as a meal. The three of them shared breakfast and the easy conversation of old friends, even though they had only recently met.

Carlos reappeared within the hour, reacquainted himself with the map, nodding as he traced and memorised the route, his army ranger training kicking in. He left with a good Arnie rendition of "I'll be back". And with that, he was gone, heading off with a small backpack and slung automatic rifle. Once he had left, the three of them talked about what the best plan of action from here on would be.

Robert called a special meeting that night, the whole camp was to attend if they could, excluding a skeleton sentry crew. Everybody knew that a strange visitor had called and had spent the night talking with Robert, and that Carlos, their best scout, had headed out at short notice that morning, leaving his pregnant partner behind. There were no secrets in a place like this. And the previous raid and losses still burned in their memories.

After the chores had been all done and the meals prepared and eaten, the entire camp gathered. Some of the younger children played in the dark, but most sat and listened as bid by their parents, because they all sensed something important was coming up. And it paid to grow up fast nowadays; nobody could afford the luxury of being a child for too long. As they gathered, Robert sat on the high rock that acted as the podium, the old man beside him. As the people settled and the low conversation hummed, he turned to the old man and asked, quite politely, "And after all this time, what is your name? How do I introduce you?"

The old man smiled, and said, "Call me an old American Indian who wandered in from the desert, or call be Bob if you like." His stomach vibrated with suppressed laughter, and Robert joined him. Bastard.

Robert began. "Welcome, everyone. We have all come a long way over the past few years, and we have survived where so many have not. Let us remember them." He let the moment hang, and then carried on, "I will not bore you with trivialities. We know about the threat from the Zombie Dogs who live too close for comfort, and the raid on our camp two weeks ago reinforces that point. We have choices, of course, and which one you take is up to you. Sitting next to me is an old friend. We met a few years ago as the wheels were coming off our old society, and we recognised a bond. I have developed a deep respect for this man and his insight. I trust him and his word. He says the Dogs are gathering for another attack."

He let the words sink in, and when most faces were looking at him, he continued, "In the short term, we must focus on survival. There is a very cold winter coming, colder than we have ever experienced before,

     ROBERT STEVENS

to be followed by a scorching summer. Do not ask me how my friend 'Bob' knows this, but you can trust his word. I am of the opinion we should shift camp, even though we have become quite comfortable here, it is a good spot. But it is just too close to the Zombie Dogs, who will come back before the winter, and in larger numbers. All of us know this."

Again there was a general nodding of heads; no point in denying the obvious.

"I recommend we move, within a week, to a place much further north and towards the mountains. Beyond the range of the Dogs. Carlos left this morning to find and reconnoitre this place for us, an old American Indian overwintering site, and I expect him back in four or five days. We shall let the winter and the following summer thin out our enemy for us. We may return to this spot, or we may not. But we shall be alive to make that decision. If you want to stay, you are welcome to do so." He paused, and people shifted a little to try and ease the discomfort they all felt.

Robert looked out over the assembled people, trying to gauge their mood. Then he resumed, "One man cannot tell another man what to do. You must make your own decisions. If you choose to stay, we will divide our food stores equally. We will hide the batteries and water tanks because they are too large to shift easily. We may come back to collect them. Those who remain here will not know the hiding places. My wagon still works, and in it we will be able to shift some heavier stuff, the young children, and the pregnant women, for a start. But only for as long as the fuel lasts. It won't travel a long way in any case because we know the road is impassable about fifty kilometres north of us.

"And I am going to be quite direct about this. For the next ten minutes, I want you to discuss this matter amongst yourselves, any longer than that is just chinwagging. I am certainly going. We must leave nothing behind for the Dogs, only a scorched earth. If you choose to stay, then know this – you will be able to keep your fair share of the food and your own belongings, but nothing else. Now decide."

Robert had deliberately left the time frame short. He knew from his previous life that if you gave people too much time then overthinking the problem would become an issue. Doubt would creep in, and the naysayers would have time to reinforce that doubt. He knew that most people could make the decision in five or ten minutes. Once the ten minutes were up, and there was a natural pause in the conversational hum, he called out, asking if anybody had a question before he sought a show of hands.

There was only one: "Can you guarantee that we will be safer heading north?" The question was from one of the parents of two young children, one of whom had been the first child born in the camp.

"I can't guarantee anything, except that it won't be easy shifting, and that I trust the word of my friend. I can reasonably expect the Dogs to make another raid, because that is what they do. I believe it is very unsafe to stay. That's about all, Paul." There was a general nodding of heads, and when the poll was taken, all but one older couple agreed to the shift.

"Okay, it is decided. We shall all start planning for the shift, which will involve you deciding what you will take, what you will destroy, and what we will hide. The solar panels and the batteries will be shifted first and hidden. For security reasons, only a few will know the hiding spot. We are fighting to survive. We will meet again in five days, by when I expect Carlos to have returned, and you will all be ready to shift. I am, as always, happy to listen to suggestions and ideas, but don't come to me and whine. Thank you."

As the group disbanded, talking amongst themselves, Robert had made eye contact with the old couple, the Witters, for whom he knew it would be a tough ask to shift again. They had only just made it to the camp three months ago, with a lot of help from others. He walked over to them. "I respect your decision. The Dogs, when they come, not if, won't make it easy for you when they find you here and us gone."

 ROBERT STEVENS

"I know," said Dean Witter. "We kinda knew we've been on borrowed time. We could never understand why we had made it this far when so many of our friends, better people than us, didn't. I'll keep my pistol handy, but what I would really like is a couple of grenades. I like the idea of going out with a bang. And taking a couple of those parasites with us. Our time is done, and we are both okay with that. We are tired of struggling to survive." Robert nodded in agreement; there was nothing to say. He suggested that Dean call by the Winnebago in ten or fifteen minutes, and he could have his two grenades – one each.

Over the next four days, the semi-permanent buildings were dismantled and what could be used as a prefab was loaded onto the trailer that Robert had hauled up there a long time ago. The solar panels, the frames, the batteries and the wiring were well wrapped and buried in the forest, close by but not too close by. They were too heavy to transport on short notice. They could be shifted later if required. The electronic control equipment they put in the Winnebago as this would not survive prolonged exposure to the elements. The camp was a bustle of activity. The guard was doubled just in case the Dogs got wind of the change being made.

After four days Carlos reappeared, and he addressed the camp that night.

"It will take perhaps ten days for all of us, carrying heavy loads. To get there, the first five or six days will be by road, which is in mostly okay condition, but with some tricky washed-out sections. The road makes for easier walking than the bush, and we will leave no tracks for others to follow. The suggested campsite is favourable – flat land that appears to be free of floods, with a good water supply. It is sheltered from the cold northerly wind, but the snow will probably lie deep. Still, we can prepare for that. It is a good place, with good access and easy to defend."

Carlos had also confided in Robert that the road bridge was washed out at about fifty kilometres north of the camp, but there was a good layby to park and perhaps hide the Winnebago as it wouldn't be able to go any further. But more interestingly, at about twenty kilometres up the road, there was a deep cutting with a rock face on one side and a drop-off on the other – a natural ambush site. They could place the heavy machine gun amongst the rocks and it would take an armoured vehicle to get past. Two competent guys could hold that forever, meaning they could thin out the Dogs even further if they chose to follow.

The Winnebago began its shuttle mission, taking building materials and other equipment as far as it could. They also placed the heavy machine gun as suggested, and it eventually turned out be a brilliant site, built to order it seemed.

Later that night, once the camp had disbanded after listening to Carlos, the three men and Marcelle retired to the Winnebago. It was getting noticeably colder at night, so they huddled around the small kitchen table. As the level of another whisky bottle fell, Robert and Bob, names that were amusing to them both, became more philosophical than usual. The planning was all done.

"Fuck, when will it end?" asked Robert rhetorically as the whisky and tiredness hit. "We struggled to get through the collapse, billions died. We struggle to get enough food, we struggle to get enough drinking water and to house ourselves. And we have the Dogs snapping at our heels along the way. That old couple who chose to stay, they should not be asked to make decisions like that. Yet they have to. When will it end, when will we be able to stop struggling?"

Marcelle smiled both inwardly and outwardly. "You see this only from your perspective. Many people in what used to be 'normal society' struggled every day as well. We never thought of the future as such, we focused on each day as it came. So I guess an adjustment in timescale is one thing you should consider."

Robert was both surprised and impressed by these words coming from such a young woman. He looked at her, and she returned the look with a provocative smile. *Hmmmm*, he thought.

Indian Bob had noticed the exchange of looks and considered Marcelle's words as well. He had learned a long time ago that it was wise to stop and think, to consider your words and those spoken by others. Often people felt inclined to fill that short silence after someone had spoken with words of their own, but they never added anything to what had already been said. However, these were wise people, so silence amongst them was as comfortable as a well-worn coat on a cold night. The other three waited, mulling their own thoughts, for the old man to comment.

"You are a good leader, Robert, and you have learned to be adaptable. This will be the greatest thing this group will need. We will make camp in the old site Carlos rediscovered, further inland, because the coastal areas, if not already inundated by the oceans, soon will be. We shall learn to adapt and survive, doing what is necessary, which will include wiping out those Dogs in a suitable radius of where we choose to put down our roots.

"Even before the white man came, the Indigenous peoples struggled too. We fought and killed each other because that is human nature. We have a propensity for violence, which is directly linked to the survival of the species. Natural selection usually favours the most aggressive, not necessarily the most adaptable. The idea of some gentle utopia was a wisp of imagination." The old man paused and gathered his thoughts. "When the buffalo disappeared, we starved too. Even the Aboriginal Australians, who lived in very hostile environments for at least forty thousand years, and who some consider to be the closest man has ever come to a sustainable society, conducted lethal intertribal warfare and practised some of the most brutal population control. But at least they understood the concept of the number of mouths to feed and the ability of their environment to provide.

"You have all failed to recognise, over many decades, that increasingly scarce resources was the driver for most of your troubles. More people wanting more. Collectively, you failed to recognise that the escalation in violence in just about every society was a symptom of this, of the thin fabric of civilisation unravelling. Greed and hatred led to the inevitable collapse of your civilisation, but this outcome was inevitable once the steam engine had been invented. The Industrial Revolution was the start of the end. The natural environment was sacrificed. The attacks on your internet and financial systems were brilliantly conceived but quite unnecessary. Your food supply was already withering, the environment already compromised, but no one really paid attention.

"Most people just starved because of accelerated climate change, and many more will. There was limited opportunity to make meaningful change in a timely manner, but that opportunity was squandered because the thirst for money and power was too great. It's all history now. The climate feedback loops will continue, even now that our greenhouse gas emissions have dropped to zero, finally. The weather will be unpredictable, to say the least.

"We were given clear warnings grounded in science and solid evidence, yet we continued to destroy the forests, the soils, the waters, the air, and the balance that nature requires. You even elected a fool, a climate change denier, to the White House. Twice.

"Mankind evolved quickly during a period of remarkable climatic stability that enabled our species to thrive. Curiously, when you read mankind's history, it becomes obvious that we are unable to reach any kind of ecological or political equilibrium. Civilisations evolve and then collapse. It is a cycle that has repeated again and again, even during times of relative climatic stability. The climate may stabilise at some new level at some distant point in the future, but it will likely be different to that which enabled man to flourish. Mankind will probably survive; we are a very adaptable species. But it will be in a much-diminished number, with a different way of life. We will have to compete with the rats and the dogs and the cockroaches for quite some time, and there is a chance that they are more adaptable than we are. There will be life on Earth. This struggle will not end. It is called life. In answer to your question, your struggle to survive has only begun.

"I will stay with you because I do not wish to die alone, my feet are sore, and there is an attractive woman, with long grey hair, who sat at the rear of the meeting the other night. Now I shall go to bed in my tipi, otherwise known as a pup tent, and dream of how I am going to seduce that woman. Good night."

And with that he simply got up and walked out. Carlos left and went to his own tent. Robert looked at Marcelle. They were both reflecting on the old man's words, knowing they were true.

"Want somewhere a bit warmer to sleep?" was Robert's approach. Marcelle's eyes revealed her interest, and she came and sat beside him.

CHAPTER 45

Dave Underground

Work on the tunnels and caverns under the town where Dave and Caitlyn lived progressed well, but fuel eventually became an issue. The never-ending wars in the Middle East had disrupted supply, and while Australia had some reserves offshore, these were increasingly difficult to extract as the field was reaching the end of its life. The army and police were prioritised, then emergency services and hospitals for backup generators because the electricity grid had become unreliable in the extreme daytime temperatures. Councils and mothballed mine sites were well down the priority list for fuel deliveries.

There was no shortage of people wanting to help dig the tunnels, but they could not run the machinery for much longer. People started digging by hand, even though they were hungry. It was good to have something to do, to feel useful again. The project had grown, and there was now a series of tunnels and caverns under the town. In Australia there was a good pool of knowledge around mining and tunnelling; they were diggers in every sense. The townspeople had explored other sections of the riverbed, and even the Aboriginal people, who were normally treated with contempt, gave advice on where to explore and dig for water. The garden areas expanded but had to be guarded day and night. Shacks were built on site so guards could sleep on the job, especially during the heat of the day. It rarely got below 30 °C even in the middle of the night.

Each underground system now had its own name and street signs. The locals did not lack for a sense of humour, even in these tough times. People started living on streets with names like Hade's Hall, Depths Drive, Rats' Refuge, and The Dead End.

There were rules for living in the caverns. No weapons were permitted underground; they would be locked up at the entrance. No fighting either – take your disagreements outside. Fighting was, of course, an option that not many were keen on. It was hard to do anything when the temperature was 40 °C or 45 °C, let alone throw a punch. No food hoarding was allowed – it would just lead to stealing. The rats, both numerous and bold, tried to move in as well. There were numerous rules to deny them places to hide and breed. And there are many ways you can cook a rat, as they found out. Hunger is a great motivator just before it becomes too debilitating. The most important rule was to be kind: kind to yourself and kind to others. Everybody was in the same boat. The caverns could not accommodate everybody. Children, people with high-level vegetable gardening skills, young mothers, the leaders, and the sick who could still recover were the ones encouraged to live in the underground caverns. Those with terminal illnesses had to stay topside, and they usually accepted this stoically. These were tough times. There were now a few places topside set aside where people could stay a few nights just to get a good sleep out of the heat.

Eviction from the caverns was not necessarily a death sentence, but it would make life a lot harder as you didn't get the support of the community. Just as being shunned by earlier communities was often a recipe for having a much harder life. One couple, suspected meth addicts, had always been argumentative and troublesome. Stuff would go missing, food stolen. The supply of methamphetamine was all but gone, and this couple struggled with withdrawal. The couple had been allocated space in the underground because they had three children, feral little brats. One day an argument over missing food grew increasingly heated, and the sheriff of the day had gone to investigate. As she approached, the husband pulled out an old pistol he had smuggled in, and levelled it at the sheriff.

The man threated the sheriff, shouting, "No closer, or I blow you away. This cunt is accusing us of stealing her food, which we didn't do."

The sheriff had not come across this type of situation before. She didn't realise you don't argue with a crackhead – there is no point. She started by asking him to stop pointing the pistol and then to give his side of the story. He fired anyway, hitting her in the left lung. She fell, and everyone looked on in disbelief.

"Ha, that fixed that mangy, nagging cunt. Now back away and leave me alone!" he yelled.

A woman in her thirties went up to the fallen woman, knelt and looked at her injury. She could see the sheriff was losing air and blood from the gaping wound with each ragged breath. Not good. She saw the pistol in the holster on her hip, and without a second thought she unclipped it, checked that it was loaded and the safety off, and quietly stood up and walked towards the crackhead. "Hey, I've got some good stuff for you," was all she had to say, just enough to confuse him, give him a moment of hope and her a moment of grace. When within easy range, she swung up the pistol and gave him a double tap to the centre mass. He fell with a surprised look on his face.

"Used to be a cop," she said, and giving the handgun to somebody she recognised, added, "Keep an eye on that bitch," indicating the recently departed crackhead's wife. "If she moves, blow her away. No hesitation." She returned to the fallen sheriff, trying to do what she could to keep her alive. The doctor arrived ten minutes after the shooting, but it didn't help. The poor woman died fifteen minutes later from a combination of shock and blood in her lungs.

The wife of the now deceased crackhead, and their children, were removed from the caverns and the town an hour later. There was no

     ROBERT STEVENS

room for compassion now, and the kids were damaged goods. They were seen hanging around the edge of the last patch of vegetables the next day, and wandered off when a warning shot was fired into the air.

Medical options were limited, and while there was still one doctor in town, she was exhausted. The meagre supplies and equipment from the town medical centre were shifted into one of the roomier caverns. Once upon a time the town had boasted a hospital of its own, but that had been downgraded over time as money was channelled to the big central hospitals in the main cities. Locum doctors were often used to cover rural areas, but there weren't many of these around any longer. Local ambulance officers and nurses, both active and retired, were used to cover the gap, giving the remaining doctor a chance to regain her energy. Most births went well, but complications that would have been handled by the hospital earlier were now occasionally fatal. Infections were harder to treat, and old Aboriginal herbal medicine was revived, and it was often effective, but not always.

It did rain, a year after they had begun the cave system. It bucketed down. They had seen the rainclouds gathering, and the general consensus was positive. It hadn't rained significantly for years. Some of the younger children had never seen rain at all. It started with a massive lightning storm, initially exciting and spectacular. But as the strikes became closer and more frequent, many retreated indoors. Skeletal trees were blasted; the town clock tower took a direct hit and was blown to pieces. To be fair, it hadn't kept the time for many years anyway. A number of houses were hit and almost immediately caught fire; they were tinder dry. In this part of the world, people had become very good at fighting, or at least containing, fires. Individual houses were quickly engulfed in flame; they could not be saved. While still suffering from the concussion of what was often a direct hit, occupants had to get themselves and what possessions they could out of the house as soon as possible. Neighbours helped, and as others arrived, they focused on stopping the flames from spreading. Some towns had completely burnt to the ground as the fires quickly grew in the tinder-dry conditions, and with little water to fight the flames, fire spread from house to house. The town had tapped a salty underground spring many years ago and had slowly filled a large, old swimming pool and several water tanks with the undrinkable water. There had been many attempts at desalination, with varying levels of success. But at least they had some reserve for firefighting. The townspeople could not wait for the fire brigade; time was of the essence. While the pressure in the town water supply was weak, there was a trickle. Initially pots and pans would be filled and thrown over the side of the house they were trying to save. Eventually, a fast-response vehicle would arrive with the correct tools to access the fire hydrants since these had been reinforced over time to prevent water theft. While not a fire truck, the aim was to stop the fire from spreading, not fight the main blaze because this was an inefficient use of resources. And they did not have limitless water. Hoses were connected to the pumps and water played over the neighbouring houses. It was mostly successful. It did stop the whole town from burning.

While groups were focused on controlling these lightning-induced fires, it started to rain. Big fat drops, and as it built and people realised what was happening, they danced in the streets. It was *fucking raining*! The rain steadily built until it was pelting down, and it hurt to stand outside in it without a heavy raincoat, which many people just did not have. The downpour soon quelled the house fires, and the need to protect neighbouring property disappeared. People retreated inside to wait out the storm. It did not stop for some time.

Many places received a year's rainfall in a few days: it poured down. The ground was so hard from the years of baking sun that the incoming rain just ran off. As the rains intensified, those in the caverns

     ROBERT STEVENS

were informed that it was torrential rain, and the advice was to get out, and probably sooner rather than later. Many started packing up what they could, but some had found a home that was comfortable and cool and were reluctant to leave. The runoff took a few hours to develop, initially puddles formed and then they grew. As the rain continued, gravity did its job and the water started to move downhill, as it always has. The catchments in Australia are vast, and it can take days or weeks for water falling in one area to appear as flood water in another. But when that accumulated rainfall does appear, it can be in the form of a flash flood. Heavy raincloud had been swept down from the tropics, an unusual event, but there was a lot of that going on lately. These clouds carried a huge amount of water that had evaporated from the very warm waters of the equator. The currents that normally circulated this warm water around the planet had been changing and weakening over the decades.

The rain fell almost everywhere in Australia, although a large area south of Perth, a grain-producing area, stayed dry. The rain intensified, the puddles and pools grew and joined, creating surface flooding. Still it rained, and the runoff from the tar-seal roads was the first to hit the storm water system. It was dumped straight into the dry riverbeds, in hundreds of different places. The rain carried on, and the runoff intensified. Within an hour there was a noticeable stream coming down what had previously been a dry riverbed. The vegetables that could be hastily recovered were, and people were steadily moving out of the cave system. Despite repeated and increasingly strident warnings, a few resolutely remained in the caverns, where they subsequently drowned. Camps in the riverbed were quickly abandoned before they washed away in the now rushing dirty water. Logs were moving with the flood, and in places formed log dams that pooled water above them, making the flooding worse in some areas. Large parts of central Australia became a lake, and had it still been functioning, the Alice Springs Yacht Club would have had a field day. But the Alice had been mostly abandoned years before as the eponymous, life-giving springs had dried up.

The heavy rain continued, and people began to trickle into the community centre. "Fuck, all we wanted was a gentle shower from time to time," muttered one ex-farmer. "But this is not funny. What's happening?"

Low-lying areas of the residential part of town began to flood, and people moved out, carrying what they could after putting as much as possible on tables and benchtops. It made no difference because at the peak, the flood waters were over two metres high in many places, and the riverbeds and storm water drains were raging torrents. Most of the central part of town was okay since the original town had been built on the elevated outcrop of sand and mudstone above what had been a flowing river. The tunnels and caverns were unreachable within six hours of the rains beginning, and a list of the missing was started.

People continued to arrive at the community centre, looking for a dry place and someone to share their story with. It began to get cosy and was very stuffy and humid inside despite all the doors being open. Numerous cups of tea were made over the gas cookers, and the firefighters came in as their job was now finished. What they hadn't put out was now being dealt with by the rain. They would check again when it stopped raining, having put tarpaulins over those houses with roofs damaged by the lightning that were considered worth saving.

The town reservoirs began to refill. Although the water was discoloured with high levels of silt, this did not bother many people.

In a quiet moment after it had rained for two days, Dave was sitting at the kitchen table with Caitlyn, having a coffee and a quiet moment. "You know, with this rain, we could try again out at the farm. I'm not exactly sure how we would get there, or what crops we could grow, as there's no fuel and most of the seed has been eaten by rats and humans, but it is still our home," said Dave.

  ROBERT STEVENS

Caitlyn thought about this for some time. How could she respond without smashing him further into the ground? "Yes, it is still our place. Yes, all the problems you have listed are true, but I'm not sure how we would get around any of them. It is a hundred and fifty kilometres to get out there, and we have no fuel. We don't know what the roads are like, or the buildings, or anything else because we haven't been there for a year or so." She let the comments settle in. "You could pushbike out. It would take a couple of nights. It would give you, and maybe the boys as well, a chance to assess things as you went."

Dave thought about this, and he knew his wife. He responded. "Good idea. There are lots of mountain bikes scattered around town, and gear for them. What's the catch?"

Caitlin sucked in her bottom lip, a habit she had when she wanted to say something that may not go down too well. "Don't get your hopes up. Here in town we have a life, friends, a purpose. We are scraping by, just. The kids have their friends here. There is the support network at the community centre. All of this would vanish if we went back to the farm." She did not use the word 'home' once, another tell.

He let her words sink in. He had known for some time that she had grown used to, and liked, life in town. As had the kids. He looked at her, thinking. "Okay, I get it. But for me, it's important. Everything you say is true. I'll ask the kids if they want to come, with low expectations. But once the floods have receded, I want to go and have a look." And she knew her husband and knew that was the end of the conversation. Sometimes a man's gotta do what a man's gotta do.

It was weeks before the floods receded, and during that time the food situation went from dire to worse: there simply wasn't any. A few mangy kangaroos had come into the town to escape the flooding, and were promptly shot, skinned and every last morsel of meat taken from them and rationed. Tempers frayed, and then as the hunger began to really bite, people became increasingly lethargic. They struggled, many of the weaker, elderly and infirm just quietly passing away from a combination of malnutrition, hopelessness and tiredness. They were tired of the continuous struggle to live.

The town had a couple of days of pleasant weather as the rain eased and the temperatures were moderated by the pools of water, but then the humidity began to creep up, and stayed up. Mosquitoes returned in plague proportions as this is what happens in the desert after a rain. There is a deafening silence during the dry, life is on hold. Then after the rain, a cacophony of life bursts forth from seemingly nowhere to get through their life cycle before the dry returns. Grass and flowers popped out from ground that had previously been hard and dry and apparently sterile. Moths, flies, mosquitoes similarly appeared from nowhere.

It took six weeks for the central Australian desert to drain, so the rivers flowed and the reservoirs filled, and natural life flourished. The vegetables that had been hastily pulled from the ground as the flood approached were eaten, and the townspeople discussed what to do about new planting because the areas that had been garden were now under two to three metres of dirty, flowing water.

New gardens were established in the middle of town. An area that used to be the central park was dug over laboriously by hand and seeds sparingly sown. Birds appeared, eager to take even these small morsels, and a continuous watch with slug guns and .22 rifles was mounted. A small roll of bird netting was found, and this was used as best as possible.

The reservoir was overflowing, and it was decided to set up an irrigation system while there was water. Solar panels were liberated from houses and a simple array set up by the reservoir. A pumping system was developed that fed tanks at the newly established gardens. It took three times as long to get stuff done now because everybody was low in energy from lack of food, and they had to scavenge for materials.

     ROBERT STEVENS

Wildlife had no need to congregate around waterholes now, and became more dispersed. The hunters took to bicycles to forage further afield.

Dave, being a reasonable shot, was rostered to hunt the following day. He prepared himself as usual, packing a small tarpaulin to create shade for the midday siesta, as well as binoculars, a small medical kit, a portion of dried meat, two litres of water, and a can of spam. They had found an unusually large stash of canned spam in the basement at the home of a survivalist who hadn't made it back. You had to be pretty hungry to eat spam. He also took along five rounds in his bolt action .270 rifle, a skinning knife, and a simple trailer behind the bike for returning the kill if he was successful. The few times they shot a camel, which was way more meat than one man could cart, a team would return ASAP, fight off the dingoes and rats, and recover what was left. He slept well that night. The caverns were being returned to a habitable condition, but for the moment they slept in the original house they had rented.

As he lay awake, Caitlyn quietly snoring beside him, he smiled. They had got this far. The three kids had survived and were doing okay. The kids had their clique of good friends, went about their chores faithfully, and had a sense of humour that only teenagers have. They suspected that their daughter was pregnant, but that was okay too. She hadn't plucked up the courage to tell them yet. Her boyfriend, Tom, seemed a good enough lad. Life was good; he was happy. Yes, he would go to the farm, one day, but not just yet. He had responsibilities here.

It was 4.00 a.m. He hadn't slept for an hour, and it was time to go. He got up quietly, kissed his wife's shoulder. She smiled in her sleep. Shirt and shorts, boots and socks waited by the door. He quietly went outside and rode off towards his designated quadrant.

He had been biking for an hour, and was perhaps fifteen kilometres out of town. You couldn't go too fast with the limited visibility of the early light of dawn. He got to the first bridge over what had been a dry riverbed. Although, now there was no bridge, and it wasn't dry. Instead, it was a fast-flowing mass of swirling muddy water. He could see the remnants of the bridge railings poking out of the water about three hundred metres downstream. No crossing here, not today. He dismounted, and leaving the bike and trailer by the road, started making his way on foot up the right bank of the river, thinking this would be as reasonable a place to start as any. The day was brighter now, perhaps 6.00 a.m., when he saw movement ahead, and he instinctively froze. He lowered himself down and slowly, steadily stalked whatever it was he could catch glimpses of. As he approached, he noticed they were small people, crouched beside something on the ground. They looked about furtively. He came up behind them, and when perhaps a hundred metres away, crawled underneath a straggly salt bush and quietly got his binoculars out from his backpack.

It was two people. He immediately suspected the crackhead mother and her kids. Who else would be out here? How had they survived this long? He studied the shape on the ground and, after some time, realised with horror that it was another person, and they were using a knife to cut off lumps of meat and eat them, raw. The leaders had discussed, quietly and privately, what the response would be when they came across cannibalism. They had read enough of human actions, historically, when food supplies ran out, and cannibalism had been regularly recorded, even amongst the Aboriginal people. While he could intellectually understand that this type of thing could happen, emotionally it hit him hard seeing it in person.

He quietly positioned the rifle on his backpack, centring the crosshairs on the spine, just below the shoulder blades, of the larger of the two people. The shot was deafening and true, the person was flung forward over the corpse, totally unaware of what had just happened. The remaining one stopped and gawked in surprise, and looked around

     ROBERT STEVENS

for who had been responsible for this. This pause gave Dave a chance to crank another round into the chamber, and centring on the chest cavity of the child, who was now standing, he blew her away with a single, clean shot.

He waited a moment, checking for any further movement. There had been four people cast out from the community; there was one missing. He slithered out from under the bush, and leaving his pack where it lay, cautiously approached on foot, rifle at the ready. He quietly cursed that he only had three rounds left. He'd been too proud to take additional ammunition. Fuck.

The flies were already thick around the bodies. It was a young preteen girl who had been the second shot. She lay on her back, naked, a tiny hole between the small mounds of her breasts and a large pool of blood underneath her. It was the mother who had been the first shot. She lay across the body they had been dining on. He rolled her body over. Her rotten teeth and ravaged face stared vacantly at him. "Cunt," was all he said. He looked at the third body. It had been the second daughter they were eating, and the bloody rock they had used to crush her skull had been casually thrown only a metre from her body. There was a mass of blood under her head, and he guessed, correctly, that the murder had only happened recently. They were all naked, indicating that the heat and the lack of food had made them completely feral. What had happened to the outcast boy remained a mystery.

Dave sat there for a bit, reflective. He then recovered his swag, took a drink and chewed slowly on some of the dried meat. Realising the shots would have scared off any other game in the immediate area, he began a fast walk further upriver in search of the original target: game. It took another forty-five minutes before he came across a kangaroo, which was showing a good level of condition, as the grass was plentiful. The thirty kilograms of meat weighed heavy on his shoulders, but it was comforting. He returned along the same route, and as he came upon the remains of the three humans, he saw a snarling mass of dingoes and dogs fighting over the feast. He had two rounds left, and quickly decided that bypassing this potentially dangerous situation was better than firing off his last two rounds and hoping the rest would scatter. They were just part of the food chain; no point taking your rage out on animals doing what animals do. He paused. In a previous life he would have shot as many as possible, trying to preserve his stock and livelihood. Now he realised that they were going to have to learn to live with each other, not try and manipulate it to human expectations.

The long bypass added another thirty minutes to his trip back to the bike and trailer parked on the road. It was now 11.00 a.m., and the temperature was already well into the forties. He thought it best to find a place to lay up until the evening, and putting the meat in the trailer, he went another five minutes back down the road before he found a suitable bush to sling the tarp over, to create shade for himself, the bike, and trailer containing the meat. Dave slept soundly for four hours, waking groggy and dry. He dozed in and out and waited until the sun was lower on the horizon and the temperature began to fall. The tar-seal had melted in the heat, but it had done that for many years now. The townspeople had discovered that there was a thin strip at the edges that was still firm. It didn't hold the heat as well as the main part of the road, since it was a mix of dust and gravel and tar, or something along those lines. If you were careful, you could still bike on this strip and not get a great build-up of sticky tar on your tyres.

He got back to town at about 8 p.m., not unusually late. The meat was taken to the old bank, where they had a huge safe that was cool and could keep the flies out. The designated butcher for the week took charge of the load, thoroughly checking for fly eggs as he carved and boned the back steaks and legs. Gruesome humour was the norm. Tomorrow it would be laid out to cure in the sun; they had a fly-proof area in which to do this.

     ROBERT STEVENS

After dropping off the meat, he sought out Brenda, one of the community's leaders, a very bright and thoughtful woman. The two of them didn't waste much time on small talk; they knew each other well. Dave relayed his story of the people he had shot, and the circumstances.

The brutal reality was that there were still too many people for the meagre supply of food they could generate through hunting and gardening in this tough place. They couldn't afford freeloaders or troublemakers. Where to from here? Clearly casting people out of the community was cruel in the extreme. Would it just be better to shoot the misfits in the future? Fuck.

The Aboriginal people had had a number of answers. After all, they had lived here in the harsh conditions for more than forty thousand years. But the white man wasn't ready to hear them. Yet.

CHAPTER 46

Carol Struggles On

Steve's death devastated Carol. She lost the will to eat. Everything about life just seemed so hard. She was now on her own with two young children. Before, they had all been steadily losing weight as the needs of two growing girls and two adults simply could not be met by the limited food in the shops and what the vegetable garden struggled to produce. The combination of persistently hot, dry conditions that would then be followed by a downpour of rain, either scorched or drowned seedlings. Or the humidity that frequently followed the rain created a flush of mould or bacteria that wilted and killed the crops before their eyes. The local supermarket had closed some months earlier after a particularly brutal attack by dozens of Zombie Dogs left five staff dead, including the three security guards.

But the offering at the supermarket had steadily declined over the years. Initially, it had been just one or two products that were out of stock, most often in the fresh vegetable section. Then it just deteriorated to the point where you could get lots of cleaning products and toilet paper, but not much to eat. There had been a small fresh vegetable stall just down the road from where they lived, in the outer suburbs. But it had been robbed and vandalised so many times, she guessed the owners decided it just wasn't worth it and were probably eating all they produced on their piece of land anyway. It remained a burnt-out shell on the side of the road, but she didn't bike out that way at all now. Too much energy required, which she just didn't have.

Now Carol had to travel over an hour by bus to buy whatever she could find on the shelf of the more heavily guarded city supermarket, managing two hungry kids all the way there and back. But they seemed to be growing up quickly, and the tantrums were infrequent. Perhaps they had some innate recognition that Mom was trying her best. They knew she cried most of the night, even though she tried to hide it.

Stephanie had a cough which steadily got worse, and she waited with both the kids at the hospital for ten hours one day before she was seen by an emergency doctor, Isabelle. Both Carol and Isabelle were drained, and initially they just looked at each other with sympathetic eyes. But sympathy doesn't cure sick children.

She listened to Stephanie's chest front and back, and after a suitable amount of umming and ahhing, concluded that she probably had pneumonia. Carol was devastated and took this as a sad indictment on her mothering ability. Isabelle, noticing the look of shock on Carol's face, being as kind as she could after twenty-four hours on her feet, told Carol that it had nothing to do with her mothering and probably a lot to do with poor food availability. She asked Carol what her husband did, which sent Carol into a complete breakdown. She slumped to the floor, howling in despair.

Isabelle, too tired to think straight and not sure what to do, pressed the buzzer for security, who quickly appeared. Security was confused, normally they would be dealing with aggressive patients or family members, often on drugs. Isabelle collected herself and advised the two burly guards that the woman and her children needed to be taken to twenty-four-hour respite care, a section the hospital had set up in a converted parking lot underneath the main building.

The two guards understood. They retrieved two wheelchairs, and lifted Carol and Stephanie into one and Jane into the other, which Jane thought was just a marvellous adventure. She was scrawny too, and was used to seeing Mommy crying. She was also sad and missed Dad. And her little sister, while a pain, was sick too. But she had never been in a wheelchair before. She smiled as the family was wheeled down the long ramps to the basement, where plywood walls and rolled-out vinyl flooring had created a large kitchen and dining area, and a communal sleeping space. They went straight to the dining hall, where rows and rows of tables and chairs were laid out like a boarding school refectory. It was half-full, which was the normal situation.

The hospital had realised some time ago that many of the patients they were seeing were simply malnourished, and had teamed up with several aid agencies in town who were struggling under the increased demand for all types of services. In a brutally frank and often heated meeting, the decision had been made to combine their limited resources and concentrate on those in greatest need: the people presenting to the hospital. They could not help everybody, and while the intellectual argument could be made that it was better to feed people before they needed to go to hospital, there was just too much need coupled with a rapidly diminishing supply of food. A large amount of rationalisation was required. This included shutting many of the smaller aid agency offices, which was an anathema to many. But they had few resources and increasingly staff were being assaulted by people desperate for help.

The respite area was conceived and built within two weeks, and all food supply vehicles routed to this location, arriving at night to limit detection by the gangs who had started to recognise and target these vehicles for what they were. Each truck now carried an armed guard. Everybody was hungry now, and to reduce pilfering by staff, they were fed as well and given a small extra ration to take home.

It was into this place of last resort that Carol and her two kids where regally wheeled. The guards, sensing the moment, wheeled the two chairs up to the counter and advised that if they wanted to be fed, they had to walk from here. Carol, still struggling to control the deep

    ROBERT STEVENS

sobs that racked her emaciated frame, all the while cradling Stephanie, smiled a weak thank-you and got up out of the chair. Jane wanted to be wheeled some more, but the smell of the cooked meat and vegetables overcame this desire, and she too got out of her chair and with wide eyes approached the counter. She had never seen so much food in one place.

"Remember your manners, young lady," admonished Carol as Jane quickly scooped up a plate and held it out to be filled by the kind-eyed ladies behind the counter.

"Can I have some more, please?" whispered one of the ladies to the other, and they smiled in sadness as they had seen this all too many times before. They heaped up the plates, one held by Jane, one by Carol and one by the security guy who realised that Carol could not handle the child in her arms, her own plate, and a plate for the child at the same time. As he laid the third plate down beside the lady, Carol looked up at him with tears in her eyes. "Thank you for your kindness. It has been some time …" and she burst out crying again. How many tears does a woman have inside? How many angels can dance on the head of a pin? He smiled back, and holding on to his own emotions, quietly walked back to his mate waiting at the now redundant wheelchairs, and the two men headed back up the ramps.

It was easier dealing with drugged-up arseholes than having to see such good people in a situation like this. At least the arseholes were responsible for their own situations, and it was satisfying dealing with the aggressive ones. While he was trained to respond 'accordingly', he, too, was a person, albeit a big strong one trained in street fighting and MMA, and sometimes the accumulated frustration boiled over.

The meals were too much, their shrunken stomachs no match for the full plates. After a surprisingly short time, all three were full and there was still food left on their plates, the first time for as long as any of them could remember. "What do we do with the spare food, Mommy?" asked Jane. She hadn't seen this before.

One of the server staff came up with a cardboard box. "You guys put the leftovers into this and keep it for later. Tastes just as good for breakfast. We don't waste anything now. Unfortunately, because of the shortage of food, you are allocated only one meal while here, the remains of which are in front of you. We would like to be able to give more, but we just don't have the resources. You have been allocated a bed, well, a stretcher actually, for a night, just to get your energy back. You are welcome to stay or go, you decide."

Carol sat for a moment, not sure what to do. She was exhausted, and acute enough to realise this. There was no one at home to worry about where they were. It had been Sophia who had nagged her to take toddler Stephanie to the hospital, so she knew that they wouldn't be worried if they hadn't made it home. So it was an easy decision to make.

"How do we find our stretcher?" was Carol's simple question.

"Just find a couple that have clean sheets on them. They get made up fresh every day. Go and sleep, I think you need it," replied the woman.

"Thank you all for your kindness. I'm just a bit lost at the moment," said Carol. She gathered up her things and did as suggested, finding new sheets on three adjoining stretchers in a far corner. She lay Stephanie down, who was already asleep on a full stomach but still wheezing away, and turned to Jane, who was surprisingly full of beans with this new adventure.

"Promise me you will not leave this hall without me," started Carol. "I am very tired and must sleep. I can't keep my eyes open. Find out where the toilets are and come back and tell me. You are allowed to explore, but do not talk to anyone not wearing one of the hospital uniforms. I need you to be very grown-up for me now, Jane. Please help me with this."

Jane listened and understood. "Yes, Mommy, I understand. I will." She hugged her mother who was sitting on the side of the stretcher. Stephanie was fast asleep, and would be for some time. Her breath

    ROBERT STEVENS

gurgled with the fluid on her lungs, but it didn't seem as bad as it had been at home.

"Thank you, babe. You are so grown-up. Sorry I am so tired all the time."

"That's okay, Mom, I know you are working hard to look after us. And we both miss Daddy."

Carol lay down and, quietly thinking about her lost husband, fell asleep. Jane, all of eight years old, felt this weight of responsibility as she watched her mother go to sleep, and after a moment, went off to find where the toilets were. She needed to pee.

Carol woke ten hours later, taking a moment to orientate herself and remember where she was. In a quick panic she looked at the stretchers beside her: Jane was curled up asleep, as was Stephanie, whose breathing was still ragged and raspy. A bottle of antibiotics stood on the floor beside Stephanie, prescribed by Isabelle once the family had been wheeled away.

She smiled and noticed the spare food was still under their beds in the simple cardboard container. Somehow they had managed to keep the rats and mice out. She needed to go to the toilet.

Carol returned from her ablutions and just sat still for some time, watching over her children. While emotionally drained, she felt buoyed by the kindness she had just come across, and was just quiet in the moment.

They had to leave, of course, and the big question was whether to finish off the remains of last night's meal straight away, or not. After much banter, it was demolished right then and there, and they laughed at themselves, even Stephanie laughed although she didn't understand why. She was full, and Mommy was laughing, and that was enough.

CHAPTER 47

Shifting Camp

The Winnebago managed three trips to the flood-destroyed bridge before it spluttered and choked on the remains of dirty diesel that came from the bottom of the tank. They had moved the youngest children and the heavy materials they did not care to leave behind. It took them eight days to get the entire group, less the Witters, to the new campsite which was exactly as Carlos had described it. The mornings were frosty, and everybody quickly went about the process of setting up the new camp and rebuilding the more semi-permanent structures. Toilets were dug and firewood collected, and that which they shifted was all put into rainproof shelters. Game was hunted and the surplus meat dried. It was cold already, and as predicted, it got a lot colder very quickly. Two weeks after they arrived, fifteen centimetres of snow covered the ground, and it stayed like that for the next four months.

Also, as expected, a group of perhaps forty Zombie Dogs arrived at their previous, almost deserted campsite three days after the last of the materials had been either shifted or hidden. Only one solitary tent remained, which the Dogs looked at as they struggled to comprehend that there were not going to be the rich pickings they had anticipated.

Patience was not their strong point, and despite the command to stay put, a couple of young bloods decided to make an early foray and see what had been left behind in the tent. They raced out of the tree line prematurely, whooping and hollering as though in a western movie. What they hoped to achieve was unclear, as all they did was alert the Witters that the inevitable moment had arrived. Dean looked at his wife of fifty years, and then moved her into his arms as he had so many times before.

"I love you as much as I ever have. You have been my everything. If there is an afterlife, I want to share it with you. Thank you."

She wept and smiled, as she knew their love had been a rare thing. They had survived the Great Collapse, yet their children had not. Dean had been a good husband, the best any woman could hope for. She could utter no words in these final moments. She leaned back and smiled at him through tear-filled eyes brimming with love. It was all the answer he ever needed.

"Once the mongrels open the tent, I am going to pull the pin from my grenade. You may want to do the same, as there will be a few seconds' delay. I forget how many, but it won't matter. You won't feel a thing. It will be so quick. I am content to be with you at this moment. Don't let them catch you. I love you," Dean said in a gentle voice.

And less than thirty seconds later, the zip on the tent was pulled upwards and a bedraggled head of hair with a smirking face below looked in.

"Surprise, dickhead," was all Dean could get out before his grenade went off, followed instantly by his wife's. They died together, which was what they had planned.

Carlos watched from the edge of the wood. He had been tracking the group of Dogs for the past two days, and smiled at the courage of the two who had been left behind. He said a quiet prayer for them, even though he was not a churchgoing sort of guy. He then made his way north because he knew the remaining Zombie Dogs would try and follow where the main group had gone. As the mob of Dogs had come up from the south, the most logical option was to continue heading north and find some kind of sign, a trail to follow. He had an hour's lead on them, but could travel much faster because he was relatively well nourished, well trained and disciplined. The Dogs were none of those things.

It took the main group of Zombie Dogs until the middle of the next day to arrive at the rock bluff where the surprise waited. Carlos had laid out the trap well: a heavy machine gun on the narrow shoulder of the road, positioned behind the largest boulder they could find and shift, and a couple of bushes they cut off and used as additional camouflage. To a trained soldier, it was an obvious anomaly in an area that screamed 'ambush site'. They had also placed a Claymore mine just before the start of the rock bluff, and had four more men with AR-13 assault rifles ready to pop out from hiding spots when the time was right.

It went well, but not for the Dogs. They walked into the ambush totally oblivious, and twenty-odd were instantly killed by the barrage of fire and the Claymore mine, and at least another two were grievously wounded, evidenced by the blood trails observed. Another four lay wounded on the road, and were summarily dispatched with no remorse. They had chosen their path.

The men involved in the ambush decided not to chase the Dog survivors. It carried a risk for little apparent gain apart from sheer hatred. The greatest safety was in distance, and it had started to snow. They threw the weapons of the dead into the river below the bluff, and left the bodies where they lay. A gruesome reminder of what awaited others was considered useful. The rats and the wolves left little behind anyway; they were feeling the cold as well.

The ambushing group then made its way north to the new camp, tramping through snow and burdened down by their weapons, but satisfied with their work. They had suffered no casualties. The Dogs had not managed to fire an effective shot in reply, so complete had been the surprise.

— ◈ —

     ROBERT STEVENS

Carlos made his report to Robert, Bob and a few of the senior members of the camp. "It was good," was how he summed it up, and they polished off one of the few remaining bottles of whisky to celebrate a reprieve from that particular danger. Now they could get on with the job of surviving: more shelters and hunting were on the agenda.

The Yuki people had chosen the site well. While the snow collected, it was not as deep as it was in every other area. It only took a ten-minute walk, out of the lee of the great stone buttresses that lay to the east, north and south, to find snow that was metres deep, far deeper than they had around the camp. But more importantly, there was virtually no wind. Most of their group survived. Two women died in childbirth, first births for them both. Although they had an ambulance first responder and a trainee doctor in the group, the complications were just too great. The camp quietly reflected that childbirth had been one of the great slayers of mankind before people became 'civilised', and although there were herbs around the campsite that may have saved one of the women, they did not know this. The old knowledge was not theirs, yet.

Survival, which Robert was beginning to understand, was all they had to focus on. Because, in addition to the deaths of the two women and their babies, another six had perished from assorted causes, most of which could be attributed to age, the cold and the inability to adapt to their conditions. But three children had been born over the five months of the bitterest winter that was ever *not* recorded in modern times. The saga became another part of the stories they wove and passed on to their children.

Robert and Marcelle were in love and lust, and even though they were reduced to living in a tent with air mattresses like all the others, this did not dampen their enthusiasm for each other. Marcelle propped herself up on her elbow and faced her lover after a satisfying bout of lovemaking, and said, "You know I just can't pop down to the drugstore to buy contraception any more. And I haven't seen a condom for a long time. There is a real chance I could get pregnant, you know."

Robert looked up at her face in the pale morning light. "Yes, that thought had occurred to me." He paused. "And clearly the risks of giving birth and raising a child are much greater now." There was a comfortable silence between them. "Put brutally, we could say that we need to populate or perish. But I believe that is old thinking. It is up to you. As much as I love you, if you chose not to have a child, then I would do my utmost best to prevent it. But if you chose otherwise, then I would be thrilled. But you run a risk, as we have seen just recently with Gail and Debra."

Marcelle smiled. "I love you too, and I would be thrilled to have your baby, including taking the risk. My second mom, Dor, said it was hard to find a man who would truly love you, and finally I have. Even though you do fart in bed when asleep!" Her teeth shone in the near darkness. "Let's try now!" she suggested, and they did.

The winter decimated the Zombie Dogs. Foraging returns in the city were nearly non-existent. Wildlife took much longer to return to the big cities, and the plague of rats and wild dogs generated by the numerous dead consumed a lot of other edible material, including the weak. Cannibalism was rife, but even that source of nourishment did not protect the perpetrators from the cold, and few had survival skills. The cannibals had usually just preyed on others, the easiest meal to find, but now there were so few people remaining. Few survived. No loss.

The camp in the enclave endured, and winter's bite eventually weakened, and the first buds of spring appeared. Carlos and another ex-army ranger type went out to investigate the old campsite and conduct a general reconnoitre.

     ROBERT STEVENS

It was as they had left it, with only a few tattered remains of the Witters' tent still visible. They checked on the hidden materials, all of which were fine. They stayed the night, and in the morning, gathered up what could be found of the Witters' tent and possessions, and lacking any other remains, buried that in the graveyard as a testimony to their courage. They would make a headstone later; now it was time to return to the camp in the north. They had gardens to establish and game to hunt. Surviving was a full-time job.

CHAPTER 48

Carol on Her Own

The sense of contentment provided by the kindness of the hospital staff and the full stomachs lasted a few days. The antibiotics prescribed for Stephanie seemed to work initially, with the barking cough decreasing in intensity and frequency. She slept better, which meant that Carol slept better. The gnawing hunger returned after three days, and one of the more disquieting aftereffects of the massive dinner and leftover breakfast was some modest constipation, as their digestive systems struggled to cope with the massive, short-term change. But it had been worth it.

Carol, though, was struggling mentally. While at an intellectual level, she knew she grieved for Steve, she also felt an overwhelming sense of inadequacy because she couldn't feed her kids properly. Karl and Sophia, as well as the squatters, Stan and Samantha, all harped on about the shortages in the supermarkets and the closure of the little bakeries, butchers and fresh produce shops. But this did nothing to assuage the feeling that she wasn't a good mother. Steve's mother, Jacqueline, had returned to her own house some weeks prior.

Carol was severely clinically depressed, and cried every night once the kids were tucked up. Everything seemed such a struggle.

Karl and Sophia did what they could to help. Food from the supermarkets was now rationed – people were restricted to how much of a specific food product could be purchased per person, with particular regard to perishable items and vegetable seeds. Parents soon learned to take birth certificates along when out shopping as proof that they were feeding more than just themselves. Many went to multiple markets to maximise purchases, as the loss of the internet made shared record-keeping between stores virtually impossible.

The kids would sometimes stay over with Karl and Sophia. The offer was made one night around what was now the obligatory backyard bonfire. They had started burning the furniture from Steve and Carol's original house, and then the wooden trims. They figured it didn't matter; there was no housing shortage anymore. It was now all about those who survived and struggled on.

The conversation usually started around what part of the house was being offered to the gods of heat and comfort, and then the drinks would begin. It was a coping mechanism, the drink.

"Why not let the kids stay with us for a night?" Sophia blurted out. She hadn't even discussed this with Karl, but he was a married man: he knew his wife.

Carol thought for a bit, surprised by the offer. "I don't know, they are kids and may not want to … and it would be a great imposition …" she stumbled through the objections.

"That would be great, Mom!" said Jane, who was sitting with them this night. By now, she was becoming all grown-up, aged all of eight, nearly nine. "And if Stephanie cries or gets all worried, we can just walk back. It's only next door." It was an adventure for her, and after some more token objections from Carol, she conceded, and the kids started staying over one night a week on the weekends. They shared a room, but nothing special about that. It was fun for the girls, and while it gave Karl and Sophia two extra mouths to feed, they knew it gave Carol some respite from the full-time stress of being a solo mom. Doubly so in these difficult times. They played card games, Monopoly and other board games with the girls: old-school entertainment.

Carol could not shake the depression that had settled on her. She struggled with her feelings of inadequacy brought on by her inability to feed her children properly, and her crushing loneliness without Steve. Not having a job meant little social contact beyond the immediate neighbours, and quite frankly, she didn't like Stan and the grudge he had against the world, not to mention that he and his wife were just squatting there. It didn't sit right with her upbringing and standards. Karl and Sophia were the best neighbours you could hope for, but even so, it did not provide the intimate moments that she needed, or the confidential sharing of ideas. Or the just knowing there was somebody else who loved you, even when they weren't there. She continued to lose weight, and her immunity system and mental processes were compromised.

Stephanie's barking cough, which earlier had seemed to abate, returned. She started coughing up green phlegm, which Carol knew meant a lung infection of some kind. Stephanie became increasingly lethargic and listless as the toxic mix of borderline malnutrition and pneumonia sapped her strength. Karl and Sophia could hear her coughing from next door and were worried. They hesitated about suggesting Carol take the child back to hospital, knowing that she had been there some weeks earlier and thus was aware of the issue.

But Carol's thinking was muddled, and for reasons she could not understand herself, she had decided not to take Stephanie back. In her mind, she had exhausted that option. They had gone to the hospital, were given some drugs, and now it was time for something different. The hospital visit had not worked. She just wasn't sure what the next step would be; she couldn't get to that level of decision-making. The default option of doing nothing played out. Perhaps Stephanie would get better tomorrow. The nearly four-year-old struggled to breathe, and increasingly just stayed in bed. One weekend it was just Jane who appeared for the weekly sleepover at the neighbours. "Mommy decided

     ROBERT STEVENS

to keep Stephanie home tonight. She is really sick, and …" her voice trailed off.

Karl saw the unhappiness and uncertainty in the child's face and voice and reassured her. "I am sure your mom is doing the best thing. And you are welcome, as always, and we will play Monopoly tonight and I'll clean you up, young lady! No mercy."

Jane looked at the adult in front of her, and showing wisdom beyond her years, replied, "Perhaps."

And they played Monopoly, with Sophia winning the first game. They both regularly reminded Karl about it. The laughter and banter and fun could be heard next door, and it was. Carol was tired, tired and sad beyond belief. She could hear what was going on at the neighbours' house, and it made her sadder. To her, it simply reinforced that 'play' and 'fun' did not happen in her house. Here it was just the daily struggle. She began to think that perhaps Karl and Sophia were better parents than she was, and this idea rapidly became the dominant though. This quickly evolved into the notion that perhaps, Jane, and the world, would be better off without her.

Carol had been unable to help Stephanie, who was obviously dying a slow, noisy and painful death. Would Jane follow if she remained this completely inadequate shell of a mother? She sat in the darkened house as the most morbid of thoughts overcame her, and she could no longer bear to hear her beloved child constantly struggle to draw a breath.

Next door, they did not hear the gasping, wheezy cough stop, because, at first, you often don't notice something that is no longer in the background. Nor did they hear the muffled shot as Carol, who had held the pillow on Stephanie's face long enough to stop the coughing and wheezing that had tormented her soul for too long, placed the small pistol between her breasts and squeezed the trigger. It was done in a fit of utter helplessness and shame at being an incompetent mother. At least she had given Stephanie a release from her suffering and Jane would be better off with Karl and Sophia. Next door they were halfway through the second game, laughing and joking as Karl was slowly and ruthlessly ruined financially on the Monopoly board.

They did not discover the tragedy until Jane reappeared at their back door about three minutes after she had returned home mid-morning the next day. She had a mystified and anguished look on her face, with tears brimming. "I can't wake Mommy or sis!" was all she could say before she rushed into her second bedroom and hid under the pillow, deep sobs racking her skinny body.

Karl looked at Sophia with a fatalistic expression of his face. "Fuck," he said, and quickly walked the short distance between the back doors of the two houses. He saw Carol slumped in the living room armchair. Nothing apparently wrong on first sight. But then he saw the pistol on the floor in front of her. He lifted her head and still did not see the small bullet entry wound in her chest. She was obviously dead. He checked for a pulse as he had been trained, but nothing. "Fuck." He then went to Stephanie's bedroom. Carol had placed the pillow beside the child and had straightened the blankets and her hair. Stephanie looked like a large white porcelain doll in the bed, her blonde hair arranged perfectly around her face, the classic pose of a child at peace. But there was no rhythmic rise and fall of the blankets, no chesty rattle or wheeze which they had been listening to for the past three or four weeks. Nothing. He checked for a pulse. Nothing.

"Oh, double fuck," he said to himself, and he walked back home to tell Sophia.

He stood at the back door, and his face said it all. He couldn't find the words, and tears dribbled down the cheeks of this hard man. She looked at him, and as the horror dawned on her, she rushed past him to go next door and look for herself. Surely not!

The scream could be heard down the street, but there were not many to hear it. Samantha did, and she appeared at Carol's back door a minute

    ROBERT STEVENS

later. She saw Sophia sitting on the living room floor, holding Carol's hand, weeping uncontrollably. She did not understand what was going on. Karl had stayed behind, wondering how to soften the blow for Jane.

In a normal world, they would have beaten themselves up as they wallowed around in 'what more could we have they done to help Carol?'. But these were not normal times, and there was nothing to be gained from it. Karl explained to Jane that her sister must have died during the night. They all knew that she had been very sick. And that the loss of her baby had been too much for her mom, who they knew was sad and struggling ever since Dad had died. And it was a very sad time for everybody. And that Jane was welcome to come and stay with Karl and Sophia, and they would go and tell Nana Jacky, and they would all decide what to do next. All very practical and sensible steps. There was no room or energy for wasted effort on self-recrimination.

Karl biked around to the police station, where he explained the situation, and because of his stature amongst the force, his word was taken as the truth. From the station Karl rang Jacky's phone, but it continuously went straight through to voicemail. A search of Carol's belongings eventually revealed an address, so Karl pondered what to do. A beat cop came around that lunchtime and inspected the scene, and he advised Karl that they would get in touch with Jacky.

After a few hours, with Jane still in shock, they explained to the child that the custom was to bury the dead, and asked where the best place would be so Jane could go and talk to them whenever she wanted. Jane blinked through tear-filled eyes and, after a bit of thought, decided that a spot by the old oak tree that overlooked the gardens would be good. It was an excellent place. That evening as it cooled down, Karl sweated and swore as he dug through the tangle of roots, eventually forming a hole big and deep enough for the two. They were buried with Carol cradling Stephanie, wrapped in a sheet, and a simple cross erected once the hole was filled. They were all too drained to say much. The big old armchair where Carol had ended it, and the bed that Stephanie had slept and died in, were burnt on the bonfire that evening.

Jacky was finally contacted by her local police, and a week later, appeared with two suitcases. After a couple of days, Jacky suggested that she live in the house that Carol had been in. She wanted to be closer to Jane and recognised that Karl and Sophia were now the closest thing to parents that Jane had. Shifting the girl to a completely new neighbourhood was something that probably wouldn't help. And the vegetable garden that spread over four backyards was in need of attention.

It was a good idea. Under her care, both the vegetable garden and the grandchild did as well as they could, given the circumstances.

Sophia had given up teaching. It had become just too hard with too many problems in the classroom. Normally a teacher is a combination of educationalist, social worker, confidante and role model. But with the steady breakdown of social norms, including the loss of the internet for generations that were previously a hundred per cent wired, it was too dislocating. This all came out in the classroom. The school had set up a breakfast programme many years previously, and the demand steadily grew as the years went by. But as food shortages became increasingly severe, what they were able to supply did not come even close to the demand. Those who missed out took it badly, and verbal and physical assaults on staff became increasingly frequent and violent as frustrations erupted. The breakfast programme was discontinued, and consequently there was a significant increase in long-term truancy. Many had been going to school just to get a feed.

The attack on the internet and financial institutions had negatively affected the government's ability to pay its employees, including teachers. So after four weeks of becoming increasingly insecure in her

     ROBERT STEVENS

own classroom, and in spite of reassurances that she would be paid somehow, she had handed in her resignation, effective immediately. Many other teachers and support staff did likewise.

She had extra time to dedicate to the vegetable garden, and found herself becoming good friends with Samantha, enjoying the sisterhood and company. They had 'accidentally' brushed by each other once, and Sophia had been surprised at the feelings created by this physical contact. She kept this to herself.

CHAPTER 49

Weird Weather
The Polar Vortex

The rotating mass of cold air called the polar vortex is created by the cold conditions of the Arctic and Antarctic winters. The lack of sunlight during these periods does not change, but what does change is the amount of ice on the surface of the ocean and the inflow of warm waters from the surrounding areas, particularly in the Arctic. The Antarctic is anchored on land. Warmer fresh water is less dense than ocean water, and tends to sit on top of the colder saline water. Therefore, the increasing inflows of this fresh water created by the great floods now periodically sweeping Northern Europe, Russia and Canada, all played their part.

The joint effect of less sea ice around the North Pole, and diminishing landlocked ice in Greenland and Iceland, warmer inflowing fresh flood waters, and the instability of the Atlantic Meridional Overturning Current (AMOC), all combined to create massive instability of the polar vortex, normally 'anchored' above the Arctic Circle. A similar but less pronounced effect was developing around the Antarctic region, but its geographic isolation and absence of the impact of freshwater inflows, meant the impact of the Southern event was much less than that being experienced in the Northern hemisphere. As the ice melted, less sunlight was reflected back into space, and the waters normally underneath this reflector shield heated, melting more ice.

The swirling mass of cold air initially relocated over Europe.

Combined with the almost absent AMOC, the initial effect was mostly felt in Europe. But then it swung eastwards, and hit the Western United States. California, a place fabled for idyllic sunshine and beaches, froze. Thirty centimetres of snow fell in San Francisco, and then polar cold temperatures followed. The great Sacramento and San Joaquin Valleys, amongst the greatest wine, fruit and vegetable producing areas in the world, were devastated.

The following spring, as farmers considered their options for replanting, an increasingly common atmospheric phenomenon known as an atmospheric river began. Carrying huge amounts of water from the heated oceans, it rained on the US western seaboard. Downpours unlike anyone could remember. Two and a half metres in three days. The ground had been baked hard by many years of drought, which accelerated water runoff. The resultant floods didn't destroy many crops; precious few had survived the winter cold. But the floods did wipe out roads, bridges, railways and fences, and the fertile topsoil was stripped away. If the country had had the ability to recover, it would have taken decades to rebuild the infrastructure. The soils would have taken hundreds, if not thousands of years to rebuild.

But there was no rebuild. There was no longer the capacity to rebuild. The shortages of materials that had started in the early 2020s had compounded: forests had burnt so there was a shortage of lumber. Supply of products from China and Indonesia was sporadic at best. Anyway, paying for the goods had been a problem since the banking system and internet crash. And the massive amount of debt accumulated by successive US Governments meant that few suppliers were prepared to extend any more credit. The US had already defaulted on previous loans, and thus was not considered a good customer. People lost hope. When would it end? Would there be a return to some semblance of normality? They slowly realised that unfortunately the answer was *no*. And with that came the dawning realisation that this was a permanent change, that the new normal was climatic and financial chaos, and hopelessness descended.

There was no food. Even the few who had home vegetable gardens had seen these destroyed by the extended period of freezing weather. There was no federal help. There was nothing they could do. Grain reserves, what precious little there were, were being held for the country's army and 'critical' personnel. The army had to be well fed because law and order was rapidly disintegrating.

Coping mechanisms included alcohol and other drugs; violence against the symbols of government or authority; violence against one another, which was often disproportionately high against the ones closest to you; and denial. Denial could involve trying to fix hopeless situations, avoidance by watching TV if you had electricity, or refusing to get out of bed or go outside. Drugs, of course, were simply another coping mechanism, and for a short moment people could forget their woes. But even drugs were in short supply. Starvation became common. Many lost the will to fight on; it was too much of a struggle. Consequently, large numbers took the permanent way out, and people created novel and interesting ways to achieve this. Parents chose to end the suffering of their children, undoubtedly the most terrible thing any loving parent could ever do. Since the crash of the internet, one small grace was that these tragic instances could not be shared on social media.

    ROBERT STEVENS

CHAPTER 50

Karl, Sophia and the Sisterhood

It took some adjusting: life with Jane and Nana Jacky. Jane grew up even more quickly, and while she sometimes felt sad about the loss of her sister and parents, she learned to shuttle between houses as the whim took her. She never learned the truth. She believed her sister had died from her sickness and her mother had died of a broken heart because of it.

Sophia welcomed the opportunity to work one-on-one with this beautiful little child, aged nine going on twenty. When the weather was good, Sam, Sophia and Jane would bike into town in the morning and go to the library and take out books on a wide range of subjects. Or they would go into town extra early to see what was available at the supermarket. Sometimes there may have been a delivery overnight and they could get a few food items. Jane's first period started unexpectedly, and Sophia and Jacky were ideally placed to welcome this young girl into womanhood. It was a four-way relationship that perhaps saved them all.

Time was spent in the garden and so the Sisterhood of the Street was born. Sometime earlier, Stan had failed to return from one of his midnight jaunts, which they all suspected was related to a series of arsons across town. But the targets of the arsons had become aware of what was going on and had responded by employing armed guards. They never heard any gunfire the night he vanished, nor was there a functioning 'news' system to report on events. But it was not unexpected; he had made his choice and must have realised the potential consequences.

Samantha did not seem overly distressed by the loss, which spoke volumes.

They all missed his distilled firewater, or more correctly, the opportunity for a head buzz and a chance to just chill out and talk around the bonfire. After much debate and spectacular failures, the girls started making their own from overripe fruit scavenged from neighbouring properties when the time was good. "Woman does not live by vegetables alone" was all they needed to encourage themselves in this endeavour.

Karl kept going to work and increasingly felt out of place, but he couldn't put his finger on why this was the case. Perhaps he had already fought his part in the greater good-versus-evil battle.

The adults could argue that the loss of Sophia's income was a blow, but as she hadn't been paid for some time anyway, they found that they had already adjusted. They were surprised at how little they could get by on and had decided not to make any more payments on the mortgage. Nobody was paying the banks now, the collapse of the banking system had taken care of that. And the insurance was not renewed. There was a lot of that going on as well. What money Karl was being paid was flat out paying for groceries, which had skyrocketed in price as availability decreased. The car sat in the garage and hadn't moved in months. Petrol was severely rationed and, while he would have received some for a police car in normal times, these were not normal times, and he did not have access to a vehicle that was not a pooled one. And these were increasingly less available to be taken home – too many were getting broken into, vandalised or set on fire. They travelled mostly by bike now, and had set up a small workshop in Steve's old garage for the necessary repairs and maintenance.

The four women were establishing a routine, quite content in their own way. Mornings would be for tending the gardens or for the twice-a-week trip to the impromptu market that had been established to trade surplus produce or just gather for a chat. Afternoons would be spent out exploring away from their houses, which was code for scavenging the neighbourhood fruit trees and seeing who else was still hanging on in this part of the suburbs. Surprisingly few as it turned out. When it was too hot to go out, they would retire to one of the garages to get on with brewing or distilling, or preserving and bottling, or just sit reading together and arguing over some issue or another. It was the best education any young lady could ever have.

Then, as life does, change came in a cascade of events. Or put another way, life comes in lumps.

— ◆ —

Karl was struggling at work, and management had noticed this. For a while he had been a tremendous source of insider information on the drug, stolen goods and burglary scene. He had never revealed his sources, which they respected. But policing had changed. There had been several arson attacks on upmarket homes and lawyers' offices. There was a large increase in attacks on supermarkets and supply vehicles, essentially hit-and-run affairs. All reports indicated a general decay in law and order, and the old structures weren't working any more. The police were devolving into a heavily armed response and protection squad, working increasingly alongside the army to protect what they could. Pro-active policing was devolving.

He was called into the commander's office at the start of his rostered day shift.

Once the traditional pleasantries were dealt with, the commander jumped right in. "Things are changing out on the street!" She was a kind but hardened veteran of thirty years of service. She smiled at Karl.

"I'm not sure if that is a question or a statement," said Karl. "But let's not talk about the weather or other trivial bullshit, shall we," he carried on. "Give me a clue as to why I was summoned."

She smiled again; she had always enjoyed this man. He was straight up and had achieved great things, past tense.

"You have a great record, Karl. But policing has become something different to the force you joined nearly twenty years ago, or when I joined thirty years ago. The days of a regular beat cop, detectives doing detective stuff, and the police being respected by most people are long gone, I'm afraid. I am not sure I agree with what we are becoming, which is more like an enforcement and protection service, but there are a lot of things I am not sure I like at the moment."

Karl was smart enough to just nod his head slightly; there was no need to add anything. He also had a sense for what was coming. But it wasn't that at all.

"How would you feel about returning to the countryside? There are a number of rural centres, one- and two-man stations, crying out for a cop with your skills and experience. And frankly, you are a spare wheel here now. Eventually we would wind up hating each other, and I would have to do something to move you on, one way or another."

She paused, letting this sink in. "Your old haunt on the outskirts of Banff wants you back, by the way. Fucked if I know why," she added just to make this man smile.

Karl was stunned. He had been expecting some kind of redundancy, early retirement, something else, not this. He gathered his thoughts quickly. Initially, the idea appealed, but there were many what-ifs and wherefores and Sophia to consider. His thought process must have seemed somewhat transparent, and the commander read him like a book.

"How about you take the rest of the day off? Go home, talk it over with Sophia. Think about it. Come back to me within two days. And yes, it is a rushed decision. If you choose to go, we can get you on a scheduled military flight." Commercial domestic and international air travel had spluttered to a halt long ago.

     ROBERT STEVENS

So he went home on his trusty ten-speed just one hour after he had cycled to work, and found the sisterhood laughing and singing a popular soul song in the ever-expanding vegetable garden, stretching between the four properties. He watched them for a while. They were completely unaware that he was there. And in that moment, he knew that they were in a good place – helping each other, supporting each other, a group collectively raising a young woman. And he was the outsider – the wrong gender.

He left them to it. They didn't need an interruption at the moment, and being honest with himself, he did feel like he was increasingly unsettling to this band of sisters. *Getting paranoid?* he silently asked himself. He biked down to the local reserve and sat by the picnic area.

A group of three layabouts approached him, asking, "What the fuck you doing in our park, old man?"

Karl sighed, stood up slowly and smoothly drew his police automatic. He immediately cranked a round into the breach and pointed it at them, with a nasty look in his eyes. "You know, fuckheads, I could drop the three of you cunts before you had time to turn and run home to mommy. And the world would be a better place for it. Now I am just trying to spend a bit of quiet time to think things over, which would be a novel thing for any of you. So decide, who wants to be the first to die, or shall you just fuck off yourselves? Go on, make my day."

Quite quickly the bravado of the group disappeared, and there was no further discussion as they all turned and fled. Karl smiled to himself; his pulse rate had not altered.

"Still got it, you gunslinging, badass cop, you," he said to himself, then smiled and sat down. And he knew he had made his decision.

He wasn't bothered by anyone else as he sat there quietly in the sun for an hour or so, not thinking about much at all. By eleven it was becoming hot, and the women would have come in from the garden and be either drinking tea, drying seeds, or making hooch. He smiled again, and biked quietly home.

They were all surprised to see him, and after the usual pleasantries and exchanges, he asked to talk with Sophia alone. They all gave each other the 'gosh, what's going on here?' look, and left to go to another house. They had a few to choose from.

Karl relayed the conversation he'd had with the commander, and the events at the park as he had left the women to get on with their tasks. And the fact that he had enjoyed drawing his pistol, but he did not pass on that he had been hoping for an opportunity to use it. And that, to him, perhaps a return to Banff wasn't a bad idea.

Sophia digested this. She knew that he wasn't settled at work, that he just didn't seem to fit any more. That the world had changed, and was continuing to change around them. She didn't have to like it but did have to cope. She knew her husband well enough by now to know that he had already made up his mind, and if she were to pout and create a fuss, it would only come between them.

"Do you want me to come with you?" was all she said after she had processed it all.

"Only if you want to. I know you have a good thing going on here, I can see that. The relationship between us has changed, but shit, what hasn't changed? Since the attack on you all those years ago, the intimacy has all but disappeared, and that makes me sad. I guess in all relationships there is an evolution, and the initial lust fades and is replaced by a general contentment. Each should grow in their own way, and the best a couple could hope for is that they grow alongside each other. I suspect we have grown apart just a bit too far.

"And let's face it, we would be living on opposite sides of a large country with limited chances to travel back and forth. Which is quite a change from what I recall, from well over a decade ago." And they

   ROBERT STEVENS

smiled at each with the precious memories; these could not be taken from them.

And that night, once it had cooled down a bit, they made passionate love like they hadn't for a long time. And they both knew she had made her decision as well. She was going to stay. There was a bond between the women in this little coven that was growing stronger and deeper.

"What happened to us?" she asked, and then, "Is there someone else?"

Karl took his time answering. "Easy one first. No, there is no one else and never has been. It has always been you." She smiled in the darkness on hearing these words. She still loved him. "I still love you, and always will," he continued. "I don't think anything happened to 'us' as such. When we first met, there was a lot of lust, as it should be." She smiled at that as well. "As I said earlier, we evolve, or should evolve, grow, mature, develop, whatever. So as a couple we should also grow, and perhaps we grow in different directions, or at different rates. I am not sure. But to expect that initial infatuation and lust to endure forever is perhaps a bit unrealistic." Karl paused, letting his own thoughts catch up.

"I have done some things in my job that I am not proud of, and I am not talking about the information you supplied so long ago. I want to start new, afresh, in my work, in my life. I can't undo what I have done, but I want to atone. I need to get out of the city." He paused again, and she let the silence linger. She did not want to interrupt the flow from this man beside her.

"We have both grown in our own ways, and I do not want to leave you. But I see what you are creating here and raising Jane with the other women. It is good, an oasis in this world of uncertainty. I just know that it is time for us both to continue to grow, and not inhibit or constrain each other. I am not sure of the words ..." A long silence prevailed while they both just lay there.

"I want to stay married to you, although it won't be a traditional living-together situation. I love you, and perhaps we are both setting the other free."

The tears rolled silently down her cheeks, and then a deep sob racked her body, and she snuggled in closer. They were the words she did and didn't want to hear.

And she knew that her relationship with the women was growing stronger and perhaps a more intimate one with Sam had crossed her mind. And she had been scared about that. Now she and Karl had both taken the step off the precipice.

And two weeks later, he was back on the Canadian West Coast, a rural station where nothing and everything had changed. And he was back in a place he understood better. There were still lots of bad guys, and people struggled to put food on the table. But as station leader, he thought he could make a real difference again and would work hard to succeed.

 ROBERT STEVENS

CHAPTER 51

Weird Weather
Wind

Wind is created by differences in atmospheric pressure. As one area heats, warm air rises, creating a flow of air into this 'vacuum' to compensate for the 'loss' of air upwards. There have been great cycles of air movement around the globe for as long as Earth has had an atmosphere. The wind is also what creates the waves: the stronger the wind, the larger the waves. This is what the surfing community worships. People living in hurricane- or cyclone-prone areas have also known this for as long as people have lived there.

Increasing greenhouse gas emissions create additional heating. Carbon dioxide molecules, like all molecules, vibrate more rapidly as they heat. This is one way that 'energy' is stored, namely kinetic energy. And there are a lot more carbon dioxide molecules now, so a lot more energy is being trapped under the enhanced greenhouse blanket, and some of this energy is being stored in the very air around us. The increasing temperature of the oceans had also been faithfully measured and reported. Not surprisingly, this extra 'energy' in the system has led to more dramatic weather events, including those involving wind and the waves that wind creates.

But a few tenths of a degree change in ocean temperature was not front-page news; few did the maths and multiplied it by the volume of water affected. And over the years, the rising temperatures were not consistent. In fact, water temperatures off the coast of the eastern USA and Western Europe fell as the AMOC current faltered. So heat from the tropics was no longer being transported north, and the resultant effect was additional heating of the waters around the equator – the breeding ground of tropical cyclones. And the higher the water temperature, the greater the energy that is stored, and the greater the cyclone. The number of cyclones had been fairly steady for many decades, but the incidence of severe storms was increasing.

Sea water surface temperatures approaching 40 °C (100 °F), well over 10 °C higher than 'normal' were being recorded around the Cocos and Christmas Islands, south of the equator and northwest of Australia. This was too high for many of the fish species, and those that could not swim far enough away died from lack of oxygen in the heated water. Millions of dead fish floated on the surface, and birdlife flocked to this feast; they didn't mind the stench.

The fishing fleets that used to come to this ocean region from all around Asia and Australia, no longer came. The fish were gone, and many fishing families became even hungrier as boats were tied up indefinitely. The price of fish soared as the supply dwindled. This was not the only part of the world where this was happening

Western Australia has been exposed to wind and waves for a long time. A drive along the coastal road shows many old trees growing sideways, such is the persistence of the pressure created by these unrelenting winds. It is also a very popular surfing region, home to some of the monster 'unrideable' waves that pepper surfboarding lore. Cyclones impacting Western Australia usually number three or four a year, and some of the highest windspeeds ever recorded have been in northern Australia, especially during the cyclone season at the 'top end' of Western Australia and the Northern Territory.

     ROBERT STEVENS

The city of Perth, on the southwestern coast of Australia, had moved to harness the power of the wind, with large wind turbines dotting the landscape two hundred kilometres inland, around Merredin, in this mineral-rich but water-poor area. Water scarcity had become a serious problem as rainfall became increasingly erratic, so the power from these mighty turbines was harnessed to desalinate seawater, providing potable water to some 1.6 million people. One problem with wind-powered electricity generation is the inconsistency of the wind. No place has consistent wind at ten to fifteen metres per second day and night. There are calm days and days when the wind exceeds the tolerance of the turbine and they automatically feather themselves, turning sideways to the wind to reduce pressure on the massive masts that hold them upright. Large solar electricity farms had also been established because a place that suffers low rainfall normally endures long sunny periods as well.

Investment in solar generation had also boomed in the sunny and hot desert state of Western Australia, so this form of 'green power' increasingly complemented the wind generation.

Initially, the extra wind was profitable. More wind generally meant more power, even if the frequency of the 'too windy' days slowly crept up, so the turbine installations were becoming more and more profitable. Increasingly, the Indian Ocean, to the west, which provided the prevailing wind, was heating like the rest of the planet.

The tropical storm that was rapidly developing into a cyclone was noticed by the weather satellites above, and high atmospheric pressures, the likes of which had never been seen before on the planet, were automatically detected and relayed back to Earth. Meteorologists looked at the figures in disbelief: 1,080 KPa and above. *Surely not. Wind speeds in excess of 350 kph, unbelievable! Never seen or heard of figures like these before!* But a lot of that has been going on as well.

The message went out about a system that had the potential to become a superstorm, developing eight hundred kilometres northwest of Carnarvon, a location which happened to have a satellite tracking station and hence useful access to what remained of the internet. So the Federal and State Governments were warned well in advance. The cyclone rapidly moved from Category 3 to 4, and then to Category 5. As wind speeds increased to a never-before-seen figure of 450 kph near the eye, the term 'superstorm' was used. The Category 5+ had been introduced years before but was seldom used. It steadily tracked at 12 kph towards Perth – a steady running pace. It took three days to make landfall, and people there had made whatever preparation they could. Wind gusts in excess of 500 kph were recorded, and satellites measured the diameter of this monster at five hundred kilometres just as it hit land.

The wind turbines, even though situated two hundred kilometres inland from the coast, had almost all feathered as required because the wind speed increased above 25 m/s (90 kph), and those that didn't subsequently flew to bits at 60 m/s, well above the design strength of the blades. As the first blade detached from the nacelle, the mechanism became unbalanced, and the stresses on the tower and nacelle became such that the top simply flew off. But only a few failed to feather as designed, and thus the destruction of these turbines, while spectacular to those who had decided to stay and watch, was reasonably infrequent. At 45 m/s (160 kph or 100 mph) wind speed, people have trouble standing up, and thus the few hardy souls who had stayed to observe and record events on their phones, wisely sought shelter behind the massive masts of the turbines that did feather and hence not break apart. The footage they recorded was spectacular, but unfortunately not many ever got to see it. The internet didn't work any longer.

The wind continued to build in ferocity, escalating to a screaming shriek that beat against the senses. Walking away from the lee of the turbine mast was not a good idea at this stage. The first to try it was

     ROBERT STEVENS

whisked off her feet and then violently rolled along the ground until pushed into a nearby gully, breaking arms and ribs as she went.

The small building that housed the load sharing control equipment was the first to fail, with the roof lifting off and being carried over five kilometres before crashing into farmland. The walls did not survive many seconds after the loss of the roof, as structural integrity was lost. These simply disintegrated, flying off after the roof.

The large towers of the feathered turbines are held in place by massive threaded rods in huge concrete footings. As wind makes its way around a structure, it actually accelerates to allow for the fact that it has a bit further to travel around the structure. And on the downwind side, there is a loss of pressure. These turbine structures were designed to withstand high wind speeds, but every structure has a design point beyond which it is not practicable to build, and engineers work to this. The wind turbine masts oscillate as the wind builds. Just as skyscrapers are designed to sway in the wind, the turbines also rock backwards and forwards. If you stand beside a wind turbine and look up along the mast, you notice this swaying; it can be quite disorientating.

With the severe winds now sweeping the wind farm, these oscillations became increasingly large, and the massive bolts that held the masts in place began to fail, spectacularly. The fifty-millimetre steel rods failed explosively, snapping off at ground level like thunder cracks. Surprisingly, these sounds were not noticed because the wind shriek was now in excess of 160 dBA, and the people cowering behind the masts had their hands clamped over their ears while they huddled in the only shelter they could find. As the masts failed, they simply fell over. Three technicians were crushed to death, very quickly and comprehensively, when the masts they sheltered behind fell on them. At that stage, they had been on the ground in the foetal position and were not aware that the towers above them were falling down. Perhaps a great mercy. They couldn't comprehend that the wind farm they had invested so much effort into was being destroyed, let alone that the tower above was going to crush them.

The destruction of the wind farm was complete. The final maximum wind speed could only be guessed at because the recording equipment was also destroyed.

Two hundred kilometres to the southwest, much closer to sea level, the city of Perth did not fare any better. The wind speeds were even higher.

Generally speaking, the large warehouses were the first to go, but it was always the older buildings with less strength in them that failed first. In the end, that was all academic, as the peak wind speeds easily exceeded the design strength of even new buildings. As sheets of corrugated iron began to peel off an increasing number of roofs, they became horizontal scythes, cutting through power poles and the remaining buildings like a hot knife through butter. Thousands were killed by flying debris, many in their own homes as timber and iron flew through walls of the remaining houses and apartments, as if they were made of paper. As houses disintegrated around them, people inside were plucked up by the wind like tissue paper and hurled around like confetti. Thousands more would be killed by the injuries sustained as they were thrown against standing walls or debris. Amputations and subsequent shock and loss of blood took more.

Solar farm panels were stripped from their frames. Wind will lift a five hundred-tonne aeroplane – the difference in pressure between 'on top' and 'below' the plane's wings. Similar differences were created by the high wind speeds over the solar panels, the forces creating an uplift that easily exceeded the design strength of the bolts that held the panels to the racks. These, too, flew like sheets of paper. Fortunately, there were few downwind to endure these missiles.

On the coast of Western Australia, the waves that rolled in were estimated to have exceeded thirty metres in height. Not even the most foolhardy surfer bum tried to catch a wave. But they couldn't have got anywhere near the coast even if they had wanted to.

Most of Perth is less than ten metres above sea level. And the Swan River provided an easy access path for the storm surge to penetrate directly into the city centre and the airport. The direct damage to coastal communities and the port at Freemantle was just as devastating. Again, engineers had designed rock barriers to meet a certain level of threat, taking into account the level of wind and wave that had been recorded before, plus a bit extra as insurance. As the threat of sea-level rise and increasingly severe weather events had become apparent, and eventually responded to many years later, some additional strengthening of the seaward defences was underway. But money had always been a constraint. Shipping companies would only pay so much in port fees, and the long-suffering ratepayer was already forking out for new, more resilient infrastructure on the land.

The storm surge swept inland, up the rivers mostly, for kilometres. As suburbs began to disintegrate in the wind, the remaining residents in the low-lying areas noticed water being forced out of the storm water grates in disturbingly strong geysers, sometimes a metre or so high. This grew in intensity and was soon supplemented by water flowing uphill along the storm drains as the surge pushed further inland. Initially, water came up over the steps to the front doors, then in through the front doors, and then up the sides of the houses until water started to come in through any open windows. Many properties floated off their foundations at that point, the water pressure shearing off the holding-down mechanisms. If anybody had been watching, there was the unusual sight of streets of houses floating downwind like demented dodgem cars, slowly disintegrating as they went. Many still contained their occupants because they just didn't know what to do when the tide came in. And in.

As the wind eventually abated after twenty-four hours of sheer terror, and the wounded were tended to as best they could – the hospitals had been destroyed as well – there came the realisation that there was no fresh water. The desalination plant had also been totally destroyed. But there was no power to run it anyway. The wind and solar farms simply did not exist any longer, nor did the power lines. And any bottled water reserves that had been in houses or supermarkets or warehouses had vanished along with the building. A good find was to discover an unopened bottle of water that had been washed up somewhere. The potential for faecal contamination became a distant secondary consideration to the punishing thirst that the survivors now felt. Hyper-ventilating in extremely stressful situations uses a lot of water.

And as the temperature rose to the mid-thirties and then the forties in the days that followed, many more perished from heat exhaustion and dehydration.

The death toll was never fully determined. The airport had been destroyed by the combination of high wind speeds and the storm surge, which covered the runway to a depth of nearly four metres in salt water. The overflights came out of Sydney and Melbourne, four hours' flight time away.

Relief trucks from the eastern seaboard took days to arrive because debris from the storm had been blown inland, littering highways, and that needed to be cleared first.

Storm surges bring seawater inland, perhaps kilometres, depending on topography. Seawater naturally contains salt, and as has been known for centuries, if you want to destroy the productive capacity of the land to deny your enemy, you apply salt. The more significant effect of storm surge-induced saltwater intrusion into low-lying agricultural areas is a long-term loss of production. Rainfall will eventually leach the salt away, but how rapidly this happens depends on the amount of rainfall and the amount of salt that has been left behind. Southern Western Australia, which had been one the great grain-producing regions of Australia, was now a basket case for ongoing supplies of fresh water and food.

     ROBERT STEVENS

CHAPTER 52

And When Will It All End?

The conclusion to climate-change induced global catastrophe won't be like a war, where there is eventually a victor and the vanquished, even though both sides are diminished once the fighting ends. Ploughshares turned into swords, which would then be turned back into ploughshares and the cycle would carry on. Not with climate change.

The climate feedback loops will continue to feedback, accelerating the warming and instability, even if we cut emissions to nil tomorrow, which won't happen. Most people want the consumerist party to carry on. The point behind this story is that we are fiddling while the planet burns. Our news stories will be about economics and power struggles and regional conflicts, as these sell papers and click time. The Zombie Dogs – the outcasts, the gangs, the druggies and dealers, and the criminals – they exist today, and we have no real idea about how to address the cause of this societal carbuncle. Massive inequality exists in just about every society, and it is rapidly getting worse. Many Westerners, who essentially control the wealth of the planet and hence have the power, like things the way they are. Few know of hunger or deprivation. "Where's the problem?" is their response.

We are sleepwalking to oblivion.

For many it will be a cataclysmic end. The sustainable carrying capacity of the earth is only so many people, and we passed that number a long time ago. As we destroy the forests, the soils and the water cycles, that carrying capacity reduces daily. The end for many will come in the form of starvation. While storms and floods, tornadoes and wildfires will ravage the planet and will make the news, the creeping yet accelerating decline in agricultural production and the destruction of the ecosystems that support all life will ultimately come to a head. The graph of dramatic population increase will peak and then fall, quite possibly almost vertically. As it has done for every other species that goes through such a dramatic population explosion. The graph of the number of humans surviving will *not* stabilise at a nice, steady level after the correction, but will fluctuate like a heartbeat, as it has done for every other species we have observed.

Mankind will probably survive, as we are a very adaptable species. It will be in a much-diminished form, though. We will have to compete with the rats and cockroaches for quite some time, and there is a good chance that they are more adaptable than *Homo sapiens*, the wise, thinking man. There will be life on Earth. It is a planet that encourages life, but not all species survive. More species are extinct than exist today, and we are well into the next mass extinction event.

Long-term climatic stability is not typical of the geological history of Earth. Mankind evolved quickly during a period of remarkable stability that enabled this particular species to thrive. That stability is now coming to a premature end because of our actions, or lack thereof. And similarly, mankind has not yet learned how to live peacefully with his neighbour, or how to build enduring leadership. For six thousand years we have had civilisations establish and flourish, and then collapse. The only variable is the timescale over which this happens.

The Aboriginal Australians had come close to a 'sustainable' society. After at least forty thousand years in that inhospitable place, they did come to live with the land, not on it. But it takes a staunch stomach to read how this occurred, and the 'unpalatable' truths that are revealed. We are not yet ready to consider such methods ourselves.

     ROBERT STEVENS

And could we reverse climate change? *If* we had the will? Perhaps with difficulty and at great cost through geo-engineering. But there is no will, no desire to change the wasteful ways of the West. Many tipping points have come and gone, so *no*, we cannot reverse what we have created.

A population adjustment is inevitable. It is only the mechanism that will achieve this that is debateable. Evolution and ecological processes will not stop just because we don't like the results.

ABOUT THE AUTHOR

The author is a biological scientist who grew up in the 1960s and 70s. Back then, the threat of nuclear war was real, but as long as everybody did nothing, we were fine. That is not the case with climate change: Doing nothing is not a good option.